Needs Must

By

Kerry Barnes

Copyright

Needs Must by Kerry Barnes ISBN 978-1-7393019-7-2

ISBN 978-1-7393019-7-2

Needs Must by Kerry Barnes

For more information, address: kerrybarnes999@gmail.com.

Publishers Once Upon A Book

www.authorkerrybarnes.co.uk

Warning

This book contains graphic details of murder, kidnapping, violence and profanities.

Other works by Kerry Barnes

Ruthless

Ruby's Palace

Raw Justice

The Hunted

The Rules

The Choice

Deceit

Cruel Secrets

Wicked Lies

Ugly Truth

Raising A Gangster

Outcast

Voice of Reason

Voice of Rage

Trusted

Taboo

Torment

Nemesis

Malice

Callous

Acknowledgements

To all the readers who have supported me along this journey, I am forever grateful. All the wonderful reviews and kind words keep me doing what I love most – writing stories.

I would like to thank NotRights Book Club for their support and enjoyable posts.

I want to thank my editor, Robert Wood, who once again worked tirelessly to ensure my story reads the best it could. We have worked together since 2016, and we have still managed to stay friends, even though I put his patience to the test at times. It has become a partnership that has made me feel confident, knowing he can always unpick the mess I weave into the pages. Thank you again, Robert.

CHAPTER ONE

March 1982
The leaves that had fallen on the uneven pavement were crisp under foot. So as Dottie Ellis turned on to the estate, she was extra careful not to slip. She now had another reason to take her time. Slowly, she took a deep breath and blew out a long plume of frosty breath. Then, she paused momentarily at the foot of the red brick steps, before pulling her coat tighter around herself and staring ahead. She couldn't help it. Her stomach churned with excitement and anticipation. Because she hadn't really gauged how Jimmy would react to the news. They had never discussed the possibility, although they should have, really.

The house was much like her own. It was a very nondescript three-bedroom semi council house with the usual bay window and a wooden front door. And it was in an area of St Mary Cray that was made up of known criminal families, many of whom were related in one way or another. Jimmy Carson's home was in the middle of a street and surrounded by his friends and family. It was lucky she was Jimmy's girl, or there was no way she would have walked along that street alone. She would have been stared at, probably questioned, and then chased with sticks or metal poles.

Jimmy lived with his mother and brothers, although Dottie hadn't got to know the family well. If she ever went to his house, he would whisk her upstairs, away from the others.

Much like the neighbours' houses, Jimmy's was unkempt. The red brick steps were not so red now – unlike her steps at home – but only because her mother liked to keep them polished.

Her mother's garden was awash with colour in the summer. Her father grew roses and hydrangeas, which he fed with pigs' blood and ground-up chicken bones. But the hydrangeas were also given further treatment: he liked to add iron filings as well, so they turned blue.

Jimmy's house, in contrast, had an old motor rusting away in the front garden. Where there should have been a small front lawn there were two deep tyre tracks, a few broken pieces of concrete slabs, and what looked like a car engine, black with oil.

She shivered and wished she had put on a longer jumper under her overcoat. But her Jimmy liked her wearing crop tops. He said they suited her flat tummy, which he found sexy, and she always wanted to please her Jimmy, especially now, and all she hoped and prayed for was that he would be as excited as she was with the news. She ran her hands over her middle and took a deep breath before knocking at the door.

She knew someone was at home because she could hear music blaring from one of the bedrooms upstairs.

Then she heard Ginty's voice. 'Turn that fucking racket off. I can't hear meself bloody think.'

The door flew open, and there, larger than life, with her arms folded under her huge bosoms and with her long black ponytail and a row of loop earrings in each ear, was Jimmy's mother, Ginty Carson.

Her stare alone made Dottie shiver. 'Good morning, Mrs Carson.' She smiled, hoping the woman would invite her in.

However, Ginty merely leaned against the doorframe and looked her up and down. 'What are you doing here, Dottie? And at this hour? Jimmy ain't in.'

It was nine o'clock in the morning, and she knew that Jimmy would never be out of his bed before ten o'clock. She desperately wanted to catch him before he went out, but only because they hadn't seen much of each other in the last few weeks. He said he'd been busy.

'Oh, do you know where he is?'

Before Ginty answered, the music began blaring again. She craned her neck and bellowed up the stairs, 'I said, turn that fucking music off!'

'All right, Muvver,' came the man's voice, the moment the music was turned off. 'You don't have to shout.'

'I do if I'm to be heard over that shit you call fucking music.'

Ginty looked back at Dottie. 'Listen, girl.' She lowered her voice and softened her tone. 'Do yaself a favour, right, and forget about our Jimmy.'

Those words cut Dottie in half. She loved Jimmy with all her heart, and she had even lied to her parents to see him. 'But—'

'No fucking buts, Dottie. I know your family.' She smiled gently. 'They're a good lot. You know what I mean. They work hard, speak nice, and go to the Baptist Church on a Sunday.'

'But I'm not like them, Mrs Carson, I'm not. Really, I'm not. I don't even go to church. If you didn't know already, I *love* Jimmy.'

'Yes, well, as hard as it sounds, he doesn't love you. He's back with Carrie.'

Dottie staggered down the steps, in shock. '*Carrie?*'

'Yeah, look, girl, my Jimmy has always loved Carrie. She's like him – wild. And I think the truth of it is, he wanted to date other girls to make sure Carrie was the one for him.'

Dottie felt herself turn inside out, her heart pounded like a drum inside her chest, and she suspected she would vomit at any time. 'But I was with him only *three* days ago. We've been seeing each other for *five* months. He said he loved me. I . . . I don't understand.'

'It's fucking cold, and you look frozen to death. Get yourself off home, put my Jimmy out of your head, and meet a good bloke, an educated sort – not one that's likely to spend half his life in prison.'

'No, Jimmy ain't like that. He's a decent boy.'

Ginty felt her level of patience diminishing. 'Listen to me, do you think you can tell me about me own boys? Do ya?' Her tone was aggressive.

Dottie quickly shook her head, her eyes wide with fear, because no one pissed Ginty off and walked away without a bruise or worse.

'Good, 'cos I know *my* boys better than anyone, and I'm telling you now, girl, you're no good for my Jimmy. It would never work 'cos you're from a different lot. My Jimmy is what he is. You would try to change him, dispirit the boy, like breaking in a wild horse, but it would only turn him into either a lily-livered wanker or a monster, and that ain't who my little Jimmy is!'

Tears filled her eyes as Dottie shook her head, desperate for Ginty to be on her side, but in her heart, she knew she would never convince a woman like Jimmy's mother.

'Stop the tears, for fuck's sake. You can't understand our ways. You ain't brought up like it. But, see, Carrie, she is. I know her muvver, her farver, and all her sisters. Carrie would be the right woman for Jimmy. She'd know what to do if the police came knocking. She'd be his alibi, she'd wait for him if he served time inside, and she'd look after his babies, if, Gawd willing, they have any. And she'd keep a clean house and know how to behave around other men.'

'But I would do all those things as well.'

Waving her finger, Ginty replied, 'You won't because you're different. I can see your pretty little face now horrified 'cos Jimmy has the police knocking at his door, or cringing 'cos you have to queue in line to visit me boy in prison. And don't think it won't be like that because all me boys are the same. They never went to school. They learned to sign on before they could spell their names, and they've never done a legal day's work in their lives. 'Cos my boys would never work for anyone else. They are their own people.'

'But Jimmy has changed. He said he would get a job. We'd have a nice home, and children, and—'

'Oh, stop, Dottie. You are so naïve. Jesus. If I were you, I wouldn't see any fella until you've grown up a bit. My Jimmy was saying those things just to get ya fucking knickers off. Didn't your muvver teach you anything?'

Dottie's face melted and huge tears plummeted down her cheeks.

'I'm sorry, Dottie, but there's no use in sugarcoating it. Go on with ya. Find a decent bloke. Just don't come after my boy.'

Dottie put her hands over her face and crouched down sobbing. It was too late to find anyone else. She was pregnant with Jimmy's baby, for Christ's sake.

Ginty tutted before clutching Dottie's elbows and pulling her to her feet. 'Go on, love,' she said, steering Dottie away from the house. 'Go home, Dottie. Forget about Jimmy. Go on with you.'

Glancing over her shoulder at the door wide open, Ginty growled, 'I'm letting all the heat out,' before she went back into the house and slammed the door, leaving Dottie outside in the freezing cold.

CHAPTER TWO

How could he? They were together only three days ago.

She thought back to the day he had been quiet, and, in fact, he had been spiteful, suggesting she was a snob. She hadn't argued before. She had just said 'sorry', but she had been saying this a lot lately.

She should have seen it coming. The more she apologised for being herself, the more he became irritated. The only time he seemed to appreciate her was when they were having sex. Although he had suggested she should start using a sunbed since her skin was so pale, and he had also mentioned she should have highlights in her hair so it was less ginger. More tears streamed down her cheeks as she walked back towards the lane. She couldn't get his face out of her mind – his blue eyes and charming smile. Even his neck tattoo of a bomb was attractive.

***

He had liked her initially when he asked her out. It was six months ago.

She recalled it vividly as it had been one of the happiest times of her life. She was hanging around the Walnuts Shopping Centre in Orpington, leaning against the wall of the job centre. Her friend Margaret Webster, from school, had dragged her along. They were going to go to every shop along the High Street looking for a Saturday job.

She was lucky enough to have pocket money from helping her mother at the church, where her mother arranged the flowers and organised charity events. She helped and got paid three pounds a week, enough to treat herself to a top or a skirt from Martin Ford.

She remembered wearing a long navy-blue pencil skirt and a blouse. Her shoes weren't high because she wasn't allowed any above an inch and a half, but they had big enough heels to show off her legs in the skirt. Margaret also wore a pencil skirt, but her legs were chunky and made worse by the flat shoes she had on. That time had been such a happy one for her.

***

There was a group of skinheads hanging around together; she and Margaret knew them all by name or nickname. Everyone from The Crays and Orpington knew each other.

She watched the lads re-enacting a fight they'd had with a bunch of others from Deptford. Whether they were exaggerating to boost their egos or to show off as if they were hard, who knew. Still, when Jimmy suddenly came striding over with a cigarette in his mouth, his 501s held up with red braces, everyone cheered.

Seeing his shoulders look as though they were shuffling cards, the way he bowled along, she couldn't help but be mesmerised by him. He air-boxed two of his mates, and it was then clear to her that Jimmy had been in a real fight because the others were hanging on to every word of his. He was talking and laughing.

Unexpectedly, he turned his head and caught her staring at him.

Margaret nudged Dottie. 'Dot, he's looking at you.'

'Shut up.'

'He's coming over, Dot,' Margaret said, with excitement in her voice.

'Shut up, Margaret.'

As soon as he was a foot away, he stubbed out his cigarette, ran his hands over his number one haircut, and smiled on one side of his face.

She knew she had fallen in love, right then and there. She was particularly attracted by his eyes. They glistened in the sunlight, and she noticed how blue they were against his tanned skin.

'All right, Dottie?' he said, his face now beaming.

Feeling shy, she sensed her face turning red. 'Yeah, I'm good, and you, Jimmy?'

'Better for seeing you, Dot. Are you going up the Civic tonight?'

'What? Oh, er . . . who me?' She stumbled over her words because she couldn't imagine someone like Jimmy asking her out on a date, but then again, was it a date?

'Yeah, you, Dottie.' He eyed her up and down, and then he winked. 'You look lovely in that pencil skirt and top, but I bet you'd look good in anything. So, how about it? Say eight o'clock outside the Civic Hall?'

She bit her lip because there was no way her mother would let her out past ten o'clock, and yet Jimmy wasn't the type to have a curfew; he was his own man, a rebel her mum would say. And she did say, if she was ever referring to one of the Carson clan.

On that first date, she was feeling as nervous as hell. Margaret agreed to go with her only because she fancied his mate Spud, who was only given that nickname because his father owned a chip shop in Carlton Parade.

Spud had money because his father was loaded. He was an ugly man with acne scars and a nasty sneer that showed his tiny teeth.

Spud's mum was a pretty woman but a real snob. She thought she was a cut above the rest because her old man owned not only the chippy in Carlton Parade but one in Marion Crescent as well. She knew her husband was shagging the pretty girls that worked in the shops, but she acted as if she was oblivious to all of that and would drive around in a flash motor, without a care in the world.

Jimmy hung around with Spud, whose real name was Thomas Tilby, because he had money and would buy the cigarettes and the booze. But Jimmy wasn't a complete ponce; he would also share any wins he got, such as the cash for the scrap metal that he'd knocked off from the dealer in Bromley, who stupidly left his copper pipes in the back of his van.

That first night, Jimmy was there bang on eight o'clock outside smoking a cigarette with three of his mates, including Spud, who was bigger than Jimmy by a foot and who had a cleaner-cut skinhead look without tattoos. His skin was pitted and spotty; nevertheless, his fingernails were clean. But all the lads were dressed exactly the same – all in Ben Sherman check shirts, red braces, and Levi's rolled up to show off their fourteen-hole cherry-red Dr Martens.

Jimmy pushed himself away from the wall, nodded to his mates, and reached to take her hand. 'Looking beautiful, Dottie,' he said, as he snatched a kiss.

She didn't mind; in fact, she was thrilled. She smiled at Margaret, who now had her attention on Spud, which was the plan all along.

That night, she felt a million dollars. He complimented her on her hair, her short black pencil skirt, and her short top. She felt shy to dance in front of him, but she knew she could dance to reggae all right and to Madness, which was her favourite band and apparently his as well. The night flew by, and it was eleven o'clock by the time he walked her home and midnight when they stopped snogging and she said goodbye. He asked her out on another date; he wanted to see her the following night, but she knew that since she'd broken her parents' curfew, she would be grounded. Still, she agreed, between hungry kisses, to meet him. She would find a way to see him again because in all her seventeen years, she had never felt more alive, more wanted, and more fancied. And fancied by none other than Jimmy Carson. She was feeling so excited to tell everyone. After all, she was the shy one at school, the girl who the popular girls left alone. She wasn't bullied, but she heard them call her boring once. Still, she couldn't wait to tell them on Monday, if, of course, word hadn't already gone around, because he hadn't been shy about snogging her face off in front of everyone at the Civic Hall.

***

Recalling that time, her parents were furious and indeed they grounded her. They guessed she was lying about escorting her sick friend home who lived in Bromley. But there was no way she was going to stay in, not when Jimmy had asked her out on a second date. So she lied to her parents while keeping her fingers crossed behind her back. She told them she was going to bed as she didn't feel well. And she asked them to leave her alone. They did because once her bedroom door was closed, neither of them would enter. They respected her privacy, at least.

***

So, the next day at seven o'clock, she climbed out from the bedroom window and jumped onto the outbuilding that had once been the outside toilet. She then clambered down, hitched herself over the neighbour's garden fence, and then ran along the side alley to the street, where she headed for the bus stop.

Wearing her jeans and a blouse, she had applied only a little lipstick and black eyeliner. She wasn't one for make-up. But all the girls she knew were. They were into black eyeliner and lip liner. She, however, only had eye make-up and some lipstick on, which was one of her mother's old ones.

As soon as she got off the bus and walked towards the Walnuts Shopping Centre, she felt a level of confidence she'd never felt before. She flicked her shoulder-length hair away from her face and marched towards the group congregated by the job centre. It seemed to be where all the Orpington and Cray lot hung around. And there was Jimmy. He wasn't dressed as smartly as yesterday. In fact, he had the same shirt on and a pair of old jeans. Still, the gang was circling him as if he was the lad they aspired to be. She suddenly felt uneasy and slowed down as she approached, but as soon as he saw her, he jumped up and dismissed his mates. With his Harrington jacket in one hand, he slid his arm around her shoulders and walked her away from the Walnuts Shopping Centre towards the main road and on towards St Mary Cray.

'So where are we going, Jimmy?' she asked, leaning her head into his arm.

'Me muvver's over at me aunt's place. Me bruvvers are up the West End. So me and you, babe, have the house to ourselves.'

Dottie felt her heart skip a beat and a mass of butterflies doing backflips in her stomach. 'On our own, Jimmy? And what do you propose we do?' She realised she sounded posh, the moment those words left her mouth.

He laughed and mimicked her.

'Don't you like the way I speak, Jimmy?'

''Course I do, babe. I'm only teasing. I like a bit of posh.'

She thought about that remark: 'a bit of posh'. But she didn't think she was. She lived in a house that was built under the same council and in the same era. The owners where she lived looked after their houses – neat curtains, tidy gardens – and all the streetlamps were lit properly and there was no graffiti. But there was no community atmosphere. It was quiet and everyone kept themselves to themselves.

Walking along with Jimmy, she was in such a state of elation – on cloud nine, in fact – that she didn't notice the level of degradation on this side of the main road.

But she quickly became aware of the kind of people who were living on the street. It was impossible to ignore them. Here the people were in their front gardens, leaning on their garden gates and chatting to neighbours while drinking tea from chipped mugs. The house dead opposite Jimmy's had a group of men surrounding a makeshift barbeque and they were all laughing while drinking cans of beer and wearing holey vests, braces, and old workingmen's trousers. Some were sitting on old tyres, one was half asleep on an old sofa, and two were sitting on wooden school chairs. Their huge beer bellies were hanging over their trousers. When they called out to Jimmy, their accent was slightly different from hers; they mumbled as well, and yet they spoke so quickly. Jimmy just laughed and told her quietly to ignore them. It suited her. She couldn't understand them anyway.

The late sun that evening lit up the street and gave it a false sense of warmth and pleasure. The smell of burned meat, the sound of various records playing, and the buzz of activity all added to her excitement. As they walked along so casually, she saw more of the occupants of the street. An old couple were dozing in two old Margate beach deckchairs, which were placed on either side of the front door, barely visible through the four-foot-high weeds. Flea-ridden dogs with matted fur roamed the streets. Some lay on the pavement soaking up the last of the sun. Looking around, she saw some kids chasing each other barefoot. They hardly had any clothes on but they seemed oblivious to this as they chucked bottles or buckets of water at each other and screeched with excitement.

One mother made Dottie jump when she screamed out, 'I'll 'ave ya, Sizzy-Lou, you fucking little scaggy tike.' The child, no older than four, shot past her laughing while holding an empty bucket.

***

Looking back to that time – the initial introduction to Jimmy's street – it had certainly been an experience and one that she'd enjoyed; it was the level of untamed spirit of the people.

***

Finally, when they reached his home, she suddenly felt so out of place. He opened the door to a glaring-coloured hallway where everywhere was painted red. There was even a red carpet. On every wall, there were photo frames. And when she entered the property, there was a smell of old fat and bacon mixed with aftershave and stale cigarette smoke, which lingered in the air. She paused nervously before he gently took her hand. 'Come on, Dottie, no one's in. We'll go to my room. No one comes in there.'

She smiled at him, but she was young, and this was a different world from hers. Her parents' house smelled of Shake n'Vac and bleach. There was only one photo, and that was of her grandmother. And there was no way in a million years that her parents would ever allow her to bring anyone into her home while they were out – male or female.

She ran up the stairs behind him and noticed the layout was exactly the same as her house, except she could see that the large room at the front of the house had two doors, where the council had turned it into a four-bedroomed home. *Probably to accommodate all of Ginty's children*, she thought.

Jimmy's room was the small boxroom at the front of the house. He opened the door, dragged her in, and closed it again. She was surprised at how cramped it was. His bed was on the left-hand side, and above it were shelves stacked high with boxes. To the right, there was a side table, a wardrobe, and a chest of drawers. On top of the chest was a bottle of aftershave and boot polish. On the floor were some of his clothes. His bed, which was covered in a thin blue blanket and a candy-striped cotton sheet, was barely made. She smiled to herself because her bedroom was immaculate; she wasn't allowed out of the house unless her bed was made.

She was gazing around when he suddenly pulled her to the bed and began kissing her. She didn't struggle because it was what she wanted too. He was gentle, and his fingers tenderly caressed her neck and cheeks. She felt different, in a womanly way; she could feel a tingling sensation, which her mates had told her about, and yet at the time, she had dismissed it as make-believe. The sensation began in her stomach and continued down to her thighs.

Then she felt him wriggle his body between her thighs, pushing her legs apart. He wasn't forceful, but she felt uneasy. She had never done anything more than kiss before. Kissing Jimmy was different, though. It was mature. He groaned and moved, and then he slid his hand inside her top. Her first reaction was to stop him, so she grabbed his wrist. He relaxed his arm and pulled away. She assumed he respected her wishes and accepted that touching her breasts was a no-go – not yet, anyway. It was too soon, surely.

Now he was whispering such irresistible things, telling her how much he liked her, how beautiful she was, and how much he wanted to make love to her. But he told her he would take it slowly. This feeling between her legs – this tingling sensation – was growing, and she now wanted him to discover her body with his hands. His lips parted slightly as he explored her mouth with his tongue, and then gently, he used his mouth to delicately tantalise her neck. As his lips returned to meet hers, his hand caressed her stomach. Slowly, he moved his right hand up to her breasts, sliding it under her bra. But she didn't stop him.

They were now connecting with a new language. There were no words, only touch and sensation. She relaxed her legs and allowed him to push his erect bulge between her thighs, knowing that she had her clothes on, and so had he. She wanted him, but she was afraid that her parents would be ashamed of what she was doing. She was only seventeen – she and Jimmy were not married – but she liked him so much, and she really liked what he was doing.

His lips became harder against hers, his movement firmer, and then he stopped straddling her and unbuttoned her blouse, unclasped her bra, and looked down at her breasts.

She watched his eyes, wondering if he liked what he saw, but before she could tell, his face was brushing against her left breast, and he was sucking and biting her. The tingling feeling became intense, and when he looked up, he smiled.

He moved down the bed, and in a sweeping movement, he unbuttoned her jeans and pulled them away.

Just when he was about to grab her knickers, she held them. 'No, wait.' Her voice was fast, her breathing was increasing, and then anticipation and fear took over. Should she allow him to take her virginity, or should she save it?

He quickly climbed off her. 'Sorry if I'm going too fast. I thought you were more mature, ya know. Maybe I made a mistake, Dottie. I'm sorry.'

Panic filled her lungs. She didn't want him to stop. She really wanted him. She needed him to be her boyfriend. He was the hardest man she knew. And he was so hot. The girls at school would be so jealous.

'It's okay, Jimmy. I just need us to take it slower the first time.'

Suddenly, she saw his face beam and a little chuckle left his lips. 'Are you a virgin?'

She blushed. 'Yes.' She couldn't lie. She knew she would bleed; the girls at school said you bled on your first time.

'Don't worry, I'll be ever so gentle.'

He sat beside her and removed his boots, his jeans, and then his pants. Her eyes glanced at his manhood, and for a moment, she wanted to get dressed and run. It was huge. She had never seen one erect, not even in a picture.

'It's okay, Dottie, just relax. I won't hurt you.'

She looked up to the ceiling and allowed him to remove her knickers. When he climbed on top of her, he began by caressing her breasts before putting his hand between her legs. She gasped. No one had ever touched her there before, and then she felt him insert his finger.

'There, now, I bet that feels good, eh?' he whispered.

She nodded, but she felt so tense. She wasn't sure how she felt. But once he was kissing her again, she felt the tingling sensation return, and then she liked what he was doing to her.

However, when he pushed her legs wider apart, she knew he was going to enter her, and the moment he did, she wanted to scream. It hurt so much, but she bit her lip and held her breath. Once he had finished, she realised she needed to wipe the mess from her navel. But he was one step ahead of her. He grabbed the toilet roll that was on the side table and handed it to her.

While Jimmy got dressed and rolled a cigarette, she felt cold and empty. She was left to wipe herself clean and scramble around to look for her underwear and the rest of her clothes.

Sitting on the bed, he lit up the cigarette.

'That was all right, babe, eh?' he asked, as he blew smoke away from her face.

She nodded but she felt so embarrassed as she put her underwear back on and climbed into her jeans. 'Was it okay, Jimmy?'

'Yeah, sure it was. Put it this way, Dottie, I want to do it again. You're pretty, and you're special. And you've got nice tits.'

Still feeling so self-conscious, she pulled her blouse across her breasts before she buttoned it up.

Once they left the house, he walked her home and made plans to see her again.

***

Looking back at that time, when they'd first dated, it seemed like a lifetime now. She wiped her eyes again as they burned against the cold wind. Going over and over the conversation with Ginty, she realised that that experience with Jimmy had been so fake. Feeling totally used – and utterly furious with herself for letting it happen – she realised that Jimmy had probably just wanted her for sex.

CHAPTER THREE

Still sobbing, Dottie walked towards her home. Thinking back to her visit to Ginty's made her feel as gloomy as the estate she was now walking through. What had once been an exciting place to come to, she could now see it for what it was.

The street was gloomy. The frontage of each house was tatty. In some, the curtains had been virtually ripped from their rails, and now they were hanging from the windows. Two burned-out cars were left abandoned on the kerbs. And strewn across the road someone had left a bin bag full of rubbish. But the contents had been attacked. The culprits undoubtedly were the urban foxes now fat on left-over turkey and uneaten mince pies. But at least the crisp dusting of frost had made the strewn rubbish seem less unsightly.

Dottie looked up at the overhead telephone wires and saw six old trainers hanging by their laces. A car tyre that had been cast out on to the pavement forced her to step into the road before she tripped over it. And there were piles of warm dog shit nearly everywhere she looked. She almost had to step around them like a ballet dancer to avoid messing up her shoes. *However,* she thought, *the saying went that if you trod in dog muck, it was supposed to be lucky.* So maybe she should jump in it and smother herself in it: because right now, she felt anything but lucky.

The cold stung her wet cheeks, and the feeling of self-pity reached its summit. Self-pity had migrated to feeling lonely, frightened, and depressed. Not only would she now have to break her news to her parents, but she could almost play out the outcome. It had been instilled in her as a child – *no unwed mothers in this house.*

***

By the time she reached the lane, she heard the clip-clop of shoes ahead, and as she looked up, she saw three girls walking towards her. Her heart was in her mouth. This wasn't her manor, but she knew that these girls lived on this side of the main road. She'd seen them in the high street, and even though she didn't mix with them, she was aware of who they were, and, more relevant, of their reputation.

'Oi, oi, it's that silly little slag that your Jimmy was seeing.'

Fear hit Dottie like an earthquake. It rumbled menacingly through her bones and held her around the throat. She guessed the best move would be to run, but she didn't have suitable shoes or the strength because right now she was feeling too sick.

'What ya doing around here, Ginger Minge?' asked the lanky one of the three, who Dottie knew was called Misty Jacobs.

Misty had long black hair, as did all three of them. They were all wearing jeans, high boots, and sheepskin coats. The coat was one that she had longed for. Most of the girls at school had one; they had bought them from Petticoat Lane.

But Dottie's parents couldn't afford a fashionable coat, apparently, not even for her birthday.

Lena Ashcroft, the shorter of the three girls, with giant hairspray flicks on either side of her face, laughed spitefully at Dottie. Like one of the girls in *Charlie's Angels,* she was pretty, but she definitely wasn't as attractive as Carrie Verne, the girl in the middle of the group.

Not wanting to look at Carrie because she knew she would burst into tears, Dottie deliberately avoided eye contact. Carrie was the reason that Jimmy didn't want her anymore. And she was like him, so Ginty said. And she was right. Carrie was well known. She was always with other girls who looked up to her because she could handle herself. She had other qualities as well: she was cheeky, daring, and probably a hell of a lot more fun than she herself was.

Feeling nervous, Dottie chose to ignore them and walk by, minding her own business, but in her heart, she knew it wouldn't be that simple.

She got that right.

'Hey, I'm talking to you,' said Misty, as she stood in front of Dottie, blocking her way. 'I said, what ya doing over this way? You don't fucking live here.'

'Nothing,' replied Dottie, now feeling so afraid because she was in the lane off the main road. No one could see her, and there was no one to stop these girls if they chose to give her a good beating. And she knew how hard these three were. They had a reputation for fighting. Especially Carrie. She wasn't a girl you messed with. Understanding the inevitable aggression surrounding her, she looked to the pavement in submission.

Misty shoved her shoulder. And that alone hurt. 'Answer me, you fucking slag.'

Dottie looked up, but she didn't answer Misty. She directed her answer to Carrie. 'I didn't know. I'm sorry.' That was all she said.

But it wasn't Misty who punched her. It was Lena. Pulling Misty back, she threw a punch. The fist alone wasn't what hurt. It was the number of rings on her fingers that did the damage. The force knocked her to the pavement, and as she tried to get up, Lena relentlessly threw a load of punches to either side of her head, which were enough to rattle her brain. Still, she didn't fight back. Instead, she curled herself in a ball to protect her unborn baby while Lena laid into her by using her boots.

'Stop!' yelled Carrie. 'Get the fuck off her, Lena. What's the matter with you! The girl ain't done nothing to you.'

When the punches and kicks stopped, Dottie removed her hands from her stomach and uncurled herself.

Carrie reached down, offering her a hand, which Dottie gratefully took.

'For fuck's sake, Lena, look what you've done to the poor chavi's face. There was no fucking need for that.'

'Carrie, she was seeing Jimmy, the fucking whore.'

Too afraid to move, Dottie held her head down. She could feel the blood trickling down her cheek and her right eye swelling up.

'You're Dottie Ellis, ain't ya, from over Poverest way?'

Dottie nodded but still she wouldn't make eye contact.

'See, Carrie, that's the slag who was fucking your Jimmy.'

'Shut up, Lena,' spat Carrie, before she turned to Dottie. 'Did you know me and my Jimmy were back together?'

Looking from one girl to the other, Dottie's right hand shook, and her tongue glued itself to the roof of her mouth. She guessed they were going to beat her up again, and if they did, she didn't know if she would survive another beating. She'd come close to passing out minutes earlier. 'I didn't know, no. But Mrs Carson told me just now. I'm sorry, Carrie. I don't want any trouble. I swear to you, I didn't know.'

'Fucking liar! You're sniffing around here after him, ain't ya. Well, he's fucked you off good and proper. He chucked ya, you fucking ugly bitch. Look at ya. As if he would fancy you. Alls I can say is you must have given him a good blow job, 'cos what else could he see in you, eh?' said Misty, almost nose to nose with Dottie.

'Get away from her, Misty. What's the fucking matter with yous two? Anyone would think you were dating Jimmy, or you fancied him yaself,' hissed Carrie, before she folded her arms, tapped her foot, and glared at Misty.

'What? Me? Nah, Carrie, I don't fancy your Jimmy.'

'Oh yeah? So what's wrong with Jimmy, Misty?'

Dottie could see how much kudos Carrie had because Misty and Lena now seemed on edge. Especially Misty.

'Nuffin, nuffin at all. He's your fella, that's all.'

'That's right, Misty, and I can fight me own battles, so I don't need you. What d'ya take me for? A fucking chicken?'

'Nah, o' course not, Carrie.'

Feeling the heat had been taken off her, albeit probably momentarily, Dottie looked up at the girls. 'I'm sorry, Carrie. I should never have dated Jimmy. But I know the score now. His mum said you were back together and that . . . you're right for him. She told me I should get on with my life. And I will.'

Carrie glared before she pulled out a packet of cigarettes and lit one up.

It was then that Dottie realised that Ginty was right. Carrie *was* a no-nonsense girl. She could handle herself, and at that moment, she imagined Carrie giving the police her middle finger if she was minded to.

Perhaps Ginty had sussed her out good and proper. Because she certainly wasn't like that. She'd just curled herself into a ball at the first few punches; she was weak and naïve – and now, foolishly, she was pregnant.

'So what else did mouth of the south say to ya?'

Dottie didn't know who she feared most, Carrie or Ginty. 'Er, do you mean Mrs Carson?'

Carrie nodded. 'Yeah. What did she say? 'Cos that fat bitch has a lot to say about fuck all.'

'She said you would be good for Jimmy. She said you'd be his alibi. You'd visit him in prison, have his babies, and keep a clean house, or something like that.'

'I bet she thinks I'd be sucking his dick on a daily basis an' all. The stupid mare. And what else did she say?'

Dottie felt a tear building but she managed to blink it away. 'She said I was from a different lot—'

'Posh, ya mean?' Carrie laughed. 'See, that divvy woman thinks that if you live on the Poverest side, then you're posh, a snob, you're not like us. But you ain't no better than me, Dottie.'

'I know I'm not. I never said I was.' Suddenly, she felt she had found her tongue. Perhaps it was the hormones kicking in. 'I actually admire you, Carrie.'

'*I actually admire you.* Are you taking the fucking piss out of us?' snapped Lena.

'Shut up, Lena. In fact, go home. And you, Misty. Go on. I'm going to see Ginty, anyway.'

'Aw, fucking hell, Carrie. I thought we were going to hang out at mine. I've got fags and a bottle of Muvver's Ruin,' said Misty, pulling out a bottle of gin from inside her coat.

'Fuck off, Misty. Anyway, I don't need no gin and I've got me own fags. Go on. I'll catch up with yous later.'

She waited until both girls walked away before she looked at Dottie. 'So, come on, Dottie, why do you admire me? I mean, I bet you've got nice things in your house. I bet it don't stink of fucking greyhounds.'

'No, it doesn't stink of greyhounds, but it does stink of bleach.'

Carrie took another drag on her cigarette while she thought about this girl. 'So, go on then, why do you admire me?'

Dottie touched the deep graze across her cheek and then looked at the sticky blood on her fingers. 'Well, it's obvious, really, Carrie. You're very pretty, you're confident, and you're smart. And you can stick up for yourself. That counts for a lot.'

She sighed. 'I don't go to school, ya know.'

'I know that, but I think you're smart. You're street-smart. And everyone likes you.'

Carrie laughed. 'Are you having a laugh? They don't fucking like me. See, that Misty and Lena don't really like me. I bet they're slagging me off now behind me back. What it is, Dottie, is that they both know I can give them a right royal beating, and if I lost – which I wouldn't, no way – then I've got me sisters, Mary, Rosie, and Dilly, who always have me back, and they would be next in line to finish them off. Have you got sisters?'

Dottie shook her head. 'I wish I did, or even have a brother, but my mum and dad only had me, and I think I was a mistake.'

'Oh yeah, my muvver calls us all mistakes and says she regrets having any kids. But she still kept on breeding 'em.' She laughed. 'Well, she did until her womb fell out.'

Dottie started to laugh at that joke, but as she tried to, her right cheek stung. 'I bet it's fun to live in your home with sisters and greyhounds.'

Carrie laughed. 'Yeah, it is. I just wish I had more privacy.'

'And I wish I had more company.'

'What else do you admire about me, Dottie?'

'Well, as I said earlier, you're stunning, you've got tanned skin, and you wear such lovely clothes.'

'Thanks, Dottie. But why don't you get yaself some nice clothes, then?'

Looking down at her black coat, which was coated in fluff and was so plain, Dottie felt embarrassed because it didn't fit any fashion. It wasn't a Harrington, a leather hunter's jacket, or even a warm sheepskin. 'My mum and dad can't afford them. Not really. Not nice things, anyway. I get a tiny bit of pocket money, but it doesn't go far, really.'

'I chore mine.'

'Do you?' A sudden chuckle left Dottie's mouth. 'See, I wouldn't have the guts. I'd be too scared to, and that's another thing I admire about you.'

'You haven't asked me what I admire about you, Dottie.'

Not knowing if she was being sarcastic, Dottie smiled sadly. 'Well, why would I, Carrie? I'm such a loser, in every way possible, actually. Look, I must go.' She touched her face. 'I'm sorry. I will stay away from Jimmy. Not that he would come near me. Not when he's got you.'

'Before you go, Dottie, there is something I do admire about you.'

Dottie sensed Carrie was being sincere and so she nodded. 'Really?'

'You have freedom. The world, as they say, is your oyster. You can go anywhere, even live in Spain, if you want to. You can talk to other men, even when you're married. You can do any job you want. And you can say "no" to having babies, if you want. I can't, Dottie. I can't do any of those things.'

Sensing a deep sadness in Carrie's voice, and the vulnerability that she was obviously displaying, Dottie paused in deep thought, and a puzzled frown began to crease her forehead. Then she said, 'What? I don't understand.'

'We live a different life, Dottie, us girls.' She pointed down the lane to the estate. 'We are raised to get married young, have a brood of chavis, and keep a clean home. I'm not allowed to drive a car. Only me ol' man, who will have to be Jimmy, can do that.'

As if an unspoken connection was formed, Dottie felt for Carrie – a girl she had always admired. It seemed that they did have something in common. Carrie, it appeared, was a trapped soul. Trapped through family expectations and family honour. But so was she, in a way.

'Don't you want to marry Jimmy, then?'

Carrie straightened up as if she was in pain and sucked the air through her teeth, which made a whistling sound. 'When Jimmy and I dated, my fate was set in stone. So now, I *have* to marry him.'

Intrigued, Dottie asked, 'But why?'

''Cos I slept with him, that's why. And so I have to get wed or stay single for the rest of me life. Everyone knew me and Jimmy would be wed before we were outta nappies. We're both the youngest of big families. Me sister Mary is married to one of his brothers. It's just how it is. So, Dottie, when he was seeing you, girl, I knew it wouldn't be long before he knocked at my door again.'

'He used me, Carrie. He never loved me. I was stupid.'

'Dottie, I don't even know if he loves *me*. It's what's gotta be done. Me muvver's booking the dress fitting already.'

Feeling suddenly ashamed of herself, Dottie looked down again. 'Look, I, uh, I am sorry. I just wished I'd never met him.'

Carrie laughed. 'He is a good catch if you like a bad boy, but the one thing ol' motor mouth is right about is that you're not like us. You live on the other side of the main road, so your life will be different. It will be what you want it to be.' She poked herself in the chest. 'With me, it's different. My life will be what Jimmy says it will be. Mind you, I won't suffer him beating me, not like my sister does with her ol' man, the poor cow. Nah, when we're wed, and if he lays a hand on me, I'll knife him through the chest when he sleeps.' She laughed, letting Dottie know that she was joking.

'I have to go,' said Dottie again, as she was about to walk away.

'I don't hold any grudges, Dottie, and I'm sorry for what Lena did to ya face.'

Dottie could see the girl genuinely meant it. 'You're kind, Carrie.'

'Hard on the outside, soft on the inside.' She winked and put a finger to her lips.

'Carrie, would you ever change the way you live?' Her eyes suddenly widened. 'Sorry, that's none of my business.'

With a sad smile, Carrie nodded. 'I can't. But I will raise my babies to be different. If I have girls, they'll work if they want to, carry on at school if they want to, and marry who they want to.'

'And if you have boys?'

'I'll raise my boys to be educated and to be who they want to be, villain or copper. Although copper is a dirty word in my home.'

'And you will be such a good mum. Jimmy is so lucky to have you.' Dottie's face paled before her eyes filled, and she walked away.

Pulling her coat tighter around her and allowing the tears to sting her grazed cheek, Dottie heard Carrie call out, 'If you ever need me, girl, find me.'

Those words echoed in her head as she begrudgingly trudged her way home.

CHAPTER FOUR

As Dottie approached her house, the man who lived three doors along from her home, who was smartly dressed in a camel-coloured Crombie coat, tilted his hat to her as he passed by.

She was aware that he was a policeman – a detective, in fact. She harboured a fondness for him, yet she couldn't help but feel an overwhelming sense of sympathy. It had been well over a year since the tragic car accident. But, whenever she encountered him, she greeted him with a shy smile, understanding the difficulty of engaging in conversation with someone who was mourning the loss of his daughter.

Jenny, a sweet and unassuming girl, had been a cherished presence in their lives. Their summer holidays had often been spent playing board games together. The memory of Jenny lingered, and Dottie couldn't fathom the depth of sorrow her father must have endured, having survived the same accident that claimed his daughter's life.

Sliding her key in the lock, Dottie realised this would be her day of reckoning. Would her parents show any sympathy towards her current position, or would they keep their noses in the air and verbally propel their righteous words to make her feel even more shameful, foolish, and worthless than she felt already? She shivered because she was afraid of the unknown and the shame they would undoubtedly cast on her, but she also shivered because it was bloody freezing outside.

As soon as she entered her home, the warm air instantly made her nose run. Pausing, she listened to hear if anyone was there. Then, she looked up at the hall clock. It was eleven o'clock. Her mother would still be at church. Her father used to accompany her mother, but over the past few months, he had elected to stay at home and do the chores. He made quite a thing about doing the chores before work on Monday, although what those were was anyone's guess.

She knew her father wasn't in the kitchen so perhaps he had popped out. Quietly, she crept up the stairs. She really hoped her father was out of the house. She wasn't ready yet to explain her bruises, which she was sure she had because her face was throbbing.

As she reached the top of the stairs, her ears pricked up. There were strange groaning sounds coming from her parents' bedroom. Wiping her nose with the back of her coat sleeve, and being very careful not to make a sound, she stepped towards their bedroom door, which was slightly ajar. Holding her breath, she peered in. Instantly, she threw her hands to her mouth. The shocking scene sucked all the air from her lungs. She blinked furiously, hoping that what she saw was a figment of her imagination.

But it wasn't. Her father was sitting at the end of the bed, with his trousers down around his ankles, and Lucas Martin from number twenty, a lad nearly three years younger than herself, had his hands wrapped around her father's penis.

At that moment, she felt as if *she* was an intruder for even being in the house, as well as feeling utterly repulsed by a vision that she could never unsee. After the shock of the events of this morning, she never dreamed her life would get any worse. But it had – in spades!

Slowly, she crept back down the stairs, opened the front door, and gently closed it behind her. Her mind was all over the place. Where could she go? And, more to the point, what could she say?

She wasn't the type to confront her father; she'd never even had the gumption to answer him back. Or her mother, for that matter. Her father was old-fashioned, and he had rules that were never allowed to be questioned. Dinner was always at six. On the dot. And she wasn't allowed to leave the table until he had.

The main living room was for her parents only and also for guests. The exceptions were Christmas and birthdays. Oh, and when they'd had the funeral of her grandmother.

So, apart from her bedroom and the bathroom, of course, the kitchen and the dining room were really the only parts of the house that she had access to. In the dining room, there was a small table and four chairs. These were at one end of the room. At the other end, there was a three-seater sofa, and a small portable television was perched on a mahogany table, which was nestled in the corner.

The TV was only on if *he* allowed it and only on the channel *he* wanted to watch. And this wasn't done for any particular reason. It was just done so that he could show that he was the head of the house. She was never even allowed to sit on the sofa. She had to plonk herself on a pouffe or on the floor if her parents were watching a film. Mostly, though, she would go to her room and read a book or a magazine. Anything, really, just to be out of their way.

Creeping along the short path, past her father's wilting rose bushes, she headed towards the main road. But she was caught in two minds. If she wasn't going to return to her house until she saw Lucas Martin leave her home, where could she go? Her predicament underscored how alone she actually felt.

She decided in the end that she would head off down her street. But as she did, she couldn't shake off that vision of her scrawny pale-skinned father, who was half naked, perched at the end of his bed with a kid on his knees fondling him. She shuddered. Every bit of respect for the man she thought she had loved could, as far as she was concerned, be flushed down the toilet.

But had she ever actually loved him at all? Had she really? Okay, she knew she had always obeyed him. But loving someone like him? Biting her lip in anger, she decided she would head towards the church.

And then her mother popped into her thoughts. She could see her always nodding in agreement with every rule her father laid down. 'Make sure that slit in your skirt doesn't allow for your legs to be on show. You, Dorothy, are not a slut, so don't wear too much make-up. You're only seventeen.' Her mother was by his side, like a nodding dog, affirming every word he said. It was pathetic to see, but now she knew the truth. The real truth. It seemed that her mother was merely a puppet – just like herself.

It was devastating to think that her father believed he was acting in her best interests. To be strict purely for her own good. Making sure that she spent her entire childhood at the whim of her lord and master. He would tell her when to take a hot bath – morning and night – and remind her to wash her hands thoroughly before every meal. A clean, spotless individual, she was only asked to speak when he deemed it necessary. To be seen occasionally but certainly not heard. Because as far as he was concerned, her opinion counted for nothing.

What was the point of this? Well, of course, it was to make sure that she turned out to be a well-respected young woman. But only in his eyes, that is. God forbid, she ran, skipped, raised her voice – or even sang, except in the choir. Her father would speak down to her in such a way that she felt dirty.

Still, she couldn't say her parents abused her. Not physically, anyway. Her father had brought her up military style, except he had never been in the military. He was a little effeminate, in many ways, if she was honest with herself. But he was harsh, all the same. Now, she felt everything he stood for was a lie, every damn bit of it, and that included her mother. Did she know what was going on? Why had she never questioned his lack of church attendance on a Sunday? What were these chores he had to complete before the start of the working week? She shook her head and huffed in annoyance. The only chores were getting this kid around to their house to toss him off or whatever they did. She would have gone screaming to a neighbour if the kid was in distress, but he wasn't. Not that it made it all right – it certainly wasn't – but it was, nevertheless, sordid behaviour, in her mind, especially as the boy was so young.

In fact, the more she thought about it, the more disillusioned she became, and then, from nowhere, she momentarily gasped and dry-heaved.

The stone wall at the end of her road was as good a place as any to sit down and take a break. She heaved again, but then, with no difficulty whatsoever, it seemed, she practically emptied her stomach contents. She thought she should have felt better, but she didn't. She felt hot and dizzy. So she remained seated until the sickness passed.

As she peered down the road towards her house, Lucas, the young lad, was heading towards her. For some reason, she felt as if she should be the one who was ashamed because she was a member of her father's family. But the cocky grin on the boy's face as he approached his house really got up her nose. There he was holding up a five-pound note and kissing it, for God's sake, before he shoved it in his trouser pocket and skipped into his house. Despite her anger towards Lucas, any feeling of loyalty towards her father evaporated there and then. And respect for him? Well, after what she had just seen, that too, of course.

'You dirty bastard, a fiver for a toss,' she hissed, under her breath.

No wonder she was shivering, wearing a thin, unlined black monstrosity of a coat. It was the lack of care for her that made her even madder. She thought back over the past few months. It was obvious now what had been happening at her home. The boy had almost certainly been there every Sunday. In a month, that would amount to twenty pounds. She could only dream of what she could have bought with that.

Wistfully, her mind cast back to seeing Carrie earlier. If she was like her, she would have done a bit of shoplifting. She grinned to herself. That would have put the cat among the pigeons. She imagined explaining the appearance of a brand-new expensive outfit to her parents. They would go apeshit, naturally. But if she did decide to do a bit of 'choring', her parents would have a difficult job of claiming the high ground if they tried to moralise on her behaviour. Especially now she knew her father's perversions.

Getting up from the cold concrete wall, she felt a little happier. Self-reflection had done her a bit of good. For the first time in her life, she had confronted her demons – her parents – and that chat she'd had with Carrie had made her see things in a different light. She'd never had that kind of conversation with anyone else before. Not even with Margaret, her closest friend.

So heading back towards her house, she mentally played out how she would tell her parents about the baby. She would be confident and hold her head up high. Besides, this family of hers was so fucked up, so what difference would a pregnancy thrown into the mix make? Perhaps it would take them down a peg or two, and maybe they could all live like other families. A baby would bring them all closer, wouldn't it?

Once more, she put the key in the lock, pushed it open, and headed for her bedroom. But before she reached the stairs, she took a quick glance in the kitchen. Her father was humming a tune, which was so unlike him. He was busy straining boiled vegetables and shoving pots and pans into the sink. The room was so full of steam that every window was covered in condensation.

Without looking her way, her father said, 'Hey, Dorothy, where's your mother? I assume you went to church earlier this morning to have a little confession session.' He then laughed, but underneath the jovial tone, she thought she detected an element of seriousness. Or was it sarcasm?

She ignored him. 'I'll be in my room. I need to clean up before dinner.'

She hated it when her parents called her Dorothy. Everyone else called her Dottie.

He still didn't turn around to face her. He carried on by filling a pot with water and continued with his humming.

Pushing her bedroom door open, she stood for a second and stared at the small pink bedroom with her old teddies and dolls, her neat bed covers, and the pretty pink fluffy rug beside her bedside table. Anyone would have thought she was living in a loving family with no dark secrets. She wanted to laugh out loud. This picture of a perfect childhood was all a damned lie. She didn't cry because she was beyond crying now. Instead, she stared at her face in the oval mirror above her chest of drawers.

Dottie gently wiped the blood away and pressed the swelling under her eye; she was definitely going to have a shiner. Still, who cared? She didn't have anyone to impress, and, anyway, she had more important issues to deal with.

When the front door slammed shut, she heard her mother's shrill voice. 'Sorry, Malcolm, the wind did that. Gosh, it's so cold today. Hmm, something smells lovely. Did you get your chores done, darling?'

'Yes, yes, all done, and dinner will be ready in ten minutes. Let Dorothy know, will you. She can lay the table. Tell her to wash her hands – twice – before she joins us, sweetheart.'

Sitting on the end of her bed, Dottie shook her head at the absurdity of it all, and yet even though she knew what he'd done, she still felt herself preparing for an uncomfortable conversation over Sunday dinner.

Once her mother had called up the stairs and repeated her father's orders, Dottie opened her bedroom door and braced herself, knowing there would be a barrage of questions.

Her mother, Harriet, had her back to her; she was busy in the kitchen stirring the gravy.

Dottie removed the cutlery from the small wooden cabinet and placed the knives and forks on either side of the brightly coloured bamboo placemats.

Their conversation about the churchgoers was more about her mother having a good gossip, which to Dottie sounded like the faint buzzing noise of an annoying wasp. She waited until her father, with a roast beef dinner in each hand, followed by her mother, who also held another roast beef dinner and the gravy boat in each hand, trotted into the dining area.

Dottie stood there wondering when either of them would notice the huge swelling around her eye, as well as the nasty graze on her cheek. They didn't spot either until they were all seated, and her mother looked to ask her to say grace. Then, everything went tits up.

'Oh, dear God above, what on earth has happened to *you*?' she screeched.

'Have you been fighting, young lady? Because I will not tolerate thuggish behaviour in this family.'

Dottie wanted to laugh out loud, but she didn't. Instead, she bit her tongue and shrugged. 'I wasn't looking where I was going, and so I clumsily fell over a kerb.'

She was pleased with that response. But only for a second or two. Because the look on her father's face was enough to make her realise that years of subservience to him couldn't be undone in a heartbeat. Her earlier bravado was just that. Bravado. True, she had discovered something very deviant about him, but the bottom line was that she was still afraid of him. It meant that she couldn't voice her thoughts – not her honest thoughts, anyway.

'So why weren't you in the church today, Dorothy?'

Pushing a burned potato around her plate, which was laden with overcooked carrots and a mountain of stewed cabbage, she even noticed her mother turning her nose up at the sight of the meal in front of them.

'Mum, Dad, I am expecting a baby.'

There was absolute silence apart from the slosh of the soggy carrots sliding off her father's fork and onto the plate.

'*What?*' said her father, as he looked over the top of his thick-rimmed black glasses.

What made her announce something of such importance but in such a down-to-earth manner, she didn't know. But probably the only one way to deliver such a startling announcement was just to say it.

'So I am pregnant,' she said, firmly this time, since there was no going back.

'Is this some kind of knock-knock joke?' asked her mother, with her eyes like saucers.

'This definitely *isn't* a joke. I am having a baby.'

Her father jumped up from the table, slammed his fork down, and stamped his foot. 'Who is the father? Do you even know, or are there various possibilities?'

'Oh, shut up, Malcolm, let her speak!' Harriet said, as she turned to Dottie. 'Were you raped? Did someone hurt you? Are they from the church, from school, a neighbour?'

'No one raped me. I had a boyfriend and now I'm pregnant.'

Harriet grabbed a linen napkin and put it to her mouth, in an exaggeration of despair.

'And we are not together, now,' said Dottie, knowing she might as well let it all out. After all, she didn't want to endure a staggered backlash.

'My God, Dorothy, how could you. You're only seventeen years old.'

'Eighteen next week and almost nineteen when I have this baby, actually.'

As her father stomped around the room seething, her mother stared at her daughter in absolute horror. 'Who *is* this boyfriend?'

'It doesn't matter now because we are not together. He is back with his girlfriend, and that's that.'

Suddenly, out of the blue, her mother slapped her daughter's cheek, as if she was blind to the fact that it must be hurting already. 'You are disgusting, Dorothy. We've never brought you up to be a hussy. We've been good to you. And yet, this is how you repay us by getting pregnant. My God, what will they say at church? Our daughter, Malcolm, shortly to become an unmarried mother!' Harriet used the napkin to wipe away her tears. 'It's so *humiliating*. I'll not be able to show my face in church *ever again*.'

Malcolm came over and placed his hand on his wife's shoulder. 'Now, now, Harriet, this isn't your fault. Our daughter is wayward. I knew it. She's a trollop. Well, there is only one thing for it. You, Dorothy, certainly can't keep it, so you either have an abortion, or you put it up for adoption. I have a so-called aunt, my late mother's best friend, up in Scotland. You can go there until this bastard is born, and then we will arrange an adoption.'

'No, I am keeping it,' Dottie replied firmly, gently rubbing her bruised cheek.

This conversation was certainly not going how she thought it would. Her father, it seemed, was already on the attack. But his anger was making her angry as well. She was beginning to feel rebellious. And whether she wanted to have the baby, or not, there was no way her parents were going to decide for her, that was for sure.

'Now, you listen to me, young lady. You will damn well do as I say, and that'll be the end of it.'

'I am keeping my baby, Dad.'

Seemingly from nowhere, her father ran around the table, grabbed her by her hair, and pulled her head back.

'You will go to stay with Elspeth in Scotland, or you will have an abortion. I won't have you in my home with some delinquent's baby growing in your belly because you couldn't keep your legs together. Do I make myself clear?'

He let go of her hair.

'Yes, Dad, you have made yourself perfectly clear,' Dottie replied, as she rose abruptly from her chair. 'And you can hit me, slap me' – she glared at her mother – 'but you will *not* decide the fate of *my* child.'

Now white with rage, Malcom lifted his hand, ready to swipe his daughter.

'Don't you dare!' yelled Dottie, as she stepped back, astonished at how her own voice was laced with an aggressive shrill.

'*What* did you say?'

'I said, don't you dare. If you hit me, I will tell Mum what you really do as a chore when she's at church. Or does she know? If she does, no doubt she is trying to find a way to absolve your sins in your absence.'

As soon as the words left her mouth, she realised she couldn't take them back. Without a doubt, she understood that what she had just said had been wholly unwise.

It began with Dottie seeing her mother's reaction, which was to put her head in her hands and sob. Then, flicking her eyes from her father to her mother, the sudden realisation that her parents were perfectly aware of her father's fetish for young boys was so shocking, it was hard to comprehend. She had been bluffing before with the mention of her mother knowing about her father's goings-on, but now, that notion suddenly gripped her.

'Shut up, Dorothy, you don't know what you are saying.'

When she saw his body shrink as he squirmed, she said quietly, 'Yes, I do, Dad, and you know I do, and clearly, she does too.' She pointed to her mother, who wouldn't even look up.

The authoritative and harsh expression on her father's face instantly dissolved into unease. He backed up and stood behind his wife's chair. 'What are you saying, Dorothy?' he asked, in a whisper.

'I know what you were doing,' she said, not glancing away. 'I saw him. That kid. I saw *both* of you. And what I saw was despicable. You're a grown man, and he is no more than a *child.*'

His eyes narrowed. 'So you were spying on me, were you?'

'So you don't deny it, then?'

She watched him nudge her mother to speak, and slowly, she lifted her reddened face as tears streamed down. 'It is not your business, Dorothy. We are adults, and this is private. We are still a family. He is still your father, and I am your mother, and you have no reason to treat us any differently.'

'Yes, I do, and that is because every ounce of respect I had for my father and as a man has gone, and what is worse, the respect I had for you as a mother and as a woman has also gone.'

Dottie sighed heavily and sat down.

'I can't change who you two are, and yet I feel sick to my stomach that you, Mum, parade around the church as if you are Mary, Mother of God herself. The one who looks down on the parishioners, the one who gossips, and the one who revels in their misfortune. *The one who snubs the unmarried mothers!*'

'Stop it, stop it!' Harriet yelled.

'It's true, Mum, and yet you and him' – she pointed to her father – 'have the nerve to dictate to me how *I* deal with my pregnancy. Not only that but you are attempting to force me to feel less than a person. In fact, a whore! Which, by the way, I am not. I don't go looking for sex.' She shot a look at her father. 'Not like someone else does in this family.'

Those words not only stung Malcom but they compelled him to bow his head in shame. It was evident he didn't know where to put himself.

'I am having my baby, not at your so-called aunt's in Scotland but in my own home until I can get the council to get me my own place, away from this house of fucking lies.'

‘Dorothy, don’t you dare . . .’ Her mother stopped, realising that hearing profanity in her home was nothing in comparison to what her daughter now knew. She lowered her chin and stared at the uneven edges of the bamboo placemat that had been dyed purple. She pushed the fine bamboo strand to level it.

‘I’m going to my room. I don’t want to talk anymore.’ She rose again from her chair. As she walked out of the room, she turned back. ‘Oh, and just so you know, the father is Jimmy Carson.’

She didn’t know if she felt elated by the look on their faces or guilty for hurting them more. In fact, she simply didn’t know what she felt anymore. Except alone, very much alone.

CHAPTER FIVE

It was eleven o'clock in the evening when Dottie heard the voices. For some reason, she hadn't closed her bedroom door, which she always did. But in her heightened state of awareness, she could hear exactly what her parents were saying. Her mother's voice, although a whisper, had such a shrill tone to it that no matter how much she tried to lower it, her nasal whistle made it pitch at a level that even a dog could hear.

Slowly, Dottie sat up and edged herself off the bed. Knowing every creaky floorboard, she could subconsciously dodge them. She approached her bedroom door and listened, having thought she was imagining the bizarre content of their conversation. But what her parents were saying was even clearer to hear since they had not closed their bedroom door either.

'Malcolm, you will go to prison if she talks to anyone. I told you ten years ago that if you liked men, then fine, but keep your secret away from the home. But, Malcolm, you were having sex with a fifteen-year-old *boy*, for Christ's sake!'

'Harriet, don't look at me like that. You have secrets too.'

'Oh, for goodness' sake, giving my mother a few extra pills does not make me a killer. Christ, Malcolm, I told you she was dying anyway.'

'Okay, okay, let me think, Harriet. But it is clear that she must have seen me.'

'Of course, she bloody saw you! And with that creepy boy Lucas, too. And before you dare to say you weren't doing anything you shouldn't have been, don't waste your breath. We have a more worrying problem.'

'You seem more concerned about this issue, Harriet, than I would have given you credit for.'

'Yes, because if you go to prison . . . Well, then I won't be able to pay the rent. And your debts have mounted, Malcolm. We are struggling as it is. We must make sure Dorothy keeps her mouth shut.'

'Harriet, I cannot live under the same roof as a child who is holding me hostage. It amounts to bloody blackmail. She will end up running this house instead of me. I'm the bloody man of this house, and I won't be dictated to by a seventeen-year-old. A pregnant one at that.'

'Oh, Malcolm, she's not just pregnant but she's been with one of those Carsons,' she added, deliberately throwing oil on the fire.

'So, let's get back to this idea of yours, shall we. So tell me again what you said earlier. You're suggesting we have her sectioned?'

'Yes, yes, Maggie Lawson at my church said her daughter had made some wild accusations about her father, and they called a psychiatrist who apparently called another doctor because you need two professionals to sign the papers and her daughter was then taken to a mental hospital.'

'Really?'

'Shuuush, Malcolm, keep your voice down. I can make the call to Maggie and get the details, and that will be the end of the matter.'

'Are you sure about this, Harriet? What if they don't believe you? What if it backfires and opens up a whole can of worms?'

'Malcolm, will you keep your bloody voice *down*. Of course, they will believe me. Why wouldn't they? I'm a religious woman. Everyone knows my values, my morals, and who in their right mind would ever question me? No, Malcolm,' she said, without whispering, 'if I say she is mad, then they will most certainly believe me.'

'You do understand that this is the eighties not the fifties, Harriet. They won't section her because she is an unmarried mother.'

'I am not suggesting it's because she is up the bloody duff. I will tell them that she is acting like a delinquent and making ludicrous accusations, and I'll add a bunch of other stuff.'

'I'm still not sure, Harriet. What if they do believe her and the police get called?'

'Will you stop panicking? Leave it all to me. I will arrange everything. Think about it, Malcolm. Why would a psychiatrist have any reason to doubt me? Look at us, look at our home, our jobs. We amount to nothing short of model citizens.'

Dottie felt her insides churning. She could hardly believe her ears. But what shocked her the most was that her mother had killed her grandmother, the only woman she had ever related to. She had loved her grandmother so much and was devastated when she died. It made sense now. She was only seven at the time when her grandmother came to stay. Pneumonia had restricted her breathing and limited her movement, so a clumsy moment led to her falling down the stairs and breaking her foot. Sadly, she died shortly afterwards.

But with every cloud comes a silver lining, or so it seemed at the time. Within a month, her father was driving a new car, her mother had a new kitchen, and the pair were in seventh heaven. However, she wasn't. She would cry herself to sleep every night, wishing her grandmother would come down from there and whisk her away.

What more were her parents capable of doing if they had killed her grandmother and were now planning to have her sectioned? And what really happens to people if they get sectioned? All she knew was what she'd heard from Dale Morgan at school. His mother was sectioned and she ended up in a cage in

Cane Hill Asylum where she was sedated every day so she wouldn't scream for her kids. Well, so Dale said. That thought filled her head with absolute fear. As if suddenly overcome with a sense of survival, she held down her rising panic and took a few deep breaths. She would have to get out of the house before they stopped her. Her mother may have been right because to the outside world, they were the perfect family. She thought back to Ginty's description of her parents. If she saw them as a model family, then it would be wise to assume others would as well. It was all about perception at the end of the day. But this was a right old mess. With nowhere to go, she couldn't easily plan where she would go. Her only option, it seemed, was to pack a small case, empty the piggy bank, wrap up warm, and run for her life.

Quietly, she tried to listen to their conversation. At the same time, she pulled on an old pair of jeans over her pyjama bottoms and carefully opened her middle drawer, praying it wouldn't squeak. She retrieved her thickest jumper and put it on over her pyjama top. Once she was fully dressed, and she had her pixie boots on, she decided not to bother with a bag; her main concern was escaping these two nutcases she called mum and dad.

She listened until there was silence. With her pink piggy bank under her arm, she cautiously pushed her door ajar and looked to see if the coast was clear. The landing light was off, and her parents' bedroom door looked shut.

She was filled with a sudden sense of relief.

But that didn't last long.

To Dottie's despair, her parents' bedroom door opened a fraction, and then – horror of horrors – she saw her father sidestep into view. Her heart thumped inside her chest as the light from her parents' room highlighted the pointy features on his face. She noticed him glare like a devil she'd often dreamed about. Behind his dark expression lurked evil. She knew it because she was seeing him for what he was.

‘What are you doing?’ His voice was so cold, she hardly recognised it. Then her mother appeared behind him. Strangely, she was dressed in her long pink negligée like someone from a nineteen fifties film. All she needed was a cigarette holder and a glass of martini, and she would look just like a film star, except it was nineteen eighty-two, and her mother was ugly. The image of the two of them, with their painted-on fake smiles, ran like ice through her veins. And dread twisted around her gut.

Her mother was sneering at her as her father pushed her door open and forced her back into her room. She couldn’t believe that these two monsters seemed to be taking pleasure in her terror.

‘I promise, Dad, I will never say anything to anyone. Please.’

‘Your mother wants you to take some medicine. We have all had a terrible time, and we need to calm our excitement. So take your medicine like a good girl and sleep well. You will feel better in the morning.’

Those words somehow stirred a buried memory. But what was it? Her mind raced back in time. When she was younger, she was often told to take her medicine, which did help her sleep, even at five in the afternoon, when their guests arrived around that time. She recalled waking up a few times to hear the laughter, and then, one evening, she saw her mother wearing that same negligée. She was entertaining a strange man in the spare room. The realisation hit her like a bolt of lightning: these two monsters had been exhibiting deviant behaviour all her life, and yet they had portrayed themselves as the epitome of righteousness.

‘You must take your medicine, Dorothy.’

‘*What?*’ Her eyes were round with fear. ‘No, I won’t take any medicine. I’m pregnant, for God’s sake.’

Her mother moved quickly into the bathroom, and just as quickly, she was back on the landing. Sidestepping Malcolm, she was now in her bedroom with a glass of water in one hand and pills in the other. She uncurled her fingers showing four tables.

'Now, you be a good girl and take the pills. I promise you that you will feel better. Sweetheart, I know you've had quite a shock, and your father and I are sorry for that. But with a fresh mind, we will explain everything in the morning.' Her voice became sickly sweet. It was the same way she spoke to the women at the church. 'Now, come on, Dorothy, swallow them.'

Dottie couldn't believe her ears. But when she looked over her mother's shoulder, she saw her father holding a long blunted instrument. It was a metal cosh. He slyly lifted it as a warning.

Unable to get her head around the idea that her parents were about to drug her, or, worse, bludgeon her, the thought turned her legs to jelly and sent her pulse racing. She was forced back inside her room, and as her calves hit the base of the bed, she automatically sat down.

Her father nodded as if she was doing the right thing before he intimidatingly loomed over her. 'Now, don't cause a fuss, Dorothy,' he said, as he lifted the cosh.

Her mother pushed him aside and gripped her daughter's jaw, yanking her mouth open. 'Take these.' She popped the tablets onto Dottie's tongue and forced her mouth shut. Then, she handed her a glass of water.

Gripped with fear, and staring at the metal cosh, Dottie took the glass and sipped the drink, ensuring her parents could see the gulp she made before she opened her mouth to show them that she had swallowed the tablets.

Her mother's painted-on smile finally flattened as she looked Dottie up and down as though she was a piece of shit at the bottom of her shoe.

Dottie stared, like a robot, momentarily too appalled for words, before her parents left the room and slammed the door shut behind them.

The thought that in a few minutes she would be comatose compelled her to stick her fingers down her throat, which was something she'd never done before. But it wasn't something she needed to practise because instantly she felt her stomach flipping over and her throat contracting as if she was going to birth a dinosaur via her mouth. She peeled back the bedsheet and braced herself before she stuck her fingers down her throat again. This time, she jolted and wretched, almost gagging on the vomit that landed on her bed. And there intact were the four blue tablets – Valium. She quickly covered the vomit with the bedsheets and then sat at the head of the bed with her head in her hands, half expecting her mother to come in again. She was lucky that there wasn't a lot of vomit and it wasn't pungent. But there wouldn't have been much because she had vomited that morning and hadn't eaten since.

Much later, the door opened, and there, still in her pink see-through negligée, was her mother, with a smirk and a look of righteous indignation fixed on her face. 'Now, you get some sleep, madam. It's been a long evening for all of us.'

The rage that bubbled inside Dottie was aimed mainly at her mother for allowing her life to be this way. But for her mother to even consider conspiring with her father to send her to an asylum was too much to bear. Still, all she could do to stop herself from jumping up and slapping her was to nod in silent defeat and pretend she was already falling asleep by lowering her eyelids to slits and sliding sideways as if she was about to lie down. Closing her eyes, she heard her bedroom door brushing slowly over the carpet and the almost silent click as the door closed. Her act had worked.

She remained in the same position for an hour until she could hear her father snoring and her mother grunting like a pig. Now, it was her chance to escape. She saw it as a desperate measure to save her baby. She hadn't thought much about it except saving its life. Out of the blue, she had a disturbing thought. What if they locked her away in an asylum and they managed to secure custody of the child? What if it was a boy? Her head was hot, and her mouth felt dry. She had to get away. Her parents were so fast asleep, they wouldn't hear her now.

She hurried from her room, still in the same clothes, but, this time, instead of putting on her own thin black coat, she slipped her arms into her mother's, and the difference was instantly noticeable. She felt so warm. She knew then that whatever happened to her, she would always put her child first – unlike her parents. She would be a *good* mother.

The moment, however, she opened the front door, she was faced with a blizzard. The snow blew in her face. It had already blanketed the street and the cars and was almost three inches deep. She took one step outside and realised she would die out there in the freezing cold. Not even a cat would survive these cold temperatures, even with a fur coat on. There were no tyre marks, no footsteps, but it was one o'clock in the morning, and the streetlamp cast a creamy orange glow over the street. If she hadn't been in such a state, she would have admired the view – the peaceful silence and beauty of it.

But right now, she couldn't imagine her life being anything like beautiful. Not one bit. She was, without a doubt, trapped. Her parents would have her locked up by lunchtime tomorrow, and they would have the rights to her child. She would live such a miserable existence to the extent that there was no purpose in living at all. What the hell would be the point? She stepped back inside the house and closed the door behind her.

As she entered the living room – the forbidden part of the house – she turned the light on and gazed around. The photo of her grandmother drew her close. Her pretty blue eyes were smiling, and her plump cheeks were soft. Staring at the photo, she recalled that the only person to have hugged her, apart from Jimmy, was her grandmother. Her father couldn't be bothered, and her mother was too stuck up her own arse to be concerned with any affection. It made her wonder if her mother liked the idea that her father had a deviant side to him so that she could lord it over him and do so in such a pseudo-submissive way. It was so bizarre. Everything was. She had always assumed her mother had been the nodding dog, with agreeable eyes, every time she spoke to her father. But that was then and this was now. Now, she was beginning to believe that what had gone on in her past was all a front. Her mother was the real puppet master, and her father was the actor pretending he was the soldier in charge. Maybe that was her mother's fantasy? Who knew.

The green Dralon three-piece suite was covered in plastic and looked as new as the day her parents bought it, a month after her grandmother had passed away. She glanced back at her grandmother's photo and felt grief like a calling from the pit of her stomach. But now? Now, she knew the truth. She mulled over her parents' conversation, and she knew that she wasn't mistaken when her mother had said she had given Granny a few extra pills. What would her parents do to her?

One thing was for sure: they were never going to get their hands on her baby. Even if she couldn't look after her child, she would be damned if her parents would ever have the opportunity.

Seeing that she had nowhere to go now, she took off her mother's coat, her own jumper, her jeans, and her boots and left them on the floor before she headed towards the kitchen, which, even after their heated argument, was left pristine. There was not a dirty plate in sight. Her eyes paused on the knives in the wooden holder, all in a sequence of size. She lifted the largest one. When she ran her finger along the blade, she felt a sharp pain, and instantly, blood dripped onto the kitchen counter. Of course, these knives were sharp; everything in the house would have been fit for purpose, so her father would have sharpened the knives until they could slice through meat like slicing through butter.

She removed a second knife as well. It was a tad smaller but it was still deadly, and then she marched up the stairs gripping what would now be her weapons. Pushing her parents' bedroom door open using her foot, she crept inside, and stood at the foot of their bed. The orange streetlamp positioned outside their home threw light into the room. It was enough to make out their bodies in the bed. She expected them to appear peaceful while they slept, but they didn't. Her mother's nose twitched like a rabbit's, and her father had his mouth so wide open, he looked deformed. But that didn't stop him from snoring and moaning. Turning her gaze to her mother, she watched as her mother gave out a little grunt and snuffle and then let out a whining deep breath.

Her eyes were suddenly drawn to the foot of their bed, where she had caught her father in his compromising position. Her gaze then lifted to look once more at her mother, who knew her father's secret and was even prepared to condone it. The enormity of what she had learned in just one day of her life would stay with her forever. And to discover that she had been living with two monsters for almost eighteen years was all too much for her.

Suddenly, she became so clear-headed that she could not only see through their façade but see them for what they were.

Looking around the room, she couldn't help but swear silently at the sight of her mother's clothes, which had been left on hangers outside the wardrobe. Those clothes, which she had worn today, were classy and very expensive. She thought back to the times when she had attended church with her mother and how she had 'peacocked around' in various suits and freshly pressed blouses as though she owned the place. Even her shoes, which were practically new, were lined up in boxes under the window. Not ever having been allowed to enter her parents' bedroom, she hadn't comprehended how much attention her mother had paid to her appearance – even at the sake of her own child's. Her mother had never cared for her as she should have.

Strangely, she wanted to count the boxes. There were fifteen pairs of shoes in total compared to her two pairs. One pair she had bought for herself and the other her parents had chosen for her for school. She also had a pair of the pixie boots that a friend had given her because they hadn't fitted her. She was forever using a black felt-tip pen to colour the scratches on the heels. The measly three pounds her mother gave her every week was pathetic in comparison to what her friends received, and it wasn't as if she had an army to feed. Her parents had only one child, and that child understood that she was never wanted. *Probably never had been*, she thought.

Dottie thought about that. Never wanted. She had so obviously interfered with their strange lifestyle. They had always treated her as if she was a relative who had been placed in their care and they were left to do the honourable thing by raising her as their own. She felt as if they were doing her a huge favour by having her live in their home and eat their food. But, sadly, she was their child. After all, her mother had given birth to her.

Dottie once again crept like a burglar to her mother's side of the bed. She stared and wondered if she felt anything, but she didn't. Not an ounce of love, a minuscule drop of compassion – nothing whatsoever.

Without guilt or in fact any feeling whatsoever, she lifted the larger knife above her head and rammed it down so fast that the huge wide blade went straight through her mother's ribcage directly into her heart. The noise was like a thud, then a squelch, but it wasn't loud enough to wake her father. Blood shot out like a geyser, and for a split moment, her mother's eyes opened and stared in horror before letting out a burbling sound as the last bit of air left her lungs. But it was long enough for her to see who was killing her. The blood then covered the sheets; it turned what was a pale lemon duvet cover to a deep claret.

Dottie didn't bother to run around the bed to her father's side. She leaned over her mother and raised the knives once more. But as she was about to thrust them into her father's chest, he moved. He must have been startled. Without his glasses, he wouldn't have been able to see clearly, but she knew it was enough for him to see the outline of his daughter brandishing a weapon in each hand. He tried to sit up, but she wasn't going to give him even a moment. There was no way she was going to talk or bargain with him for his life. This time, she rammed the smaller knife into his neck and pulled it out. She saw his eyes widen as he faced the reality that she had stabbed him. He threw his hands to his neck and instantly felt the blood pumping out.

Dottie watched him trying to stop the bleeding. First came the panic on his face. Then the begging in his eyes. But he knew he was going to die, and, within seconds, his face turned into someone she couldn't recognise. This wasn't her father. He was a stranger.

Malcolm fell back onto his pillow. His eyes rested on his wife and his mouth gaped open as he tried to gasp for air. As his hands slipped away from the fatal wound, the blood pumped twice more, spraying over his daughter's pyjamas.

Dottie staggered back. Frozen to the spot while drenched in her parents' blood, she started to shake uncontrollably. The knives, which were dripping with claret, were still in her hands. Her knuckles were white as she gripped their handles, but all she could do was stare at the carnage – the blood-drenched bed and the grotesque expression on her parents' faces.

Dottie wasn't aware of how long she had stood staring at the dead bodies, but it must have been a long time because now the first rays of the early morning sun were shining in through the curtains. Opening one of them, she saw that the snow outside was untouched. There were no footprints, no tyre tracks even.

Lowering her stiff arms, she stared down at the blood-covered knives before she dropped them and put her arms around herself. She backed out of the room, almost expecting her parents to sit up and berate her.

After closing their door, she walked down the stairs and into the living room to find her clothes still in a heap. Stepping over them, she looked at the photo of her grandmother. 'I'm sorry, Gran, but I had to do this. I couldn't let them have my baby.'

Taking a deep breath, Dottie opened the front door and left the house. But with nowhere to go, and in a state of deep contemplation, she sat down on the doorstep, which was covered in snow.

***

Three doors away, Raymond Clarkson came out of his home. He was dressed in his camel Crombie coat, his trilby hat, and his Wellington boots, which protected his tailored trousers. He walked along the street and was about to tip his hat to say good morning when he stopped. Staring for a minute, he struggled to comprehend what he was looking at.

But there was no mistake: Dorothy Ellis was sitting on her doorstep. Her face and hair were covered in blood, and her bare feet, which were also covered in blood, were blue from the cold. His eyes fell to her hands, which wouldn't stop shaking, and they too were dripping in claret. She was staring at nothing, as if she was in another world.

Clarkson, a man in his late forties, was a detective, although at the moment he was on long-term leave. He could take an educated guess that Dorothy had murdered her parents or at least one of them because they didn't have a dog, and the amount of blood all over her would suggest she had slaughtered someone. He wanted to comfort the girl, but he knew that he had to call the police first, so he turned on his heel and hurried back to his home, where he dialled 999. The operator told him to stay away from the scene and that officers were on their way. He replaced the receiver. He thought about what the operator had said, but then he decided he couldn't leave Dorothy there, cold, alone, and in shock.

He hurried back, but when he reached her garden, he walked slowly along the path towards her. She was still staring into nothing. As he sat beside her on the doorstep, he whispered in his most compassionate voice, 'Dottie, love, are you hurt?'

She didn't answer, so he briefly looked her over. He couldn't see any evidence of blood coming from her, but then, without lifting her top, he couldn't really make a judgement.

'Dottie, are your mum and dad inside the house?'

Dottie snapped out of her gaze and swivelled her head to face him. 'Yes, Mr Clarkson, they are in their bed . . . dead.' A tiny tear escaped her eye.

He slid his arm around her. 'Are you all right, Dottie, love?' he asked, as he felt her shivering body.

'I am now, Mr Clarkson. I am now.'

He removed his coat and wrapped it around her. Then he held her close until the police arrived. He wanted to make sure that they wouldn't manhandle her because he knew that Dorothy wasn't a bad kid. However, as for her parents, that was probably another matter entirely. Her father had been under scrutiny for a sick crime a few years ago, but there had been no real evidence to convict him of having sex with a minor. Maybe today was the day young Dorothy had discovered the truth.

CHAPTER SIX

Detective Chief Inspector Raymond Clarkson offered his hand and smiled at Detective Inspector Kenneth Granger. 'Hello, long time no see. How are you, Ken?'

'I am okay.' They shook hands.

'The doctor believes I will be as good as new in a few months.'

Scratching his wild nest of grey hair, Ken worriedly asked, 'But you're not planning to return to work though, are you?' He had been promoted to Detective Inspector and was running the show since Clarkson had been signed off indefinitely. The car crash had left him in a bad way, and no one could have imagined that he would ever walk again, let alone string a sentence together. However, looking at him now, he appeared as bright and fit as he was before the appalling incident.

'I thought you would be pleased to welcome me back.'

Granger's jaw dropped. 'What? Are you coming back?'

'Of course, I am returning to work. Why ever did you think I wouldn't?'

'Well, because it's been so long and word has it that you are opting for early retirement. I mean, of course, we would find a place for you in the team. That's not—'

'A place for me? No, Ken, when I do return, I will take up my former position. I'm so sorry. I thought the Commissioner made it quite clear to you that when you took over my role it would be on a temporary basis.'

‘Yes, right o’ course, Ray. So when do you think the doctors will sign you fit for work?’

Clarkson laughed. ‘Don’t worry, Ken, you can fill my boots for a good three months yet.’

With his hands in his trouser pockets, Granger swayed back and forth. His pleasant tone had dropped a notch because he had hoped that Clarkson would never return.

‘So one of my officers told me that you know Dorothy Ellis and would like to be present while we interview her since she’s a young person.’ He frowned. ‘Not really the done thing, though, Ray, is it?’

Clarkson, who had spent all his life taking particular care of his appearance regarding his attire – even his hair and nails – was one of those people who didn’t seem to age. This was despite having suffered such a horrific accident. He walked and talked in such a calming manner that he could talk anyone down from a cliff and appease the most violent offenders just by a few well-composed words. His ex-wife saw it as a fault but also not grounds for divorce. *Irreconcilable differences* she put on the petition. He didn’t argue: of course their marriage was over when she slept with her swimming instructor and the gardener and the milkman – and probably scores more.

‘Isn’t it, Ken?’

Granger, who had recently celebrated his forty-eighth birthday, had worked under Clarkson for ten years, and he had a great deal of admiration for the man. His record in the murder squad was impeccable, and his excellent reputation was second to none. Suddenly, he felt under attack. Even though what Clarkson actually asked was so straightforward, it was expressed in such a casual – almost deceptive – manner that he felt Clarkson should be the one who should be apologising for asking the question. But that was Clarkson all over. He had this knack of putting you on the defensive. But he knew that undertone of Clarkson’s was certainly not one of politeness. The man was a master at getting what he wanted from people.

'Sorry, I didn't mean anything by that remark. Er . . . so you know Dorothy Ellis well, do you?'

'She is just a neighbour. No more than that, Ken. She's a sweet girl who always leaves for school dead on time. Rarely do I see her with friends. She's not the type to be hanging about on the streets causing any trouble.'

'She's not talking to us, Ray.'

'Fair enough. But I bet she doesn't have a solicitor present, does she? You know how I feel about police protocol, Ken, don't you?'

Granger felt his ears burning and he knew his face was turning red. Clarkson probably could see that he was having that effect on him. *But the thing was: why hadn't he taken the trouble to give the kid some support?*

'Er, no, no, not yet.'

'Hmmm, so, Ken, let's look at this logically. We have a child – because she *is* a child – let's not kid ourselves – and no pun intended by the way – who is unaccompanied and with no legal representation. That's where we are with this, isn't it, Ken?'

'Well,' said Granger, half laughing, 'you know how it is, Ray. We want to get as much out of her as possible.' But as soon as he said that, he could have kicked himself in the shins. He knew how stupid, callous, and utterly unprofessional that sounded, especially to someone like Clarkson.

The pause was a long and uncomfortable one. 'So would you take me to her, then, Ken?'

'Er . . . sure. Why not? She could probably do with a friendly face,' he said, not knowing what he could say to prevent Clarkson from getting involved.

***

As Clarkson followed Granger, he stopped at the open door to the serious incident room, where smack bang in the middle of the whiteboard there were the photographs of the Ellis family. The images were macabre, to say the least, even to someone of his considerable experience.

'Sorry, Ray, you can't go in there. Er . . . you know what I mean.'

But Clarkson just ignored Granger and walked right up to the whiteboard. The team, who were busy in an animated conversation about the murders, stopped talking immediately. However, a couple of them, who had been on the force for a number of years with Clarkson and who respected him for his professionalism and integrity, acknowledged him by the customary 'Sir' or 'Gov'. The whole team either knew him or knew of him. He would never be a shrinking violet.

'She killed them like a pro,' said Brian Colt, a young detective who was Granger's sidekick.

'Like a pro?' Clarkson said, with his hands on his hips, as he swivelled to face the young detective.

'Yeah, definitely. She stabbed them once each and clearly knew where to plunge the knives to cause fatal injuries.'

One of Clarkson's pet hates was dealing with officers who liked to be presumptuous. But he wasn't going to express his annoyance. A fair man, and super critical of himself as well as of his colleagues, he had to concede that maybe he was being somewhat too sensitive about Dorothy Ellis. The fact was he liked her – a lot.

'May I suggest that if you were to kill someone, most people would go for the neck or chest? That doesn't make you a pro. And a pro suggests she has killed before. I think we can establish quite easily that this is a seventeen-year-old girl who has had no previous convictions. In fact, Detective, if she hasn't said a word to anyone yet, then how can you be so sure she killed her parents?'

The room fell silent, and Colt – who had not worked under Clarkson – gave him a respectful nod.

‘I’ll take you to see her, Ray,’ said Granger, quietly.

Clarkson smiled at everyone and turned to follow Granger.

A police officer was outside the interview room, and as soon as Granger pushed the door open, Clarkson’s heart sank, and his fists clenched in anger. He glared at Granger and then looked back at Dorothy.

‘Has Dorothy been photographed, and have her prints been taken?’

‘Yes, sir, I mean Ray.’

‘So why is she still in those clothes? Look at them, Ken. She is plastered with blood from top to bottom. If I hadn’t given her my coat, she would have had no form of comfort whatsoever.’

‘Well, we, er . . .’

‘You were trying to get her to speak, were you not?’

‘Ray, I don’t think this is a good idea, mate, you being here. She’s just a neighbour to you, and she’s old enough to be questioned, so—’

‘Hold up, Ken.’

He stepped closer to Dorothy and took the seat opposite. He wanted to hold the girl and comfort her because she appeared absolutely terrified. Her hands were shaking, but behind that Charles Manson stare, he could see she was a very frightened young lady.

‘Dottie? Dottie, love?’

She snapped out of her gaze then, and her eyes desperately searched his, seeking help.

‘Dottie, would you like me to stay with you as your accompanying adult?’

Clarkson glared back at Granger with a hint of a smirk because they both knew that she only had to agree and he had the right to act for her. And Granger would understand that that could be disastrous, especially since no one knew the law better than his former boss.

She nodded and whispered, ‘Yes, please, Mr Clarkson.’

'Right,' he said.

Clarkson stood up. 'Ken, I don't see any empty cups. Has Dorothy had anything to drink? Has she seen a doctor? Has she even been to *the toilet*?'

With every question, Granger's face glowed redder and redder. It didn't go unnoticed by Dorothy and Clarkson.

'I'll see to it right now.'

'Oh, and please have a female officer take Dorothy to the bathroom. She needs a shower and to warm up. She's bloody freezing. Turn the heating on in here, and fetch a McDonald's.' He looked at Dorothy. 'Dottie, would you like something from McDonald's? A large burger and chips, and perhaps a Coke to go with it?'

She nodded, gratefully.

'Good, and can we get a doctor to check her over. If you don't have any change of clothes, then we must get an officer to go back to the house and bring them over. Oh, and as for the refreshments, I'll pay for them.' Clarkson pulled out his wallet from his long black coat and slapped a twenty-pound note on the table while also keeping his eye on Dorothy.

'Yeah, sure. And in the meantime, we'll find her a tracksuit to wear.'

Clarkson peered up. 'In her size?'

'Oh, er . . . I don't know about that.'

Clarkson went back to his wallet and took out another twenty-pound note. 'Look forget what I said about asking an officer to go and fetch Dorothy's clothes over. It'll be quicker if someone goes out and purchases some. I can see she is a size ten. I want jeans, underwear, a vest, sweatshirt, and a thick jumper, socks, and boots.' He looked down at her feet. 'Size five.' Then he looked up, and this time, he pulled out two fifty-pound notes from his wallet. 'Make them fur lined. No shit boots either. Oh, and I want receipts for the lot.'

'Gov . . . I mean Ray, it's a bit outside our remit all this, isn't it? I, er . . .'

'Outside our *remit*, Ken? Are you being *serious*? I think this case calls for a detailed understanding of what happened to this young lady. And right now, leaving her sitting in congealed and dried blood in a cold room with no food or drink, no doctor, and no accompanying adult amounts to what? How can I put it delicately? I would say that what she's enduring right now is torture. Wouldn't you agree? This means she won't give you a detailed account, will she? Unless your interviewing techniques have reverted to bullying to get a confession, that is.'

'*What?*' said Granger, knowing he was not only in a sticky situation but he could be seen to be acting prejudicially against Dorothy Ellis. 'No, Ray, that's not how I do things. And as for the cold, come on, yeah, all right, it's a bit chilly, but it's bloody freezing outside.'

'Ken, she's shivering. And yet you have beads of sweat on your face.'

'Ray, you're not the lead here anymore. You've been signed off, so let me do my job. And another thing. Maybe you need to take a step back.'

A smile stretched across Clarkson's face, which uneased Granger. 'I am her assigned adult because Dorothy has just assigned me. Haven't you, Dottie?'

Dottie nodded, her eyes ping-ponging from Granger to Clarkson. In a small way, she felt safer.

'And I guess you haven't organised legal representation for her, have you?'

'What do you mean? We were waiting for a duty—'

Clarkson cut him off. 'Well, there's no need. I have employed one.' He looked at Dorothy. 'You need a lawyer, Dottie. I have the best. Would you like him to take on your case?'

She nodded again.

'Who?' asked Granger, but then, he knew it was a waste of time asking that question. It was perfectly obvious who it would be.

'Clive Clemence.'

Granger rolled his eyes, took the money, and shook his head. 'I'll organise the food and clothes. And just so you don't think me a monster, Ray, I have already called the doctor to come and see Miss Ellis.'

As soon as the door closed behind Granger, Clarkson lifted Dorothy's chin. 'Have you said anything to the police?'

Her eyes dragged to the side. They were full of fear and exhaustion. 'No, Mr Clarkson.'

'Good. When Clemmy, I mean Mr Clemence, gets here, he will advise you what to say, and, more importantly, what not to say.'

'I want to tell the truth. You know I killed them, and I did. I stabbed them.'

Clarkson peered over his shoulder and put his finger to his lips. 'You may have done what you have just said, but there would have been a reason for it, and that's the point. The reason for murder defines a person's motivation. Look at it this way, Dottie. If this was a crime based on pleasure, one could argue that the killer would have psychopathic tendencies. But if a person was compelled to act the way they did, that is a whole different matter altogether. And, Dottie, I don't believe that you are a psychopath. Not one bit.'

'What makes you so sure, Mr Clarkson?' She looked at her hands, which were covered in blood.

'Because do you remember last summer when my little dog, Jack, was knocked down? You came running to me, tears streaming down your face, and you held my dog like a baby. You willed my dog to live, and, thankfully, he did. Every day, you came to my house to check he was okay, until you saw me taking him for a walk. That, young lady, is not the actions of a psychopath. So, we have to establish what is called mitigating circumstances and also to establish whether it was manslaughter or murder. And there is a difference. Although the outcome is the same for the dead person, the outcome for the accused would be different.'

Dottie continued to stare at her hands and slowly turned them over, scrutinising both sides. 'They were going to lock me up in a mental hospital or an asylum, Mr Clarkson, and I couldn't let them do that. I couldn't let them take my baby, not after . . .' She clammed up and took a few deep breaths. 'Not after what I saw.'

Clarkson was stunned that Dorothy was pregnant. He had all kinds of twisted thoughts weaving through his head. He leaned closer, and without mentioning the pregnancy, he said, 'What did you see, Dottie?'

She shook her head. 'I can't. I can't . . .' Tears rolled down her cheeks.

'You can, and you must, because you need to have a defence. What did you see, Dottie?'

She looked away and stared at the wall.

'Your father?'

She shot him a wide-eyed glare. 'How do you know?'

'Was he with a minor?'

She frowned. 'How do you know?'

'Dottie, who was he with, and what was he doing?'

'It's so disgusting, I can't say.'

Clarkson sensed she was uncomfortable, so he knew he would have to tease it out of her. 'Was he with a boy?'

She nodded but kept her hand over her mouth.

'Was he younger than you?'

She nodded, and huge tears fell over her hands this time. 'Almost three years.'

'I'm sorry to ask, but was what you saw sexual in any way?'

She nodded and squeezed her eyes shut.

'I know it's hard. It must have been quite a shock.'

She wiped her face. 'It was . . . He-he-he was in the bedroom with the boy, Lucas Martin, from our street.'

Clarkson knew who Lucas Martin was. But he hid his shock. 'Okay, Dottie, you are doing well, love. So, did your father see you?'

'No, he didn't. I left the house. That was when I saw you, Mr Clarkson. You walked past me.'

'I remember, so I understand why you may have wanted to kill your father, but why your mother as well?'

'No, Mr Clarkson, I had to kill them *both.* They were going to have me sectioned, and I knew that they wanted to lock me away. Then they would have given my baby to my parents, and if it was a boy, then my father . . .' She swallowed hard. 'My mother gave me the pills, but I threw them up on my bed and covered the vomit up, and then, I waited until they were asleep.' She sighed and looked up. 'I am certain now that my mother knew all along that he was doing this dirty stuff with young boys. And they acted like I was in the wrong for getting pregnant. They tried to drug me. My mother believed that she could convince a doctor I was mad.'

Clarkson leaned back on his chair and let out an almighty sigh. It all made sense because when he investigated Malcolm Ellis, he never dreamed that his wife would ever have been used as an alibi. That man had gotten away with it for years because his wife knew all about his sexual tendencies. So the woman had protected him the whole time.

He placed his hand over Dorothy's. 'You did well, love, and now, when this solicitor comes, you tell him the same as you told me, but do not talk in front of any policeman. Whatever you do, do not say anything in front of Detective Inspector Granger, or anyone else, because it will go against you.'

She nodded, and for the first time, her cheeks lifted into what he could only describe as a sad smile.

A female officer entered the room. Clarkson knew her and was grateful that Granger had sent her along. She held a towel and a washbag. Her blonde hair was pulled back tightly in a bun, and her fresh pretty face glowed when she smiled.

'Hi, Dorothy, I'm Detective Constable Susan Ring. You can call me Sue. Everyone does. Come with me and we'll get you cleaned up.'

Her words were so gentle that Dottie wanted to cry. Apart from Mr Clarkson, it was the first time anyone had been kind to her in ages.

'Go on, Dottie, Sue will look after you.' Clarkson smiled encouragingly.

As Dorothy stepped out from behind the table, Susan looked at the young girl's feet, which were bloodstained and yet blue from the cold. Susan met Clarkson's eyes, shaking her head in disgust at how the girl had been left. 'I will take care of her, Ray.'

He nodded. 'I know you will, Sue.' And he did because she was a great member of the team.

As Dorothy left the room, Clarkson noticed how fragile she appeared. The fact that she was pregnant was undoubtedly a concern. As if the young girl wasn't going through enough.

While Dorothy was getting cleaned up, Clarkson made his way to the reception.

As if on cue, Clive Clemence arrived. He was looking less like a typical solicitor, dressed as he was in jeans, a marl grey crew neck jumper, and a woollen jacket. With a tatty briefcase under his arm, he hurried to meet Clarkson. 'I was about to go on a breakfast date, Ray. With a beautiful woman, and all.'

Clarkson laughed. 'Clem, you go on a date all the time with the same pretty woman. I am sure your wife won't miss this one morning. It's the double murder case, a young Dorothy Ellis, my neighbour and a sweet kid.'

'Yes, Madeleine and I heard it on the radio. She told me she wouldn't be surprised if I was called in, but I never dreamed it would be by you, Ray.'

As they huddled in the reception area, talking about the case, the door opened and in bustled two officers carrying shopping bags and a McDonald's meal.

'Oh, the force are clamping down on the shoplifters, I see.'

'No, Clem, that's for the girl. They bloody had her here for hours – without a drink or any food – and she was still wearing her pyjamas that were soaked in blood, may I add. The bastards turned the heating down in the interview room, and by the time they allowed me to see her, she looked like that character "Carrie" out of the Stephen King film.'

'I saw that film too. Right, let me get up there and throw some weight around.' He laughed, rubbing his hands together. 'I'll be frank with you: the team have been like headless chickens running around and pushing their luck since you left. That Granger bloke needs to get the shove. He comes to work and leaves his moral scruples behind. Anyway, Ray, the one thing I can do is ensure she is treated fairly. From what you've told me, she will serve a prison sentence. Let's hope we have enough to get a manslaughter conviction and not one for bloody murder.'

'Clem, all I ask is that you do your best. That kid has no one, now. No family, that's for sure, and she is a bit short on friends. One other thing, and it's very important. You also need to know that she thinks she's pregnant.'

'Right, but tell me this: why the interest on your part?'

Clarkson looked down. 'She reminds me of . . .'

'Oh, Christ, sorry. Yeah, your daughter would have been the same age. Forgive me, Ray. I can be a bit clumsy with the details.'

Clarkson waved his hands. 'No, listen, it was some time ago now. But I guess it has something to do with it. If my little Jenny had been in trouble, you would have done the same for her, wouldn't you?'

Clemence nodded and gave a compassionate smile. 'Yeah, of course, I would. Now, let's meet this kid.'

By the time they reached the interview room, Dorothy was looking much better and tucking into a burger as if she was starving.

'Well, now, there's a difference,' said Clarkson, smiling.

He couldn't believe the transformation. The colour had been restored to her face, there wasn't a speck of blood on her, and she looked warm, with her thick blue-and-grey ski jumper, well fitted jeans, and, when he looked down, he saw she had on a decent pair of boots.

Dottie stopped eating and put the burger on the wrapper. 'Thank you, Mr Clarkson, I feel so much better. I thought I was shivering from the shock, but it may have been the cold.'

Clemence stepped forward and introduced himself before taking the seat opposite.

'Ray has filled me in on what happened, but listen to me. I will instruct you to say nothing, okay, because I need to gather some evidence. For starters, I want your bedding checked for those tablets.'

She nodded. 'I understand. You must think I'm a monster.' She looked down.

'A monster? Gosh, no, not at all. If my friend, Ray, here says you are a good kid, then you are, Dottie. May I call you Dottie?'

She nodded.

'Now, let's go over everything before they come in to interrogate you.' He chuckled. 'I mean interview you again.' He put his finger to his lips. 'And remember, you say "no comment" unless they offer you a drink. Then ask for two. I like a black coffee.'

As soon as she smiled, Clemence knew he had gained her trust. He could feel Ray's body relax, too. Because, of course, it was all about trust, and by the sound of it, Dorothy Ellis had probably given up pretty much on everyone.

CHAPTER SEVEN

It was half past four on Monday afternoon when Carrie traipsed through the front door into the hallway of her family home.

'Is that you, Carrie girl?' called out her sister from the living room.

'Poxy snow has turned to slush, and it's ruined me bleedin' new boots,' Carrie said, as she sat on the bottom tread of the stairs and removed her fur-lined suede boots and her sodden socks. 'Fuck Jimmy. The bastard, he should have come here if he wanted to see me.'

Dilly appeared in the hallway with a steaming mug of tea in her hands. At nineteen, she was two years older than Carrie and a lot less spirited than her youngest sister. 'Do you have to shout? You knew it was snowing, girl, before you left the house.'

Carrie looked down and suddenly covered her face.

'Hey, Carrie, what's the matter? It ain't like you, girl, to cry. Don't tell me he beat ya, the fucking little scrotum. I'll have Farver give him what for.'

Carrie shook her head, her face red, but there were no tears. 'I'm not crying. I'm fucking angry. Who's home, Dilly?'

'Muvver's upstairs. She's got one of her migraines, and Farver's in the shed, probably brewing beer or whatever he does up there. Mary is back at Lenny's. They've stopped arguing. Rosie's with Zachariah's lot for dinner. Why?'

'Jimmy's pulled a right royal fucked up stunt on me, the bastard. I swear I ain't gonna marry him. If he thinks he can get me in the family way to trap me, then he'll have another thing coming, I swear to God.'

Dilly flicked her long wavy hair over her shoulders and sat beside her sister on the stairs. 'What's he gone and done, Carrie?'

'He got all amorous and didn't put anything on it.' She sighed heavily. 'Dills, I'm at the middle of the month. You know what that means. Muvver's always warned us. If we want a break from breeding, then don't fuck in the middle of the month, 'cos you're most likely to have a belly full of baby.'

Dilly put her arm around her sister. 'Carrie girl, what the hell does it matter? In a few weeks, you're gonna be wed, and you know babies are gonna follow. We have a mile of babies. That's what our lot do.'

'But I'm too young to have babies, Dills. I'm not ready. I'm not. I ain't even lived.'

Dilly was a good foot taller and a size bigger than Carrie. Still, she was like a Mediterranean beauty, with black hair and the darkest skin with hazel eyes and dimples when she smiled. 'Listen, Carrie, you know you can't go off acting foolish now. You have to get wed. We are brought up this way. Still, look at us. Our life ain't that bad. We've all got each other, and we all look out for one another. And besides, you're not too young to have a little chavi.'

'You ain't, Dilly. You're older than me. You ain't got wed or got chavis, so why should I?'

Dilly chewed the inside of her mouth. 'You can be a nasty bitch sometimes, Carrie. Farver might call you spirited. But me, I'd call you a spoilt, selfish cow. You know full well, Toby, the only man I ever loved, was killed the night before our wedding.' She jumped to her feet ready to storm off.

Carrie suddenly felt very guilty. 'Sorry, sis, I didn't mean anything by that. I'm just not ready to be a muvver, that's all.'

Dilly paused and stared at her sister, her voice now compassionate again. 'You will be, kid. Our muvver had our

Mary when she was sixteen, our Rosie when she was seventeen, me when she was eighteen, and you when she was twenty, and look at her now. She's still a stunner and all of us grown up.'

'What's that about me?' asked Luanne, from the top of the staircase.

'Dilly was saying you are still a stunner, Mum.'

'You're talking out of your arse. I was, when I was younger. Just like you are, my Dilly girl. I had your wild ways, Carrie, and ya farver loved me for it until I got wed. Then o' course you have to settle down, don't ya,' she said, as she walked down the stairs to join her two daughters.

'Dills, make us a brew, love. Me headache's only just easing off. That fucking beer your farver brewed gave me a bloody migraine. So get us two tablets, babe.'

As soon as Dilly headed to the kitchen, Carrie followed her mother into the living room, where her father had left the fire on full blast.

'Lucky that fat bastard has fiddled the electric 'cos we'd never afford the fucking bills,' Luanne said, as she sat down in an armchair.

Carrie turned the fire down from four bars to two and then sat down in one of the other armchairs. 'Mum, do I have to marry Jimmy?'

'No, you, Carrie girl, don't have to do anything. We can't force ya. But what do you think yous gonna do, eh? What respectable boy is gonna wed ya? You've slept with Jimmy. He is a big part of our family. He's Mary's bruvver-in-law. I've been on the phone to Ginty and booked the flaming hall.'

'That fat-mouthed bitch—'

'Oi, Carrie-Ann, mind ya fucking manners! Ginty will be your muvver-in-law, so you'd best start showing her some respect. You speak when you're spoken to, and you make sure you're a good daughter-in-law. Don't you disgrace the family.'

'But do I really have to marry Jimmy?'

'Girl, if you wanna call it off—'

'He ain't even proposed to me, Mum. I've only been back with him a week, and now you've ordered the dress and booked the hall.'

'Listen to your ol' mum. You are getting on—'

'Mum, I'm *seventeen.*'

'Nearly eighteen, and that's not too young to be wed. The other boys will wonder why you ain't.'

'They don't say nuffin about Dilly.'

'Shut your mooi, Carrie. She's got a good reason, and that's that. A man will come along for her soon enough, but only when she's ready. Your other two sisters were married at seventeen.'

Carrie jumped to her feet. 'And look at our Mary. She's always got a shiner or a fat lip. I wanna stab the wanker in the throat for how he treats me sister.'

'Shut up, Carrie. Your sister Mary is learning to be a proper wife to Lenny, and she has too much of your wild spirit in her, and it ain't good for any marriage.'

'That's bollocks. And he is lucky she even sleeps in the same bed as him. He's got a face like a camel's cunt.'

Luanne wanted to laugh but she held it in. 'Carrie, stop it. You're too pretty to be talking like a man. Now, what were you moaning about to Dilly?'

'I wasn't moaning, Mum,' Carrie said, as she returned to her father's armchair. 'Jimmy didn't use protection.'

Luanne smoothed down her bed of hair and pulled her heavy cardigan tighter around herself. 'Put those two bars back on. It's bloody cold.'

'Mum?'

'So what? There's many a young bride getting wed with a baby in their belly. That don't matter none. I will get a grandbaby sooner than expected, but that's not uncommon.'

'But I don't *want* a baby.'

Although Luanne was just getting over the throbbing pains of a headache, hearing Carrie's whining voice was getting on her nerves. She had spoken calmly to her daughter, but Carrie was irritating her now, and having raised three others, she hadn't done so without a firm word. 'Carrie!'

Carrie looked at the fire in her mother's eyes, that set jaw, and she knew she was pushing her luck.

'If you didn't want a baby, you should never have laid down with the boy.'

'But he should've used a condom.'

Luanne jumped up from her armchair and pointed a finger in Carrie's face. 'Do my words ever go into your head, eh? Was I fucking wasting me breath trying to educate you? Well, was I?'

Carrie almost shrank into the back of the armchair. She shook her head. 'No, Mum, I'm sorry. I know I should never have laid down with Jimmy.'

Her mother retook her seat and smiled. 'That's better, love. Carrie, you are the apple of your farver's eye. Do ya know why?'

Carrie shook her head.

'I'll tell you, girl. It's because your mouth and attitude were like mine, which was all well and good, but when we wed and I was his wife, he couldn't have that. But you, you're different. You're his daughter, and he laughs at your antics. He tells everyone that you are wild, but not a tart, not a slut. He boasts about how you can handle yourself. He reckons you box better than a lad, and you could chore a pig's notebook right from under his nose. And you, girl, have played up to your farver's boasting. And I know he sees you as the son he never had.' She paused and smiled sadly. 'But ya farver knows if you lay with a boy, you have to marry him. Everyone knew you would end up with Jimmy because you're like two peas in a pod. That's fine as little chavis but not as husband and wife. Remember, he'll wear the trousers. You'll have to keep ya mouth shut, keep a clean home, and give him babies. It's how it is.'

Carrie felt sick because as much as she was familiar with how it worked among their kind, she didn't want it. She wanted her freedom, to be able to sleep with whoever she wanted, to go wherever she wanted, and to speak to new friends, even boys, without being talked about and given a bad name.

'Your farver was like Jimmy. He was a bad boy. All the girls had an eye for him, and I got him. I thought he was a lucky catch, but what he loved about me as a kid wasn't what he wanted in a wife. So I had to grow up and mellow. Look, we've been together now for twenty years. I've got older, he's got fatter, but we are still together.'

Carrie nodded. 'But do you still love him?'

In a huff, Luanne glared at her daughter. 'Now, that's not a question you should ask your parents. What is love, anyway?'

That was the question Carrie had asked herself. Many times. Because did she love Jimmy? Could she love him? She didn't even know what love was. She had thought about Dottie and could see the heartbreak behind the girl's eyes. Dottie *had* loved Jimmy. There was no doubt about it. Strangely, she felt nothing short of envy of Dottie's feelings towards Jimmy. She really wished she loved him as much as Dottie had. Life would be so much easier that way.

Just as Carrie was about to re-challenge the idea of marriage, her father bustled into the living room. He was holding up a chicken. Its head was still attached, blood was dripping from its beak, and the rest of its body was completely featherless. It was apparent that he had been the one who'd plucked it because there were feathers in his thick mop of hair, which had stuck to his stained vest.

'Jed, get that bird out of me clean living room. You've got the brains of a peanut.'

His round rosy cheeky face was beaming. 'Here's our stew, my Lulu.'

Luanne waved her hands, shooing him out. 'Put it in the kitchen, and I'll get to it in a minute. I'm still smarting from a headache your rotten beer caused me.'

Jed looked at his daughter. He laughed and winked. 'She can't handle a bit o' beer. Not like the old days, when she could knock 'em back. The days of your muvver singing at our family gatherings are long gone now.'

'Oh, shut up, Jed. You make me out to be a party girl, and you know damn well I wasn't like that.'

'Yeah, you were, before we had our baby girls. You would be swigging those gins and singing to Elvis Presley. You always said I looked like him.' He looked at Carrie and winked again.

'Elvis Presley, and now you favour Humpty Dumpty.'

He laughed and left the room, singing an Elvis Presley song like a drunk.

When Dilly returned, she was carrying a tray of her mother's best china. There was a large pot of tea in the rose garden pattern, three tea cups, a plate filled with biscuits, and a bottle of milk. There was no matching jug because Carrie had smashed the milk jug in one of her rages. All because her sister Mary had ruined her suede jacket. She'd borrowed it without asking and got caught in a rainstorm, buggering up the suede and making it as stiff as a board. When Mary tried to explain that she hadn't meant it, Carrie threw the only thing she had in her hand, which happened to be the milk jug. Which was part of her mother's best china tea set, bought as a wedding present by *her* own mother.

'Here, Mum, take these two tablets. I made the tea strong, just how you like it.'

Luanne smiled compassionately at Dilly. It was always with the same look that said: 'I feel your pain.'

Carrie had seen it a year ago and understood it was because Dilly's fiancé had been murdered. It was only a few days ago, when her mother had explained to her that Dilly was still hurting over her man because she had loved him so deeply.

A thought crossed her mind. Maybe there was a difference between loving someone because you were used to them being a part of your life and loving them so deeply that you couldn't bear to be apart from them.

Dilly's fella, Toby Murphy, had been a well-known face, and she had to admit it, he had been really handsome. But, then again, all the Murphy brothers were good looking. Toby had been generous and thoughtful too. He had never arrived at the door without roses for her, and often, he'd brought her a nice piece of gold. The engagement ring had everyone talking. It was a single yet enormous diamond.

While Carrie watched her sister pouring the tea, she could see the ring; it stood prominently on her finger. Of course, being the person she was, she didn't think before she engaged her brain.

'Dills, if you want to meet a man, ain't it worth you taking that ring off? I mean, you could spot it from across the room. It's like putting a shield up.'

No sooner had she said that than she wanted to run from the room.

Dilly shot her such a glare.

But it was her mother who jumped up from her armchair and poked a finger in her chest. 'You, my girl, have too much to say for yourself. You need to keep your mooi shut and be mindful to your sister's pain.' Her face was red with anger. 'Maybe it'll be a good thing if you *are* in the family way. It might piss on your brazen ways. Now, fuck off to your room or say sorry and keep your mooi shut.'

'I'm sorry, Dilly. I just don't want you to be unhappy, that's all. I would like you to have a bloke – to be in love again.'

Tears filled Dilly's huge round hazel eyes and tumbled down her cheeks before she brushed them away. 'I don't *want* a man. I can't love another man, not yet.' She looked at her ring. 'Don't ever talk about it again, Carrie. I'm older than you, so, in future, show me respect.'

Those cold words somehow cemented a divide between herself and Dilly. The two of them had been so close, just like Mary and Rosie were.

But now, it seemed that she had gone too far this time. She watched as her sister sat nearer to her mother and hold herself like a grown woman, establishing herself, Carrie, as the child in the family.

***

By six o'clock that evening, Jed had taken a bath, put a fresh vest on, slipped his feet into his carpet slippers, and entered the living room. 'Cor, that chicken smells good.'

Luanne peered up at his fresh face and smiled. He always looked handsome when he had got out of the bath. His eyes sparkled, and his hair was shiny and swept back with hair cream.

Carrie, who was still sitting in her father's favourite armchair, which faced the television, jumped up and took a seat on the four-seater sofa, which was against the wall opposite the electric fire.

'Put the news on. It's gone six, Luanne. Let's see who's been nicked, who's dead, and what's happening in the Falklands.'

'Shit, are we at war? I never knew,' said Carrie.

'That's why, my baby girl, you need to watch the news. The answer is no, we're not, but we soon will be. I can guarantee it.'

Carrie hurriedly got up, turned the TV on, and sat back, worrying that they could be bombed at any moment. However, what came on was a bit closer to home. A news reporter was standing outside a semi-detached house that was cordoned off with crime tape. In the distance, there were police officers and forensics toing and froing.

'Fuck me, that looks like the other side of the main road,' said Jed, pointing at the screen.

'Shuush, Dad.'

'A couple have been found murdered in their beds,' said the reporter, as he pointed to the house behind him. 'Detective Inspector Granger has informed us that the couple are Mr and

Mrs Ellis. It is unclear as to what has taken place, but we know for sure that their daughter Dorothy has been taken to the police station for questioning.'

'Shit, that's Dottie Ellis.'

Jed stared at his youngest daughter. 'Do you know that family, then?'

'Yeah, that's Dottie, the girl who was seeing Jimmy before . . . well, up until last week.'

Jed sat up straight and leaned forward. 'Now listen, my girl, if anyone asks, you don't know her, okay?'

'Dad, I won't bring the filth to our door, but fucking hell, do you reckon she killed her muvver and farver?'

'There are more things in Heaven and Earth. I bet the gavvers will be knocking at Ginty's door. She'll be telling them to do one,' said Luanne, with a smirk.

Carrie bit her nails. 'Poor cow. I bet she never killed 'em. She's not like that. She's sweet.'

All three pairs of eyes were on her, their mouths gaping.

'What? Don't look at me like that. I met her yesterday, all right?'

'You *met* her? Fucking *yesterday*?' asked her father.

'Yeah, she was walking towards the lane. Misty and Lena got right fucking nasty with her and had a bit of a ruck.'

'They beat her up?' questioned her father, who was now tight-faced and concerned.

'Yeah, 'cos she had been seeing Jimmy. Anyway, I fucked them off, and me and Dottie had a chat. She was gutted about Jimmy and said she was really sorry, but it wasn't her fault. She didn't do anything wrong, did she?'

Luanne tilted her head. 'Well, she should have known that Jimmy was off limits. Everyone knew he was yours. So you reap what ya sow.'

'She ain't like us, Mum. She's, well . . .'

'A snob?' her mother retorted.

'No, actually, she ain't a snob. She not horrible, either. I feel sorry for her.'

'I'd lay my horse on it that she is a spoiled rich kid who was not getting her own way and so she butchered her parents. See, ya never know what goes on behind closed doors. And you, my baby girl, may have dodged a bullet there. Hey, 'cos if she was jealous that you've got back with Jimmy, she could have come for you. Nutcases like that are better off in a nuthouse. She'll be in Broadmoor, no doubt.' He shook his head. 'Would you fucking believe it, and practically on our own doorstep—' He was interrupted by the phone ringing.

Luanne jumped up. 'I bet that's Ginty wanting to have a good gossip about the news.'

'They'll be questioning Jimmy. He's got a record, ain't he, and if they knew he was seeing this Dottie bird, they'll haul him in, and I bet they'll try to pin it on him.'

'Oh, leave it out, Jed.'

'You listen, girl. Never you mind what Ginty has to say, 'cos we both know she is full of bullshit. The Carsons have been down the station for various crimes this year. Tongues have been wagging 'cos they've got off scot-free, with most of them. So either they've got a bloody good brief, or they're grasses. Anyway, I bet the gavvers will wanna nick young Jimmy.'

'I'll answer the phone,' Luanne said, shaking her head at her husband's theory, which was always on the dramatic side, before she hurried out to the hallway.

'You've gone quiet, Carrie. Are you worried about Jimmy?'

'No, Dad, I'm not worried about him. He ain't got the guts to kill anyone. He's a bit of a flash wanker, truth be told.'

'Carrie.' He exaggerated her name. 'This is your future husband you are berating. That's no way to start a marriage.'

'What, Dad, by speaking the truth? He *is* a wanker.' She got up and was about to storm out of the room when her father grabbed her arm.

Dottie was completely stunned. Of all the people in her universe who she would hope would want to speak to her – like Margaret or her other friend Sophia Paxton – it was actually Carrie who had bothered to come to the courtroom today to wish her well. An unexpected tear trickled down her cheek, but she quickly brushed it away. She looked at Carrie again, who unexpectedly blew her a kiss. Was this a joke? Was she rubbing salt in the wound? But it didn't look like it.

The case had barely begun when the judge asked Dorothy Ellis one question. When asked her intended plea to the charge of double murder, she said in as strong a voice as she could muster: 'Not Guilty'. On hearing that, the judge ordered her to be briskly escorted back down the stairs.

Once inside the holding cell, Officer Tanner removed the handcuffs and smiled tenderly at his charge. 'Your lawyer will be here soon to explain everything. The prison van will take you to Holloway Prison.'

The authorities had made Dottie aware that this would happen, but on hearing Officer Tanner say it with such sadness, she wondered if it was hell that awaited her in prison.

'I am doing a changeover for my lunch break, Dottie. Do you need anything?' He looked at his watch. 'The van taking you to Holloway won't be here for a while yet.'

'A drink, please. My mouth is so dry.'

As he nodded and was about to leave the holding cell, Dottie suddenly had an idea. 'Please, if you see that girl – her name is Carrie – would you ask . . . Oh, er, I actually don't know what to ask her. Sorry, just water would be fine.'

Tanner nodded again and left.

Graham Tanner had been posted to the Old Bailey but he worked for the Metropolitan Police. He had aspirations of being a senior police officer at some point in his career – sooner rather than later – but time and time again, he had been told that he was too soft for the job and was, therefore, ideally best suited to the courts. It sickened him that officers above him had taken that view of him. After all, they didn't know him. But in any case, he didn't care what they thought of him, and he certainly wasn't going to change who he was. And why should he make the prisoners feel worse than they probably already did? As for young Dottie, she was no more than a frightened child.

He wandered out on to the street and saw the endless horde of reporters. Scanning the vicinity, his gaze fell on the pretty dark-haired girl who was in the courtroom earlier. *She was more than pretty*, he thought. She was a real stunner. But to him, she looked a little lost and was clearly on her own.

Tanner hurried across the road. When he came face to face with the girl Dottie had called Carrie, he tilted his policeman's helmet. 'You were in the gallery, right?'

Carrie nodded. 'Yeah, that's right. I wanted to talk to Dottie, that's all. But I don't know how to get my address and phone number to her. Unless I can see her. Can I do that?'

'No, sorry, she'll be off to Holloway Prison in a few minutes' time. But I'm just about to get her a drink. If you want, I'll pass on a message to her.'

Carrie put her hand in the pocket of her sheepskin coat and pulled out a crumpled piece of paper. 'Can you give this to her?'

'Sure.'

'Is she okay?'

'She's brave, but then, again, she has no idea what it will be like in prison and with no parents.' He coughed. 'Sorry, I mean, no relatives to support her. I should think having a friend to write to will keep her, at the very least, sane.'

Carrie shivered at the thought of what prison could be like. 'So she has no one? Is that what you're saying? No one at all?'

Slowly, Tanner shook his head. 'That's about it, yes. But I'll be sure to pass this message on for you.'

'Ta. Can I ask, did she kill 'em?'

Scrutinising the girl's expression, he wondered if she was asking out of morbid curiosity or whether she would want to stay friends with Dottie if she had murdered her parents.

'Sorry, I shouldn't have asked. It doesn't matter, none. Please ask her to call me.'

'Are you friends?'

'Yeah, I mean, no. Well, what I mean is, I will be. I want to be. She ain't got no one, and I dunno, I s'pose I feel for her.'

'Okay, Carrie, you get off before those reporters start asking you questions,' he said, spotting one eyeing them.

'Blimey, that's all I need, me face splashed all over the bleedin' news. Me family don't even know I'm 'ere.' She laughed. 'See ya, mate.' She gave him a cheeky smile and scooted off along the street.

Before any of the reporters spotted him and crossed the road, Tanner hurried towards the small parade of shops where he bought a sandwich, a packet of crisps, a chocolate bar, and two bottles of juice for Dottie.

By the time he returned to court, the reporters had gone, and he found that he could go in without shooing people out of the way.

When he reached the holding cell, Dottie was sitting at a small table and leaning against the cold brick wall. Her eyes were heavy, and she looked so young and innocent to him.

She sat up straight and smiled as he placed the refreshments on the table.

'Has your brief been to see you yet?'

She nodded. 'Yes, he just said he would let me know when my trial date is set.'

'Here, memorise this phone number and address because they may take this off you.' He handed her the crumpled note. 'Carrie gave it to me. She said to call her.'

Dottie stared at the note, which looked as though it had been written left-handed. 'Did she say anything to you about me? Only, we're not friends.'

Tanner shrugged. 'She said she felt for you.' He sat at the small table. 'It won't do you any harm to call her. She came to court, so if she wants to be your friend for whatever reason, you hang on to that thought, okay.' He winked.

'Why would she, though?' Dottie asked, her eyes glassy like those of a sleepy child.

'Dottie, they've charged you with double murder. The stuff on the news was quite shocking, so there will be people out there wanting to know you because of what they believe you did. The world is full of morbidly curious people. Maybe it's in our nature. In prison, there'll be inmates for whom the newspapers have promised money, favours, whatever, to get the scoop on you. So choose your friends inside very carefully, please, Dottie. Don't be fooled by a smiling face. Not everyone is who they pretend to be.'

Dottie wanted to laugh. 'I know that more than most. My parents weren't, that's for sure.'

'Okay, now I suggest you eat the food. I don't know when you will get another meal today.'

'Will they starve me in prison, then?'

'No, but they govern when and what you eat, so get stuck in,' he said, pointing to the sandwich.

***

When the van arrived, Dottie wasn't ready to go. Her feet felt as though they were glued to the floor, and a sudden sense of terror enveloped her.

Tanner saw the blood drain from her face, and he had the urge to hug her, but his superior, Officer Stoney, had entered the cell, and his voice was firm. 'Come now, Miss Ellis, the van is waiting.'

Her eyes flicked back to Tanner, and she mouthed the words 'thank you'.

'Remember what I said, Dottie, and look after yourself. I'll see you again.'

The older officer, distinguishable by his white hair and a black moustache, glanced at the empty wrappers on the table and then glared at Tanner. 'I doubt that, PC Tanner.'

With a prod in her back and a rattle of keys, Dottie was taken outside the holding cell to be greeted coldly by two harsh-featured men. They weren't police officers, but they were in uniform. They, too, had clinking keys, swooshing chains, and walked like soldiers towards the large oak-panelled doors. Unexpectedly, her legs felt weak, her body shook, and she had to swallow a few times to hold down the vomit that threatened to rise up and burn the back of her throat.

'No dawdling, Miss Ellis. Get moving,' said Stoney.

As the outside door opened, the cold air hit her. It provided some much needed light relief since she felt that she was now burning up. When waves of sickness ran over her, she had to pause to get her breath.

'Move along, for goodness' sake. Anyone would think this is the walk of death.'

Tanner, who had decided to follow Dottie out to the waiting prison van, wanted to jump in and stop Stoney, who probably spent most of his waking hours with his hand around his truncheon as though it was an extension of him. When he saw how hard Stoney prodded Dottie in the back, he wanted to beat the man with it.

All he could say was 'Hold up, Gov. She's not at all well. I'll escort her.'

'No, you won't, you soppy sod. She'll soon learn that there is no one to pamper her in Holloway, so she's better off getting used to it now.'

Dottie looked back. 'It's fine,' she said. 'I just thought I was going to be sick. I'm all right.' But when her eyes locked on Stoney, for the first time in her life, she glared back with hate.

Seeing that death stare and knowing the circumstances in which Dorothy Ellis was here, Stoney looked away, feeling distinctly uncomfortable. And at that moment, he truly believed she was a cold-blooded killer.

But being the unfeeling son of a bitch that everyone knew him to be, he hadn't accounted for who Dorothy Ellis really was.

She was merely afraid, and her eyes were searching for empathy. That was all. At least Officer Tanner saw the true side of her, and her last view of him was of him giving her a thumbs-up.

CHAPTER NINE

Having never even seen a picture of Holloway Prison, it alarmed Dottie when the prison van opened its door, and a heavy-handed officer suddenly handcuffed her wrist to his. All the while, he glared silently at her, she stood there showing a stoic resignation of the fate that awaited her. Together, they waited for the assistance of another officer.

It allowed her a brief moment to take in the enormity of the vast imposing building that looked like one of those medieval castles she had learned about at school. Never in her wildest dreams had she believed that she would enter one as an inmate.

Built in 1852 as a mixed-sex prison it was now a female-only establishment, with all-female officers. Ingrained in its brickwork was a sense of the Dark Ages, and the imposing turrets added to the ominous vampire-like appearance, while the pillars on either side of the enormous door loomed like two sentinels.

Her heart raced, her throat tightened, and it hit her that she would never be the same again. Life would be a very different picture for her, probably for many years to come. *Would she be out of here before the turn of the century?* she wondered. The tall walls cast shadows, the bitter cold tore through her – even wearing Mr Clarkson's coat – and she shivered relentlessly.

Without further ado, she was rudely prodded in the back to cross the threshold of this monstrous building. Trepidation crept inside her like an evil snake worming its way around her very being. The cold damp stone floor beneath her feet sucked the life out of her, and as she gazed around, she could feel the air heavy with endless past regrets. She imagined so many secrets and stories, and hers would probably be one of them. The smell of institutional disinfectant, mixed with unfailing disappointment and remorse, created a tapestry of senses impossible to ignore. But this was going to be her home, whether she deserved it or not. Nevertheless, she was determined to live not for herself but for her unborn child – because she didn't care about her own life anymore.

Before the thought of running away gained any credence, another officer shackled herself to her. 'We are taking no chances with you, Miss Ellis.' She then sniggered. 'Are you any relation to Ruth Ellis, by any chance? She was hanged here in 1955, ya know.' She laughed again, not waiting for a response.

The heavy iron gate grunted and squealed as it was pulled shut behind her. As if she was a serial killer, the prison officers marched Dottie to the reception area, where there were four others ready to receive her.

Dottie didn't want to look up again because she had already glimpsed them staring at her. She wasn't sure who was more nervous – herself or them. As soon as an officer locked the door behind her, two others removed the handcuffs. Rubbing her sore wrists, she suddenly had to hold the counter before she fainted. She didn't want to say she was feeling ill because even though Mr Clarkson and her solicitor knew she was pregnant, she didn't want anyone else to know, in case they forced her to have an abortion. She wasn't sure what the rules or laws governing a prison were because she'd had no reason to know about them.

Moments later, a tall woman strolled into view. 'I'm Officer Audrey Jennings, the number one governor.'

Dottie looked up at a middle-aged woman who was dressed in a tweed suit. Her hair was short but set in large waves, a bit like her mother's had been. With eyes that were sunken, again like her own mother's, and a pinched mouth, Dottie felt very uneasy.

'You will be in your own cell after you see the doctor. Officer Kelp will show you where you are to go and inform you of the set times for your food and exercise.'

Dottie nodded in acknowledgement.

'Yes, Ms Jennings! You cannot merely nod. You must answer. Do I make myself clear?'

'Yes.'

'Yes, *Ms Jennings*!' Her voice was high-pitched, irritated, and piercing. 'And I warn you, this prison has held notorious female inmates, and it appears from the news that you will no doubt, Miss Ellis, be amongst them. I run a very tight ship, and any nonsense from you, and you will be held in solitary confinement. Are we clear?'

'Yes, Ms Jennings.'

'Good. Now, I will hand you over to Officer Kelp, who will settle you in before you see the doctor.'

'Why do I need to see the doctor?'

Jennings raised an eyebrow. 'You do understand that you are in prison, Ellis, don't you?'

She nodded. 'Sorry, yes, Ms Jennings.'

'Good. Then don't ask questions unless you are unsure of the rules. You must go through our process, keep your head down, and get on with it. I suggest you keep yourself to yourself because there will be a lot of unnecessary excitement following your arrival, and that, young lady, can be a problem for the staff. So I advise you to say nothing about your alleged crime.'

'Yes, Ms Jennings,' Dottie replied, before looking deep into the woman's eyes. At that moment, a feeling struck her. Unbelievably, she was looking into her own mother's eyes. It sparked a gut-groaning hatred of this female officer.

'What are you staring at, girl?' shrieked Jennings, as if Dorothy had suddenly spooked her.

'Sorry, Ms Jennings, I didn't realise I was.'

‘Officer Kelp, would you take charge of her. I want her processed and then taken to her cell. The doctor is late, and I don’t want Ellis cluttering up reception.’

***

Once they were in the next room, Kelp looked Dorothy over. She spoke with detached professionalism, while stripping her of everything that had held even a smidgeon of her own identity.

However, Dottie didn’t have anything to identify herself by – not one that she could talk about, anyway. All the items of clothing that she had with her in a bag, as well as the clothes she had on, had been bought for her by Mr Clarkson, and these were now confiscated. Even the washbag Sue had given her in the police station.

With a spiteful sneer, Kelp pointed to the necklace around her neck, and for a moment, Dottie forgot she had it on. It was a present from Mr Clarkson for her to wear in the courtroom.

‘May I keep this?’

With her pale expression matching her bleached hair, Kelp held out her hand, not even bothering to answer.

Dottie unclipped the necklace and placed it in Kelp’s hand before she looked up and glared. She was angry because she couldn’t see any reason for that to be confiscated as well, and it meant so much to her.

Kelp wouldn’t maintain eye contact. She glanced at the cross. ‘I am surprised you would have the nerve to wear a cross. You are far from what I would call a Christian.’

Those words and that tone opened a part of Dottie’s brain that had been brainwashed to suppress her own thoughts and feelings for most of her life. Except that was until she met Jimmy. For all his faults, he had treated her like a woman. And that remark by Kelp only served to remind her that her former life had actually been no life. Not for her. How could it have? It had done her no favours at all. Being the obedient daughter, the helpful schoolgirl with top marks and a positive attitude, hadn’t gained her any more respect, and she had no real friends to call her own. Where were they when she needed them? Where were the letters of hope and faith from the congregation or a friendly face in the gallery? No one had come to give her any support – except Carrie.

Dottie looked up at Kelp and thought that there was no way Carrie would have been saying *yes, sir, no, sir, three fucking bags full, sir*. And being a shy, quiet mouse would only compel others to shit on her from a great height.

Knowing she had nothing to lose – apart from her baby, who would go into care sooner rather than later – Dottie smiled and stared because she had noticed that when she stared, it made people uncomfortable, maybe because of the news reports. She imagined the headlines: **Teenage girl butchers parents**. They wouldn't be wrong. She *had* butchered them. She didn't flip out and stab them in self-defence. She wanted them dead, and she had no remorse, not even a flicker of guilt.

As the thoughts flew through her mind, she maintained her stare.

'Why are you staring at me, Ellis?'

'Oh, you remind me of the number one governor, that's all.'

'What?'

'Yes, Officer Kelp, and she reminds me of my mother.'

'Are you threatening me?'

'Not at all, Officer Kelp. I was merely pointing out that you both remind me of my mother.' She smirked. 'There was no threat implied.'

Kelp suddenly handed back the cross as if it held off the demons.

'Thank you, Officer Kelp.'

CHAPTER TEN

As the officer jangled her keys and unlocked the heavy metal door, Dottie stared. She felt as though a trapped bird was fluttering its wings inside her ribcage. It caught her breath as the enormity of the situation gripped her around her throat.

She stared inside the cell and looked at what she would probably expect to see every day for what would seem like eternity. The cold grey brick walls, the miserable-looking narrow bed and thin mattress, the corner sink and toilet, and the small table and chair beside that. There was a single arched window but the bars obscured her only view of the outside world.

Despite all these basic accoutrements, which would be a part of her very existence, she was adamant that she wouldn't show any fear, at least not to the officer who had brought her to her cell. Instead, she turned to face her and smiled.

'This is great. Thank you,' she said, much to the surprise of Kelp, who looked gobsmacked.

As Dottie crossed the threshold of imprisonment and the door clanged shut behind her, she let out a deep jittery sigh. Okay, she was locked in, but at least she was safe for now. No one could hurt her. The only things that could were her own mind, her emotions, and her memories.

She dropped the bag of prison issues and sat on the bed. It was cold and damp, so she knew she wouldn't have a good night's sleep. Instinctively, she flipped the mattress over and then felt it. It was drier. The prison bag contained a blanket and two sheets, but, unfortunately, they were not enough to keep her warm. The cell didn't have central heating, and one of the panes of glass in the window was broken.

Having made the bed and laid out all her toiletries by the sink, she realised she had nothing to occupy her mind. That thought amounted to torture. Still, for the moment, she was safe – cold but *safe*.

Staring at the second tracksuit she had folded neatly on the table, she contemplated wearing it over the one she had on. But she was pulled from her thoughts by a sudden movement in the corner. Her instant reaction was to leap onto the bed, and when she saw the furry creature looking at her with its glinting eyes, she squealed. It was a mouse. She feared mice but mainly because her mother had. She would scream the house down at the very glimpse of a tail. Even her father, the cowardly weasel, had to get the pest control man in to remove a stray field mouse that had nested in the back of the cereal cupboard. Shaking all over, she couldn't take her eyes off the little brown animal. It almost mesmerised her. It wouldn't move at first. But then it did, and it scurried under her bed. Then, unbelievably, she saw another one. It was cleaning its whiskers on the water pipe that led to the sink. Breaking out into a cold sweat, she wanted to scream for help, but what the hell would anyone do? The small mice were harmless, weren't they? *Maybe*, she thought. But to her, they were vermin with poisonous pointed teeth.

As she tried to slow her racing heart, she heard the rattling of chains and keys before her door opened again. A different officer, one with a round puffy face and wearing her hair in a sleek jet-black bob, stood there smiling. 'Tea?'

Dottie climbed down from the bed. 'Sorry, what did you say?'

'I said it's teatime. Follow me. You're not allowed anywhere on your own until the professionals assess you.'

'Assess me?'

'Well, we need to know what we're dealing with here,' she replied, still smiling and in an upbeat tone.

Cautiously, Dottie approached the woman. 'Dealing with?'

'Ellis, you are on remand for killing your parents. I mean, let's be honest, if you did, it's pretty wacko, eh?'

She looked at the woman's lanyard. 'I see, Officer Wells.'

'Are you wacko?' the officer asked, with a friendly smile.

'Probably,' Dottie replied.

'Well, whether you are or not, you must still eat, so follow me, and don't worry. I'm not going to feed you to the wolves. I recommend you keep yourself to yourself, though.'

'Thank you, Officer Wells.'

'Oh, for Gawd's sake, call me Helen. Everyone else does.'

Dottie realised that this was a far cry from the way she had been treated by the number one governor and Officer Kelp. 'You can call me Dottie.'

Helen stopped and turned to face Dorothy. 'Sorry, love, I have to call you Ellis. We call all the inmates by their surname.' But then, she lifted her brow. 'Ellis is a pretty surname, though. It's better than Ramsbottom.'

For the first time in what seemed like ages, Dottie chuckled.

And it was then that Helen noticed that Dorothy was no more than a child. She would keep a keen eye on her. Most of the women in here would eat her for breakfast.

'Why were you standing on the bed?'

'There are mice in my cell, and I'm terrified of them.'

'That's the problem with parts of this place. Some are still very old and unfit really for anyone, let alone a prisoner. Hopefully, you might get a cell in the refurbished part of the prison in due course. But, in the meantime, I'll organise some traps for you.'

'Thank you.'

***

The food hall was busy, and the smell of food was certainly not inviting. The room smelled more like a public toilet than a canteen. Still, she would have to get used to it. But more disconcerting to her was the sight of all these women. Instantly, they made her panic.

She had imagined it would be more like a boarding school with older women thrown into the mix. But what she saw initially made her shudder. There were so many hard-looking bulky women with tattoos, missing teeth, and scars. That was all she saw. No doubt there were others who were not like this. But the room seemed like a giant onion. Layers of women with different physiques and different personalities. In time, she would peel back the layers, and the women would reveal themselves for who they really were. And when she did, she wondered if she would see an even darker side to those inside.

All the women she'd ever known were mainly church-goers, the twinset-and-pearls type. Compared to this bunch, the women she knew were almost frail in comparison. She decided there and then that she wouldn't make eye contact with anyone, fearing she would upset the wrong person. But when the hall suddenly became very quiet, she looked up to find a lot of them were staring at her or whispering to each other. But some were not. They were looking away as if they were more afraid of her.

An inmate, possibly in her fifties, who was dressed in jeans and a tracksuit top a good three times her size, marched over. 'So who do we have here, Helen? Is this the girl who killed her mum and dad?'

'Cribb, leave her alone. You know you can't ask that.'

'We've all seen her boat race on TV, so we know it's her.' She lifted Dorothy's chin. 'I'm Cheryl Cribb. Pleased to meet you.'

Helen pushed Cribb away. 'Back off, Cribb. She's just a kid, right. She's eighteen in, what, two days, so treat her as such.'

'If she's inside this shithole, she's a woman. End of.'

Dottie didn't like Cheryl's tone. She shot her a look, not meaning to, but it clearly resonated with the woman.

'Well, anyway, I just thought I'd introduce myself, but if you ain't in the mood to make friends, I'll leave you to it. The potatoes are shit, by the way. Go for the chips.'

Dottie kept her eyes on Cheryl because, for whatever reason, this new staring thing she was doing was evidently making people feel ill at ease.

By the time she joined the serving hatch and selected her food, she realised that Cheryl was right. The potatoes looked disgusting, and the chips seemed the better option.

Helen pointed to the table in the corner where no one sat. 'Eat yours over there. You can't really speak to anyone until—'

'I understand. You need to know if I'm mad or not.'

Helen smiled again, but when she did, Dottie could see the sadness in her eyes.

'Just for now, stay away from them, especially Cribb, who thinks she's the top dog in here.'

'Is she?'

'Apart from one woman, she is, and she will try to bring you into her fold. We discourage it.' She peered over her shoulder. 'Every one of those women wants something.' She leaned in closer. 'Don't accept even so much as advice from them. You don't want to owe them a thing.'

'I understand,' Dottie replied, before walking over to the table that Helen had pointed to. She sat with her back to the wall, sensing it wouldn't be a good idea to have her back to anyone. She hadn't realised how thirsty she was until she began to drink the water from the plastic beaker. After forcing down a few chips, she used her plastic fork to move the processed meat around the plate. Moments later, deciding that this was virtually inedible, she glanced over at the small bowl of pudding. She could only make out a few slices of apple floating on top of what looked like lumpy custard. Deciding that it was far from appetising, she went back to her main course. After scoffing a few more chips, she pushed her plate away, and without thinking, she looked up.

Some women were so engrossed in eating their food, they were shovelling it in like starving street dogs. But Cheryl and a few others at her table didn't seem particularly interested in their food. They were more focused on watching her.

Dottie sensed her adrenaline surging through her veins and began to panic, but when her eyes fixed on Cheryl, she recognised that this woman looked uneasy once again. It shocked her because no one at school had been wary of her.

But that was then and this was now. The difference now was that she had killed two people, and worse, her own parents. She thought about what that would look like if someone had said it about her friend Margaret. Of course, she would be very wary of her. Her mind cast back to the last time she saw her friend. Why hadn't she bothered to make contact?

The stench of the prison, the hardness of the women, and the brutality of the officers gave her the only weapon at her disposal: she would use what she had to stay alive. And what she had, it seemed, was the ability to instil fear in people. Not through fighting but through fear of the unknown. If these women saw her as a potential psychopath, that would suit her nicely for the time being.

Just as she took a large mouthful of water, another woman, who was clearly much older, possibly in her seventies, called over. 'So why did you kill 'em, Dorothy Ellis?'

When Dottie automatically glanced in her direction, she saw what she could only describe as a witch. Her face looked like old tanned leather. It was deeply creased with numerous wrinkles. She displayed other tell-tale signs of an unkempt appearance: her hair, for example, was a mass of long grey curls, which looked as though it hadn't been washed in weeks. But it was her eyes that really defined her as strange: one eye looked one way while the other looked straight at her.

While Dottie was appraising this woman, in a matter of seconds, the inmates around her were looking at her for a reaction.

She knew then that this was a kind of do-or-die moment. What she said next would define her for the person she was. It would either make her or break her. Swallowing hard, she got up, deliberately making sure that the screech from the chair sliding across the floor was loud enough for the whole hall to hear her. Then, she smiled while locking eyes with the witch.

Helen returned to the table. 'Enough, Milward, you can't ask any questions.'

'Yeah, I can. You can't fucking gag me, you numpty.'

'I'll have you in solitary.'

'For what? Asking a fucking question? We all wanna know why she did it. I mean, look at her sitting there as cocky as fuck. She could be a right fucking nutter, for all we know.'

Dottie was shocked. It had never crossed her mind, even for one minute, that she would give them the impression of being cocky. Still, if this was the way she was coming across and it was working, she'd continue to bamboozle them.

However, the thing was, she didn't quite know what to say. As her pulse quickened and throbbed in her neck, she stared at the witch, and a broad beaming smile, which forced her cheeks to lift, radiated across her face. A psychiatrist or a body language expert would say that this was down to displaying a nervous demeanour, and she knew that this was partly true in her case. She *was* nervous. Very nervous. Who wouldn't be?

'Milward, I said, *enough*. Now eat your food, or you will be escorted back to your cell. It's your choice.'

Lucy Milward decided she wanted her pudding, so she looked away.

Helen flicked her head for Dorothy to follow her, but as she walked around the table, the door at the end opened and in walked another inmate.

Dottie found it hard to judge her age; but at a pinch, she thought she could be in her late twenties. She wasn't tall or particularly large, but as she walked, she did so with giant-sized steps. And with each one, there was a level of indescribable confidence. Four officers were escorting her. Suddenly, the atmosphere changed and there were angry mutterings among the other inmates.

Dottie could taste the foreboding. It was as if the devil had walked in and needed to be heavily guarded. The woman, who was approximately five feet six inches tall, was dressed in jeans and a sweatshirt with the sleeves cut off. Her olive skin defined her muscles and her short black hair framed her face. But the thing that was most striking about her was her eyes. They were as black as coal and they looked right through her.

Helen put her hand back to stop Dorothy from walking in front of the guarded woman. She turned and whispered, 'This inmate is Billy Cardel. Stay away from her.'

But Dottie showed no signs of distress. She was actually intrigued by Billy's confident demeanour, and the way her eyes shot around the room. At first, her face showed a complete lack of expression. But then the hint of a smile – or was it a smirk – was sufficient to let everyone know that she had their cards marked.

Dottie watched as two officers walked on either side of Billy as she approached the serving counter. But then, as she was about to lift a plate to the first serving hatch, her head twisted, and her eyes locked on her.

Placing her plate down on the counter, Billy took a step towards the young inmate.

Dottie knew nothing about the woman except that she clearly attracted much attention. Keeping her eyes locked on Billy, she added a genuine smile this time.

'*Dorothy Ellis?*' Billy dragged out the name.

Dottie remained dead still.

Billy tilted her head from side to side as if she was sizing her up. 'You must be the double murderer. Killed ya mum and dad, didn't ya?'

'Leave her, Billy. She's just a kid, yeah?' said Helen.

But Dottie sensed the nervousness in her voice, and the hairs on the back of her own neck stood on end.

Billy's eyes shot a glare at Helen. 'Do I fucking look stupid? I can see what she is.'

'She's not been found guilty yet, Billy.'

The devilish look, which was enhanced by her widening her eyes, to the point where it was possible to see the sclera or the white around the pools of black, just added to her defiance. 'Fuck me, so what, Helen. What are you worried about anyway, eh?'

She stepped closer, looking Helen up and down as if she was shit.

'Ha! You fucking thought I would come in here throwing me weight around and act all hard in front of a kid, didn't ya, *Helen*. As a matter of fact, can ya see what you're doing, *Helen*?' She dragged out her name again. 'You're making it extra hard for the kid by giving her protection like she's a china doll or somink. That means you're not preparing her for a long bird.' She flashed a look at the new inmate. 'Mollycoddling you, Dorothy, will only piss off the other inmates.' She turned to face them. 'Yeah, I'm talking about you lot, ya fucking bullies.'

Most of the prisoners looked away when she said that. It suggested to Dottie that something serious had recently taken place.

'Billy, move on! Get your food,' Helen said, with a harshness to her tone.

Another officer gave Cardel the most gentle push that she could to move her back to the counter. But in a millisecond, she had her back to it and faced the officer, her lips tight and her eyes red with incandescent rage. 'Don't you *ever* fucking touch me again! You have no right and no fucking reason!'

The officer put her hands up. 'All right, Billy, calm down. Just get your food and sit down.'

'And what if I don't, eh? What ya gonna do about it? Whack me back in solitary confinement for another month? If you do . . .' She pointed a tattooed finger in the officer's face. 'You'll be missing a fucking ear, like your pal Letchford did!'

Dottie watched the dynamics play out in front of her. The officers were all on edge, giving Billy Cardel space, but Dottie could see their white knuckles gripping their batons, ready to wade in.

Helen decided to push Dorothy in the back and usher her on.

But then, without thinking, Dottie turned back and smiled at Billy. 'It was nice to meet you, and you can call me Dottie.'

The silence in the hall spoke volumes. Even Helen stopped in her tracks, stunned as she was by Dorothy Ellis's gumption.

'Dottie, eh. That's a cute name. You can call me Billy.'

As Dottie walked away, she smiled again, but she noticed that Helen seemed annoyed. And as she was escorted back to her cell, she heard Helen mumbling under her breath.

'May I ask why those officers were surrounding Billy?'

'Ellis, listen and listen well. You stay away from her. Lucy Milward and all those women have absolutely nothing to lose by messing you up. They're in here for the rest of their lives. So just mark my words: getting mixed up with them will do you no good. You would be fair game. They'll beat you up just to prove they're still a force to be reckoned with.'

'But why were there so many officers surrounding Billy?'

Walking at a slower pace now, Helen said, 'Billy Cardel has spent most of her life behind bars. She's gone from detention centres to various prisons. When she erupts, she's like a tornado, and it takes four officers to contain her, so she ends up in solitary. We leave her in there until she's ready to come out. And sometimes that's months.' She paused and looked Dorothy straight in the eyes. 'Ellis, you need to be careful of Billy. She will try to get you on her side.' She huffed. 'She killed her own father when he was asleep.' She put her finger to her lips. 'I am not supposed to tell you any of the inmates' crimes, but, in fairness, everyone in this prison knows who Billy is, so it's an open secret.'

'Oh, I see. So, you think that she and I have a crime in common, then?'

'Ellis, I didn't say that, but it's a possibility that Billy will see it that way. She has never connected with anyone in prison, and that also makes her dangerous. She has no friends, only enemies, so please, Ellis, stay away from her.'

'I will probably end up like her, with no friends.'

'You are very different from many of the hardened inmates, Ellis. You're not like them. You don't have any criminal history, and that presents itself differently from the other inmates. Firstly, what you are accused of isn't out of a history of violence, like a lot of the women in here. But that presents a problem in itself. It's all about perception. The inmates may *think* you could be very dangerous, and so you could be a threat to them if they believe you're a psychopath. When they find out the truth about what you did to your parents, they may look at it as though you can kill a person without anger or a particular reason for doing so. So, as far as they are concerned, the prisoners will give you a wide berth until they know who they are dealing with. Psychopaths are segregated, but until you see the shrink, none of us are going to know, are we?'

Dottie shook her head.

'And secondly, Ellis, if you befriend these women and they turn on you, believe me, love, you wouldn't stand a chance. Billy has carried out some hideous crimes while being in prison.'

'Oh, I see,' replied Dottie.

'Hmmm, but, there is always the exception to the rule, isn't there.' Helen smiled. 'I have never known Billy to show an interest in anyone, but she even smiled at you, so she must have seen something about you that made her do that.'

'Maybe she understood what it takes for a person to even think about killing a family member.'

The depth and seriousness of that statement compelled Helen to consider that Dorothy had suffered extraordinarily if she hinted that she was driven to it.

Once Helen opened the prison door, she peered inside. Even though she had walked the corridors for twenty years and seen inside the cells numerous times, she suddenly felt the magnitude of the situation and what these women went through each day locked up in such an uninviting place. Her eyes were drawn to the old mattress and the thin brown blanket. She tutted. 'This is bollocks!'

Dottie was stunned that the officer, whom she considered to be a person of authority, had just sworn.

'Ellis, I'm going to source one of the new mattresses and a couple more blankets. It's freezing in here. Actually, bollocks to that as well. I'm going to relocate you to another cell. This one is never used unless the prison is overflowing. Bag up your stuff. I'm going to the office to get this sorted.'

Helen locked Dorothy back in her cell.

As the officer walked off, Dottie could just hear her cursing Officer Kelp under her breath.

Within five minutes, Helen had returned, and she flicked her head for Dorothy to follow her. 'Right, the wing isn't ideal for you, but the cell you are going to is much warmer, and the plumbing in this part is not so ancient, so the mice don't squeeze in. We rarely find mice on this wing.'

'May I request just one thing?'

'You can try, but I cannot promise anything.'

'May I have a book, any book? I like to read.'

'You can use the library.'

'There's a library?'

'Yes, of course. We don't stop education. You can go on a course and study.'

'Really? I'd like that.'

'I will grab a couple of books for you for now until you get to know your way around, understand the rules, and find your feet.'

'May I ask another question?'

'Sure.'

'You called Billy by her first name. Why is that?'

Helen rolled her eyes. 'She killed her father. His last name was Cardel, and she hates it. I don't fancy getting a black eye, or worse, so all of us officers call her Billy. And before you say it's not fair, it's one rule for one and all that, we do it because we also need to protect the other inmates, so we would like to keep this prison as peaceful as possible.'

As soon as Helen unlocked the door of the new cell, Dottie's face lit up. The room was much brighter and warmer, the bed had a thick mattress, and everything looked clean. The window was the same size, but at least it didn't have a broken pane.

While Helen went off to collect more blankets and the books she promised, Dottie stood awkwardly and waited for her to return. She assumed that the footsteps she heard coming her way were Helen's. However, she was shocked when she saw Billy Cardel standing in her doorway.

'Well, look who we have here. Little Dottie. So I guess we're neighbours.'

Dottie's eyes bulged in fear. 'Hello again,' was all she could say.

'Dottie, look, I'm not as fucked up as they think I am. I won't hurt you. You're different.'

With her head inclined, Dottie pointed to herself. 'Me? Am I?'

Billy entered the room and sat on the bed. 'Yeah, little 'un, you are, and before Helen, the so-called friendly screw, tells you otherwise, I wanna tell ya, I am not the fucking bully they make out I am. Look, see, if they fuck me over, I do the same back. And I ain't about to start asking you about your parents.'

Dottie leaned comfortably against the sink. 'They said everyone wants to know. They think I'm a psychopath, and I haven't tried to prove them wrong, as yet.'

Billy suddenly laughed at that last statement. She liked the girl's wit. 'I bet they fucking do.' She chuckled again. 'I'm not going to poke into your business, Dottie. Those women questioned me night and day about what I did. It does ya nut in. They thought *I* was a psychopath as well, but I ain't. So, anyway, have you got everything you need?'

With a sad smile, Dottie replied, 'And they also told me not to even ask for advice, or I'd end up owing someone something.' She showed the palms of her hands. 'But I have nothing to give. I've got no one.'

'Yep, I knew they would say that, too. I don't want nuffin, either. Debts cause heartache, stress, and pain. I don't owe anyone a thing. It's best that way. And I don't lend anything to anyone either because when they don't pay it back, well, I resort to violence and then end up down in solitary.'

'Thank you, Billy.'

'Nuffin to thank me for.'

'Coming in here and talking to me like I'm a person, I suppose.'

'You remind me of me. I don't know what it is, but you just do.'

'Not about the murder thing, is it?' asked Dottie, assuming it probably was.

'No, funnily enough, it ain't. Maybe we're kinda kindred spirits and all that.'

Dottie suddenly felt comfortable enough to sit next to Billy on the bed. 'You know what, Billy, when we were in the food hall, and everyone was shitting themselves expecting things to kick off, I didn't feel scared. Maybe because, well, I don't know you, but I just saw you as a *person*.'

Billy laughed. 'You're right, little 'un, you did. They fucking treat me like I'm a caged animal. Anyway, I'd best go back before they fucking start on me again.'

Dottie jumped up from her bed and followed Billy to the door. She watched her enter her own cell dead opposite. 'Thanks, Billy.'

Billy put her hand up without looking back, a sweet gesture of acknowledgement.

CHAPTER ELEVEN

Carrie curled her knees under her chin and stretched her baggy jumper over them. She listened to Ginty going on and on about how the police had pulled her Jimmy into the station all on account of his name being mentioned when they had questioned Dottie's mate Margaret.

'So why, Carrie, haven't you gone to the station? I bet my boy will be expecting to see his future fucking wife in the waiting room when they're done with him. 'Cos they can't charge him with anything. You were with him the night that the Ellis girl killed her muvver and farver. Fucking shocking. He dodged a bullet there.' She looked up and smiled at Carrie. 'Cor, imagine if he'd married her. He'd have had to sleep with one eye open.'

Carrie stared at Ginty. She could imagine a long line of people who would probably want to put a knife into *her* neck while she slept. No doubt, Ginty's husband may have contemplated doing just that, when he was alive.

'Ginty's right, Carrie, you should be at the cop shop waiting for Jimmy,' said Luanne, who had always been wary of Ginty since she was a woman known to fight. She'd once gone to the pub where her husband was having a good Sunday lunchtime drink. Armed with his dinner on a plate, she closed the door behind her, walked right up to him as he sat laughing with his mates, and then she threw the dinner at his face. His two brothers, who were also there, tried to grab her. But she beat off the pair of them and then walloped her husband again and threatened to take on anyone else if they dared to interfere in her private business, although it wasn't so private since half the men in the street were at the pub that afternoon. So, ever since that day, no one had ever really argued with Ginty, let alone her browbeaten husband, before he died.

Carrie, who wasn't in the least fazed by Ginty's harsh ways and fearless reputation, uncurled her legs, faced her mother, and sat up straight. 'It's freezing out there, so you reckon I should sit in that waiting room while the gavvers get a good ol' butcher's at me face and wait for Gawd knows how long, just so he can see me when they're done with him, do ya?'

Her mother nodded nervously because she knew her daughter only too well; she wasn't the type to do as she was told.

'And you know exactly what Jimmy will do when they release him, don't ya? He'll be straight in the pub, and he won't give a flying fuck if I'm there or not.'

Ginty had her meaty arms folded under her ample bosoms. 'He'll be your husband soon, so you'd best get used to it, girl.'

Carrie curled her lip. 'He'd best get used to me *not* being there, is all I can say. Or me and him ain't gonna get on.'

'Don't be surprised, Carrie girl, if you don't get a backhander. When my lad is providing for you and the chavis, you need to show your support and some respect.'

Those words were like a red rag to a bull. '*What?* Are you fucking serious? Ginty, who the fuck do you think will be at home looking after his chavis?' She poked herself in the chest and jumped to her feet. 'Me, Ginty. It'll be fucking me, but I ain't a slave. This is nineteen eighty-fucking-two, if you haven't worked that out for yaself.'

Ginty's eyes widened and she shot a look at Luanne. 'Are you gonna put your girl in her place?'

Luanne shuffled uncomfortably on the sofa and shook her head in shame. 'Carrie, sit down and shut up, will ya. I didn't bring you up to be so disrespectful. Say sorry to Ginty.'

'I'd rather shit in me hands and clap!'

'*What* did you say?' hissed Luanne, through gritted teeth.

Carrie clocked her mother, who had protruded her bottom jaw. That facial expression alone would have had any of her sisters running up the stairs. She realised she'd overused her mouth. Glaring at Ginty, she said, 'I'm sorry, Ginty.' She sighed. 'I am so cold and I don't feel too good.'

Ginty's eyes widened, and she smiled. 'Have you got a little chavi in that belly of yours, girl?'

That thought made Carrie want to heave and slap the woman, but, instead, she held down her anger, smiled sweetly, and said, 'No. One day I will, when we're wed,' she replied, before leaving the room.

The awkward atmosphere improved a little more when Dilly gracefully entered the room with a tray of her mother's best china and a plate of lemon puff biscuits.

'Cor, now, there's a nice tea set you have there, Luanne. I was thinking of getting Jimmy and Carrie one for their wedding.'

Dilly glanced at her mother with a smile. They both knew the joke behind that. Jimmy would be lucky to have a cup left over if Carrie got into one of her rages.

Ginty leaned forward and snatched a lemon puff before she looked Dilly up and down. 'My Arthur's out of prison next month. Well, he is as long as he ain't punched another screw up in the air. You two are the same age, ain't ya, Dilly?'

Dilly almost froze to the spot because she knew exactly what Ginty was getting at, and that was never going to happen. Not now, not ever. She looked at her ring, and for effect, she turned it around on her finger.

'Arthur would make an honest woman of ya, Dilly. You know he's always liked ya.'

Usually, Dilly would smile politely and choose her words very carefully, but the cheek of the woman forced her to blush before she retorted, 'No disrespect, Ginty, but Arthur really isn't my type, and I—'

'Your type? There ain't nuffin wrong with my Arthur. He's a good man, and as for your type, I hate to tell you, Dilly girl, but you're getting on, so turning away a catch like my Arthur is a big mistake.' She looked at Luanne for support, but even that comment prickled Luanne's rage.

'Ginty, you have my Mary as one daughter-in-law, and Rosie as your nephew's wife, and by the end of the month, you'll have my Carrie,' she spat, her jaw tightened in anger, 'but please don't insult my Dilly. She's been through a lot, and if she says she ain't ready to wed anybody, then she ain't ready. Do we understand each other?'

'I was only just saying. I mean, there's a mile of girls, pretty girls an' all, that would be knocking on my Arthur's door. So, I was thinking, since, as you say, two of your girls are already part of my family now, and Carrie will be soon, why not Dilly an' all. That's all.'

The fact that Ginty wasn't getting it or she was simply being too bloody-minded only increased Luanne's fury. 'My Dilly is a fucking good catch. Look at the girl. She's a real beauty. And you know she is, Ginty, so tell me what your Arthur can bring to the table 'cos let's be honest, 'ere, it ain't his looks, is it?'

Ginty pursed her lips and looked sideways, now thoroughly embarrassed. 'He ain't that fucking bad, Luanne. At least he's got his own hair and teeth.'

'And my Dilly ain't? Oh, come on, Ginty, your Arthur looks like a pot-bellied swamp donkey.'

Ginty had to laugh at that analogy. There was one thing going for her. She could always have a good laugh at herself. 'Luanne, you are a cheeky mare.' She laughed again. 'A swamp donkey. Yeah, all right, I'll give you that one.'

Dilly felt every muscle in her body relax and not just because there was no way she would marry Arthur. She hated arguments and this had had all the makings of one huge blow-up a moment ago.

The phone in the hall rang, and Luanne nodded to Dilly to get it. But before she had a chance to get to her feet, she could hear Carrie pelting down the stairs to answer it.

'Looks like Carrie's getting the phone, then. I wonder why?'

Ginty grinned, knowingly. 'She'll be thinking that's my Jimmy.'

'I wish she was more ladylike,' said Dilly, rolling her eyes. 'She jumps down those stairs three at a time. One day, she'll headbutt the wall.'

'Who is it?' called out Luanne.

'It's just a school friend!' Carrie shouted back.

Dilly frowned and glanced at her mother. 'But she don't go to school.'

Waving her hand dismissively, Luanne replied, 'But she did once, although these days, I ain't got a clue who she hangs about wiv. Anyway, where were we? Did you say a few days ago Kelly girl is doing the bouquet?'

'Yeah, she wants to do all the girls' hair as well.'

Dilly knew who Kelly was. 'Ginty, what about Kelly for your Arthur? She's not engaged, and she's nineteen.'

Ginty grabbed another lemon puff. 'Oh, I dunno. I've heard she's been around the block a bit.'

Dilly watched as Ginty seemed to stare off into space, but she would bet a fiver on Ginty considering it as a possibility.

***

Carrie sat next to the small telephone table, holding the phone closely to her ear so that no one could hear what was being said. 'Fucking hell, Dottie, I didn't think you were gonna call me.'

'Well, you asked me to.'

'Yeah, I did, didn't I.'

'What did you want from me, Carrie?'

'Nuffin, actually . . . Well . . . I dunno. I kinda thought that maybe you didn't have anyone.'

'I don't, Carrie. I really don't.'

'Listen, I know you're a bit green behind the ears, like, so listen to me. Never say anything on the phone 'cos the screws listen in all the time, okay?'

'Okay, I won't. The truth is I don't have much to say really. As for my mum—'

'Shut *up. Shooosh.* Don't mention anyone on the phone. Don't mention them at all. Only when you are wiv your solicitor, all right?'

'Yeah, okay. How do you know *so much*, Carrie?'

'I was born knowing the law. All of us lot are. Listen, Dottie, send me a VO, will ya?'

'What's a VO?'

'Oh Christ, girl, you've got a lot to learn. It's a visiting order. You've got my address, so send me one in the post. You *are* allowed visits, you know. I'll come and see ya, yeah?'

'Why, though, Carrie? I mean why would you even *want* to?'

'I hate the thought of you in there, and if it's my fault what's happened, I couldn't live wiv meself.'

'Carrie, believe me, it was *not* your fault. Not even close.'

'Well, send me a VO anyway.'

'Okay, I will. I have to go. The others are poking me to use the phone.'

'Don't forget to send a VO.'

'Bye, Carrie.'

Carrie put down the receiver and hurried back to her room before her mother or Ginty asked any questions. And as soon as she was inside, she closed the door and sat on her bed. Even the thought of having this strange relationship with Dottie was bizarre. She was at a complete loss as to why she even wanted a friendship with her, but something was compelling her to do it. And, even more important, she always trusted her own instincts.

She went over the conversation she'd just had with Dottie. Was she going to be friends with her? It certainly looked that way. She was pleased she'd given Dottie some advice about using the phone. The poor kid really hadn't a clue about life in the real world. But the one thing that really stood out in that conversation was when Dottie asked her why she was keen to make contact with her. It was a fair question, and being true to herself, she couldn't exactly answer that. Not right now, anyway.

She couldn't imagine what it was like for Dottie to go to a women's prison because she had always had her family to support her and protect her from anything. But for Dottie, the reverse was the case. Dottie was now being accused of killing her parents, and she herself was aware that Dottie had no siblings or relatives. The one and only thing that they really had in common was Jimmy.

Propping herself up with the pillow behind her neck and staring up at the Artex ceiling, she thought about the look on Dottie's face when she'd first clapped eyes on her after getting back with Jimmy. There was so much pain there. Behind that frightened expression, she knew Dottie was heartbroken. And it made her bite down on her bottom lip. She should have left Jimmy to Dottie, but, in some ways, she had been a little jealous of their affair. So when he had come back sniffing around, she was happy to jump into bed with him. But she could never really love him, not like Dottie probably did. This fact alone was why she was so angry with herself and it explained her mood recently.

Her main concern boiled down to one thing: was Dottie in prison facing a life sentence because she had been so upset with breaking up with Jimmy that she decided to kill her own parents? It was a possibility. Maybe, one day, she hoped Dottie would tell her. For now, she felt she had to treat Dottie with compassion because everything that had happened may have been partly her fault.

Another vision that wouldn't leave her mind was how Dottie had stood in the dock like a frightened lamb to the slaughter. But she recalled the two of them making eye contact, and she hoped that this might give Dottie some reassurance that there was someone out there who she could call on if needed. It was a thought, anyway.

Just as she was about to fall asleep, she heard her mother shout up the stairs, 'Ginty's off home. Are you gonna come down and say goodbye?'

Carrie mumbled, 'No, I ain't, the fat ugly old mare.'

'Carrie?'

'Yeah, sorry, I was falling asleep!' she shouted back, before getting up from her bed and making her way downstairs to face Ginty's mean grimace. It was her trademark gossiping wife's stance with her arms folded over her breasts and that suspicious look in her eye.

'There you are! So, Carrie girl, are you off to the gavvers' shop to give my Jimmy support?'

'I'm not feeling me best, Ginty. I feel like me guts are gonna spill over.'

Ginty looked Carrie up and down. 'Hmm, you do look a bit white, girl. Well, he'll probably call me anyway. So when he does, what shall I tell him?'

Carrie wanted to say *'Tell the rat I've changed my mind. I don't wanna marry him.'* But, instead, she smiled and said, 'Tell him to call me when they let him go. If they let him go.'

After Ginty gave her a sharp nod and slipped out of the door, Luanne swiftly closed it behind her. 'That *fucking* woman eating all the *fucking* biscuits. *And* the bleedin' cheek of her. As if my Dilly would even look twice at that ugly bastard of a son, Arthur! As God is me fucking witness, she'll not have another daughter-in-law from my family.' She glanced at Carrie. 'After you, that is.'

Carrie sighed. 'What if they keep Jimmy inside and blame him for Dottie's parents' murders, Mum?'

'Well, if they do, you can still get wed inside prison these days, ya know.'

'*What?* I ain't doing that, Mum. No way. If I'm getting married, I want it done proper.'

Luanne raised her eyebrows, now quite concerned. 'What do you mean by if?'

Carrie lowered her head, realising what she had just said. 'Oh, I just mean if Jimmy still wants to marry me.'

Waving her hand, Luanne dismissed the idea. 'Of course, he does. Who wouldn't wanna marry one of my beautiful girls, eh?'

Dilly appeared in the hallway. 'I'm so glad she's gone. I was sweating there for a bit. I mean, she was deadly serious about me marrying her Arthur. Do you know what they call him?'

'An acquired taste?'

Dilly chuckled. 'No, not that. They call him "trophy", Mum.'

'Yeah, I heard that. So?'

'Mum, it's not because he's won so many boxing matches. It's because his ears look like trophy handles.'

'Yeah? Ha, and that stupid cow thought she could ask for your hand for her fucking daft ugly boy.'

Carrie wasn't in the mood to laugh along with them. She was annoyed that she was marrying one of Ginty's sons. 'I'm going to my room,' she said, as she gave them a sad smile and sauntered back upstairs.

She needed to be alone to digest everything that was happening. It was a real mindfuck. She had imagined that the life she thought Dottie had lived – in a quiet house with all the lovely things around her – would be what she would want for herself. But now, learning first-hand that Dottie had all but admitted she had murdered her parents – having lived a life that she herself would have liked to experience – she wondered if her ideology of life on the other side of the main road was all it was cracked up to be. Besides, she had never hated anyone enough to want them dead, especially her mother and father. She loved them too dearly for that to happen.

CHAPTER TWELVE

Officer Kelp glared at Dorothy, the moment she replaced the phone receiver.

'I heard you. Why lie, Ellis? No one is here to push or poke you. Who were you talking to on the phone?'

Dottie frowned. 'Er, my friend, why?'

'You lied. You said you had to get off the phone. Why?'

Dottie wondered if she was supposed to tell the officers everything, but what did she have to lose? Even her baby would go into care, so apart from her life now, there was nothing they could take from her. She smiled, fixed her eyes on the officer, and realised Officer Kelp was uneasy again.

'Can I go back to my room now?'

Kelp's eye twitched. 'It's a cell. Get used to calling it that.'

She stared again. 'Can I go back to my cell, Officer Kelp?'

'I asked you a question, Ellis.'

'I know you did.'

'I expect an answer.'

'I know you do.'

'Well, Ellis?'

'Can I go back to my cell?'

'Have it your way. I will escort you back, but then you are down to see the doctor, so don't get too comfortable.' The officer laughed, which would have riled up most women.

But not Dottie; she didn't care. She had spent half the night tossing and turning and the other half sobbing. She hadn't gone for breakfast since she felt so sick.

Billy had been kind: she had made her a cup of tea and given her a ginger nut biscuit and even a quick hug before she shot off to get her own meal.

By the time they reached Dorothy's cell, Kelp was annoyed with herself for allowing this young slip of a kid to trouble her. She looked at her watch. 'I will be back in fifteen minutes. Be ready.'

Dottie stared at her dead in the eyes and nodded slowly.

But Kelp didn't wait around to be unnerved. She stormed off along the corridor.

As soon as Dottie sat on the bed, she took a few deep breaths to stop this constant nauseous feeling. Within a few minutes, she knew she hadn't imagined how she felt. Only just making it to the toilet, she found herself heaving as she emptied her stomach contents. With sweat pouring off her forehead, she hung on to the toilet rim as she gasped for breath.

Suddenly, she felt a pair of hands pulling her hair away from her face. 'You poor kid, I'll fetch you a cold glass of water.'

Dottie turned her head to the side to see Billy there with a face full of compassion. Slowly, she got to her feet, wiped her mouth, and sat on the bed.

Billy returned with a paper towel and a plastic beaker of water.

'Thank you, Billy.'

'Drink it slowly, kid.'

With her hands shaking, Dottie sipped the water and felt her body cool down; she took another two deep breaths and relaxed her shoulders.

'So how far gone are ya?'

A sudden stream of tears fell down Dottie's cheeks. 'I don't know. Two or three months at the most, I guess.'

'Was it you father's?'

Dottie looked up, and a deep frown crossed her forehead. 'My father's? No, no, it wasn't. He liked boys, not girls, I think.'

Billy nodded slowly. She understood: this young woman may have had a reason to kill her parents. It was no random psychopathic act of violence. With that thought, she had an idea. 'Dottie, listen, being pregnant may help your defence, ya know. 'Cos hormones make you do all sorts of strange things. Are you gonna keep it?'

Dottie was taken aback that Billy was so matter-of-fact about the pregnancy – that she wasn't judging her.

'Yeah, I'm definitely keeping it. Well, until I can't, that is.'

'The quack might suggest an abortion, ya know.'

Dottie's eyes widened. 'What, no, no, I won't do that. I have to protect my child.'

Billy saw the change in the girl's expression and guessed then that she probably had killed her parents to protect her baby.

'Dottie, I won't pry, but in this shit pit, you must stick up for yourself, like. The doctors, even the nurses in here, can get pushy—'

Suddenly finding her gumption, Dottie jumped up. 'If they dare to try to take my baby before it's born, I swear I'll—'

Billy gestured with her hands for Dottie to keep her voice down. 'All right, Dottie, they can't make you, anyway. You're on remand, and by the time your case comes up, you'll be full term. Tell them you're five months pregnant. Tell them you're a Christian. Then at least you will get to go to the new part of Holloway Prison instead of this rat and flea-infested hellhole. I've heard they've even got a swimming pool.'

Dottie smiled. 'Like Butlins then, is it?'

Billy shrugged. 'Me, I've never been. In fact, I've never even dipped me toe in the sea or felt what it's like to walk on the sand.'

Having seen the fear Billy could create, Dottie also saw a person who had been denied probably a hell of a lot that most people took for granted. Another tear trickled down her face, but it wasn't for herself. It was for Billy.

However, Billy hadn't a clue because no one had ever felt sorry for her; they never had and probably never would. So she put her arms around Dottie and hugged her, believing those tears were from a frightened and confused young woman who had no one.

'Oi, get away from her, Billy. We'll have none of that here, thank you very much!' yelled Kelp.

Billy instantly jumped to her feet and turned to face Kelp. 'What the fuck do you mean?'

'You know what I mean, Billy.'

'You, ya ugly cunt, might be a first-class rug muncher, but, see, me, I'm not, so don't put me in the same category as you.'

'One more word, and you'll be back in solitary.'

'Go on, Kelp, do it. Call for fucking backup an' all 'cos by the time I'm done biting chunks out of your ugly fanny face, you'll need it, *and* an ambulance. So, go on, make it worth my while,' she said, showing her bottom teeth as she stepped closer.

Dottie could see the sudden change of colour in Kelp's face, and her eyes widened in terror. To stop the officer from pressing the alarm, she got up from her bed and slid past Billy. 'Aren't you supposed to be taking me to see the doctor?'

Relieved by Dorothy's subtle intervention, Kelp turned to the girl. For one moment, she really thought her passable looks – such as they were – were numbered.

'Yes, and you, Billy, you'd better watch yourself.'

Billy huffed and laughed, mumbling under her breath, but it was loud enough for Kelp to hear the words 'cowardly cunt'.

Officer Kelp held her tongue and marched along the corridor, jangling her keys, with Dorothy on her heels.

The walk was long and tedious since every corridor was locked and unlocked, magnifying the idea of prison. Dottie could tell that Kelp's silence was masking her rage at being talked down to by Billy.

When they finally reached the medical centre, Kelp opened the door and shoved Dorothy in..

It was utterly unnecessary. Dottie hadn't given Kelp cause to be manhandled.

A nurse, who was dressed in a pale blue starched dress and wearing a white swallowtail cap and holding a clipboard, peered up. 'Dorothy Ellis?'

Dottie nodded.

'I'm Nurse Pippa Humphrey. Take a seat. The doctor will be in shortly.' She then glared at Kelp. 'He will want to speak to her alone, Officer.'

'She hasn't been assessed. She may be—'

'We are aware, Officer. We have read her details. Nevertheless, the doctor will see her alone. If there is any issue, we will call for you.'

Kelp sighed, shook her head, and left.

No sooner had the entrance door shut than a door at the back of the room opened, and in walked a middle-aged man. He was tall, with dark hair neatly trimmed and a thick moustache, and he was wearing square-shaped black glasses and a white lab coat. He took a seat, scanned his notes, and then placed his hands together on the table.

'Right, Miss Ellis, what's going to happen is this. I'm going to fill out this form.' He picked up his pen and stabbed the file. 'And then the nurse will take your blood pressure and a urine sample for testing. Before we begin, is there anything you need to tell me?'

Dottie bit her lip, unsure whether or not to say she was pregnant.

'I can see you have something on your mind. Spit it out, girl.'

He was like an army sergeant, and his harsh words took the option away from her. 'I'm pregnant.'

Those words made him sit up straight and stare. 'Really?'

She nodded. 'About three months.'

'Right, this poses a problem because I have read your charges, and if you are found guilty, you could potentially be in prison for a very long time, and so there would be no point in continuing with a pregnancy. We can arrange a termination this week. But we need a urine test first.'

'I'm keeping it!' she quickly piped up.

'Er, that's not my advice. You cannot keep it. You are in prison, and the rules are you will have to hand the baby over to the authorities. This isn't a place to have a baby. What do you think you are in? A hotel?' He leaned back with a smug smile that reminded her of her father. It was that holier-than-thou look.

'I am a Christian,' was all she could say without losing her temper.

'Ha, a Christian. And yet you are charged with double murder. How can you, in fact, how dare you, call yourself a Christian?'

Something inside Dottie snapped. All she saw was her father sitting there looking down his nose at her and spouting his righteous words. 'So you are judge and jury, then, are you?' she retorted.

The doctor's face tightened. 'I am a doctor who is offering advice. Being a martyr won't help your unborn child and—'

'But my unborn child *will* be born.'

The doctor waved his hand dismissively. 'Nurse, please do a pregnancy test and take her blood pressure.' He picked up the file and shook his head. 'I'll have to write a report on the present circumstances because it looks like we have a stubborn one here.'

'Doctor, far be it for me to interfere. You are the doctor, and I am merely the nurse.'

Dottie sensed an atmosphere between the two of them.

'Dorothy has the right to have her baby and she will be managed in the new section of the prison as soon as possible.'

His face suddenly reddened, but it was clear he didn't have an answer to that. Instead, he slammed the file back on the desk. 'Well, let the medical team over there assess her.' He rose from his chair and left the room, slamming the door behind him.

'Dorothy, sorry about that. Let's get you checked over, and I'll let the governor know you are pregnant, so we can get you moved ASAP.'

Dottie rose from her chair, her legs feeling a little wobbly. 'I won't be made to have an abortion, will I?'

The nurse slid her arm around Dorothy's shoulders. 'No, pet, you won't. Ignore him. Now, you probably don't know this, but you may be treated a little better since you're with child and remember this: you are on remand. If you are found not guilty, you will be released, and there will be nothing to stop you from keeping your baby.' She paused and rubbed Dorothy's arm. 'And if the worst happens, at least you will have given a baby its life, okay? Be proud of that.'

Dottie could feel her eyes welling up from the gentle and kind words from the nurse, who she guessed was from the north-east, judging by her accent.

'I read your file, Dorothy, and you have no past, do you? I mean, you've never been in any trouble before.'

'No, I haven't, apart from, of course, getting myself pregnant, but I thought I loved him. He just didn't love me, though.' She stopped talking, suddenly realising that she was opening up about Jimmy.

'We all love someone at some point. Some of us are lucky enough to have a long-lasting love that spans a lifetime. My husband and I have been married for twenty-three years, and, hopefully, we will have another twenty-three, God willing. And you, Dorothy, will find someone special for you one day.'

'I don't think I want a relationship with anyone but my son.' She rubbed her belly.

'Oh, so you think you are having a boy?'

'I have to be because if I'm not, then what I did may have been a mistake.'

Pippa frowned but she didn't push for an explanation because she had an idea that Dorothy was referring to the murders.

While taking Dorothy's blood pressure and giving her a thorough check over, Pippa was careful to remain gentle, and all the time she was carrying out her tests and checks, she spoke to her patient about the rules and what food she would be entitled to and what to expect in the new prison because she covered both sites.

'So everything seems okay. You are in good shape. Now, you may be entitled to a buddy, someone who will be like a partner to help you.'

'Really? I have someone already who has been very kind and supportive.'

'Oh, that's great. Who is it? I might know them.'

'Billy Cardel.'

Pippa's eyes widened. She removed her stethoscope and placed it on the metal trolley. 'Billy?'

'Yes, she is in the cell opposite. She has been so kind.'

'And she's been kind in what way?'

Dottie sat up on the bed and tilted her head to the side. 'Well, she hugged me when I was very upset. She helped me when I was sick. And she warned me about the doctor and to stand my ground if he suggested an abortion.'

Pippa nodded. 'Billy is a very violent woman. I have had the displeasure of sewing up her victims, mainly staff, so I am aware of how vicious she can be. Having said that, inside that tough exterior is a heart of gold. If she is good to you, then I believe there isn't a hidden agenda because what you see with Billy is what you get. And, Dorothy, if she likes you, then she likes you.' She turned away to wash her hands in the small sink hanging on the wall, before drying them with a paper towel.

'Thank you, nurse, for your help.'

Pippa spun around. 'I'm not here to judge. I'm here to add a little help. Most of the women shouldn't be here, so if I can help them, then I feel I am doing a good job.'

'Nurse, if I'm allowed a baby buddy or whatever it's called and they take me to the new prison, what can I do about Billy? I could do with her help.'

Pippa leaned against the sink and chewed her bottom lip. 'I can recommend that Billy joins you in the new prison.' She winked. 'The governor would love to get her out of here. Obviously, she is out of solitary. Let me see what I can do.'

'You would do that for me?'

Pippa smiled. 'I'm actually doing it for Billy too.' She looked at the door. 'Billy deserves it. Some women in here have been treated pretty badly.'

When the nurse looked at the door again, Dottie knew that the doctor had had something to do with it.

***

As Dottie locked eyes with Officer Kelp, she noticed a fake smile on her face.

'All done, Ellis?'

Her voice was higher pitched, giving herself away. Her attempt at friendliness was fake, and Dottie spotted that straight away.

'Yes.'

'Okay, let's go straight to the food hall, shall we. Only, they've got burgers today, which is a good choice. We can beat the queue.'

Dottie didn't reply. There was nothing about Kelp that she could possibly warm to.

'Ellis, while you are here, I can make your life a lot easier, you know.'

Kelp paused, waiting for Dorothy to say something, but there was an uncomfortable silence. 'It's all about scratching each other's back. That's how prison works and how women survive in it. I could be your friend in need.'

Dottie walked on, remaining quiet.

'But to be your supporter, I need to get to know you. And, so far, you seem a nice person. I'd be very wary of Billy Cardel. She's hurt a lot of people. She has razor-sharp teeth, you know. I just don't want you getting carried away believing she is a friend. She's not. She's dangerous and always after something. I can protect you.'

'Can you?' asked Dottie, knowing where this was going.

'Yes, absolutely, Ellis. But I have to understand you before I lay my career on the line because if at any time we show favouritism, we are up for reprimand, even the sack.'

'Hmm, well, there's no need to do that with me. I don't need it.'

'Oh, believe me, Ellis, the women in here are animals, and I know you're not like them, so you come to me if things get rough.'

'Thank you,' was all Dottie could say because she trusted Kelp as far as she could throw her.

'It must be hard for you, Ellis, now you've not got your parents to support you. Mind you, I'm sure they weren't particularly nice, were they?'

Dottie wasn't surprised at all by where this conversation was going. She shrugged her shoulders.

'It's okay. I understand. I mean, my parents were not nice to me. They were abusive, in fact.'

'Were they?'

'Yes, cruel, to be exact. I felt like killing them myself. So I think we have much in common, you and me.'

'Do we?'

'Yeah, sure we do. I understand you more than you know. I've been there . . . almost. I just didn't have the guts to kill my parents.'

‘Hmmm, what makes you believe I did?’ Dottie asked, knowing perfectly well the game Kelp was playing.

‘Did you, Ellis? Kill them, I mean?’

From nowhere, Dottie felt an overwhelming sense of bravery. She stopped dead and turned to face Kelp. With a half smile, she said, ‘I don’t believe you have the right to ask me that question. No matter how much you have been offered, I will not tell you a thing about it. My solicitor has told me not to speak about it, so, if you don’t mind, I’d rather not answer your prying questions.’

Kelp was fuming. Having been offered a substantial price for a good scoop from a tabloid newspaper, and wanting to leave the prison anyway, this would have been an enormous help to make that move. Her right eye suddenly twitched relentlessly, and she glared at Dorothy, wanting to strangle her. She hated herself as well for ever uttering the words that her parents were cruel. They were far from abusive. In fact, they had spoiled her rotten. And with her being an only child, this was probably the only thing that she and Dorothy had in common.

‘No one has offered me money. Don’t expect me to come running to help you when the alarms go off and the prisoners are beating the crap out of you. I’ll be the last in line to come to your aid. Are we clear?’

‘Crystal,’ Dottie replied, hoping that she wouldn’t have to face Kelp’s wrath in one way or another and that the nurse would be true to her word and help her to get a transfer to the new prison.

CHAPTER THIRTEEN

Carrie was woken up by a loud banging on her bedroom door.

In came Jimmy barging his way into her room. He was looking flustered. 'For fuck's sake, Carrie!' he bellowed. 'Where have you fucking been?'

Still half asleep, Carrie slowly swung her long legs around before pushing herself off the bed. 'What are you doing here, Jimmy? Coming into my room like this. Me farver will have your guts for garters.'

'He ain't here. Dilly let me in, and never mind all that, why weren't you up the station? I've been inside that fucking place for two days, so where were you when they finally threw me out?'

Carrie looked him up and down and noticed how dishevelled he was. Even his cropped hair looked greasy, a sight she rarely saw in Jimmy. If there was one thing he always did, he ensured his skinhead was neat. His sheepskin coat had stains down it, and he didn't smell so much of aftershave as he did of sweat and morning breath.

She yawned and then ran her fingers through her long black curly hair before she took a hairband from her wrist and tied her hair in a ponytail. 'Have you even been home, Jimmy?' she said, looking him up and down once more.

'No! I came straight here since you weren't at the station waiting for me.'

'Jimmy, don't expect me to be hanging around no nick for you. For fuck's sake, it's taters outside, and like I told your muvver, I don't want the gavvers to get a good look at me. And besides, I ain't feeling too clever.'

'Well, ain't you even gonna ask me how *I* got on?'

Carrie slumped back down on her bed. 'Well, you're 'ere, ain't ya. So they didn't nick ya, then.'

Jimmy sat beside her. 'They showed me the photos of that Dottie's parents. Fucking hell.' He ran his hands over his spiky hair. 'She's a nutcase, Carrie. Cor, it's lucky I dumped her. That could have been me. She sliced one of 'em open and the other was sliced in the neck. There was blood everywhere, and her muvver was staring up into space. She must have seen it coming.' He shook his head. 'I can't believe it. She seemed sweet, if you know what I mean. Quiet and certainly not violent.'

'Why do you think she did it, Jimmy?'

He tapped his head. ''Cos she's a fucking lunatic. Why else?'

Carrie chewed her thumbnail before she sighed. 'You don't think she did it because you dumped her, do you?'

'*What?* Are ya saying it was *my* fault? No, Christ, just 'cos I dumped her, it ain't a reason for her to murder her own muvver and farver.' He frowned. 'Why? Do you think it was the reason?'

Carrie shrugged. 'Maybe. Who knows?'

'Look, can we change the subject. I missed you.' He stroked her cheek.

'What did the police say?'

'Nuffin, just where I was, who I was wiv. You know, all that bollocks. So, did you miss me?'

'Bloody hell, Jimmy, you've only been gone for two fucking days. Besides, I thought you'd be up the pub with your mates by now.'

'The pub? No, I wanna spend time with you. We're getting wed soon, and I want us to be happy like before. You know what I mean.' He leaned closer and placed his hand on her right breast.

Straightaway, she slapped his hand away. 'You can't let up, can ya, eh? You've just got out the nick, and right away, you want me knickers off.'

'Carrie, you're beautiful, and you're gonna be my wife soon enough. What's wrong with sex now? You loved it before.'

'*Hello*, it's my bedroom, and I'm in my farver*'s* house. Have some respect.'

Jimmy sat up straight. She was right, and if her father caught them, he would beat him with a stick or worse.

No sooner had Jimmy realised the consequences of actually being inside Carrie's bedroom than the banging at the front door had him leaping off the bed. 'Fuck, is that your farver?'

Carrie wanted to laugh at the horror on Jimmy's face. 'Probably,' she said. But she knew he was with her uncle. They were trying to get an old banger out of the River Cray before the police found it. So she reckoned he would be gone for a long time.

Dilly had once again opened the front door.

Jimmy listened, frozen to the spot, until he recognised his own mother's voice. 'It's me muvver.' The colour returned to his cheeks.

'I can tell. So can all the fucking neighbours!'

Jimmy flashed Carrie an angry look. 'I hope you ain't bad-mouthing her, 'cos you know I won't have it. She's gonna be your new mum once we're wed.'

Carrie got up from the bed again, crossed her arms, and widened her eyes. 'I'll tell you something for nothing, Jimmy. Your muvver might end up as me muvver-in-law, but no one, and I fucking mean *no one*, will ever replace me own muvver.'

Not having seen that look before, Jimmy recoiled only slightly before realising he needed to correct himself. 'Er, you know what I mean. She's gonna be a big part of your life, that's all I'm saying.'

Carrie pursed her lips and then kept them closed because she didn't want to cause a massive row. Not today.

Jimmy left the bedroom and hurtled down the stairs to see his mother carrying two large shopping bags.

'There you are, you little fucker. I was worried near to death about ya. The filth said they'd released you, and your mates are all supping fucking beer at mine waiting for ya. I might have known you'd be here. So Carrie came to the station after all, did she?'

She looked up the stairs at Carrie, who still had her arms folded.

'No, I didn't. I was tired, and it seems it's lucky I didn't, 'cos otherwise, I'd have waited another fucking twenty-four hours.'

'Never mind that, get down here, Carrie girl. I've got a load of knocked-off silk flowers straight off the lorry going to Harrolds.'

'Harrolds?' said Carrie, as she descended the stairs.

'Yeah, you know that posh shop in London. All the famous people shop there.'

'Ya mean Harrods, don't ya?'

'Whatever. Anyway, have a look. There's bouquets for you and the bridesmaids.'

'Nice one, Muvver,' said Jimmy, eager to get involved and inject some enthusiasm because he could tell from Carrie's face that she wasn't impressed. In fact, she didn't seem all that keen on him at the moment.

Carrie peered inside the bag and pulled out a bouquet of white and pink flowers. She had to admit they looked pretty, but she wasn't interested, not right now. This incident with Dottie was playing on her mind.

Ginty looked at Dilly. 'Are you gonna put the kettle on, girl? I've got some news for you as well.'

While Dilly hurried to the kitchen, she prayed that her mother would be home soon. She didn't like Ginty because the woman was a manipulator and a bully. And there was another thing. For some reason, Ginty always gave her an uneasy feeling that made her shake inside.

Nudging Carrie's arm, Ginty winked. 'My Arthur's coming home sooner than we thought.'

Jimmy punched the air excitedly. 'Blimey, Muvver, that's cause for a party.'

She winked again. 'He's interested in Dilly, and I think he is just the ticket to take her mind off what happened and help her to get on with her life.'

Carrie chuckled. 'Ginty, me sister ain't interested. I thought me muvver told ya.'

Ginty wagged her finger. 'Yeah, only on account of his, well, what can I say, less than handsome features. But you know what prison can do for free? They can fix your railings. And now me boy has a nice set of pearly whites, so he's a bit of a looker now, ya know.'

Carrie stood with her hands on her hips. 'What? Did they do plastic surgery an' all?'

But it was Jimmy who replied. 'Oi, Carrie, leave it out. Don't be so rude to me muvver. I reckon our Arthur's a good match for your Dilly.'

Carrie felt her face redden as her anger built up.

'The only match is Dilly's arse and his face.'

She laughed at her own joke before Jimmy grabbed her arm and squeezed a little tighter than he should have, with the intention of putting her in her place.

But it didn't work. Shaking him off, she glared at him. 'Grab me like that again, and I'll fucking hurt ya, Jimmy Carson.'

Ginty tried to laugh it off, for fear of another breakdown in their relationship, which would be a nightmare considering they were three-quarters of the way to organising the wedding.

'Jimmy, you've always been so fucking heavy-handed. Now, learn to treat the girl like a girl and not like one of the lads.'

Carrie would have appreciated Ginty's support if it was genuine. But she wasn't stupid. She was fully aware of how much the marriage between herself and Jimmy meant to her future mother-in-law.

Jimmy looked at his mother and then back at Carrie. 'Sorry, Carrie, I didn't mean to hurt ya. It won't happen again.'

'You bet ya fucking granny's life it won't happen again!'

Putting the bouquet back inside the bag, Carrie left the pair in the hallway and stormed into the living room, where Dilly had placed a mug of tea on a coaster.

'Ginty, your tea's here!' shouted Carrie, as she rolled her eyes at Dilly, who seemed a little off-colour.

Carrie mouthed the words 'Go back to the kitchen.'

With a hint of a smile, Dilly hurried through the dining area, and turned right into the kitchen.

In the time it took for Ginty and Jimmy to enter the living room, Carrie made an educated guess that they had been whispering about something. No doubt, it was either about herself or Dilly.

After plumping up a cushion and placing it in the small of her back, Ginty sat in the armchair with her back to the window. She leaned forward and snatched the mug of tea.

'Dilly!' she called out. 'Any biscuits to go with me tea?'

'No, Ginty, sorry. Me mum's out shopping,' said Carrie.

'Dilly girl, are you gonna come and join us?'

But, again, it was Carrie who answered for her sister. 'No, she ain't. She's got that bug going around. I think I had it yesterday. Cor, I was violently sick, I was, and she felt the same, so best she doesn't get too close to you. You don't want to be vomiting out of ya arse, 'cos that's what it does to ya.'

'Carrie, for fuck's sake, do you have to talk like that? You're gonna be me wife, and you ought to act more like a lady.'

Carrie turned and growled with her jaw clenched. 'I'll 'ave you know, I've always been ladylike when necessary, so don't pull me up on how to act.'

Ginty waved her hand and smiled nervously. 'Take no notice, Carrie. He's just nervous. And being in the station, he's hardly slept, by the look of things. So, boy, they obviously didn't charge you with anything, then?'

Jimmy shook his head. 'No, the gavvers took for ever to check out my alibi and asked me loads of questions before they told me not to leave the country. The wankers, they didn't even get me a burger. Just a couple of manky sweaty cheese sandwiches.'

'So what did they say about that Dottie bird? Anything?'

'They showed me photos. Fuck me, I'll have nightmares for a week. Cor, proper gruesome, it was. She's looking at a long life sentence, that's for sure.'

'So they don't think you were a part of it?'

Jimmy shook his head fast. 'No way. I gotta be honest.' He hung his head sheepishly. 'I threw up. I think they knew then I couldn't have done that. I ain't got the stomach for it.'

'And they didn't try to dig for information on the family, did they?'

Jimmy shook his head. 'No, this was all about Dottie and her parents. They never asked about anyone else.'

'Good, right, so let's get back to the wedding. The hall and church are booked, and your uncle has promised the vicar as much holy water as he likes.' She winked again.

Carrie knew the vicar in the local church was prone to a few whiskies, so no doubt they would have bribed him to get the wedding done as soon as possible. The hall was attached to the workingmen's club, but she didn't care about that. She was getting less and less interested in it. The problem was the wedding. And the other problem was marrying Jimmy. So as

Ginty rambled on, she only nodded and smiled, not even taking in what she was saying.

An hour later, her mother finally returned home with bags of shopping. It was a relief for Carrie to escape from hearing Ginty's ugly voice droning on and on.

Since Dilly had already gone to her room, Carrie helped get the bags out of the back of the taxi and began unloading them.

Ginty bustled her way into the kitchen to be nosy. 'I was just going over all the details about the wedding with Carrie.'

Luanne wasn't in the best of moods. The taxi was late, and her shoes were soaking wet. So much so, she couldn't feel her toes. 'Couldn't you have waited until I was home?' She pointed to the bags almost overflowing the kitchen worktop. 'Or at least until I'd got me shopping put away.'

'Well, anyway, Carrie's agreed to everything, so I might as well head off home.'

Luanne rolled her eyes and shook her head. 'I'll be over later, Ginty, to discuss the arrangements. Since Carrie is my daughter, her farver will be giving her away and putting his hands deep into his pockets to pay for it.'

Ginty frowned. 'I hope you ain't implying I'm diddling your ol' man out of money?'

Luanne glared. 'I'm not implying nuffin of the fucking sort. What I'm saying is we have a big say in our girl's wedding since we're footing the bill.'

Ginty was surprised that Luanne's voice had become firm and forceful, but she wouldn't get into a row. Well, not until after the wedding, because then things would be very different.

CHAPTER FOURTEEN

Four weeks later

Dottie was sitting with her back to the headboard and her feet resting on Billy's lap. 'So this afternoon, they are going to transport me to the new prison, and I don't think I want to go now. At least here I have you, Billy.'

Billy was massaging Dottie's feet. 'You will have so much more over there, from what I've heard. It's not like a fucking ice box and it's supposed to be spotless, no mice or rats. And there's more to do. It's so fucking boring here.' She looked around Dottie's cell. 'This place is so old and angry from ghosts of the past that it makes the women mad. Over in the new building, it will be all nice and fresh with no bad energy or spirits from the old ages. And 'cos you are pregnant, you will get treated better.'

She sighed because she wished she was going there too but there was no chance of that. She believed she would leave the old prison in a wooden box. She noticed Dottie chewing her bottom lip.

'Now, I see you keep looking at that letter. Are you gonna tell me what's in it?'

'This is the third letter. It's from Carrie.'

'Yeah, so?'

'She says she's getting married this Saturday and wants my blessing.'

'Blessing? That's a bit fucking weird, ain't it?'

‘Yes . . . and no. We somehow have this strange connection. I don’t know what it is, but like I said before, she came to the courts and asked me to call her. I did, and she wanted to visit me. Well, that hasn’t happened yet, but she keeps writing to me hoping I’m okay and asking me if I need anything. Strangely, she doesn’t ask for anything in return.’

‘Maybe she’s filled with guilt because she’s marrying the father of your baby.’

‘Yeah, that might have been so, had I told her, but she doesn’t know I’m pregnant.’

‘What?’ Billy sat up straight. ‘So there I was thinking you’ve told this Carrie bird everything. Except you left out the most important bit. You, Dottie Ellis, are carrying his baby, and now, if she’s getting married in a few days, then she will be your bubba’s stepmother. And also, don’t you think she has the right to know before she marries the prick? ’Cos she may not want to marry him if she knew.’

‘You know what, Billy. I really didn’t think of it that way. And to be honest, I wasn’t ready to tell anyone. Well, except you, obviously. And Mr Clarkson, my solicitor, and the nurse, of course. But not anyone else just yet. And, Billy, I will have to give it up, so she will never know anyway.’

Suddenly, Officer Kelp appeared in the doorway. ‘Give what up?’

Dottie’s face reddened, knowing she had to think quickly. ‘My toiletries and hot chocolates.’

‘Oh, right, yeah. Anyway, Ms Jennings wants to see you, Ellis.’ She glared at Cardel. ‘She’s being moved to the new prison, so it looks like you’re gonna be alone again, ready to prey on the next innocent victim.’

Kelp was expecting verbal abuse from Cardel.

But it was Dottie who retaliated. ‘No wonder Billy has attacked your officers when you come out with shit like that. She has been the only real honest, decent person here who has made me feel safe and who has cared for me.'

'This ain't a care home, you silly little—'

'No, I am well aware of that, but there is still no need to be so nasty, sly, or deliberately bloody-minded.'

'Oh, look at you! Suddenly, you've found your balls, have you, Ellis?'

Dottie grinned lopsidedly as she stared demonically into Kelp's eyes. 'I actually never thought I'd lost them.' Slowly, she rose from her bed and stepped closer to the officer.

Kelp staggered backwards. 'What are you doing, Ellis?' she asked nervously, since Dorothy's stare was freaking her out.

'Er, didn't you just say the governor wants to see me?'

Realising she had shown a moment of fear and weakness, she replied, 'Yes, so get your plimsolls on and follow me.'

Billy was laughing because she was surprised that little Dottie could put the fear of God into anyone. But, clearly, she had. She watched her friend slip her feet into the prison issues and disappear out of sight.

Billy wandered back to her room and suddenly felt a deep sadness. Because she would miss the girl. There was something about her that made her feel comfortable in her company. She'd never felt like that with anyone before and she knew she would genuinely miss Dottie. And the idea that the girl had asked to have her as a birthing buddy had really pulled on her heartstrings. At no time in her whole life had anyone ever been that kind. But she knew there was no way they would allow that. Not with her history of violence.

***

The jangling of keys and the smell of metal as each door opened made Dottie feel sick. She hated the odour of prison, mainly because she was suffering from morning sickness, but also because it was such an uninviting smell, she could taste it at the back of her throat.

Kelp tapped twice on the door before Governor Jennings shouted, 'Enter!'

Dottie was gently pushed inside the room and the governor pointed to a chair for her. 'Take the weight off your feet.'

Also in the room were Officer Helen Wells and Pippa Humphrey, the nurse.

'It has been agreed that you will be moved to the new prison, considering your condition.'

Kelp hadn't been informed of the facts. 'Condition? What condition? I wasn't informed of any issues.'

Jennings glared at Kelp. 'Well, you have now. Ellis is pregnant. That's the whole reason for the move.' She waved her hand dismissively. 'Now, Ellis, I have all of your paperwork and your medical notes in front of me. Mrs Humphrey will escort you to the new prison, and there, you will be under the control of Governor Cobain,' she said, as she curled her lip slightly.

But it didn't go unnoticed by Dottie. Evidently Jennings didn't like Cobain. *Was it a power issue?* she wondered.

Jennings sat behind her desk and signed some paperwork before looking up. 'I understand you wanted Billy Cardel as your birthing buddy.' She chuckled. 'Was that a serious request?'

Dottie frowned. 'Of course it was.'

'Then your request is granted.'

'*What!*' snapped Kelp.

'The sooner *she* is out of here and in the new Holloway, the safer my staff will be. Now, Officer Kelp, if you have a problem with that, then I suggest you put it in writing to me, but we both know that you are already skating on thin ice.'

Everyone in the room could tell that Kelp was absolutely furious, having been humiliated in front of other staff and prisoner Dorothy Ellis.

Dottie glanced at Kelp and smirked before returning her attention to the governor. 'Thank you so much.'

‘Hmmm, good luck for the future, Miss Ellis.’ She waved her hand, again dismissively. ‘You may go.’

Inside, Dottie was so excited that she grinned all the way back to her cell, but she didn’t go inside. Instead, she went inside Billy’s cell, only to find her friend’s eyes red. ‘What’s the matter? What’s happened?’

‘Nuffin. Go on, fuck off, Dottie. Leave me be for a minute, will ya.’

‘I can’t do that, Billy.’

Billy’s eyes widened. ‘What do you mean you can’t do that? Go on, fuck off, and leave me alone. I hate goodbyes, and . . . What are you grinning at, ya sick prat?’

‘You are coming with me, Billy. The number one said so.’

Kelp slyly appeared in the doorway with a face like a slapped arse. ‘Get ya gear, Billy. You’re on the move.’

‘What? This ain’t a fucking joke, is it?’

Dottie’s smile stretched encouragingly from ear to ear. ‘No, seriously, you’re going to be my birthing buddy in the new prison.’

Just as Billy was about to fling her arms around Dottie, she clocked Kelp staring at her, so she decided not to hug her best friend and risk jeopardising her chances, just in case this whole thing was a wind-up. But assuming it wasn’t, inside, she was shaking with excitement. And to think that no one in her life had ever been so trusting as to allow her to be a birthing partner or any kind of partner, not even at school. But then again, her school days had been filled with kids bullying her because she had nothing, not even shoes without holes, and she probably had smelled a bit.

It took Billy less than five minutes to sling all her belongings into a clear plastic bag and be ready to leave before the prison staff changed their mind.

As Kelp escorted them both towards the main reception area, she said quietly in Dorothy's ear, 'You kept that little pregnancy nugget a secret, didn't ya?'

'No, I didn't, actually. I just didn't tell you I was pregnant. But my guess is now you know, the whole world will because I am sure that bit of information will come with a financial reward from the press.'

'Yep, it sure will.'

Billy stopped in her tracks and spun around to face Kelp, but Dottie quickly grabbed her arm. 'No, Billy, leave her be. She's really not worth the trouble. Let's get to the new prison. Remember, Billy, they've got a swimming pool.'

Billy glared at Kelp, but she had the sense to keep her hands to herself. Otherwise, she risked being sent to one place only – solitary confinement.

***

The level of security was at its maximum. The women were going to be escorted separately by foot to the new Holloway Prison. It had been built inside the grounds of the old prison where a huge section of the old building had been demolished.

The idea of being separated initially caused both Dottie and Billy to kick off, but Pippa assured them that they would *both* be going to the new prison, which was only minutes away. She wanted to keep Dottie as calm as possible because she couldn't afford for her to lose the baby. Her case was too high profile, and there would no doubt be some do-gooder fighting for her rights. The press loved prison gossip on high-profile cases, so Pippa was eager to ease Dottie on her way, while assuring her that Billy would be arriving soon afterwards.

Once Dottie arrived, she looked at the new building, which was so different from the old one. It was more like a school, except the walls were much higher.

One of the officers had handcuffed her to herself while Pippa walked on ahead. Another officer stood to her left and held her plastic bag and transfer papers.

After being escorted to the main reception door, Dottie looked back to Billy, who was only just behind her. The officers were not so gentle with her as they yanked her cuffed hand while marching her along. Still, it didn't take the massive smile off her face as she winked at Dottie.

They were processed separately. Dottie met the new governor, Claire Cobain, first. And what a difference she was compared to Audrey Jennings. Dressed in a loose blue jacket, fashionable trousers, and a thin jumper underneath, she seemed more chilled out. Her blonde hair was permed and cut shorter at the sides and her cheeks were coated in pink blusher. She smiled when she introduced herself and looked directly at Dottie when she spoke.

'Now, this prison runs slightly differently from the old one. We have more facilities, and, obviously, we are equipped to house the pregnant ladies, yourself included. One of my officers will take you to your room, and tomorrow, you can go over the rules. They will be very similar to the previous prison. But food arrangements and exercise may be different. You will have more free time to maybe go for a swim or enjoy some classes, and we encourage association times.' She paused and smiled again. 'Now, Miss Ellis . . .' She looked down at some notes. 'You have asked Billy Cardel to be your birthing partner, or buddy as we call them. I know of Billy. In fact, her reputation precedes her. I am hoping that you are a good influence on her because if she so much as looks at my officers the wrong way, she will be shipped out of here and placed in a prison probably up north.'

'I understand, Ms Cobain, and I promise I will try my best. I want her to stay, too.'

'Yes, maybe you have one thing in common—'

Instantly, Dottie was angry and snapped back. 'Just because she killed her father isn't the reason we have become friends . . . Sorry, I didn't mean to—'

'It's okay. It is *I* who should be sorry. I wasn't implying that at all.' She looked at Pippa Humphrey. 'Does Miss Ellis know about Billy Cardel?'

Pippa shook her head. 'It wasn't my place to mention it.'

'Well, there are some inmates in this prison who know her history, so it's no secret.'

Dottie frowned. 'Please may I know?'

'I was a senior officer in the old prison before I became governor here, so I might as well tell you. You will find out soon enough. Billy gave birth in prison, in her cell alone. And the baby was taken right away into the care of social services.'

Dottie put her hands to her face in shock. 'She didn't say. Oh my goodness, and I asked her to help me with my baby. How must she feel?'

Cobain waved her hand. 'Listen, I know Billy. If you upset her, all the prisoners will know. You would hear her shouting from the next block. But, strangely enough, I think she will make the best birthing buddy for you.'

'Thank you.'

'Right, one of my officers will see you to your room, and I will tell Billy that I have told you about her past.'

Dottie nodded. The notion of Billy giving birth alone was still weaving in and out of her thoughts.

***

Dottie was delighted to find that the room was clean with a linoleum floor, curtains at the windows, two beds, and there was so much more space. Making her bed, she noticed how much softer the sheets and blanket were, and the room was warmer. She wouldn't be spending a night shivering herself to sleep.

An hour later, Billy arrived and she was all smiles. She was escorted by Officer Petworth, a soft-spoken woman with a friendly smile. Her deep burgundy hair was pulled into a top knot bun with a stiff hair-sprayed fringe. 'There you go, Billy. Your new accommodation. If you get yourself sorted . . .' She looked at her watch. 'Say in ten minutes, I'll come back and take you both to the food hall. You'll be having chilli-filled baked potatoes for tea.'

Billy was still smiling. 'Thank you, Miss Petworth.'

Linda Petworth winked and closed the door behind her.

Billy sat on her bed, lay back, and said, 'Fuck me, Dottie, this is the life, eh.'

Anyone would have thought she had just inherited a fortune.

'It's much better, and the officers seem friendlier.'

'Cor, not half. Cobain seems to be a nice woman, anyway, and as for Petworth, she's a real sweetie.' She sat up straight, her eyes suddenly downcast. 'Dottie, I didn't tell you about my baby, but not 'cos I didn't trust you. Nuffin like that. I just didn't want to make you feel uncomfortable since you've got one cooking in the oven, that's all.'

Dottie suddenly felt awkward. 'I, er, I don't really know what to say, except I'm sorry.'

'Ahh, it's okay. I knew I had to give her up before she was born. A right little stunner she was, an' all. Black curls and rosebud lips.' She paused before jumping off the bed. 'Right, chilli and jacket potatoes sounds pretty good to me, and you get extra helpings of vegetables and fruit, so make sure you eat them.'

Dottie could sense that Billy didn't want to talk about her baby, and she knew it would be on her terms if she did. So she didn't press for any more information.

CHAPTER FIFTEEN

Feeling like a trussed-up chicken, Carrie descended the stairs slowly. She could see her father's face beaming and his eyes brimming with proud tears. He looked smart in his new suit, yet the pink carnation wrapped in silver foil and pinned to his lapel was wonky. She could smell the distinctive aroma from the carnation. It always reminded her of weddings.

'Look at you, my baby girl. You look . . .'

'Like a fucking meringue?'

He laughed because he hadn't really expected any demure reply.

Reaching out for her hand as she approached the last tread on the stairs, he said, 'You look beautiful, like a princess.' And the fact was she did. Her hair was piled high like a Grecian goddess, with gypsophila weaved into it. The underskirt layers gave the dress a fairytale look, and the bodice gave her a more womanly shape. With the puff sleeves being all the rage, Carrie looked like she had stepped out of a wedding magazine.

'What's up, my baby girl?'

She held back her tears and shook her head, but her father knew her only too well.

'Forget the carriage. Come in the living room and talk to your ol' man.'

'I'm fine, Dad.'

'Nah, you're not. Come on.' He steered her into the living room while navigating the side tables out of the way of her dress.

She sat on the sofa, and the endless layers of netting circled her, almost swallowing her up.

'Now, I know that look, so don't tell me nothing is wrong. Is it cold feet? Believe me, my baby, you can cancel the wedding if you don't wanna marry him.'

Carrie looked at her father. She was surprised because he was strict on marriage and always said *If you lay with a boy, be prepared to marry him*. And she had lain with Jimmy all right.

'You made our Mary get wed 'cos she was sleeping with that prick.'

He sat in the chair under the window and sighed heavily. 'I am gonna tell you something. It's our way, and you know that, but I regret telling our Mary she had no choice, and when I see her bruises, I feel so much guilt, girl, like you wouldn't believe. And as for our Rosie, I did the same with her, and as much as she pretends she's happy, I know she ain't. So, I'll say this again: if you don't wanna wed Jimmy, then don't.' His serious expression changed into a smile. 'I can think of one reason to run a mile, and that's the muvver-in-law, Ginty.'

'Dad, I don't want to marry him.'

'Okay, so now there's something I need to tell you—'

'Forget it, Jed. She's got no choice,' interrupted Luanne, as she swanned into the room, trying to fix her earrings.

Jed looked at his wife, who was dressed in a satin skirt and a jacket in a dark peach colour, her hair piled up in defined curls. Looking so pretty and classy, she could easily have been one of the daughters. He was proud of his wife and his girls, and he had to admit it: they had got their stunning looks from her.

Once Luanne had secured her earrings, she straightened her jacket and looked again in the mirror above the fireplace. 'Get in the carriage, Carrie, and no more sulking, girl, or you will ruin what is a pretty face and a fucking expensive dress. Now, Jed, no more talk of choices, 'cos she ain't got one now. Have you, Carrie?'

Carrie looked down in shame. ‘No, Dad, I ain’t, really. I’m having a baby.’

Jed hopped up from his chair in disbelief. He looked from Luanne back to Carrie. ‘Really? So I’m gonna be a grandfarver?’

Luanne smiled. ‘Yep, Jed, you are. Our Carrie did a test yesterday, and she’s with child.’

‘Ahh, come ’ere, my baby girl. Give your ol’ man a cuddle.’

He held out his arms, and Carrie shuffled forward, put her hands on either side of her, and launched herself off the deep cushioned sofa to hug her father.

With his arms around her, she could hear the emotion in his voice when he said, ‘A baby, eh?’

‘Yeah, a baby.’

Her voice was flat because she was still numb from shock. The whole revelation had knocked her sideways, and in her head, she hated Jimmy for not using a condom that day. She didn’t want a baby. She wasn’t ready, and she wasn’t happy, and yet she was in the middle of the living room in a wedding dress, which had cost a fortune, which she didn’t choose either, and which would put her on parade for all to see. But she didn’t want to be looked at and have to perform in a certain way. It was going to be hard work putting on such an act.

Luanne fixed Jed’s tie for him, and then she stood back and admired her husband. ‘Now, Jed, no flirting with the others or drinking too much. This is our baby’s wedding, and you are the farver of the bride, so just keep that in mind.’

‘You are a fine one to talk. All I can say, my little beauty, is we need to hide the mic and the vodka.’

She pinched his cheek. ‘We have a lot to celebrate, so let’s get in the cars, shall we.’

As they bustled out of the room, Carrie’s dress caught the side table and knocked it over. Automatically, she bent down to pick up the magazines. As she did so, her eye caught the front page of the local newspaper, which was just peeping out from inside a copy of *Woman's Own* magazine.

Luanne had also spotted it and tried to move Carrie on. But seeing the headlines, Carrie moved her mother's hand away and picked up the paper.

Luanne and Jed looked at each other, knowing that at any moment, their daughter could go into a tantrum and start yelling from the rooftops.

'*Dottie's pregnant!*'

Luanne nodded. 'Yeah, she is, but listen, no one says it's Jimmy's child. We know nothing about the girl except she dated him for a while. She could have been sleeping with other lads. Who knows?'

'*I* know, Mum. *I* fucking know.' She poked herself in the chest, her eyes filling up.

'Now, come on, love,' said her father. 'You *don't* know. Your muvver's right. The paper doesn't say how far gone she is or who the farver is.'

'So you knew about this as well, did ya?' She shoved the paper under his nose.

'I did, and that's why when you looked so unhappy, I said you didn't have to marry him, but, babe, you're pregnant now, so you have to do the right thing for the baby. That baby is gonna need a farver. Now, don't you go getting yaself all upset. Put that Dottie girl out of your head.'

'Can you go on ahead? I need a minute.'

'Carrie, listen, your sisters are outside freezing their tits off, waiting to see you in your dress. So, come on, girl, no stalling. The vicar is probably three parts pissed already.'

Jed put his arm around his daughter's shoulders and was smacked in the face by her substantial puff sleeves. 'Yeah, it's a meringue, all right,' he said, trying to make light of the situation.

Carrie let the newspaper drop to the floor and did as she was told. When the front door opened, she knew there was no going back. Her three sisters were there already to see her and to offer their support. They wore pink satin dresses with colossal puff sleeves matching hers. They were all the rage now, a cheaper version of Princess Diana's. Every little girl's dream was to wear a dress and look just like the princess, and her mother had seen to it that her girl had one as close a match as possible.

Half the street had gathered to see Carrie leaving the house. It was warm for February but not warm enough to stand in a dress without a fur shawl.

Carrie noticed that Mary looked thinner than ever. She was shivering in the dress, the remnants of a bruise still evident on her cheek. She then looked at Rosie, who seemed to be wearing a fixed grin.

But Carrie knew she was constantly clenching her jaw underneath that smile. Her husband wasn't a wife-beater, but he did call the shots, and if he said 'jump', she said, 'How high?'

It made Carrie wonder why her sisters had become so damned submissive. She thought perhaps it was the pressure from the families. Well, she sure as hell wasn't going to put up with the shit her married sisters endured, even if Ginty did try to bully her.

The crowd cheered, and her sisters clapped before they hurried to get inside their warm cars.

Jed had hired a horse and carriage, and the two large black horses had decided to shit all over the road, which turned Carrie's stomach. There was nothing magical or Cinderella-like about it.

She lifted her dress so it didn't get dragged along the damp and dirty path. Her father helped her clamber inside, and it was then that she realised she would rather be inside a car. The horse-and-carriage contraption was cold and uncomfortable. Nevertheless, giving everyone her best smile, she waved like the Queen to all who came out on to the streets to wish her good luck.

Approaching the entrance to the old church, Carrie sighed at the amount of guests there were. They were all dressed in their finest under their thick coats and many of them were taking a drag on their last cigarette before the ceremony. They cheered and watched as Jed helped his daughter down from the carriage.

As soon as her feet were on the ground, she paused and looked around at all the guests. Then she froze, unable to put another foot forward. She could see their faces and hear the clapping, but the sound was muffled, and everyone just seemed to merge into one mass of colours.

'Come on, girl, they're waiting, and you're getting cold.' He rubbed her back.

She allowed her father to link arms with her, and again, she slapped on a fake smile. Her sisters, who had hurried from their cars, rushed forward with bouquets in their hands so as to be in front in order to lead the way into the church and up the aisle. One of Ginty's nieces was a little flower girl who was proudly throwing petals everywhere. Most of those, though, were just being blown into the graveyard.

While the crowds oohed and aahed and they commented on how stunning Carrie looked, all she could do was shyly nod back. She couldn't speak. The tone of her voice would have given away her true feelings, otherwise.

Carrie was well aware that she didn't feel how she should on her special day. There was no anticipation, or excitement, even, about meeting her groom at the end of the aisle, or butterflies thinking about saying 'I do.' This was a formality, like signing on at the dole office or going to the dentist. Except it wasn't quite like that: she was wearing an expensive dress and there would be a party afterwards.

As she reached the beginning of the aisle, she saw Ginty adjusting Jimmy's tie. Standing next to him was Arthur, who looked like an enormous garden gnome grinning with his new bright-white teeth.

As soon as the music played 'Here Comes the Bride', which was clearly out of tune, Ginty hurried back to her seat, and Jimmy, being Jimmy, wolf-whistled and was cheered on by his brothers and a few of his pals.

Carrie wanted to spin around and run, but her father gripped her arm tighter. *Maybe*, she thought, *he felt the tension and suspected she would jilt her husband-to-be.*

When the bridesmaids took their seats, Dilly relieved Carrie of her bouquet, and her father shook hands with Jimmy.

But Carrie clocked the gentle tug and heard the words he whispered.

'You ever beat my baby, and I'll muller ya.'

Jimmy grinned, thinking that Jed was joking, but when his father-in-law-to-be didn't laugh, he had no option but to nod in acquiescence.

The vicar was, as suspected, a bit tipsy, and when the organist stopped playing, he stopped swaying and addressed the guests with a formal speech.

All the while the vicar droned on and on, Carrie couldn't look Jimmy in the eye. She was still livid with him. And she couldn't get that initial meeting with Dottie out of her head. Her mates had humiliated her – one had even beaten her up – and while they did that, she was pregnant.

Carrie assumed then that the reason Dottie had gone to see Jimmy that day was to tell him she was pregnant, and yet, as Ginty had bragged to her only a few days ago, it was she who had sent the girl packing. If only Dottie had had the chance to tell Jimmy, things would have been so different. Jimmy wouldn't have been too adamant about getting her down the aisle and having sex with no protection. He would not have wanted another baby on the way. And if Dottie had been able to tell Jimmy, then maybe the frustration and even the fear of the consequences of being pregnant wouldn't have made her kill her parents. Perhaps they wanted her to have an abortion. Maybe – and this was the most horrifying part of it – they were going to force her to have one.

There were so many maybes that Carrie knew that the only way she could get her head straight was to go and see Dottie. She had to. It was as simple as that. So, as soon as this shambles of a wedding was over, she would write to Dottie again, and this time, she would bloody well demand a visiting order!

By now, the vicar was at the point in the service where Carrie knew she was expected to say her vows. Jimmy was holding both her hands, and it was then that she looked up. He was smiling and looking at her with so much love. But she couldn't return the public display of affection. She didn't love him, and at that moment, she wondered if he probably knew that too.

Once the certificate was signed and the ceremony was over, the bride and groom walked hand in hand to the graveyard. There, the guests threw confetti, and Ginty's Uncle Rooster, the photographer, tried to arrange family photos with all the bride's family and then all the groom's. But it was virtually impossible: it was like herding cats. There they were, all smoking, some swigging on hip flasks, and every one of them was freezing, so when Ginty suggested they all go to the workingmen's club, the guests surged through the church gates and into their cars.

Jed pointed to the horse and carriage. 'You go off to the club, my girl, with your husband now.' Kissing her forehead, he then turned to Jimmy. 'And I meant what I said.'

'Jed, she's me wife now, so—'

'Oi, do you want a smack in the mouth? Don't you fucking dare talk to me without respect, boy, or I will hurl your skinny arse under a double-decker bus.'

Jimmy's face flushed bright red. 'I, er, well, I was gonna say, I'll look after her and the baby.'

'Best you do, boy, best you do.'

As soon as Jed joined his wife and headed to the cars, Jimmy yanked Carrie's arm. 'What's the fucking matter with you,

Carrie? You look so miserable. You proper showed me up! I mean, I could see you didn't look happy and so could every other fucker. How do you think that makes me look, eh?'

Carrie ripped her arm away. 'I warned you, didn't I. Don't you grab me like that again, Jimmy Carson!'

'Or what, Carrie, or fucking what?' His eyes burned into her with such intense anger.

'Don't you start getting hot-headed with me, Jimmy. I have every fucking right to be miserable.'

He stood with his hands on his hips and looked about. Everyone had gone. 'What are you on about?'

'Dottie Ellis is *pregnant*, and don't you dare pretend you didn't know.'

'So what? Who cares? She was shagging around, so it could be anyone's.'

Carrie stared at her new husband in abject disbelief. 'You what? Are you for real, Jimmy? You know that ain't true. Everyone knows that Dottie Ellis isn't that kind of girl. So unless you own up to the fact that that little chavi is most likely yours, then I will continue to be fucking miserable, and if you think, Jimmy, that I can be all fun and laughter at your demand, then fucking wake up and smell the roses. You know me too well. Your brother might get away with hitting me sister, but see, me, if you ever even think about it, I'll stab you when you're asleep.'

Jimmy glared at his new wife. 'You need to calm down, Carrie. You're a married woman now, with a baby on the way.'

That statement was exactly what she didn't want to hear, but the fact was he was right, and now she would have to make the most of it. However, she couldn't imagine any silver lining.

***

She remained quiet all the way to the workingmen's club, while Jimmy droned on and on about how their wedding would be the talk of the town, how he would call the baby Jimmy Junior, and how he would get him signed up at the boxing club.

All the things that Carrie detested.

The back double doors to the hall were now open, ready for their entrance, and so as soon as they were out of the carriage, Jimmy linked arms with her and whispered, 'If you're not happy, just pretend you are, for everyone else's sake. This wedding cost me muvver a fortune.'

'Shut up, Jimmy. I'll 'ave you know, me farver paid for it all.'

'He didn't pay for me suit.'

'Oh right, so except for your suit, me ol' man paid for it all, so if I wanna smile, I will. If I don't, I fucking won't.'

As the couple stepped into the hall, the cheers and whistles snapped Carrie out of her anger. In some ways, Jimmy was right. Everyone was happy. The music had started, the bar was three deep, and one of Ginty's sisters was removing all the clingfilm and foil from the buffet food on the long trestle tables along the back wall.

Jimmy guided Carrie to the top table, which was nothing special because no one was going to give a speech. The wedding was thrown together. After all, Ginty's family could barely read, and Jimmy's father-in-law didn't like speeches.

As Carrie took her seat, she was handed a glass of champagne. Just as she was about to take a sip, Jimmy held her wrist and stopped her. 'None of that for you. You're pregnant.'

'A fucking sip of champagne won't hurt.'

'I said no.'

Carrie wanted to stab him there and then, but just at that moment, Ginty and Arthur suddenly approached the table. 'Well, didn't that go well. I ain't had a chance to say, but you look beautiful, Carrie. A proper wife for my little Jimmy. All we need now is for my Arthur to get it on with your Dilly.'

Carrie's eyes widened as she looked once more at the oversized garden gnome.

'Cor, last time I saw you, Carrie girl, you were playing with Sindy dolls.'

'I never played with dolls, Arthur.'

'Well, anyway, you look beautiful. Now, where's that other beauty, Dilly?'

'Hiding from you,' Carrie said, under her breath.

'What?'

'I dunno, Arthur.'

Ginty, who was dressed in an outfit two sizes too small, which showed her lumps and bumps, swanned off like the queen bee. Yet when Carrie looked over at her mother, who should have been the one swanning around like the queen bee, she saw her sitting at a table with Mary, Rosie, and Dilly.

Carrie fervently wished she could be there too, instead of putting on this display for Ginty's family to gawp at. She looked to see where her father was. He was at the bar with a tray of drinks for the girls. Arthur was now by her father's side, no doubt sucking up to him.

She watched him relieve her father of two drinks and then approach Dilly. He handed Dilly hers and pulled a chair over to sit next to her. 'Ugly wanker,' she hissed, under her breath. She could see what was going on. He was now sucking up to her, all winks and teeth, and, no doubt, complimenting her.

Carrie looked away. The sight of Arthur ingratiating himself with her sister was just too much to bear.

As soon as the guests had got their drinks and were seated at the various tables and were scoffing the buffet food, the music turned up a fraction, and the kids were on the dancefloor.

'Shall we dance?' suggested Jimmy, as he got up, assuming she would say yes.

Instead, Carrie looked him up and down. 'You haven't admitted yet that Dottie's baby is yours.'

Jimmy glared at her as though she was a deviant child. 'This is my wedding day, Carrie, and I'll not fucking ruin it by talking about that business. That's to be sorted out another day. Now, the guests will be expecting us to dance, so get up, girl, and dance wiv me.'

Not prepared to argue despite her temper fairly brimming with rage, Carrie allowed him to lead her on to the dancefloor, and right away, the music changed.

The DJ announced it was the first dance and played 'Let's Get It On' by Marvin Gaye.

Jimmy placed his arm around his wife's waist and held her other hand as they slowly danced, while Carrie maintained her fake smile for the guests who had surrounded them. Then, as the song ended, the other guests entered the dancefloor and began dancing.

Carrie was about to leave when Jimmy pulled her back. 'Hang on, let's dance a bit more.'

Carrie didn't answer. She did as he asked until she spotted Dilly, who was heading for the back door. But something looked off.

Usually, Dilly was nimble on her feet with a very upright posture. She always held herself very serenely, which was probably half her beauty. However, her sister wasn't walking with her head up and looking graceful. Not one bit. She was swaying as if she'd had too many drinks. But Dilly never drank. She had only got drunk once before, and the hangover lasted three days, so she swore blind that from that moment onward, she was allergic to alcohol.

Looking around the room, Carrie could see that the table where her mother had been sitting was empty. Then her eyes fell on Mary who was with her husband on the dancefloor. It didn't take long to spot her parents, who were also dancing. Rosie and her husband, though, were up at the bar.

When Carrie tried to pull away, Jimmy gripped her tighter. 'No, Carrie, don't spoil it.'

'Jimmy, Dilly's gone outside. She looks drunk.'

‘So, let her be. She’s enjoying herself. It’s our wedding, for fuck’s sake, not hers.’

‘No, but you don’t understand. Dilly don’t drink.’

‘Well, it’s a celebration. Perhaps she’s decided to join in instead of being so fucking stuck-up.’

Carrie was utterly stunned that Jimmy had called her sister stuck-up. She wasn’t stuck-up at all. She was a good girl, sweet and kind.

‘Don’t you ever slate me sister again. You just remember, Jimmy Carson, they’re your fucking in-laws, so you treat them like your own sister.’ She shook her head. ‘Ahh, but, then again, you ain’t got sisters. I’m sure me farver will be only too pleased to show you how you’re supposed to treat the women in my family.’

‘Carrie, you are a part of my family an’ all, ya know. So you need to show respect to me. Now, let’s just dance and have a bit of fun.’

Carrie could smell the vodka on his breath. It made her feel sick. ‘I need a bit of air, Jimmy.’

‘*What?*’ He screwed his face up.

‘I’m pregnant, remember, dick for brains.’

He instantly released her, and she hurried to the back door to ensure her sister was okay.

However, it was getting dark when she walked outside, and she couldn’t see much. No one was around. To the left was a brick wall, and behind that was an area where the club’s landlord kept the empty kegs. She hurried to see if Dilly had gone around the other side of the wall and was hiding away from Arthur or just getting some fresh air. However, as she turned the corner, she was horrified to see Arthur pinning her sister against the wall. He had one hand over her mouth while he was using the other to lift up her dress. She could see the round whites of her sister’s eyes and knew that Dilly was absolutely terrified. Arthur was a big man.

Carrie knew full well that if she attempted to pull him off, he would throw her to the ground. For the moment, though, he hadn't heard her. Looking around, she spied a shovel leaning against the wall, and straight away, she grabbed it.

'Get the fuck off her, you bastard!' she yelled.

But Arthur didn't instantly let go of Dilly and run. Instead, he pushed her to the ground and turned around to face Carrie. As he was about to lunge at her, she threw the shovel like a javelin as hard as she could. The metal blade hit Arthur straight between the eyes, and he staggered backwards in shock.

Carrie helped Dilly to her feet, and they both ran back towards the hall.

'Carrie, I think you've killed him. Oh my God, Carrie, he was going to—'

'I know what that oaf was gonna fucking do.' She grabbed Dilly's hand. 'We need to tell Dad.'

'Carrie, I think you killed him,' Dilly repeated.

'Don't worry, Dills. Dad will know what to do.'

Carrie shoved Dilly into the ladies' toilets as they entered the hall. 'Wait here,' she said, pointing a firm finger at her.

Storming back into the hall, she found the party was in full swing. Everyone, it seemed, was picking up the pace with the free bar that was on offer.

Suddenly, Ginty who was drinking with a few gypsy men and behaving like a man herself by swigging the whisky neat, grabbed Carrie and swung her around. 'Look at me new daughter-in-law. Ain't she a stunner. I bet I'm gonna have beautiful grandchildren.'

Ginty was too drunk to realise that Carrie had pushed her away with such aggressive force that she toppled backwards. As she did so, she grabbed the shirt of Uncle Rooster and pulled him down with her.

As soon as Carrie saw her father, she flew towards him.

Seeing the look of panic on his daughter's face, Jed hurriedly came away from the men, who were all talking shit about the old days.

'What the fuck's the matter?'

Carrie was out of breath. 'It's Arthur. He was trying to rape Dilly outside. I, er . . .' She had to catch her breath. 'I think I've just killed him.'

Jed held his daughter in his arms. 'You fucking *what*? Where is the cunt?'

'He's out by the old kegs. I threw a shovel at his head. Dad, he went down. But I think he's dead.'

'All right, girl, listen. Where's Dilly? Is she all right? Er . . . did he . . .?'

Carrie shook her head. 'No, I stopped him.'

'You see to your sister. Say nuffin to no one. You leave this to me, girl.'

The DJ was now playing Black Lace's 'Do the Conga', and Ginty got to her feet and yelled at people to join her.

Suddenly, from nowhere, Jimmy appeared. Gripping Carrie's hips, he leaned his chin over her shoulder. The smell of vodka was even more pungent.

'There you are, me beautiful wife. Fancy another dance? Da da da dada, let's all join the conga, da da da.' He began kicking his legs to the side of him, trying to push Carrie towards the conga snake.

'You go, Jimmy. I'm having a cold drink, and I need the loo.' She winked, trying to keep him onside before he kicked off. He would if he drank too much.

The moment he joined the conga, she hurtled off back to the toilets, but Dilly was obviously inside one of the cubicles. Her own two friends Misty and Lena were in front of the mirrors, reapplying their make-up and respraying their hair.

Lena turned around. 'I have to say, Carrie, you look stunning. That dress is beautiful.'

Carrie hadn't seen Lena or Misty for a good month, not since they'd had the fight with Dottie. She looked them both up and down, curling her lip in annoyance. 'You two fuck off! I wanna speak to me sister in private.'

'What's wrong, Carrie? Are you all right?' asked Lena.

'I'm fine. Now, just fuck off and leave me alone.'

'Has Jimmy upset ya?' asked Misty. With a few ciders inside her, she felt she had the guts to push the issue. 'You wanna be a good wife to him. There's plenty of good girls out there if you don't want him, Carrie.'

Carrie tilted her head in confusion and anger. 'What bit of fuck off don't you understand?'

The girls didn't argue. They left the toilets and slammed the door behind them.

'Dills, you can come out now.'

Slowly, the cubicle door opened, and Dilly, who had a bruised lip and a ripped dress where Arthur had forced himself on her, looked down in shame. 'Oh, Carrie.'

She cried as she fell into Carrie's arms. 'He was horrible. I thought he was being kind because he told me he had bought a Coke for me. But he put something in it. I know he did. I feel so weird, but you have to get out of here, Carrie. I think you killed him.'

'I don't care if I have, the fucking rapist.'

'Carrie, I'm going back out there. I'll take the blame. You can't go to prison. You're pregnant and married.'

'I don't give a shit, Dills. This isn't about me. Arthur can't rape you and get away with it.'

'I'll take the blame, not you, Carrie.'

'Hush, listen. Dad's out there sorting it.' She stroked her sister's hair. 'Well, this has to be the wedding of the century. The fucking Carsons. I hate 'em. Even Jimmy, the wanker.'

'Carrie, what's gonna happen to us?'

‘What’s gonna happen to the Carsons, you mean, ’cos I ain’t standing for this bollocks anymore. Fuck Arthur, fuck Ginty, and fuck *Jimmy*.’

CHAPTER SIXTEEN

As Carrie sat on the floor in the ladies' toilets with her arm around her sister, trying to calm her down, she was raging inside. She thought about her sister Mary and her husband Lenny, who was only four years older than Jimmy, and Zachariah, who was Jimmy's first cousin and who had grown up in Ginty's house for most of his teenage years. They were all the same. Arthur, the weirdo, she hadn't known well because she had been much younger when he'd been locked away. And then there was Albert, Ginty's eldest, who still lived at home. But Albert wasn't stupid, although he was dangerous. And to think Ginty wanted all the Verne sisters to be a part of her family, and, as she had heard Ginty say it herself, all because they could produce beautiful babies. Except so far Mary and Rosie hadn't gotten pregnant. She wished with all her might she could say the same.

It was as if reality had slapped her in the face. She had been happy to date Jimmy because out on the street, they both had a reputation, and they used to have a laugh together, and maybe she loved him as a mate more than anything else. But he wasn't husband material, not for her, anyway, because he wouldn't give her the life she truly wanted. No question, he wouldn't take her on a plane to go to other countries. She knew he wouldn't break the Carson mould. His idea of a holiday would be a trip down to Margate or Dymchurch in a van with as many of his family crammed in as possible. She could see it now. They'd all be drinking cans of beer on the beach, followed by fish and chips and ice cream, and then they would take home a few tubs of winkles and cockles and that would be it. She'd probably be visiting him in Wormwood Scrubs on and off over the years, and money would be all or nothing.

'Carrie, I can't go out. I'm so ashamed.'

'Ashamed, Dills? You did nuffin wrong. He was trying to help himself to *your* body, the skanky, ugly, fucking troll. He is no man, he's a dirty rapist.'

Getting up from the cold quarry-tiled floor and staring in the mirror at her bruised lip, Dilly said, 'What are we gonna do, Carrie?'

Before Carrie could get her thoughts in order, Lena flew into the toilets. 'Carrie, your farver's out the back. There's a fight. You'd better come.'

Carrie barged past Lena and pushed through the small crowd of women gathered by the double doors, only to find her father on the ground, with Rosie's husband Zachariah kicking and punching him. She spotted her mother trying to get to him, but Lenny stopped her by pushing her over. Seeing her mother's head hit the ground sent Carrie into a raging temper.

The scream from Carrie's mouth was like a wolf call. Her sisters, Rosie and Dilly, appeared as if from nowhere and were by her side.

Mary, having already witnessed her husband pushing her mother, hurled herself at her husband. She jumped onto his back and grabbed handfuls of his hair. Screaming at him, she yelled, 'You bastard, Lenny, you've pushed me muvver!'

Lenny struggled to pull her off because she was like a wild cat swiping and snarling at him.

Since it seemed that Zachariah and now Albert had managed to get Jed to the ground, it was evident that Ginty felt confident enough to put the boot in as well. She was showing off as if she was as hard as the men, except she wasn't. She could never have brought a man like Jed to the ground. It had taken two of the

Carson men to do it. As Ginty was yelling at Jed saying, 'You wanker, hurting my boy,' she viciously booted him in the head.

Carrie saw red and ran at her mother-in-law.

Rosie took off her shoe and smacked Zachariah in the side of his head, whacking him repeatedly like a woodpecker. She called him every swear word under the sun, while hammering his head with her stiletto, until, finally, he fell to his knees, unable to see straight.

Carrie was even more enraged. Jumping up, she put her arms around Ginty's neck and dragged her away from her father while biting hard down on her mother-in-law's right ear, taking a chunk out of it. Ginty screamed and tried to get her daughter-in-law off her, but Carrie, now in such a state of frenzy, screamed, bit, and clawed at Ginty's face until Jimmy suddenly managed to drag his wife away.

Turning towards him, Carrie threw her most brutal punch and caught Jimmy on the chin.

He staggered backwards, stunned.

With Jed back on his feet, he was now wading into Albert and punching him into next week.

But then, Arthur came over to Jed holding the shovel in the air, ready to plunge it into his head.

Carrie would see that picture in her mind for the rest of her life. Powerless to stop Arthur, she screamed the place down.

The instant Carrie screamed, Dilly looked across the room to see what was about to happen. Instinctively, she ran in front of her father. But at that moment, the shovel blade struck her on the shoulder. With her blood spurting out like a geyser, she immediately fell to her knees and briefly passed out.

As the crowd gasped, the fighting stopped, and there was silence as Luanne and her daughters ran to Dilly's aid.

Jed was horrified. Knowing he had been just seconds away from death, it didn't make him feel any better. He would have taken the hit if it meant his Dilly was safe. Instead, he could only stare in horror at the gaping wound on his daughter's shoulder.

'Will someone call a fucking ambulance!' he bellowed, before he kneeled beside her and tried somehow to hold his daughter together. All he could think of doing was to put pressure on the wound as he'd seen the vet do to his horse when earlier it had bolted with blood welling from a large gash on its neck.

'Come on, baby, talk to me. Stay awake, darling.'

As white as a ghost, Dilly somehow regained consciousness and even tried hard to smile.

But everyone knew that if the ambulance didn't arrive soon, she could bleed to death.

Luanne had her hands to her mouth, holding back the sob trapped in her throat.

Rosie stroked Dilly's hand, saying, 'You'll be fine, Dilly, you'll be fine.'

But Carrie was absolutely raging, seeing the graze on her mother's cheek, the bruise developing under her father's eye, Mary's faded bruises, and now her sweet sister Dilly in a serious condition fighting for her life, all at the hands of the Carsons. The hate for that family was mounting at such an astronomical rate, that there was only one logical person to be cast as the fall guy at this precise moment and that was her brand-new husband.

The second Jimmy managed to see straight from Carrie's earlier punch to join her, she jumped up, grabbed him by his shirt collar, pulled him to his feet, and dragged him away. 'Fuck off, Carson!'

'Carrie, I only wanted to help,' he replied, anxiously.

'Just fuck off, Jimmy. You make me piss boil. All of you Carsons do!' She glared at Ginty.

'Come on, Carrie, please, girl,' said Jimmy, in desperation. But he knew he couldn't penetrate that cold shield she'd just erected.

And Carrie wasn't going to let up. She pointed a finger. 'Run, Ginty, run, because you raised these evil fuckers, and you are to blame!'

But Ginty, seeing that her Arthur was not badly injured and was actually scurrying away from all the mayhem, looked back at Carrie, and with a wide grin on her face, she raised the antagonistic atmosphere by another notch.

'You are too big for your boots, Carrie, and the sooner you realise you can't go around like the fucking boss, the better. There's only one fucking matriarch in my family and that's me.' She suddenly felt the blood trickling down her neck from where Carrie had bitten her ear. 'You *will* learn your place in my family, and fast, you cocky little cunt.'

But when Jimmy saw that wild look in Carrie's eyes, he knew then that his mother shouldn't have retaliated like that, not now, when Dilly could be dying at the hands of his brother. He pulled his mother away. 'Muvver, go home.'

Shaking him off, she stood there like a sweating horse, with white phlegm coating the corners of her mouth. 'Don't you tell me what to do, Jimmy.'

'Muvver, just go home. The police will be here soon, so go home.'

She pointed her finger at Carrie. 'Don't you say a word to the Ol' Bill, Carrie, because you are a Carson now, so, girl, remember that.'

'Your son is a rapist!' Carrie shouted back, her face red with rage. 'Your other son is a fucking wife-beater, your nephew is a bully, and you, Ginty Carson, breed the evil in them, so don't you ever fucking tell me what to do again. I will *never* be a part of your family, so go fuck yaself.'

From nowhere, Lenny, who was dragging Mary away from the scene, suddenly punched Carrie hard in the side of her head and knocked her to the ground.

It was the first time in her life that she saw stars and couldn't move. The punch was so fierce, it was evident that Lenny hadn't held back.

All Jimmy saw was his pregnant wife's head almost falling off her shoulders before she buckled and hit the ground.

Mary screamed, and Lenny let go of her.

But it was Jimmy who wasn't going to stand for that. As drunk as he was, he tore into Lenny, punching and kicking him.

That was when Ginty stepped in because the one thing she would never put up with was any of her boys fighting each other, no matter who it was over. Separating them, she dragged Lenny away, leaving Jimmy to see to Carrie.

'Are you okay, Carrie?' Jimmy asked, as he tried to help her sit up.

However, it was Mary who took the initiative. She was now raging. 'Get the fuck away, Jimmy. In fact, why don't you round up your entire family and piss off, 'cos the police will wanna nick ya.'

Jimmy looked back at his wife, who only allowed her sister to help her to her feet.

'I'm sorry, Carrie. I'm so sorry.'

'Fuck off, Jimmy. Just go!'

Hearing the ambulance arriving and within seconds pulling into the rear of the workingmen's club, everyone watched speechless as Dilly was put on the stretcher and taken into the vehicle.

Luanne hopped up inside to hold her daughter's hand.

Carrie's fear for her sister climbed as the paramedics began attaching tubes, wires, and all sorts. Feeling utterly helpless, all she could do was pray they would save her sister's life.

As the next set of sirens could be heard in the distance, the Carsons all vanished, even Jimmy.

A gentle tug on Carrie's arm made her spin around, ready to punch the next man.

But to her astonishment, there in a smart suit and clearly sporting a new set of teeth was the last person she expected to help her – Jimmy's best mate. She'd always liked Spud. He might not have been the best-looking fella, but he wasn't a bully like Jimmy could be. And they'd shared a laugh or two over the years. And giving him the once-over, she could see that he no longer had issues with his weight or his acne. The guy was obviously living the dream.

'Carrie, I've got my motor out the front. I'll take you, your sisters, and your dad to the hospital, if you like.' He looked over at Jed, who was standing like a frozen statue, staring into nothing, with Rosie hugging his arm.

Carrie looked Spud up and down. 'Cheers, Spud, I mean Thomas.' It was as if his nickname somehow didn't suit him anymore.

'It's a red Ford Escort. It's open. Go on. I'll get your dad and Rosie.'

'Go on, Carrie.' Jed nodded to Mary. 'Take her, Mare, will you.'

Mary nodded, linked arms with Carrie, and they walked through the empty hall.

Carrie looked around at all the mess. These were the remnants of her wedding. A pile of vomit was conspicuous on the dancefloor. Endless cans, bottles, and glasses were strewn everywhere – on the tables and the chairs. The pretty bunches of silk flowers – those same ones that had been pilfered from the Harrods lorry – had been plucked from their plastic stems and scattered by a bunch of unruly kids. One of the long trestle tables had partially collapsed – not from the sheer weight of half-eaten food, which made an unsightly spillage that no one had bothered to clean up – but from when one of the drunken guests had fallen on it. As for the DJ, Carrie could see him packing away his records and loudly moaning that someone needed to fucking cough up the money for the night. But it was the sight of the stressed-out landlord, she felt most sorry for. He was standing at the bar, just shaking his head and looking bereft.

As the police sirens became louder, Carrie faltered. She wanted to tell the police what Arthur had done. She had witnessed it with her own eyes, even. Something she would never unsee and never forget or forgive.

But Spud's car was straight ahead, and Mary had already opened the door. 'Get in, Carrie.'

It seemed that her sister had made the decision for her.

It wasn't long before Rosie squeezed in as well, and her father hopped in the front, and they were off to the hospital. The journey took fifteen minutes, and, in that time, no one said a word, except for Spud asking if everyone was warm enough.

***

As soon as Spud pulled up directly outside the accident and emergency doors, all four bundled out and tore inside, leaving Spud to park up.

The department was quieter than usual, but then again, it was two o'clock in the morning. Jed approached the desk and could hardly get his words out, he was in such a state.

Rosie stepped forward. 'My sister Dilly Verne was rushed in a few minutes ago. Where will she be, please?'

The receptionist politely asked them to take a seat and told them that the doctors seeing to Dilly would be out to give an update shortly.

But Carrie wasn't in the mood to be fobbed off. 'My sister didn't ask what she should do, love. She asked where my sister Dilly was. That's a very different question. Now, where have they taken me sister? 'Cos me muvver will be there alone.'

The receptionist, a woman in her fifties with a starched white blouse and grey permed hair, realised that this was not a family she could easily fob off. 'If you go along this corridor, the main A&E area is there. You may find who you are looking for.'

Carrie didn't thank the woman but spun on her heel, and with her father and her sisters, they marched along the corridor towards the hustle and bustle of the A&E department.

Right away, the family saw their mother. She was already deep in conversation with a doctor. Carrie could see her mother was hanging on to the doctor's every word while she clutched the top of her jacket.

Jed hurried to be by her side. 'Is Dilly okay? What's happening?'

The doctor stepped back. He hadn't expected the family to be so in his face. He glanced at the three young women standing behind their father and realised that the incident had clearly occurred during a wedding. 'You are Dilly Verne's father, I take it?'

Jed nodded, his eyes filled with unspent tears. 'Is she all right, Doc?'

'She is in the theatre now. We won't know for a while, but we have the best surgeon on hand, so if you would all wait in the waiting area, there's a coffee machine just along—'

A nurse interrupted. 'I'll take you to a private waiting room and make some coffee. It must have been quite a shock, but she is in the best of hands.'

She walked away from the doctor, and the family followed. As she opened the door to a side room, she said, 'I won't ask what happened, but I can see you are not in the right frame of mind to talk to the police because as you know they will be called, so I won't mention that you're here. Okay?' She winked.

Luanne grabbed her hand. 'Gawd bless your heart. Thank you, nurse. That's very kind of you. Do you think my Dilly will be all right?'

The nurse nodded. 'She was conscious before surgery, so that's a good sign. Just have hope and a strong coffee.'

The Verne family took their seats and were silent for a few minutes until Luanne looked up at Carrie. 'That sleeve on your dress is ripped, but I might be able to get me money back on it.'

Carrie fingered the tear in the seam. 'Yeah, I reckon you will.' But when she stood up and turned around, she said, 'Look at the back. I can feel me bare back exposed to the cold.'

Luanne sighed. 'Yeah, that's ripped, an' all. But I still want a full refund.'

Rosie got up and stared out of the window. 'There are the Ol' Bill. They've parked up. They'll be in here in a minute. What are we gonna say?'

'I don't want to see them,' said Jed. 'They can fuck off an' all. Alls I wanna know is if my little Dilly girl is gonna be all right. Then and only then will I make plans to cut that ugly bastard Arthur in half. Straight down the fucking middle.'

Carrie could see the anger in his eyes and the tight fury in his face. She'd never seen her father like that – ever. She knew he'd had a fiery reputation in his younger days and could fight. And this evening, she had seen him punch Albert to the ground. He wasn't a tiny fella either, and, by all accounts, he was the real fighter in the Carson family.

Luanne looked at her husband. 'Dare I ask why the fight started? What the hell happened?'

Jed looked at Carrie.

'Carrie,' he said, lowering his voice. 'What happened?'

'I saw our Dilly going out the back door, but she looked drunk. Jimmy was making me dance, but by the time I got shot of him, she wasn't in sight. So I went outside, but then, I couldn't see her. So I went looking behind the wall and found that fucking great fat garden gnome, Arthur, pinning her against it.' She paused and swallowed down the fury. 'She looked fucking terrified. He'd drugged her. The rotten bastard had put something in her drink. Anyway, I threw a shovel at him, and that's when I thought I'd killed him.'

'A pity you didn't, darlin',' said Luanne. 'So that bastard molested my girl, did he?'

'He was trying to rape her, Mum.'

Luanne's face glowed red. 'I will kill him. As God is my witness, I'll murder the nasty piece of shit.' She wiped her eyes on a mangled old tissue before she looked up. 'And how did you end up fighting, Jed?'

'I went looking for him, but I guess Ginty and Lenny saw me in a temper when I was calling out for Arthur. When he appeared looking a bit fucked up . . .' He grinned at Carrie. 'I could see you had hurt him good and proper. He was covered in blood and was staggering about. Anyway, Ginty and Lenny yelled for Zachariah and Albert to come because they thought I was the one who'd bashed Arthur.'

Luanne nodded because now it all made sense. 'Well, once our Dilly is out of the woods, then we will make plans, 'cos I'm not having this anymore.' She pointed to Mary. 'How many times has that fucker Lenny hit you?'

Mary shrugged. 'What tonight, do you mean?'

Jed jumped up from his chair. 'See, and that says it all, don't it. I'm not fucking standing for this, Mary. Later on today, me and you are gonna go to your flat, pack up your gear, and you, my girl, are coming home.'

'No, Dad, I can't.'

With his hands on his hips, he frowned. 'And why not?'

Mary looked down and her bottom lip trembled. 'I just can't, Dad.'

But it was Rosie who walked over to Mary and nudged her. 'Tell them, Mare. Tell them why, for fuck's sake. Tell them what he tells you on a daily basis.'

Mary looked up, tears filling her eyes. 'He said if I ever leave the flat without his permission, even if I need to go to the shops, then he will beat me. And he said if I ever have any ideas of going back home, he'll burn the house down with all my family in it.'

Jed paced the floor, running his hands through his hair. 'I need to think about all this, but first, where's that fucking doctor? Surely, they have mended me baby girl, by now.'

At that moment, the door opened, and the nurse who had shown them to the room entered. She was balancing a tray of mugs of coffee, some biscuits, a bowl of sugar, and a jug of milk.

Luanne quickly helped her with the tray and asked if there was any news on Dilly, but the nurse just smiled. 'I promise you, as soon as I know anything, I'll be straight in here. She is still in surgery.' She held up her hand before anyone jumped in. 'But that doesn't mean it's very serious. It just means they are working hard on her.'

'Thank you, nurse,' said Luanne.

'There's a lad outside called Thomas. Can I show him in or . . .?'

'That's Spud,' said Carrie.

'Yeah, show him in, please,' said Jed.

Spud entered and nodded to Jed. 'I thought I'd come in . . .' He smiled and looked around. 'I know I am supposed to be Jimmy's best pal, but I, er . . . Well, I wasn't brought up to hit women, and what I saw tonight was wrong. So I wanna help if I can. Is there anything I can do? I've got me car if you need a lift.'

'That's good of you, son. Right gentlemanly. Look, there is something you could do for me. Could you check on my house in case any of those Carsons have attempted to burn it down?'

Spud shook his head. 'They wouldn't do that. I've known Jimmy and his brothers for years. They always threaten to burn down houses, but they know that arson on that scale will cost them years inside. Ginty's brother, Arnie, got twenty-three years, but nonetheless, Jed, I will go and make sure all is okay.' He looked at Carrie. 'Are you all right? Shall I grab you some clothes?' He looked back at Jed. 'Sorry, I mean, if it's fine by you, that is.'

Jed threw Spud the house keys. 'Yeah, actually, take Carrie with you. I don't want the gavvers carting her off to the police station. There would be murders, and my poor girl will end up in court, no doubt, on a police brutality charge.'

'Dad, I wanna know how Dilly is. I can't wait at home.'

'Listen, do as I say, girl. Go with Spud, and if you have to come back, then come back, but please get out of that dress. It's a fucking dead giveaway that you, my girl, were at the wedding.'

Carrie wanted to laugh. Not because the situation was funny but because he did have a point.

Spud guided her through a back route to where he had parked the car to dodge the police. Once they were in the cold early morning air, Spud put his arm around Carrie's shoulders. 'Carrie, what a fucking mess, eh? I can't believe Jimmy and his poxy brothers did that. Anyway, I'll get you home, and you can get out of that—'

'Meringue.'

Spud laughed. 'Yeah, puffy, ain't it? I bet it wasn't your choice, was it?'

Carrie laughed as she leaned into him. 'Spud, nuffin about that wedding was my choice. Anyway, why haven't I seen you for a couple months?'

Spud opened the car door for her to get in. He put the heaters on and drove out of the car park. 'I stayed away, Carrie, because Jimmy and me, well, we don't get on much now. I got a job in the woodyard, and I said there was one for him as well if he fancied it. But he turned his nose up at it. All he said was to leave the back doors open so that he could go in late one night and rob the place.'

Carrie shook her head in disgust. 'And he could have grabbed the job opportunity with both hands, but the bastard didn't. He didn't do it for me or . . .'

‘Or what, Carrie?’

‘Me baby, Spud. I’m pregnant.’

‘Oh no, Carrie. I’m so sorry, girl.’

Spud was the first person who actually understood that having Jimmy’s baby was not cause for celebration. Not one bit.

CHAPTER SEVENTEEN

A week later

Spud was kind enough to drive Carrie to Holloway Prison. Even though he didn't like to hide anything from Carrie's parents, he knew that she would, if push came to shove, go by herself. So, since it was a fair old trek, he offered to take her.

As they set off from her home, Carrie wondered what on earth she was really doing. But something in her gut was compelling her to visit Dottie. Perhaps it was curiosity but she wanted to learn the truth about the father of Dottie's baby.

'I appreciate this, Spud.'

Spud was reeking of his new expensive aftershave, and he looked so smart in his white shirt and navy-blue jumper.

She smiled. 'If you walk in with me, they'll think you are a screw.'

He chuckled and felt his stiff white collar. 'The last thing I could be. Well, second to a copper, that is.'

He looked out of the window and then rubbed his bristly chin. 'So what are you gonna do about Jimmy? Because he is driving me around the fucking bend. He even came into the woodyard and wanted to know if I've spoken to you.'

Carrie nodded. 'He's rung the phone at home hundreds of times, begging to talk to me, but I dunno if I want to, or if I will *ever* want to.'

'I saw the huge bouquet of flowers sticking out of the bin. I didn't read the note.'

'That's not from Jimmy. That's from Lenny to me, for punching me in the head.'

'Have you forgiven them, any of them, Carrie?'

She slowly turned her head, her eyes wide and fiery. 'Spud, I will never forgive them. I hate every one of them . . . maybe not Jimmy so much. Well, 'cos he's just a fucking idiot. But the others I do.'

'Mary's still at yours, then?'

'Yep, and that Lenny's another wanker. The next day he came knocking and acting all lairy, demanding that Mary come home.' She chuckled. 'He didn't expect me farver to be hiding behind the door, so when he went to grab our Mary, me farver cracked him right on the nose. Knocked him clean off his feet.' She stopped smiling. 'But a couple of days later, when he dropped the flowers off, I saw our Mary get excited 'cos she thought they were for her. But they weren't. They were for me. It was his feeble attempt at saying sorry. But I don't want his apologies. I want him dead, really. Plus, no way was it that prat's idea to send me flowers. Oh no, Ginty made him do that. He can't even fucking read. The handwriting was clearly someone else's.'

'Why did he send you flowers?'

''Cos I am carrying her grandbaby. She will not only want to get me onside, but she will also want to get her hands on the baby. And another thing, Spud. All the while I am raging at the Carsons, hell will freeze over before she even looks at a picture of the baby when it's born. And that fat ugly bitch knows it.'

'So they are trying to get back in your good books, then? Is that what you're saying?'

'Exactly that, Spud. Ginty came around two days later with a pot of stew and an apple pie.' She snarled. 'As if stew and pie could make up for what happened. Me muvver ain't going to be taken for a fool.'

While they stopped at some traffic lights, Spud was eager to know what had happened when Ginty knocked at the door. 'What did Luanne do?'

Carrie shook her head. 'She opened the door, looked Ginty up and down, and Ginty seemed pretty upset. Her eyes were red and she had a bloody great bandage on her ear. I had nearly bitten it off. She was a little OTT, if you ask me. Anyway, me muvver was fuming. "Don't you ever step on my doorstep again. Get away," she said, before she pushed Ginty, who then toppled backwards arse over tit and ended up pouring the stew all over herself, while the apple pie' – Carrie nudged Spud's elbow – 'ended up covering the neighbour's cat. I was watching from the upstairs window, nearly pissing myself from laughing. But when me muvver slammed the door shut, she burst into tears. Rosie, who has also moved back home, spent that afternoon nursing me muvver, making sure she didn't get another migraine. As for me farver, he ain't been the same since. He is ready to fight the world.'

'It was a bad day, a bad omen, Carrie.'

'I know, Spud. Ya know what? It didn't feel like a wedding, not the moment I put that bloody great puffy dress on. It wasn't a bit of me at all. And then when Jimmy wolf-whistled at me, as me farver was walking me up the aisle, I could have died. Who fucking does that, eh? Still' – she sighed – 'I am married now. Legally. Not that I have seen Jimmy since. But I do need to make a few decisions about my future.'

When Spud smiled at her, Carrie, for the first time, realised that he was turning into a really handsome man. It was as if he had climbed out of his teenager's skin and grown into a sophisticated specimen of a fully-fledged male.

'You could always get divorced, Carrie, and then you can marry me.'

At first, she laughed, thinking he was being jovial. But when he turned to her and he didn't laugh, she frowned. 'You're joking, ain't ya?'

'No, I wasn't, actually. Listen, Carrie, I've known you for years. You're a good girl, and this way of life ain't for you. You're smart. Not A-level smart. I mean you're street-smart. We would make a good team, me and you.'

She smiled, and her eyes caught the reflection glaring off his watch. 'Just 'cos you've got the woodyard job, and you're earning now, it doesn't mean that's what I want in life, Spud. I want more. A lot more.' She frowned and stared at his watch. It wasn't cheap. It was a bloody Rolex. 'Your woodyard job pays well, though, don't it?' She nodded at the watch.

'Carrie, the woodyard pays a basic wage. It's nuffin.' He pulled the watch down towards his hand and shook his wrist. 'This little beauty is not the only one of mine, ya know.'

'What did you do, Spud? Rob a bleedin' bank or a jeweller's?'

Spud was silent while they drove through the Blackwall Tunnel. But once they were the other side of the River Thames, he glanced across at her.

'One day,' he said, as he tapped her nose, 'I'll tell ya for sure. So are we getting married or what?'

Carrie laughed again. 'Spud, me and you have always got on well. We have a laugh, you're kind, but I think at the moment, I need a good mate more than I need a husband, to tell ya the truth.'

He slid his arm around her shoulders and kissed her forehead. 'And that, Carrie, will do for me.' He winked. 'For now.'

She looked at her own watch. It was only a cheap one from the market. 'Spud, how the fuck did you get to own a *Rolex*?'

'Ha! I'll tell you, girl, but only when I really know I can trust you.'

That said it all, thought Carrie. His reply spoke volumes about the new Spud. He was so different from the spotty teenager she had known for years. He seemed so much more manly and confident. She tried to figure out when he'd changed, and then she recalled him often having to shoot off to see a man about a dog. Jimmy had called him a mummy's boy, but Spud just laughed it off. His hangouts up the high street became fewer and fewer. So whatever Spud had been involved in, she knew it had begun a while ago.

Eventually, they reached Holloway Prison with a few minutes to spare. Carrie reached behind her for her handbag and sheepskin coat.

'Carrie, you'll have to go and join the queue. I'll be here when you're done. I'll pop in the pub over the road. Come and find me.'

Carrie smiled as she got out of his car to join the queue of visitors. Seconds later, the bitterly cold wind nearly knocked her over as it whistled past her and nipped at her ears.

Hearing Spud locking his car door, she quickly glanced behind her to see him put his wallet inside his thick dark Crombie and march across the road. From the back, he looked like a grown man, but, then again, he was twenty years old. She clocked his shoes and she could see that they were clearly Italian leather. He'd ditched the two-tone trousers and Dr Martens too.

To her horror, she saw a car fast approaching him. Holding her breath, she almost closed her eyes. Surely not? Not her Spud. But then her heartbeat returned to normal, and she laughed out loud. Spud had had the confidence to hold up his hand, slowing the vehicle down, before he skipped on to the kerb, as though he owned the road.

She sighed and shivered. Life was such a tenuous thing. One minute all was good, but the next, it could slip away from you. It caused her mind to drift to her poor sister Dilly, who was still in the hospital and hanging on for dear life. She imagined what she'd do if she could get her hands on Arthur. Burning him alive was one option, or skinning him alive was another. Still, that day would come, she convinced herself.

When the queue began to move, it was not a moment too soon because she was still shivering from the cold, even in her thick coat. Once inside, she handed over her visiting order and noticed the screw looking her up and down. 'So Ellis has a visitor?'

Without bothering to reply, Carrie looked away, and she was then told to move into the next room for a search. After a quick pat-down, a small group – herself included – was escorted to the visiting room.

Carrie wasn't new to visiting prison. She used to visit her grandfather and her father, and, on one occasion, she even visited her Aunt Lizzy, who sadly died in Holloway. It gave her the shivers just thinking about the place. It was all well and good making threats and bashing ten tons of shit out of a person, but the consequences could be serious. She flinched when the huge metal gate opened and banged against the wall. The noise had just rattled her bones. Soon, though, she found herself being taken into the visiting room.

The moment she put a foot inside, she suddenly stopped in her tracks. *What the hell was she doing? Wouldn't it have been easier to ignore the fact that Dottie was pregnant with Jimmy's baby?* Besides, she knew what happened to women's babies. If the mothers got a long stretch, social services would place the babies into the care system, and a lovely childless family could adopt them. Or was that the romantic idea of the care system? She felt a stab in her chest because she knew kids that had been in care; they weren't spoiled and loved. Quite the opposite.

She stepped forward and looked around for Dottie. Expecting to see a fragile-looking stick-thin girl with dull, lifeless red hair looking down in fear, she halted in her tracks at the sight before her. Standing at a table towards the rear of the room was a young woman wearing a grey tracksuit with a red tank top, which all the inmates had on. It was Dottie and she was beckoning her.

Dottie looked well. She had gained weight, her hair shone like wet conkers, and her cheeks were peach-coloured.

Carrie hurried over and sat down quickly. Both stared at each other for a moment, until the silence became uncomfortable.

'Thanks for coming.' Dottie smiled. 'I haven't had a visitor. Carrie, you can buy some food at the tuck shop over there. They sell chocolate and lots of different drinks.'

Carrie couldn't help but continue to stare at Dottie. The situation was so bizarre. It reinforced that thought of hers moments ago about how life could change someone in a heartbeat. And she felt as though she was sitting opposite an entirely different person from the one she saw in the lane a while ago now. A girl who her mates had beaten up, a girl who had looked terrified in the dock in the courtroom.

Coming out of her introspection, she replied, 'Oh, er, yeah, sure. What do you fancy, Dottie?'

'Chocolate, chocolate, and chocolate. Oh, and a hot chocolate if they've got one.'

Carrie rose from her chair, made her way to the little kiosk, and waited her turn to be served. She remembered the kiosk the last time she visited her aunt. Her mother had bought her bars of chocolate to keep her quiet. *Was that Dottie's intention?* she wondered. Using a tray to carry the drinks and the sweets, she glanced over at Dottie. She noticed how her eyes lit up when she placed the tray on the table.

Carrie chuckled. 'Cravings for chocolate, then?'

'Oh, er, so you heard?'

'It was in the newspaper.'

Dottie peeled away the wrapper and bit into the Mars bar, allowing the chocolate to melt on her tongue and her taste buds to savour the heavenly, velvety experience. She bit into it again and wolfed it down, before clearing the sticky toffee, which had stuck between her teeth, by washing it down with a hot chocolate. 'God, I miss sugar.'

Carrie was stunned. That was twice in one day when two people had managed to take her completely by surprise. Not only had Spud changed his whole persona, but so too, it seemed, had Dottie. *What had happened to the shy, scared, and fragile Dottie?* she wondered. If she was honest, she had expected to see a battered waif of a girl with a massive black eye. But not so, apparently.

Just as she was about to take a sip of hot chocolate herself, another inmate came over and handed Dottie three bars of chocolate. 'Me ma thinks I like these, but I don't. Here, Dot, you can have them.'

'Thank you, Rita, that's very kind of you.'

'No worries,' Rita replied, before walking back to her chair.

'They said I can take back the leftovers from the visit.'

'So you've got mates in here, then?'

'Well, really, just the one. She's called Billy. We share a room. She's nice – well, she's nice to me. Maybe not so much to the others, though. She's a bit fussy who she has it with.'

Carrie raised her eyebrows at Dottie's terminology. 'What?' She laughed. 'Who she has it with?'

'Yeah, sorry, I mean who she—'

'I know what *has it with* means, Dottie.'

They stopped talking, and again, there was that uncomfortable silence.

'The baby is Jimmy's, Carrie. I'm sorry.'

Carrie put her own hot chocolate drink down on the table and sat up straight. 'No, don't be. You didn't do anything wrong. In fact, *he* should be the one visiting you, the fucking coward.'

It was Dottie's turn to raise her eyebrows. 'How did the wedding go?'

'A right royal fucking shambles if ever there was one, Dottie. Jimmy wolf-whistled at me as I walked up the aisle. I mean, what a show-up.'

Hearing that, Dottie chuckled and bit into another chocolate bar.

'My dress was the same as Princess Diana's but a cheaper version, obviously. It got all ripped in a massive fight between us sisters and the Carsons, so Dottie Ellis, there you have it in a nutshell. Oh yeah, and worse, me sister Dilly is in hospital fighting for her life 'cos Jimmy's brother nearly killed her.'

Dottie put the chocolate bar down and stared. 'No. Oh my God, Carrie, you didn't have to come, you know. It sounds like you have more important things to worry about than me.'

Carrie leaned back on her chair and looked around. 'I suppose I needed a distraction. Maybe I came out of curiosity. Oh, I dunno, Dottie. I thought seeing you in that dock, looking frightened to death, you'd need some support. I thought maybe I could do some good for someone.'

'Carrie, I am so grateful, I truly am. I don't have friends apart from Billy. But look, you and me. Would we really be mates on the outside? No, not in a million years. So, you actually taking the trouble to come and see me is a bit mind-blowing, to be honest. You see, I've got no one, Carrie. No one who knew me from before' – she threw her hands in the air – 'all of this. No one has cared about my situation. None of my friends from school or church. No one has even *written* to me except you.'

'Well, I only know you a tiny bit.'

Taking a deep breath, Carrie asked the ultimate question that had been burning inside her, but she chose her words carefully. 'I have to know, Dottie, 'cos I can't sleep at night.' She looked around before leaning forward. 'Now, I'm not saying you killed your muvver and farver, but, like, if you kinda did . . . well, *sort* of killed 'em . . . would it have been because I got back with Jimmy, and that old cunt Ginty sent you packing? I'm guessing you were there that day to tell Jimmy you were expecting his kid.'

Gazing ahead just slightly away from Carrie's face, Dottie wondered whether telling her the truth would be advantageous.

Before she could answer, Carrie sighed. 'Sorry, Dottie, it's not my place to ask, is it?'

Staring poker-faced at Carrie, Dottie said, 'I don't know if I can talk about it yet.'

Carrie nodded, accepting her response before her eyes scanned the room. The fact that all these women in here were much older than Dottie intrigued her. Many were old enough to be her mother. She'd never noticed that before when her aunt was here, but then, again, she was only interested in getting back home to see Jimmy. She wasn't in a rush today, though. 'Dottie, do you still love Jimmy? I mean, it makes no odds to me if you do. Just saying, like.'

Dottie unwrapped a Cadbury Flake and stared at it. 'No, I think I was infatuated by him. To me, Jimmy was the boy you could never take home to your parents. He was the one who led the pack. The one who was daring.' She laughed and peered up through her eyelashes. 'The good-looking one who every girl fancied.' Her cheeks turned pink before she bit into the Flake.

'Dottie, I've got something to tell you. I mean, I don't have to, but I just think it's the right thing to do, but first, can I ask you something really personal about how you got pregnant?'

Quickly swooshing down the chocolate with a mouthful of her hot drink, Dottie nodded. 'Yes, I suppose so.'

'Did he pretend to use a condom and then selfishly didn't put one on?'

With her thoughts on that day, when he was a bit forceful with her, and he hadn't used a condom, she suddenly felt sorry for herself. 'No, I don't think so. But he wasn't thinking about me, that was for sure. He wouldn't stop, and then, it was too late. I didn't think I could get pregnant. I didn't dare tell my mum or go to the doctor for that morning-after pill. I was too worried. I just hoped I wasn't pregnant, and when I missed my period, well, I knew then that I was. So, all I could do was to look on the bright side and hope Jimmy would be pleased.' She paused, and her eyes seemed heavy with regret. 'I never got to tell him. I will never get to celebrate having a baby either. I won't be able to bring mine up because he or she will be in the system. He or she will be just like all the other babies born in here – shipped off to the children's home, and no doubt abused and unloved.' She placed her hands over her eyes to hide the tears.

Suddenly, Carrie's mind was in a complete spin. So many thoughts entered her head, she felt dizzy. Not knowing what to say, she grabbed Dottie's hands and pulled them away from her face.

'Don't cry. Listen, I'll do whatever I can.' She hesitated for a second before she blurted it out. 'I'm pregnant too.'

Instantly, Dottie stopped snivelling and blinked furiously to clear the tears in her eyes. 'You are?' At that moment, she didn't really know how to feel. 'So you and Jimmy are gonna be a family?'

Carrie didn't know how to answer that.

'So is that why you came to see me, Carrie? To rub my nose in the fact that you will be having Jimmy's baby, playing happy families, while my baby is shoved in the care system. Was it because I was seeing Jimmy? Was it revenge?' The tears tumbled down her cheeks.

Aware that a few eyes were gawping and looking daggers at her, Carrie grabbed Dottie's hands again. 'Of course not. I'm *not* fucking happy I'm pregnant, I can assure you of that. Look, Dottie, I only asked you about whether Jimmy intended to use protection because that was what he did to me, the selfish prick.'

Dottie wiped her eyes. 'I'm sorry, Carrie. I'm so worried about my baby, the thought of—'

'Don't think about that, Dottie.'

'I can't *stop* thinking about it. And now, it's worse because my baby will have a brother or a sister and he or she won't even know them.'

Carrie's eyes widened. Reality had slapped her hard. Dottie was right. Her baby's half-sibling would be floating around the care system while she'd have hers tucked up warm in bed, loved, and spoiled. She'd grown up in a large family, and as much as she moaned about them at times, she wouldn't have wanted it any other way.

'Will they tell you where your baby is? I mean, I could check on him or her. Make sure the baby's all right.'

'No, if I get a very long sentence, the baby will probably get adopted, but he or she will stay in care for a long time before then.' Another tear trickled down her face.

'And you have no family at all?'

'No, no one, well, except Jimmy. He's the baby's father, but he won't want to know, will he?'

Carrie was stunned. She hadn't given that a thought. 'I'm not talking to him.' Seeing the devastated expression on Dottie's face, she couldn't tell her that Jimmy had suggested the baby could be anyone's. It would only make matters worse than they already were.

'Only he or his family can take the baby if they want to.'

Carrie thought about Ginty and how she would love to get her hands on a baby, especially if it was a girl.

But before she could say any more, another inmate approached the table, escorted by an officer. She handed Dottie a few more chocolate bars and a banana. 'The Twix is for Billy.'

'Thank you,' Dottie replied, smiling a little nervously.

Carrie clocked the Twix packet already opened, and her eyes widened. 'I'd better go, Dottie.'

Dottie flipped the Twix packet over. 'It's all right, the screws don't give me a hard time. I'm too famous now. They think I'm a psychopath, and I'm not telling them otherwise.'

'Who is this Billy?'

'She's my bodyguard and saviour in this prison. No one messes with Billy. She could take down a lion.'

Intrigued, Carrie asked, 'So how have you two become friends? You come from the posh side of the main road. I didn't think you knew people like this Billy.'

Dottie shrugged. 'I got us moved here together, or she would have stayed in the old block until it was finally knocked down. *And* I taught her to swim, so she looks out for me, and that's it, I suppose.'

Carrie smiled, as she glanced at the Twix wrapper because they both knew that inside was a stash of drugs. 'Seems she's been teaching you to be a little streetwise, too.'

Rising from the table, Carrie went over to the tuck shop to buy more hot drinks and bars of chocolate. When she returned, the two of them chatted about life in the prison, and they arranged another visit before it was time to leave. When the bell was rung again, they stood up.

Dottie flung her arms around Carrie and hugged her. 'Thank you for being a . . . whatever it is we are.'

Normally, Carrie wasn't at all tactile, but, somehow, it just seemed so natural. She hugged Dottie tightly and whispered, 'Friends, Dottie, we're friends.'

CHAPTER EIGHTEEN

Spud was already waiting in the car by the time Carrie came out of the prison. She glanced upwards and noticed that the Arctic weather wasn't letting up. Opening the front passenger door, she got in – relieved to get out of the cold – and dropped her bag on the floor.

'Thanks, Spud. I didn't fancy walking into the pub alone.'

'No, I guessed that's why, so I finished early and waited in the car for you.'

She smiled at him and then her thoughts turned to Jimmy. He wouldn't have done that. He would have been pissed by now and expecting her to find him in the pub.

'How did it go?'

'All right, I guess. But she says the baby's definitely Jimmy's, and she's gutted because if they take it off her, she's gonna have to hand the baby over to social services.'

'Or Jimmy,' replied Spud, quick off the mark.

'Jimmy won't want nuffin to do with the baby, that's for sure.'

'No, you're right there. I've known Jimmy for most of his life, and I can't recall a single day when he has ever taken responsibility for anything or anyone, not even himself. Ginty does everything for those lads, barring wiping their arses.'

Carrie stared out of the window watching the madness of the London traffic. 'It's busy now, eh.'

'I know, it's the bleedin' rush hour. Look, Carrie, would you mind if I take a detour? I need to see a man—'

‘I know, a man about a dog.’

He laughed. ‘Something like that, yeah.’

‘Yeah, sure, I’m in no hurry. And I really like the drive. I don’t often get to go for a ride. Jimmy doesn’t drive and I can’t afford a car.’

Spud laughed. ‘Sounds like our Jimmy ain’t got a lot going for him, except for his looks.’

Carrie looked at Spud from the corner of her eye. ‘I gotta say, Spud, I agree with you, and since me and you are mates, I wanna say you’re handsome, probably better looking than Jimmy.’

She could see Spud blushing.

‘Well, I’ve joined this boxing club. When I say I’ve joined it, it’s run by my Uncle Tony Tilby, my dad’s brother. He’s out of the nick – did a long stretch – but, anyway, he has a few sidelines, one being the gym, so I go there. He also paid for me to visit his dentist, and I’ve got a new set of teeth. I’ve also got fit. I’ve cut out the greasy burgers and now I feel a lot better for it. So . . .’ He patted his flat stomach. ‘This is the new me. Oh yeah, I’ve ditched the stupid antics. So I’ve grown up, Carrie. It’s a shame Jimmy ain’t.’

‘You’ve done well, Spud.’ She smiled. ‘I remember you talking about your Uncle Tony. So he’s out of prison, then, yeah?’

‘Yep, so this man I’m seeing about a dog, it’s my Uncle Tony. I’ve got to pick up some money from the hot dog stand in Brands Hatch before it closes and drop it off at my uncle’s place.’

‘Sure, I really fancy a hot dog.’ She chuckled, feeling the impending excitement of going to Brands Hatch.

***

Spud parked his car directly beside the hot dog van, and as soon as he got out, Carrie followed.

‘Er, Carrie, listen, I’ve got a bit of business to attend to. But I’ll bring you back a hot dog, yeah?’

Embarrassed, Carrie nodded. 'Okay, I just needed some fresh air, ya know, what with all this pregnancy lark.'

'Fair enough, but don't walk too far. I need to get you home, and then I've got a few other vans to see.'

She nodded again and leaned against the car. Spud's business was beginning to pique her interest now. What the hell was this sideline all about?

Moments later, a short man in a white apron came out of the side door of the van. He looked about before sliding a manila envelope to Spud and hopping back into the van.

She hoped Spud hadn't forgotten her hot dog. She was starving.

It turned out he hadn't. He returned with two, both filled with onions, mustard, and tomato ketchup. 'Here you go. One for you and one for the baby.'

He opened the door for her to get in and then he handed her the food, which smelled delicious.

'How the hell did you know I liked mustard and ketchup?'

'You always have, Carrie.'

Gratefully, she took them, and again, she thought about her Jimmy. He wouldn't have remembered how she liked her hot dogs or even bought her two, the tight bastard.

The final leg of the journey from Brands Hatch back to Orpington didn't take very long, and so less than half an hour later, they pulled in to the kerb a few doors down from Carrie's home.

'Thanks, Spud. I really mean it. Thanks for today.'

'Anytime, Carrie.'

Spud pulled out an envelope and opened it. 'Here, Carrie, take this. Get the baby some bits,' he said, as he handed her one of the notes.

Looking inside the envelope, she was astonished to see a wad of fifty-pound notes. She'd never even seen one in the flesh before.

'*Fifty?* I can't take that, Spud. You only work in the woodyard. That's gotta be half a week's wages, ain't it?'

He winked. 'I thought you might have already worked that one out for yourself, Carrie. The woodyard is just a front. But you, Carrie, keep that to yourself. Like I said, you and me would make a good team. Whatever you do, don't tell Jimmy, even if you decide to make it up with him.'

She looked at the wad of money in that envelope and the fifty he was happy to part with and wondered if she had made a colossal mistake in marrying Jimmy when Spud had been there all along hovering in the background.

Here he was looking smart, handsome, and driving his own car. But more than that, Spud was a real man.

'You *can* trust me, Spud. I'm different an' all. I've also grown up. I'm done with hanging around the high street getting into trouble, fighting and choring. Besides, whether I like it or not, I'm gonna be a muvver.' She turned directly to face him. 'Spud, you said me and you would make a good team. I think you're right, but not romantically. You're handsome and everything, but I still see you more as me mate, like a bruvver kinda thing.'

Spud laughed and held up his hands in a surrender-like gesture. 'Yeah, okay, fair enough. I know what you're really saying 'cos I saw your eyes light up when I pulled out that wad of money. Right, so here's the story. My uncle has no kids, right, just me. The bottom line is that my dad and my uncle fell out. You see, Tony gave my dad half the money to set up the chip shop. Then Tony got locked up, and my dad sold the chippy and bought another one. Well, he made a mint. We all know that. But the thing is, he didn't put any money aside for Tony, so there was a big family row and it ain't over. Tony has asked me to get involved in the business – to one day take it over – but my dad doesn't know about this. Once I have learned the ropes, I'll be managing many of the vans.' Spud looked at Carrie and grinned.

'If you want, you can help once the baby's born and if you want to go back to work.'

'Really?'

'Yeah, but, Carrie, there is a big *but* to all of this. You can't tell Jimmy what you will be doing, okay. At least not until I have everything set up for you.'

'I won't tell that wanker nuffin. Don't you worry about that, Spud.'

'Good, okay, well, you'd better go in before someone spots us and goes grassing to Jimmy.'

'Fuck Jimmy. And again, Spud, thanks for today.' She slipped the fifty-pound note into her pocket. 'And thanks for the money.' She leaned in and kissed him on the cheek.

***

As soon as she put the key in the lock, her father flung it open. 'Where the hell have you been?' His eyes were red, his face tight.

Carrie immediately assumed the worst. 'No! Is Dilly all right?'

He pulled her by her arm and slammed the door shut. 'She's okay. Your muvver and your sisters are up the hospital now. They are staying together because those Carsons are fucking circling the house like a load of sharks.'

'What? Why, Dad?'

'I've had that fucking Albert revving his car engine outside the house and Jimmy shouting through the letterbox and calling you a slag.'

'What? A slag? What the fucking hell is he doing?'

'I opened the door, and I had him around the throat, the fucking little cunt. He said you were seen in Spud's car. No one has seen Spud all day, or you, so is it true?'

'Yeah, it's true, but that doesn't make me a slag. The man only gave me a lift.'

'Were you out all day with him?'

Carrie sighed and put her hands on her hips. 'No, well, yeah, but not exactly. Look, it's a bit more complicated than you're thinking.'

'Stop talking shit. What's going on, Carrie?'

'Spud took me to Holloway Prison. I wanted to see that Dottie bird and find out myself if she is carrying Jimmy's baby.'

Jed ran his hands through his thick mop of black wavy hair. 'Why couldn't you just stay home?'

'Dad, they don't scare me.'

'Well, they fucking well should! You're a girl, Carrie, with a baby in your belly as well. And as much as I hate to say it, you're also married, and until you are divorced – if that's what you want to do – then you can't be going off in another man's car.'

'Another man's car? Are you serious? Jimmy ain't got a car and is not likely to fucking have one. He can't even drive. And it was only Spud. We've been mates for years. There's nuffin in it, and as for Albert, what's he getting involved for?'

'Jesus, Carrie, the Carsons are raging right now. Mary's fucked Lenny off, Rosie's fucked Zachariah off, and you, Carrie girl, have only been married five minutes, and you've fucked Jimmy off. Ginty is turning herself inside out. Your muvver's shown her right up in the street, and so everyone in the neighbourhood is watching out for the next episode of our family drama.'

He stormed into the living room, sat on the chair under the window, and took a swig of beer from the side table.

Carrie followed him, feeling a little guilty that her father had been suffering at her expense. 'I'm sorry, Dad. Really, I am. It's all a right mess, ain't it.' Her eyes welled up for many reasons. She never ever wanted to upset her father.

Lunging out of the chair, Jed threw his arms around his youngest daughter. 'No, baby girl, no, you shouldn't be sorry. It's me that's caused all this bollocks. You ain't done nuffin wrong.'

He pulled away. 'I can't go up the hospital. I can't see my little Dilly in that state. Truth is, it's killing me.'

'I know, Dad, but she'll be all right. We will *all* be all right.'

'Will we, Carrie-Ann? Will we? They've already arrested Arthur.'

Carrie put her hands to her mouth. 'Oh my God.'

'Yep, and Ginty's going around saying that our Dilly was caught with her drawers down, and it ended in a nasty fight. She got in the way. It was an accident. And she's saying that one of us grassed to save her dignity.'

'Well, there were a lot of people there. It was a wedding reception, for fuck's sake. Anyway, good, I'm glad they've arrested him. I hope he gets banged up for life.'

'I don't, Carrie, I really don't,' Jed said, his face tight and his eyes dark. 'I want him walking the streets so I can kill him.'

Jed looked out of the window. 'How about that, eh. All fucking day those Carsons have been either hanging about outside or driving by, and now there's nuffin. It's as if they know you're home.'

Suddenly, Carrie's eyes were out on stalks. 'Oh my God, Dad, if they ain't driving by, then they've seen Spud drop me off.'

'Well, let's hope that lad can drive faster than Albert, love.'

***

Spud was oblivious to the car following him. He had his rounds to make and money to collect. His next stop was the burger van in the DIY superstore along Cray Avenue. As he approached the car park, he could see the store was shut and the van was closed. The man who worked the burger van would have hidden the money under the griddle.

Spud went over to the griddle in the van and removed the parcel. He then stepped out and locked the van, and that was when he saw a car pull into the car park. He didn't take much notice until it stopped beside the van. Glancing at the car, his heart sank. He knew that the vehicle, the beaten-up old Cortina, was driven by Albert. Suddenly, three men, Albert, Lenny, and Jimmy got out of the car. They approached like hard men, clearly ready for a fight. Even Jimmy walked as though he had two barrels under his arms.

'All right, Jimmy?'

'*All right? All right?*' Jimmy's voice was seethingly shrill.

Spud looked at each pair of eyes in turn. He knew then they were after his blood, and there wasn't a chance in hell he would be able to fight all three of them. 'What's up, Jimmy?'

'*What's up?*' he yelled.

Spud knew he wouldn't get anywhere if Jimmy childishly repeated everything he said.

'Jimmy, what do you want?'

'*What do I want?*'

'For fuck's sake, is there an echo here?'

Albert, a man of few words, walked up to Spud nose to nose. 'You dirty cunt, you are messing with Jimmy's wife.' No sooner had those words left his mouth than he pulled his head back and head-butted Spud so hard it knocked him backwards.

With his ears ringing and his head now pounding, Spud tried to gauge his best move. Should he offer to fight them one at a time or should he run away?

Jimmy, the coward, feeling confident now that he had two of his brothers with him, swung a punch.

But Spud, using his experience as a boxer, was able to duck Jimmy's fist. It helped that he was quicker than Jimmy because he was fitter. What he hadn't expected was Lenny's interference.

'You leave Spud to me, Jimmy boy. Let me show you what I'd do if he was out with my girl.'

Jimmy laughed as he glared at Spud. 'You fucked up big time, Spud.' Jimmy's head nodded rhythmically like a human pulse.

Spud didn't see the pole in Lenny's hand until he began waving it back and forth like a scythe cutting tall grass. Spud stepped backwards and realised he had one choice – the only choice – which was to run.

However, as he turned around to leg it, Lenny cracked him hard on the back of the head. The sound was like a table leg snapping.

Spud hit the ground face-first. He knew he was hurt, and instinctively, he ran his fingers over the wound. He could feel the warm gooey blood pumping out. Through fear and pumping adrenaline, he managed to flip over, only to see the three of them ready to kick the life out of him. Unable to get to his feet, he realised he couldn't escape, so he put his hands over his head to protect himself from the onslaught of their vicious assault. He could feel every boot and every fist, and he even heard the pole snap across his hip. It was as if the Carson men had taken out their frustrations on him because they believed they had good reason to.

'Now, you even look at my wife again, I'll make sure you won't walk on two legs,' said Jimmy, almost out of breath. 'And I'll take this off ya,' he said, picking up the parcel lying on the tarmac.

Spud tried to speak, but his jaw was broken, and he couldn't see because his eyes were swelling up. He couldn't even move his hands because the Carsons had broken his fingers.

'Oi, Albert, Lenny, and is that you, Jimmy, you little shits? Leave that lad alone. Now, go on, fuck off,' came the voice of someone who sounded like an older woman.

'Mind your own business!' bellowed Lenny.

'Oh, is that right, Lenny Carson? Did you just tell me to mind my own business?'

'Yeah, I did.'

‘Shut up, Lenny, you fucking idiot,’ growled Albert. ‘If she tells her sons you’ve been lippy, then you’ll have the Murphys on your back, and James will cut your arms and legs off.’

‘Shit, er, sorry, Mrs Murphy.’

‘Go on with yer, ya fucking bullies.’

Spud felt relief when he heard their car start up, but then he felt very cold. The world was caving in around him, and a voice, which was barely audible, was saying, ‘Are you all right, lad?’ It was Mrs Murphy, who he knew, but, quite evidently, she didn’t recognise him in this state.

‘I’m waiting for my son to pick me up. I’ll get him to take you to the hospital. I think you need it, boy.’

The sound of a car screeching into the car park had Spud shaking, now wondering if the Carsons had returned to finish him off.

But as the door slammed shut, the sound of heavy footsteps signalled the distinctive voice of James Murphy. ‘Fuck me, what happened, Mother? Did someone run him down and drag him around the car park?’

‘No, lad, it was the Carsons, the fucking bullies.’

James eased Spud’s hands away. ‘Fucking hell, is that you, young Spuddy?’

All Spud could do was moan.

James was an enormous man, six feet seven inches tall, and as wide as a barn door. Using his arms like a forklift truck, he gently scooped up Spud and carried him to his car. ‘Open the door, Mother.’

Before Spud knew it, he was drifting in and out of consciousness until, finally, he woke up in a hospital bed with doctors all around him. He felt drowsy and yet, strangely, no pain. Then he saw all the drips and tubes and machines beeping. That was the moment he knew the Carsons had gone in for the kill.

CHAPTER NINETEEN

Carrie stood in her bedroom looking into the mirror. She looked exhausted and she was feeling sick. But she couldn't stay at home. She had more pressing matters on her mind. So opening her wardrobe, she found an old grey hoodie and her fur-lined suede boots. Slipping these on over her Levi's, she made her way downstairs. A taxi was waiting to take her to the hospital to visit Dilly, so that she could take over from her mum and sisters.

Spud was continually dominating her thoughts, and she hoped and prayed that the Carson brothers hadn't got to him. Since no one had called their phone, she assumed he had gone about his business and the Carsons had simply gotten bored and gone home. However, when she got out of the taxi and saw the two police cars at A&E, a dark thought crossed her mind. *It wasn't possible, was it?*

About to walk into the main entrance to go to the intensive care wards, Carrie saw a face she knew very well. It was James Murphy.

James had a reputation for being a real gentleman unless you crossed him. Then if you did, or provoked any of his family, he wouldn't leave you with a bruise: he'd leave you disabled for life.

He had the knack of evoking a sense of awkwardness in Carrie, which was exceptionally rare, because no one else came close to doing that. He was older than her, being in his early thirties, so that interested her. But the main attraction was that she found him exceptionally good looking in a very masculine way.

His movements were not just deliberate but also precise, and when he was minded to, he could speak proper English, which just made him stand out from the riff-raff where she lived. And even his piercing green eyes looked right into you, sussing you out before you opened your mouth to speak. He would undoubtedly have any person of authority in knots.

'Hiya, James, how are you?' She smiled politely but realised how childish she sounded.

'Well, hello, Carrie. I'm good, love.' He paused and looked her up and down. 'I heard about your Dilly. Mum sent some flowers. How's she doing?'

Carrie slid her hands into the pockets of her hoodie and blushed. 'She's stable but still very poorly. She's in there.' She pointed down the corridor. 'Me muvver and sisters are with her. I'm just taking over for a bit. We don't like to leave her alone.'

'Christ, is she still in hospital? Was it that serious? We never knew it was that bad. Fuck.'

'Yes, she's lost a lot of blood. She nearly died.'

'Am I correct in believing it was Arthur Carson?'

She nodded. 'Yep.'

He rubbed the back of his head and moved uncomfortably from one leg to the other. 'I know you married Jimmy, and what a fucking shame that was. I'll be honest, Carrie, I like you and your family, but don't invite me around for dinner at the Carson's place because I'm sorry, love, I'm not a fan of any of them.' He looked behind him. 'I've just brought in a lad. He's badly battered. And battered not by one cowardly Carson but by all three of them because they couldn't have a row one-on-one.'

Carrie's eyes widened. 'Oh, no, it wasn't Spud, was it?'

'Yeah, it was, as a matter of fact. Was there a feud or something between them? Because my mother saw them attack him, and they took a packet or something off him. She couldn't be sure. The lights in the superstore car park aren't brilliant.'

'A parcel, like a big envelope?'

‘Oi, don’t you walk out when I’m talking to ya. Now, sit your arse back down.’

Carrie felt her face turn crimson. She had riled up her father, and that was not a good thing to do. He was a jolly man, but if he was cross, then you were for it.

‘Now, what’s this about Jimmy?’

She sighed heavily. ‘Since we broke up and he dated Dottie, I don’t think I feel the same way anymore.’

‘Jealous?’

‘No.’

‘Really? ’Cos, of course, you would be jealous. Fuck me, if my eyes even so much as flicked at another woman, your muvver would brand me with an iron.’ He lifted his vest to show a scar in the shape of a V, where she had burned him years ago. It wasn’t a considerable scar, but it was there as a constant reminder that he should never upset his wife and then go anywhere near her if she had an iron in her hand.

She rolled her eyes, having heard the story a thousand times. ‘I’m not jealous at all, and that, Dad, is the problem.’

‘So what’s really troubling you, my baby girl?’

‘That Dottie girl, Dad. I feel so sorry for her.’

‘Are you going soft? How the fuck can you feel sorry for her? She took up with Jimmy, and then she’s gone and murdered her parents.’

‘She didn’t know I would get back with Jimmy, so that ain’t her fault, and she ain’t a fighter, Dad. When Lena kicked the shit out of her, she curled up in a ball. She never even threw a punch. So I reckon her parents did something bad to her.’

‘Or, Carrie, she is insane and lost it. Anyway, you need to forget about her and go and see if Jimmy’s okay ’cos they’ll have him down the station. You wanna show your support, ’cos with the Carsons, girl, you may have a nice home, nice clothes, but it comes at a price. You will be visiting him in the nick, so get used to it.’

‘I’ll call him later. Mum’s on the phone to Ginty.’

She rose from her seat, smiled sweetly at her father, and left the room. She wanted to be alone because she couldn’t get Dottie off her mind.

CHAPTER EIGHT

The day Dottie had to go to court, she wasn't afraid because Clive Clemence had explained in detail what was going to happen to her. She knew that she would spend some time on remand and that she would be informed about all aspects of her defence all the way up to the eventual trial date.

The fact remained that her fingerprints were on both of the knives used in the attack on her parents. Their blood was not only on the weapons used but it was also all over her, and there was no sign of any forced entry.

It wasn't going to be a case of cold-blooded murder because Clemence, with Clarkson's help, had dug up some vital mitigating circumstances surrounding her father. Also, the vomit left on the sheets was found to contain the tablets that her mother had forced down her throat. From that point of view, as well, the evidence was positive, in that it confirmed the truth of Dorothy's statement.

When the psychiatrist examined Dorothy, he concluded that she was of sound mind; but he suggested that considering the circumstances, she may not have been at the time. Nonetheless, she was only a few days away from her eighteenth birthday, so he deemed her eligible to go to a women's prison.

Dottie was grateful for the clothes that Mr Clarkson had arranged for her to wear in court. Dressed in a blue suit, white blouse, and simple jewellery accessories in the form of a tiny cross and chain, she climbed the steps to the witness box. She had been fine up until then, but that was not the case when she saw the courtroom heaving with people. At that point, she faltered and wanted to run back down, but Officer Tanner, a young man in his mid-twenties, who was handcuffed to her, whispered, 'Don't, Dottie, you will only draw attention to yourself.'

He had stayed with her while they waited in the holding cell. She was grateful to him since he was gentle, considering she was facing a double murder charge, which she earnestly hoped would be reduced to manslaughter.

Her hands shook so much that the vibrations ran along the handcuffs and rattled the chain.

Out of character, he squeezed her hand. It was not the politically correct thing to do, but he was done with all that shit. Hearing all about the incident that had happened on that night from his colleagues, he thought Dottie's parents were evil.

After taking a jittery deep breath, Dottie calmed herself down and slowly looked up. Instantly, her eyes were drawn to the gallery, and there at the end was someone she would not have expected to see in a million years. It was indeed a shock to her because Carrie was there waving frantically to get her attention. Unashamedly brazen, despite the gravitas of the occasion inside the courtroom, Carrie rose to her feet and shouted out that she was rooting for her. At that point, the court usher came across and whispered in Carrie's ear and she dutifully sat down and kept quiet.

Dottie didn't know whether to smile in acknowledgement or look away. But she couldn't have been happier than at that moment. It was also clear that Carrie was now giving her some type of sign language, with her hands working in all directions and at different speeds.

Officer Tanner glanced sideways at Dottie and whispered, 'That girl is saying she wants to write to you, and for you to call her.'

‘Probably, why?’

‘He was collecting the takings from the vans.’

‘Oh, so they fucking robbed him as well as beat the fuck out of him, did they?’

As tall as she was, Carrie still had to look up because of James’s height. Speaking in such a deep, husky voice, his solid, confident demeanour told a story. He was a hard man and on the ladder to making it big, but not through legal earnings. Although she was attracted to him, she suspected that she would never stand a chance of dating him because he was every girl’s dream. He wasn’t like Jimmy or Spud. He was in a different league. And from the way he walked, the clothes he wore, and the new motor he was driving, she was very aware that he wasn’t short of a bob or two.

Her lip quivered. ‘Is Spud going to be all right?’

‘What’s up, Carrie? You look upset, love.’

‘Well, it’s my fault, that’s why,’ she replied, her voice now trembling.

‘Hey, listen, I don’t know what took place, but you never stood there with a gun to their heads.’ He clutched her elbow. ‘Come on, I’ll walk you back inside.’

Happily, she allowed him to put his arm around her shoulders. ‘He drove me into London. I wanted to see a friend, and he waited and then brought me back, but, James, I swear I wasn’t up to anything with Spud, although, clearly, Jimmy sees things differently. But me and Spud, we’ve only been mates, nuffin more than that.’

James shook his head. ‘Listen, Carrie, I can see where you’re coming from. Even though the poxy Carsons and a lot of families on that side of the main road have their own rules and shit, there is nothing wrong with getting in a car with a friend, whether they’re male or female. So if that’s why the Carsons battered him, believe me, love, it’s not your fault! They’ve just used that as an excuse to act hard and show off. Well, I’m afraid the Carsons are pissing a few people off, lately. Mark my words, Carrie, you've married into a family who will have a bounty on their heads before long.'

'I've not been with Jimmy since the wedding. Our Mary's left Lenny, and our Rosie has stayed away from Zachariah.' As soon as those words left her mouth, she saw James's eyes glistening, and a smile beamed right across his face.

'Good, you girls are way too nice for the Carsons.'

He looked down, and she could hear the slow breath leaving his lungs.

'Dilly was the only one—'

'I know.' He coughed to hide the emotion in his throat. 'I still miss my brother, you know. I miss him every day. And we all miss Dilly. I know she loved him dearly. And as for my mum, she misses her dreadfully. It feels like she has lost a son *and* a daughter-in-law, although they never made it down the aisle.'

'Would you like to see her?'

He shook his head. 'As I said, we miss her, but it's hard. My mum still hasn't got over my brother's death. If I go in and see Dilly in such a state, I'll do something so reckless that it will put me behind bars.'

He wiped his brow with the back of his hand. 'That Arthur deserves to die for what he did. Tell me, Carrie, although I can guess the answer. Did Dilly get with Arthur? Only there is a bit of gossip going around that says as much.'

Carrie gasped. 'No! Jesus, no fucking way, James! But if I hadn't gone out to find her, God knows what would have happened. He drugged her, you see, and intended to rape her. I saw him pin her against the wall. She was so scared of him. It was me who threw the shovel at his head.'

'He tried to *rape* her?' The blood drained from his face as his eyes turned black. 'My brother will be turning in his grave to think one of the Carsons hurt his Dilly.'

'Well, Arthur's been nicked, so he'll go back to jail.'

‘Fucking shame, he’s not out here now. I’d love to get my hands around his throat.’

‘Me dad said more or less the same.’

James smiled sympathetically. ‘I bet he did, but I must go, Carrie. I need to go and tell Spud’s parents that he’s here.’

‘Where is he?’

‘He’s in intensive care.’

‘Shit, could he die?’

‘I don’t know. The doctor said he’s suffered a lot of broken bones, but there’s no internal bleeding. Anyway, sorry, Carrie, but talking about it is winding me up. I like Spud. He’s a decent young man.’

‘I didn’t think you knew him all that well.’

James smiled again and winked with a cheeky grin. ‘We’ve rubbed shoulders.’

It took Carrie a moment to realise what James meant, and then it dawned on her that Spud was having it with the bigger guns.

***

Carrie decided to head to the intensive care unit before going to her sister’s ward. As she approached the corridor, she saw two police officers walking towards her. Keeping her head down inside her hoodie, she walked past them, but neither stopped her. It seemed from hearing some of their conversation, they were too busy moaning about the attitude of the nurse in charge.

As soon as she reached the room, she peered in through the glass panel and gasped. A nurse was fiddling with a drip, and another one was feeling for a pulse in Spud’s ankles. Carrie watched as they checked him over and took his blood pressure. Tears rolled down her cheeks. She hadn’t even realised she was crying until she felt a tap on her shoulder. As she turned around, she saw another nurse in a dark blue dress; clearly, she was the one in charge.

‘Do you know this man?’

Carrie nodded, and then realising that her cheeks were wet, she wiped them away.

'You can go in, but speak quietly. Let him know you're here, but stay out of our way. Understand?'

Carrie nodded again.

'You are family, I take it?'

'Yes.' Because the fact was she saw Spud just like a brother, but as for being part of his real family, of course she wasn't.

As she stepped inside the room, she could hear the beeping sounds from the machines, and there was a strong smell of disinfectant.

'He is going to be all right. He has quite a few broken bones, and we are waiting for the swelling to go down before we can put his leg and arms in plaster. But,' she whispered, 'a friendly voice telling him he'll be okay would make all the difference.'

Carrie was struck dumb. She'd never seen anyone so brutalised before. It had been bad enough seeing her sister in the hospital bed, but her wounds had been covered up, and they weren't swollen like Spud's were.

When the nurse beckoned her over, an overwhelming sense of fear anchored her to the floor. But then, when the nurse smiled at her encouragingly, she walked towards the bed. However, on seeing Spud's eyes open only slightly through swollen slits, she nearly jumped out of her skin.

'Carrie,' he said, his voice barely audible.

The nurse moved out of the girl's way to enable her to get close enough to talk to him.

'I'm so sorry, Spud,' she said, as more tears fell down her cheeks.

'You didn't know, Carrie. But they . . . won't stop . . . They wanted . . . me dead, Carrie.'

For a moment, she thought that Spud was staring into space. Then, horrifyingly, his head flopped to the side.

Pushing Carrie out of the way, the nurse pressed a buzzer while another nurse quickly pulled Carrie out of the room. Two doctors came tearing down the corridor, and all Carrie heard one of the nurses say was 'He's gone.'

Feeling freezing cold, as if someone had thrown a bucket of iced water over her, Carrie stared through the open doorway. She had no idea what the doctors were doing except that they were pumping his chest and injecting him with stuff. Then, after a few minutes, they detached the machine, clicked the wheel brakes, and wheeled him out of the room and down the long corridor to the double doors at the end.

Carrie followed them. Watching in disbelief, she saw the doctors run with the bed along the corridor as though they had just stolen it. Two nurses ran with them, but one stayed back.

'Where is he going?' asked Carrie, the tears still stinging her face.

'He is going into theatre. He may have a clot on the brain, but he is in the best of hands. Go and get a coffee or something. We won't know any more for a while now.'

***

As she walked out through the main doors, she tried to process what she had just witnessed. The shock of the last few minutes had really taken its toll on her mental wellbeing, and she thought that the whole incident would be imprinted on her brain probably for the rest of her life.

Leaning against a wall in the cold night air, so many thoughts went through her head like a thousand buzzing bees. *If Spud died, she would ultimately blame herself.* That thought made her dig deep in her pockets for a packet of cigarettes. She needed some nicotine, even though she knew she shouldn't be taking up smoking again.

Believing no one could see her, she lit a cigarette and took a deep drag. There was silence apart from a few cars pulling away from the car park. She looked up, noticed the stars, and wondered whether praying would be a good idea. Then again, would she be praying to God to save her soul? After all, so much of this was her fault. The wedding should never have happened. Getting pregnant had been stupid, so damn stupid, when, in her heart, she had only really got back with Jimmy out of jealousy.

Just as she wiped her eyes again, she felt a presence behind her. For a moment, her heart was in her mouth. She held her breath, hoping it was just an eerie feeling and nothing more, but the strong smell of cheap aftershave, which crept into the lining of her nostrils, was enough to tell her that there was someone close by. Before she registered who it was, a voice whispered, 'All right, Carrie-Ann? I thought you'd be here.'

She knew that voice. It wasn't Jimmy's, it was Albert's, the psychopath. She spun around to see his smug face. It was strange because Albert was like Jimmy. Both were the best looking men out of the Carson brothers, yet, apart from Arthur, she hated Albert the most.

He put his hand on the brick wall and grinned. She knew he was blocking her way. All she wanted to do was to knee him in the nuts and bite a chunk out of his face, but she decided maybe it wasn't such a good idea, not after witnessing the aftermath of the damage he could do.

'You are breaking me muvver's heart.' He exaggerated a sigh.

Carrie frowned but then remained deadpan. But her poker face belied her inner feelings. She was frightened. It was a first for her.

'Yeah, and if there's one thing I can't 'ave, it's me muvver being upset.' He looked down at her stomach and then poked her. 'That baby in there is me muvver's grandbaby. Our Jimmy's gonna be a farver. So you'd best get home, and when I say home, I mean me muvver's house and back to Jimmy, where you belong.' He shook his head. 'And if you think that as a family we're gonna take this total bollocks attitude from you, Carrie-

Ann, then you are a fool. I won't stop fucking up anyone who offers to help you in any fucking way. And a word of warning. See, me, I don't care about this saying that you can't hit a woman. Because if you hurt us, I will hurt you. And I know what will hurt, Carrie-Ann. It will be seeing your family fucked up, like your sister Dilly in hospital. I bet that breaks your heart, don't it.'

Carrie's eyes burned into him with such revulsion. She could feel her stomach acid bubbling inside and the blood surging around her veins with so much pressure, she thought that at any minute her heart would indeed explode.

'So, after you're done seeing Dilly, you get your arse back to my muvver's and make it up with Jimmy, or one of your sisters will be next.'

Carrie was rigid, her mind doing overtime. 'The police will be looking for you all because of what you did to Spud,' was all she could say, hoping he would run at the thought of the police arriving.

He didn't. He laughed as though it was all a big joke. 'Oh, so you know we gave him a good pasting, then. Well, Carrie-Ann, believe me, girl, that's fuck-all compared to what I'll do to Rosie, or Mary, or even your ol' mum.'

Carrie tilted her head away. His tobacco breath was making her feel ill. But when she looked him in the eye and she saw the look of contempt on his face, her anger was beginning to boil to the point where she was finding it hard to keep her claws to herself. In her mind, she was ripping his face to ribbons.

'The police will lock you up. Spud's been rushed to surgery. He's got blood clots in his head,' she said, hoping Albert would realise what he had done and leg it.

Albert pulled his hand away from the wall and straightened up. 'He is in the hospital? You're a liar.'

Carrie guessed then that he didn't know about Spud's condition. He'd obviously assumed she was having him on.

‘Why do you think the police have parked their cars over there near the entrance?’

Albert glanced over. ‘How did you know he was in the hospital?’

‘Because I was told.’

He gripped Carrie’s shoulders. ‘Who fucking told you?’

‘James Murphy.’

Releasing her from his grip, he growled, ‘His fucking muvver is one meddling bitch.’

He glared at Carrie. ‘Well, that don’t change nuffin. You get yourself home with our Jimmy, or, like I said, your sisters will be next. ’Cos I’m not having you silly little tarts upsetting my family. Oh, and if you think it’s just the three of us, ’cos Arthur’s now inside, remember that I’ve got cousins. Lots of ’em. So you just think on.’

Carrie, who usually gobbed off, remained quiet.

As he hurried away, like a sly fox, she let out a deep breath, and her hands shook as she tried to light up another cigarette. The image of Spud’s swollen face kept coming to the forefront of her mind, and she imagined her sisters suffering the same fate. Albert wasn’t afraid of anything: not her, not the police, and not James Murphy. She’d heard stories of how evil he was, but she’d never taken much notice until now.

Going to Ginty’s was her only option to save her family despite the devastating impact it would have on her father.

‘Please, God, don’t let Spud die.’

CHAPTER TWENTY

Seeing her sister lying in the hospital bed and looking so frail, Carrie made the decision there and then to go to Ginty's. She accepted that she would have to be the sacrifice to save her family.

Still, she thought, *some good news had come her way.* It transpired that Spud hadn't died. The medical team had operated on his brain and managed to fix the issue. Thankfully, it left him without any permanent damage.

Dilly opened her eyes. 'Hello, Carrie. So you're still here. Gawd, get yourself home. You look as white as a ghost. I'm fine. I don't need around-the-clock watching. They are letting me go home today. So if farver can come up and get me, I'll be able to rest on the sofa watching *EastEnders* and at least have decent food. The crap they serve in here, I'm surprised anyone gets better.' Sitting up straighter, she ran her hand through her hair. 'This needs a good wash. I feel all lousy. You know what I mean.'

Carrie smiled. But inside, she was feeling far less confident. *How was she going to break it to her family that she wasn't going back? But Dilly would understand, wouldn't she?*

'Dilly, I have something to tell you.'

Dilly blinked and rubbed her eyes. 'What's up, Carrie?'

'I'm going back to Jimmy.'

Dilly frowned, and her eyes darkened. '*What?* How could you? But *why*? I mean, I thought we agreed we would stay away from the Carsons? Mary and Rosie aren't going back. They're staying away, and you said you were getting a divorce or an annulment.'

Carrie held back the tears. 'I'm sorry, Dilly, but I've made up my mind. I'm going back. Well, I'm moving into Ginty's until the council sort me out a place.'

'But *why*? Was it all a load of flannel? What were you saying before about being married to Jimmy? You didn't wanna get wed, did ya? Was it just you acting like the rebel you think you are?'

Carrie shook her head. This was proving much harder than she had expected. But she couldn't allow Dilly to persuade her to change her mind. Her family's safety was at stake. 'I'm sorry, Dilly, but I have to. I just have to.'

Staring away, Dilly simply said, 'Then go, Carrie-Ann. You do what you wanna do because you always fucking have, ain't ya. I'll be home today to console Muvver and Farver, so go on, Carrie, go. But know this, little sister: you do that, and you'll have sided with them, and you know Muvver and Farver will disown you. You will be a Carson through and through.'

Those words cut Carrie in half. If only she could tell Dilly what she really wanted to say. 'I'm sorry, and, Dilly, I love you. You're my best mate – you always have been – as well as my sister.'

'Oh no, I'm not. Don't start talking shit, an' all. You've obviously made your mind up, so go, because I can't look at you.' She wagged her finger. 'But I will leave you with one little thought: you are depriving our parents of a grandbaby, just so you know.'

'No, Dilly, I'm not. They can see the baby, o' course they can.'

With fire in her eyes, Dilly glared, her jaw shot forward, and her lips tightened. 'You will be disowned, you fool. They won't even speak your name. None of us will. It'll be like you never existed. You know how all of this works.'

Carrie so desperately wanted to say *I'm doing this for all of you, to keep you safe*. But she couldn't because she knew Dilly would talk her out of it. And yet the consequences of not returning to her marriage were too severe to contemplate.

***

Carrie loitered around until her family were out of the house. They had gone to bring Dilly home from the hospital.

Gathering up her clothes, she shoved them into a holdall and stared at her dressing gown hanging on the bedroom door. That dressing gown was her comfort blanket. If she was sick, tired, cold, had just got out of the bath, or she simply couldn't be bothered to get dressed, that was her go-to item of clothing. But she decided to leave it there, where she always hung it, because she knew that from now on, she would never feel comfort; in fact, she never even wanted to feel comfort. She could foresee that she would have the price of guilt to pay. And guilt was cruel. Right now, it was gnawing its way into her bones, scarring her mind with the gut-wrenching feeling that she would hurt her family so much.

Fifteen minutes later, she was standing at Ginty's front door and bracing herself for whatever was coming her way. The shouting, the violence, the belittling, and the ridiculing. But she held on to the idea that it didn't matter. She consoled herself with the fact that at least her family would be safe.

Ginty opened the door and was stunned.

Carrie could see it; it was written all over Ginty's face.

'Carrie?' She looked down at the holdall. 'So you saw sense, did ya?' Her voice was now a mix of excitement and *I told you so*.

It was at that point that Carrie felt just like a prostitute. She was giving herself for something in return: the safety of her family. Inside, she cringed as if she was having sex for money. She stared at Ginty and knew that this was the day she would have to lose her wild, rebellious side and conform. But first, she had to make a deal with the devil, the devil being Albert.

Right on cue, he hurtled down the stairs, almost pushing his mother aside. 'So you changed your mind, then.' His smug face almost compelled her to turn around and head back home. But the image of Spud's battered body flashed in her mind. If they could do that to her friend, God knows what they would do to her family.

'Can we talk, Albert, before I unpack?'

'What d'you mean, talk? If you wanna talk, you talk to me, Carrie. I'm your muvver-in-law.'

Carrie threw her hands in the air, picked up her holdall, and turned away to head home, but Albert grabbed her arm before she could go anywhere. 'Okay, okay, let's talk.' He turned to his mother. 'Muvver, go and make us a sandwich, will you.'

But Ginty wore a questioning frown. 'What's going on?'

'Muvver, just make a sandwich and don't worry yaself.'

Ginty looked at Carrie, then back at her son, and decided it was probably best not to know what was really going on. She wanted nothing to stand in the way of getting her hands on her grandchild-to-be.

Albert carried Carrie's holdall into the living room. 'Now, what do you wanna say?'

She looked him up and down. 'I'll go back with Jimmy, and be his wife, but I have conditions.'

Albert gave Carrie a fake laugh. '*Conditions?* Who the fuck do you think you are?'

Carrie smiled at him, with an air of sarcasm. 'Well, see, Albert, who I am depends on the conditions because I can leave this house, go back to me muvver, get a divorce, and I won't be a Carson. *Or—*' She put her hand up to stop him from interrupting. 'I can stay and be a Carson. But only if you lot stay away from my family. And I mean my sisters as well. 'Cos if Lenny so much as looks at Mary, I'll be gone, back to me muvver's, and none of you will see me or the baby again.'

He smirked. 'And that's supposed to be a threat, is it?'

'Oh, no, I'll go home to my family *after* I've spent a few hours in the police station singing like a fucking canary.'

'Grassing?'

'You call it grassing? I call it getting fucking even.'

Right then, Albert saw the girl become a woman. She had a steeliness in her eyes that told him she probably wasn't joking. He curled his lip into a snarl. 'Zachariah won't have it. He wants Rosie back home.'

'So with you seeming to be the head of this house and your lot, you'd best make him understand, or I'm gone.'

The satisfied smile on her face wound Albert up. Never one for controlling his temper, he lunged forward and gripped Carrie's cheeks, squeezing them together. 'Who the fuck, do you think you're talking to?'

She stared and waited until he removed his hand. 'And if you ever fucking touch me again, I'm out of here, so you may have your way with your threats, but so will I, Albert. So the fuck will I.'

He paced the living room before he turned to her. 'All right, it seems they're fucking barren anyway. My brother and cousin can do better than your lot, so you've got a deal. But if you ever walk out and break up with Jimmy, I'll come for you and make sure you'll never have another baby or walk again. And, see that pretty face of yours? I will . . . well, let's just say it will look more like a road map.'

The conversation stopped when Ginty came bowling into the room with a tray of doorstop sandwiches.

Carrie could see she had done a right number on the woman. Ginty's ear was still red and swollen and a piece was missing.

'There's your grub, boy, and you, Carrie, get some down ya neck. You're eating for two now, my girl.'

Carrie stared at the food and felt a sudden panic. It wasn't, by any stretch of the imagination, how her mother or any of her sisters made a sandwich. Ginty's fingerprints were indented in the freshly cut bread.

'I'm good, but can I just make one thing clear, Ginty: I'm not your girl.'

Ginty was about to open her mouth and lay down the law when she clocked Albert placing a finger over his lips. She knew then that Carrie needed to be eased back into the family with kid gloves.

'Well, before the wedding, me and Jimmy had a surprise for ya. I suppose you'd best see it now. Jimmy will be home later. He's got a job on, working now to pay for the baby. He's already got a few quid stashed away.'

Instantly, Carrie knew that that was a lie. And then, when James Murphy's words sprang to mind, she knew why. Jimmy and his brothers had stolen the cash from Spud. She could guess it was that envelope with what had looked like a couple of grand inside. It turned her stomach, the thieving bastards. And she saw them exactly like that. Even though she hadn't been averse to choring herself – she'd done it often – it was not from people but from businesses, like the supermarkets.

Carrie traipsed behind Ginty up the stairs, assuming they would go straight into Jimmy's bedroom. But, instead, they went to the room on the right. Ginty opened the door and gestured for Carrie to go into the bedroom. 'Albert kindly swapped rooms with Jimmy so that you two could have a double bed.' She winked and nodded, but all that did was to make Carrie feel sick.

'And look, see beside the bed? That cot was my Jimmy's when he was a baby, and it's still like new. I've spent hours cleaning it. It's not got a speck of dirt on it.'

Carrie looked around the room. On the right, there were two wardrobes, and the cot was on the left-hand side of the bed. It was clean but not what she would have chosen for her baby. Not that she'd given much thought to anything for the baby. She shivered. Why the hell was the window open?

Seeing Carrie shiver, Ginty said, 'I opened the window to air the room out. You know, you must air every room. It's good for your lungs. Oh, and another thing. That bedspread is fresh on this week, and it was me muvver's, so you take care of it.'

Carrie looked at the garish pattern, which she guessed was something from the sixties. But it wasn't how the room was laid out that made her feel so uncomfortable. It was that this was Ginty's house. It was *her* things. And *her* house smell. It was not like the smell of jasmine her own mother sprayed everywhere, especially if her father had let one of the greyhounds stay indoors.

'Unpack ya bag and get settled before Jimmy gets home. I'm sure you two have a lot of making up to do. I mean, we all wanna put the whole incident behind us and start afresh, now you're home here, where you ought ta be. I am sure Mary will go home with Lenny and—'

'No, Ginty. No. My sisters *aren't* going back. They're both getting divorced. Lenny has hit Mary one too many times and me farver ain't gonna send her back to Lenny like he has done in the past. And as for Rosie, she's not going to be bullied by Zachariah, so she's filed for divorce already, and me farver is supporting them. So there's only gonna be one girl from my family, and that's me.'

Ginty's eyes widened and she searched Carrie's face for a sign that she was joking, but it was evident she wasn't.

'People like us, Carrie-Ann, don't do divorce. Your farver should be sending them back to their husbands. It's what we do.'

Carrie smiled and then sighed. 'The old ways are dying out, Ginty, and I'm afraid my farver is obviously becoming a modern man, and more than that, Ginty, he loves his girls, and he's had enough of seeing them so unhappy.'

Ginty rolled her eyes and thought she could put Carrie in her place. 'My boys are younger than your farver, and believe me, they're no pushovers. They'll have them home where they are supposed to be.'

Carrie smiled and shook her head. 'If you say so, Ginty. If you say so.'

She was about to close the bedroom door when Ginty leaned forward, grabbed her arm, and spun her back around to face her. 'You can leave that cocky fucking mouth of yours at the front door when you step over my threshold.'

'Fine.'

Ginty let go of Carrie's arm, confused by her response. 'You should be happy, a baby on the way, my Jimmy out grafting, and you don't have a worry in the world. Look, we've even given you the double room, so be fucking grateful, Carrie, or me and you will fall out.'

Smiling again, Carrie nodded gently in acknowledgement. She wasn't going to argue; she would have to live with it anyway.

Two hours later, Carrie was still in the bedroom because she didn't want to see Ginty's ugly face or suffer Albert's growly voice. Hearing Jimmy coming into the house and what sounded like whispering, she then heard him pounding up the stairs and pushing the door open.

His face was beaming. 'Carrie, I fucking knew you'd come here. How are you?' he said, as he put his arms out, clearly hoping for some sort of embrace.

But Carrie looked away and didn't even bother getting up from the bed.

He sat beside her and slid his arm around her. 'I've missed you so much, Carrie. I'm so glad you came here. Look, Muvver's sorted us a nice room and me old cot.'

'That's fucking bad luck.'

'What?'

'The cot being up before I'm even three months gone.'

'Oh, shit, I'll take it down, then.'

'Leave it. It's up now.'

‘Carrie, I don’t get it. Why are you acting like you don’t wanna be ’ere?’

She looked him straight in the eye. ‘I want me own place, Jimmy.’

‘All in good time.’ He looked around. ‘This ain’t so bad, is it?’

‘I just want my own place for me own family. I’m not here to breed and for your muvver to take over.’

‘What? No, of course not. Look, Carrie, I’m gonna jump in the bath and then me and you can sit down with Muvver and have a nice bit of dinner and talk. Or.’ He grinned and gently pulled her hand to the bulge in his jeans.

She instantly ripped her hand away. ‘Don’t, Jimmy.’

‘What’s up? We’re married, we’ve got one in the oven, and I’ve missed you.’ He chuckled. ‘We could make it twins.’

Totally gobsmacked at his ridiculous statement, she said, ‘Do you think that’s how you get twins?’

‘Yeah, o’ course it is.’

‘You know, you are so fucking thick.’

‘I’ll tell you what is thick and that’s my prick. Now, come on, just a quickie.’

‘Don’t touch me, Jimmy. I’m not in the mood.’

‘I’m getting in the bath,’ he said, as he hung his head dejectedly and skulked off to the bathroom.

She had no sooner sighed with relief that he was not pawing at her than Albert strutted into the room. Of course, he didn’t bother to knock. Walking over to her, he leaned into her ear and said, ‘And don’t you start denying him his conjugal rights. ’Cos that ain’t part of the deal.’

Glaring back at Albert, before she jumped to her feet, she shouted, ‘Conjugal rights? It ain’t a fucking Swedish prison where he is entitled to have so-called conjugal rights, ya know. So, Albert, yes, we have a deal, but what we agreed is what we agreed. That's it. Please don't interfere in my fucking married life *or* my fucking sex life, 'cos that's just crossing boundaries.'

Unexpectedly, Jimmy returned to the room, having forgotten his aftershave. Standing dead still, he said, 'What's going on?'

Carrie saw her chance. And she was going to grasp it with both hands. Seeing that she could cause unrest between the brothers, she looked away from Jimmy as if she was hiding something.

'I said, what's going on?'

'Oh, I was just saying I'm glad she decided to get back with you.'

'You fucking liar. Look at her face, Albert. What did you say? Are you after my bird, eh? Well, are ya?'

'Don't be stupid, Jimmy.'

But Jimmy was perplexed. He and Carrie knew each other so well, he assumed she would have put him straight, there and then. But she didn't. She was sitting there quietly.

'Stupid? What are you doing in our room while I'm getting a bath?'

'Sorry, Jimmy, I was only welcoming Carrie back.'

'Fuck off, Albert, and don't you ever come in this room again. My Carrie needs her privacy. She's a woman. Not that you fucking have one to know about this stuff. Go on. Fuck off.'

Albert glared at Carrie. He realised that she had not only outmanoeuvred him, but that at some point she could cause trouble. So now he wondered if having her in their home was the best move. But the main thrust of his anger was aimed at his brother, and as he passed Jimmy, he shoved him into the wall. 'Don't you get fucking lairy with me, you little tit.'

As soon as the door was shut, Jimmy looked at Carrie. 'What did he want, Carrie?'

Giving him her best feared look, she said, 'I dunno, Jimmy. He gives me the creeps like he's undressing me in his head. You know what I mean? I don't wanna be left on my own with him.'

He sat beside her. 'It's all right. We'll get our own flat soon enough. We're on the council list, and as soon as little Jimmy arrives, they will house us.'

She glared. 'If it's a boy, *I'm* naming him because I'm doing all the hard work.'

'But I always wanted a son named after me.'

'Yeah, well, maybe Dottie will name her son – if it's a boy – after you.'

Jimmy jumped up. 'It ain't my kid.'

'Yeah, it is, Jimmy, and that's where I was the other day. I asked Spud to drive me to Holloway Prison, but you and your stupid brothers assumed me and Spud were carrying on behind your back. You beat him near to death.' She shook her head. 'I will never get the image of him in that hospital bed out of my head.'

Jimmy was about to ask what she was doing in the hospital at Spud's bedside when he thought better of it. 'I didn't mean to hurt him.'

She threw him a death stare. 'Oh, shut up, Jimmy. No one beats a man so bad as to break a load of bones and put blood clots on his brain if they don't mean to do some serious harm. And to think he and you were close.'

'Well, he knew the rules. He should never have gone off for the day with my wife.'

She nodded, and with her tongue to the roof of her mouth, she replied, 'Hmm, and him giving me a lift was a good enough reason for you to try to kill him and steal his money, yeah?'

Jimmy couldn't answer. He looked down, and for the first time in his life, he felt embarrassed because when it was put to him like that, it was a terrible and unforgivable betrayal. Seconds later, a sudden panic struck him. 'Is Spud gonna press charges?'

Carrie shrugged. 'If he does, I will be visiting you in prison for a very long time, and my baby will grow up seeing his farver behind bars. You won't mind me taking a lift off him to see you then, will you?'

The very thought tipped his anger, and he snatched a clump of Carrie's hair and pulled her face close to his. 'You stay away from Spud – from any other man. You're my fucking wife, so just you remember that.'

When he pushed her head back and let go of her, he couldn't believe what he was seeing. She was sitting up on the bed with a huge smile on her face.

CHAPTER TWENTY-ONE

A month had passed during which Carrie had been spending most of her days in her bedroom reading about babies. Anything to raise her enthusiasm about the new baby's arrival. Because feeling sick all the time and not fitting into her jeans was anything but a good experience.

All she could think about was her family. A week ago, she had seen her sisters walking past Ginty's house because they lived in the same street. How she had longed to go out and join them. But it would have broken her heart to see them literally turn their backs on her. And she had no doubt that that is what would have happened because in their eyes she had done exactly the same thing to them.

Getting up from the bed, she wandered on to the landing and gazed out of the window. As if by magic, Rosie and Mary were linking arms and skipping down the road. It was Wednesday and they were off to catch the bus to Swanley Market. She would have joined them if she had been at home. A lump lodged in her throat as she watched them laughing between themselves. Those two had always been close but not to the extent that they would have excluded her.

Just as she was about to move away from the window, she saw a car pull up. It was a Porsche 944, with the pop-up headlights, if she was not mistaken. She had walked past one only the other day and had stopped to admire it.

Carrie's heart fluttered briefly as she spotted who the driver was. It was none other than James Murphy. James got out first and went around to the passenger door to assist Dilly. A tinge of envy whipped through her. She'd always liked James and would have loved to have got with him. Maybe he was taking his brother's place and now dating her sister. She wouldn't mind; Dilly deserved a good man.

She wanted the best for Dilly. For all of her family. But witnessing what she was seeing outside Jimmy's home just brought all those regrets, which she had tried desperately to conceal, to the forefront of her mind. It was so evident that they were getting on with their lives – their now Carson-free lives – while she was effectively a prisoner in Ginty's house.

The brothers had made it all too clear to her that her job now was to be a good wife to Jimmy and to help around the house so that their dear old mum could have a break.

Cleaning the house was the easy part; she liked to keep a clean house – like her mother did – and she didn't mind all of the cooking either. But what she hated more than anything was hearing all the snidey comments and all the threats the brothers would whisper to her. The situation was becoming so horrific, she was beginning to have nightmares. In one dream a few days ago, she saw her sisters almost hung, drawn, and quartered. Of course a dream was just that – a dream. But actually hearing the Carsons describe the brutality they would inflict on her family was like a sick form of brainwashing.

When Dilly glanced up and saw her, Carrie automatically waved and smiled, but, to her dismay, her heart felt as though it had been ripped out when her sister's eyes narrowed into a look of spite before she turned away.

Hearing James's powerful vehicle roar away, a tear rolled down and burned her cheek.

'Oi, what ya doing gawping out the window? Ain't you supposed to be cleaning or something?'

Turning to face Lenny, she said, 'Am I, Lenny? That's what I'm supposed to be doing, is it?'

She hated him. When she looked at his face, all she saw was Mary's face black and blue. She had never understood what it was that Mary had seen in Lenny. With his dirty greasy hair stuck to his head, Carrie could smell his rancid beef broth bed smell, his sour breath, and sweaty armpits. She held her breath.

Lenny tilted his head to the side, his legs dancing as though he had a nervous disposition. Eyeing her suspiciously, he said, 'What are you talking about?'

'Is this how you treated Mary? Like she was Cinderella?'

'You shut your mouth, you fucking homewrecker.'

'I'm no homewrecker. You, Lenny Carson, were the homewrecker, when every single time you beat up me sister and bullied and frightened her and left her without a tiny smile of happiness. You *wrecked* your marriage. I came here to *save* my family. But, Lenny, you know that.'

Seeing his face as red as a beetroot, his fists balled, and his arms stiff by his sides, as if the rigid muscles could prevent him from punching the hell out of her, Carrie waited with bated breath for him to go that bit further. It was perfectly obvious that he wanted to.

She stared and laughed. She actually wanted him to do it. She wanted to feel physical pain because it had to be better than the mental torture that she endured day in, day out.

'You, ya pathetic lairy little cunt, will never have that much power. Our Albert only let you fucking believe it.'

Carrie wiped her tears away and stood daringly with her hands on her hips. 'Oh, is that so? Only, I don't see my sisters running back into your or your cousin's arms. It's been a month, Lenny, a whole fucking month, and they've moved on with their lives. All your family have now is me, and . . .' She poked her belly. 'This baby.'

'Oh, I'll have my Mary back, just you watch me, you cocky bitch.'

Carrie stepped forward. 'She *hates* you, Lenny. You could only force her to have sex with ya. Like our Rosie, Zachariah repulsed her. And then there's Dilly. Your ugly gnome-faced brother would never get a woman like her. Why? Because he is too disgusting. So he tried to rape her. But you lot won't touch her now. Believe me, you won't. Because we made a deal.'

Those words that were spat back at him only added to his temper. Like putting too many logs on the fire, he couldn't control the situation or himself. Suddenly, sparks flew. Lunging forward, he backhanded his sister-in-law so hard, she toppled backwards.

Desperate to grab the bannister, to save herself, Carrie pulled out two fingernails and smashed her head on each tread.

The commotion brought Ginty and Albert from the living room.

'Jesus fucking Christ! The *baby*!' Ginty bellowed, who, to be fair, also had her mind on Carrie as well. She tried to help her daughter-in-law, who had fallen headfirst to the bottom of the stairs, to an upright position.

Albert looked up the staircase and saw Lenny with his eyes wide and a worried look on his face. 'What have you done, you fucking div? She might lose the baby.'

'She's a mouthy prat. I swear to God, she's lucky I didn't stamp on her head.'

Ginty tried to get Carrie to stand up, but the girl was wobbling all over the place.

Just at that moment, the postman knocked at the door.

Ginty helped Carrie to sit back down on the bottom step before she opened the door to send the postman packing.

'I need a signature for this one.' He pulled the letter closer to his face. 'It's from the council.'

Getting to her feet, Carrie suddenly felt clear-headed enough to ask, 'Who is it addressed to?'

'Mr and Mrs Jimmy Carson.'

'I'll sign for that!' said Ginty, snatching the letter from the postman. 'You sit your arse back down, Carrie. You've had a nasty fall.'

But Carrie knew that the letter was for her. She had been waiting for correspondence and had wondered why she hadn't received anything. 'It's okay, I'll sign for it, Ginty. It's for me.'

Ginty pulled the letter away from Carrie to prevent her from getting her hands on it.

'Ginty, please give me the letter. It's addressed to me.'

The postman coughed. 'I need a signature.' He looked at Carrie. 'From Mrs Jimmy Carson.' He snatched the letter from Ginty's hand. 'Sorry, love, but this has to be handed to the recipient.' He gave it to Carrie, who used his pen to scribble her name on his paperwork.

Ginty pushed the postman off the doorstep and slammed the door in his face before she turned to Carrie. 'This is still my house, Carrie.'

Gripping the letter tightly, while trying not to get blood over it from her bleeding nail beds, Carrie ran her other hand over her stinging cheek. She looked up at Lenny. 'You ain't my husband. You can't backhand me.'

'Were you getting lairy with Lenny? 'Cos you know what he's like. Best thing for you, girl, is to keep your mouth shut.' She pointed up the stairs. 'And you, boy, keep your hands to yourself. What if she had lost the baby, eh? Then what?'

Lenny didn't even apologise. Storming off to his room, he turned on his favourite heavy-metal music that rattled through Carrie's bones.

Eager to get away from them all, she decided to go back up to her bedroom, which was the only place where she could have some privacy. Taking the stairs very carefully, she shut the door behind her, slumped onto the bed, and ripped open the letter.

When she discovered that the council hadn't received a response about the flat she'd been keen on, and that she would be taken off the council list, a torrent of tears ran down her cheeks.

The bitch. The nasty, cruel bitch.

Carrie knew what Ginty had done. She had been monitoring her post, with the sole aim of stopping her from moving out of this home with Jimmy. It was as clear as day that Ginty wanted her to stay in the house so she could get her hands on the baby.

But that wasn't part of the deal. No one had mentioned that she would be living at Ginty's for any length of time. If she had known that to be the case, she would sooner have cut her own wrists.

Rereading the letter, Carrie decided that she couldn't stay in this room all day feeling sorry for herself. She would go and do something about it. She'd given in to a lot in the past four weeks, but she was not going to put up with this. Easing herself off the bed, she slipped her arms into her sheepskin coat, tucked the letter in her pocket, and felt the fifty-pound note there. She'd almost forgotten about it. Fifty pounds was a lot of money. *A pity it was not enough to change my life*, she mused.

Before she left the bedroom, she looked into the small cracked mirror that had been glued to the wall and saw the red bump on her forehead where she'd faceplanted the bottom step. Gingerly, she touched her swollen cheek from Lenny's brutal backhander. What struck her most, though, was seeing her eyes. They weren't at all how they used to look. They were empty, and she wondered how long it had been since she had smiled, without contempt on her mind for receiving all those silent sarcastic gestures. In fact, she couldn't recall the last time she had even laughed. And it burned her insides to see her sisters doing just that as they skipped along with their arms linked.

Leaving the room, she came face to face with Albert. She stopped abruptly. 'Waiting outside me room, were ya?'

'Where are you going?'

Carrie was indifferent to the possibility of him beating her up. In any case, she was angry with the world right now.

Stepping aside, Albert grabbed her arm. 'Don't you go and do anything stupid, or you'll know the consequences.'

She shook him off, and her eyes bore into him with so much venom, he had to blink.

'I never do anything stupid. Now, if you're adding making me a prisoner to your deal, then it's all off, you sicko cunt.' She balled her fists and snarled like a dog.

'You're not a fucking prisoner. Don't get dramatic, silly little girl.'

'Dramatic? Me dramatic? You follow my every fucking move.' Her hazel eyes burned with intensity as she spat the words out. 'You even wait outside my room. *And* you're there when I get out of the bathroom.' She tilted her head to the side. 'Hoping to cop a look? Hoping me towel slips down, are ya?'

His jaw suddenly snapped to one side, and his scowl deepened as he clenched his fist.

'I know what you want, Albert. What you really want is me, don't ya? All this bollocks about me being here for your muvver, 'cos I'm carrying the baby, *is* bollocks, ain't it? Nah, I ain't buying into your shit.'

'Shut ya mouth.'

'Or what, Albert? Or fucking what?'

'I will fill it for you.'

Stepping back, Carrie looked him up and down before she shook her head. 'Fill it with what, Albert? Ya dick? 'Cos that's what you really wanna do, ain't it? You fucking want me here for your own pleasure. I bet you wank over imagining seeing me naked while you are in the boxroom and while Jimmy's fucking the hell out of me in the room next door. I bet you wish it was you.'

She could see she was hitting a nerve and now she was revelling in the fact that she was wiping that cocky look off his face. 'Now, get out of my way. I have a doctor's appointment.'

Carrie could feel her heart beating so fast she thought he could see or hear it, but she held her ground and waited for him to step aside.

'You have guts, Carrie, but if you ever speak to me like that again, I won't care about the consequences. They call me a psychopath. Maybe I will show you what a real psychopath can do.'

As she hurried away, she didn't stop to look back. She flung open the front door and walked as fast as she could – despite her injuries – along the garden path. As soon as she was on the street, she heard Ginty calling after her, but she didn't turn back. She had to go to the council offices and beg to be reinstated on the list.

***

Apart from the odd stares she received from a few commuters, Carrie arrived at the civic centre a lot calmer than when she had left the house. She had spent the journey planning what she'd say. All she could tell the housing officers was the truth, and she fervently hoped they would actually believe her. But her experience with them so far hadn't been great. Ms Clarendon had even said, 'Your kind will get what they're given or go without.' And then she had said, 'Beggars can't be choosers.' She'd taken offence to that and called the housing officer a cheeky fucking mare. She herself wasn't a beggar. Now, she hoped that Ms Clarendon wasn't in or was off sick because she really couldn't stand to be belittled by that snooty bitch again.

However, the minute she walked through the doors, behind the Perspex partition, who should be there but old Snooty Chops herself.

The moment she saw Carrie Carson, Clarendon's cheeks glowed with satisfaction. She curled her finger, beckoning the girl to approach even though there were people in the waiting area.

Carrie had no choice, after glancing at the other two helpdesks that weren't manned.

Clarendon clasped her hands as she leaned back in her chair. 'So, Mrs Carson, you received our letter, I take it?'

Carrie wondered how old the snooty bitch was. At a guess, she put her to be in her late forties, but with a little bit of lippy to colour her humourless lips, she thought she could be younger than that. All her features were pointed, sharp, and spiteful; even her poker-straight hair was sharply cut around her ears like a crash helmet.

'Look, I got this letter today, but I swear I never received any others. I'm having a baby in a few months. I can't live at me muvver-in-law's. It's crowded, and it's not nice.'

Clarendon smiled sarcastically. 'Well, I can assure you that they were sent and signed for, so don't come it with me. Like your lot, you received the letters but you were too lazy to respond. We don't chase you to sign a tenancy.' She pointed over Carrie's shoulder. 'As you can see, we have a long list of people wanting a home, so I'm sorry, but you will have to go to the bottom of the waiting list after reapplying again.' She smiled. 'I am sure your mother-in-law will love to have you at her house. Think of all the support you will get with a new baby.'

Carrie had had enough; her anger boiled over. She jumped up from the chair. 'You wicked ol' cow, I bet you knew I didn't sign any of the fucking letters you sent. It wouldn't have been my signature on any of 'em.'

'I will have you escorted out of this building. We do not tolerate abuse here.'

'Oh, go fuck yourself, you snobby cocksucking ol' bag.'

Clarendon was so shocked, her mouth opened and closed like a fish out of water.

Just as Carrie was about to leave the offices, a woman appeared from the side room. Sensing that the pretty girl seemed unnaturally agitated, she enquired, 'What is all the shouting about?' She glared at Clarendon.

But before Clarendon could answer, Carrie got in first. 'Miss, me name's Carrie Carson. I got this letter, and that woman there' – Carrie pointed at Clarendon – 'said I had been sent letters that I signed for, but I never did. And she's chucking me off the list and . . .' Suddenly, she stopped talking and burst into tears, deep heart-wrenching sobs as well.

The woman guided Carrie to a separate room, where she helped her to a chair.

'Okay, let me get you a drink. You're obviously in a terrible state here. Would you like a cup of tea, sweetheart?'

Carrie looked up and nodded. 'Two sugars, please.'

The kind officer left Carrie alone for a few minutes to get herself together, and when she returned, she placed a mug of strong tea under Carrie's nose. 'Right, my name is Nancy Cassidy.' She gestured towards a pile of paperwork sitting on her desk. 'I believe I have your records somewhere here. Let me sort this out.'

Carrie grinned. 'You're not one of the Cassidys from The Cray, are ya?' She half expected Nancy to shake her head.

Nancy slowly nodded, moved her black hair away from her ears, showing her creole earrings, and then placed a finger over her lips.

Carrie chuckled. 'And you got a job here?'

'Yes, I've worked for the council for twenty years. My old manager was a lovely woman who my mum cleaned the offices for. And she kindly put in a good word for me, so they took me on. I'm now the manager, and I know it can be tough for you,

Carrie Carson. Some of the officers here are so judgemental and bloody rude. I won't stand for it because there's really no need.'

Carrie wiped her nose with the back of her sleeve. 'Ms Clarendon said, "Your kind", like I'm an alien, and she said, "Beggars can't be choosers." She made me feel pretty shit, and I'm having to live at Ginty Carson's house . . . with all the boys . . . and I'm having a baby and . . .'

Nancy covered Carrie's hand. 'I know Ginty. Who doesn't. *And* her lads. Anyway, I have a place with your name on it. It came in this morning. Ms Clarendon hasn't had sight of it yet. So how about I take you there myself, along with the paperwork and the keys, if, of course, you find you like it?'

'Really? You'd do that for me?'

Nancy ran a finger down Carrie's puffy red cheek. 'Did Ginty do that to you?'

Carrie looked at her missing fingernails, both beds red and swollen, and shook her head. 'No, not this time. It was her son Lenny.'

Nancy gasped. 'Dear Gawd above, I hope Jimmy takes after their father, not Ginty. I shouldn't get involved, Carrie, but I know that family bullies anyone they take a dislike to. Let's view this flat and get you away from them.'

'You knew I married Jimmy?'

'I sent the two letters for you to sign, so I knew they were addressed to you and Jimmy. But I didn't send you a letter taking you off the list. Ms Clarendon did that. Right, as I said, I am the manager, so I can overturn it.' She smiled again. 'Drink your tea, and we'll get going.'

'I do appreciate this, Ms Cassidy.'

'Call me Nancy. This is my little way of getting my own back on that fat ol' cow.'

Carrie put her hands to her mouth and giggled.

'I'll tell you all about it on the way.'

CHAPTER TWENTY-TWO

Carrie couldn't believe her luck when Nancy pulled into Poverest Road. Holding her breath in anticipation, she wondered where exactly they were going because as far as she was aware there weren't any council houses on the other side of the main road.

Now, with her excitement level rising in step with her accelerating heartbeat, Carrie watched as Nancy turned left and right before slowing down to what looked like a house. A house, not a flat! The thing was, she couldn't see the front door.

'Here?'

'Is it okay, Carrie? I mean, a long line of tenants will rip my arm off for this place.'

'It's lovely. I thought you were gonna take me to a bedsit at the top of a block of flats with piss-smelling lifts and crackheads by the bins. I mean, what is it?'

Nancy laughed at Carrie's description. 'This is a maisonette. You're on the ground floor, and there is another person living here as well. Well, he actually bought the top maisonette, so he owns the top half. It has two bedrooms and inside there is a bit of a surprise for you. Come on, I'll show you around.'

Carrie was in complete shock. The front of the property had a small but very pretty garden and there was a wide path-cum-driveway that led down to a back garden.

Nancy showed Carrie to the main door, which was on the side of the building, and at the back, leading to another main door, there was a stone staircase.

Shaking all over, Carrie would never have dreamed that she would be offered a place like this. It was beautiful. *But what was it like inside?* she wondered. She suspected that it might need a lot of work to make it habitable, but even so, it was in a great location. It wasn't on the estate; it was on a leafy road opposite a green. There were no burned-out cars, no piles of rubbish, and no mangy cats and dogs roaming about. In short, it was perfect.

Nancy slid the key in the lock and pushed it open for Carrie to go inside. 'Go and have a look, Carrie.' She chuckled. 'Don't be shy.'

As Carrie stepped into the carpeted hallway, the newness of the place hit her nostrils. It had been given a fresh lick of paint, that was obvious. Taking a few steps forward, her eyes darted to the room at the right. The kitchen looked brand new, with white cupboards and a white worktop. Then she frowned. Looking around, she noticed an array of red accessories including a toaster and cups on a rack. Spinning around, she said, 'Look, Nancy, they haven't cleared out their stuff.'

Nancy smiled. 'I told you this place had your name on it. So the old woman, who had lived here for years, recently died. Her sons, who had grown up in the maisonette, had it all done up for her the during the time she was in hospital. But, sadly, she never made it back home. So her sons asked me to find a good home for all her things or give them to charity. But if you look around, everything smacks of quality.' She pointed ahead. 'Go on, go into the living room.'

The moment Carrie entered the room, she threw her hands to her mouth. It was almost too good to be true; even the sofa, the two armchairs, and the rug were immaculate.

'I'm sure you'll replace it all in time, but it'll do you a turn, eh?'

'Do me a turn? I bloody love it, Nancy. Oh my God, I can't thank you enough. Ya know, I was having the shittiest day, and now . . . Now, I feel like I've got something to live for, to look forward to. Something I can call mine. Shame me muvver and farver won't come to see it.'

Nancy gave Carrie a sympathetic smile. 'What about your sisters, Carrie? I know Rosie, a lovely woman.'

Carrie felt a lump in her throat, but she battled to hold back the tears. 'I've never told anyone else this, but, see, the Carsons . . .'

Nancy screwed up her face. 'Yeah.'

'Well, my two sisters were married to two of the Carson family. Actually, they still are married to them – in theory.'

'Yes, I know they are, and that's a shame, if I'm being truthful with you, Carrie. You girls are all very attractive, and I have never understood why you got with the Carsons in the first place. But, still, it's not my place to judge.'

'You can judge all you want, Nancy. *I* know what they are, and I've been stupid meself for marrying one. Did you hear about the fight at me own wedding?'

'Yes, I did. Your poor sister Dilly, another lovely girl.'

'Well, me sisters left their husbands, and me dad took them in, and . . .' Carrie's hands shook before she took a deep breath. 'Albert told me he would really hurt me sisters, do some nasty stuff to 'em if I left Jimmy. All because I'm pregnant and—'

'Yeah, Ginty wants to get her hands on the baby, right?' Nancy interjected.

'How did you know that?'

'That's what I was going to tell you on the way here. You didn't know me sister Joycee, did you?'

Carrie shook her head.

Nancy smiled. 'Take a seat. This place is yours if you want it.'

Carrie eased herself onto the almost new sofa and allowed her finger to run over the soft velvet while Nancy sat in an armchair opposite. 'Me sister Joycee got with Albert. He was different a few years back. You are probably too young to remember.

Anyway, they ran off together like people did in the old days. They went to a small site in Brighton. Ginty's brother runs it.'

Carrie sat still, her eyes glued to Nancy, hanging on to her every word.

'Well, me farver.' Nancy had already slipped into her natural way of talking. 'He was wild with anger, ya see. They just took off, and she was the baby in our family, like you are. Except she'd just turned sixteen. Barely three months later, our Joycee came back. She fell through our front door, in a terrible state, she was. A right terrible state. He'd beaten her up, Carrie. But worse, she was pregnant. Farver was angry, but the rules are the rules, and our little Joycee was held accountable. She was accused of acting too familiar with other men. But she told me she rarely left the house, and the only men she spoke to were his friends, in particular Vinny, a rogue mush, and only to ask if they wanted a drink or some food.'

Carrie could feel herself tearing up.

'When that fat ugly bitch Ginty found out our Joycee was pregnant, she brazenly walked into our home and took over. She took our Joycee back to her house and promised that she'd look after the girl like she was her own. She'd support Joycee, help with the baby, and make sure her son didn't get too handy with his fists again because she claimed she was the only woman who could calm her sons if they got angry. But I knew all Ginty wanted was the baby. So, anyway, me farver agreed, even though I knew our Joycee was terrified. But she respected our parents, so she went to live at Ginty's. I tried to visit her, but Ginty always said she was sleeping. I knew that was a downright lie. Me sister never slept. She was of the worrying, nervous kind. She never slept a fucking wink. Then I saw her one day, although she didn't see me. She was putting out all the rubbish, and her face was so bruised it looked like a marble. It was all colours, from old bruises *and* new ones.'

Carrie held her hands to her mouth in disbelief that this had gone on years before and Albert wasn't in prison for it. But, then again, it wasn't the done thing in their community for people to grass to the police.

'It was late one night, and we were all at home, when there was a knock at the door. Me muvver answered it . . .' She paused to gather thoughts. 'Our Joycee was black and blue. He'd hurt her real bad, this time. She showed me muvver the bruises to her stomach. She consequently lost the dear little baby.'

'Oh no, that's so bad. He is evil.'

'Evil? He is the devil himself.'

'How is Joycee?'

'Because she wasn't officially married to Albert, me muvver sent her to me auntie's place in Ireland. God love her, she married an Irish traveller. Built like the side of a house, he is. The poor man had lost his own wife, and so they found comfort in each other. No one said a word when they got together. Of course, when they came to The Crays to visit us, big bollocks Albert wanted to have it out with the man. Still, it was a joke because Mikey, our Joycee's husband, towered over him. Mikey's hands were the size of Albert's head, so the lairy little wanker retreated a bit sharpish but not before Mikey made Albert give him his blessing.'

'Does she have a family now with Mikey?'

Nancy smiled. 'Yes, she does. More than enough. Six chavis in all. Three boys, three girls, all the image of her.' She looked around. 'So, as you can imagine, I hate Ginty. She allowed that man to beat me sister, so I'll do anything to get my own back.'

Hearing all of this was definitely bursting Carrie's bubble. She wondered what it would take to ditch her husband.

Interrupting her thoughts, Nancy said, 'Now, a skip will be arriving on Monday, and anything you don't want, you can throw out. The men are supposed to clear the place, but I've told them that we will do that. I've already written down that the furniture has been collected by the charity people.' She laughed. 'This is better than my own stuff.'

Carrie stroked the sofa again. 'It's pukka. I can't believe me luck. Well, rather, I can't believe you've done this for me.'

Nancy winked. 'It was also for me, ya know. A little way of getting revenge. You won't have to live at that wicked woman's house now. And I know that will get her so riled up, she'll blow her top. I hope it gives her a heart attack.'

Carrie grinned. 'Me too.'

After Nancy had gone through all the form filling and Carrie had registered the new gas and electric readings, Nancy dangled the keys in front of her. 'It's all yours, and . . .' she whispered, 'Jimmy's name is yet to go on. I mean . . .' She winked. 'He's not here to sign it, is he?'

Carrie's eyes widened. 'But won't anyone say anything? We're registered as a married couple with a baby on the way.'

'I'm the manager. I've signed this over to you. If you want to add Jimmy, that's up to you.'

'He'll know, though, won't he?'

'Not unless you mention it.'

Carrie wanted to pinch herself. It was like a dream, and all in the space of a few hours.

As soon as Nancy drove away, Carrie decided to have a good look around. She started with the two bedrooms. Both were a good size and the beds were made up with brushed cotton candy-striped sheets, which were all new. The smaller room had two single beds, with blue bedspreads and blue curtains at the window. All the net curtains in the home were gleaming white, just like her mother's. She thought of selling one of the beds, and putting the cot in its place and adding baby pictures on the walls. It couldn't be more perfect. Out of character, she put her hands together and said, 'Thank you, God, for such a huge gift. I will try to be a good person.' Then her eyes were drawn to a small plaque on the white bedside cabinet, which read: *Love shared equally between children makes for a kind and happy home.* She instantly thought about Dottie and her baby, but she had to push the thought out of her head for now because she didn't want to muddy the euphoric feeling. So, she turned the plaque over. Staring out of the window, she realised that if she came out of her maisonette and turned left and right, she would be in Dottie's street. She shuddered because spirituality and weird coincidences were not things that she had ever given credence to.

Just as she was about to lock up and head back to Ginty's, there was a loud bang at the door. Instinctively, she assumed Nancy had forgotten something, so she opened the door and simultaneously heard police sirens.

Before she could even register what was happening, a man, who was dressed all in black, pushed past her and slammed the door shut. He had a holdall in one hand and a gun in the other. His skin was peppered with beads of sweat, and his black Reebok trainers were caked in mud.

'Keep schtum,' he growled.

Despite this huge guy filling the hallway with his beanie pulled down so low that it covered his eyebrows, making him almost unrecognisable, Carrie soon calmed her nerves, once she realised who it was. 'Sunny, for fuck's sake, you gave me the fright of me life.'

Sunny Murphy was tall and handsome, and at twenty-five years of age, he was James Murphy's youngest brother. When he recognised Carrie, he lowered the gun. 'Hide me, Carrie. Don't tell the Ol' Bill I'm here or I'll go away for a fucking long stretch.'

Hearing the sirens so close, she guessed the police were outside. Then she heard the sounds of car doors being opened and closed. 'Quick, get in one of the bedrooms under the bed.'

'You're a good 'un, Carrie.' He quickly kissed her cheek, flew into the first bedroom he came across, and slid under the bed, pulling the holdall with him. He was just in time because the police were now surrounding the maisonette and two officers were peering in through the windows.

'Cheeky fuckers,' Carrie mumbled, under her breath.

Then the police banged so hard on her door, she thought they would come through it. She slowly opened it, but only a few inches. 'Hello.'

'It's the police, madam.'

'Oh, hello, hofficer,' she said, trying to talk posh. 'Is everything all right?'

'Have you seen a man in a black tracksuit carrying a large gym bag? He ran this way.'

'No, sorry, I didn't, but I've had a migraine, so I've been lying on the settee.'

She then saw other officers running along the side of the maisonette and heard them thumping up the steps and banging on the door of the property above.

'Are you sure? You wouldn't be lying to me, would you? We have the place surrounded, and he couldn't have disappeared into thin air. Are you sure you didn't let him into your home?'

'I wouldn't have any man in my house. My husband wouldn't be at all happy with that, hofficer.'

'And no one knocked at your door, and you haven't seen anyone?'

'No, I'm sorry.'

Closing the door, she could feel her heart thumping. It was only when she heard the police drive away that she looked out of the window to confirm they had gone. She closed all the curtains and then called Sunny out of the bedroom.

He was still on edge and looked about before he let out a deep breath and pulled the beanie off his head. 'Cor, fucking 'ell, that was a close shave.'

Carrie laughed. 'Yeah, I thought they were gonna force their way in. So you robbed a bank, did ya?'

He looked down at his holdall. 'Not quite, but here, Carrie, this is for saving my arse.' He reached in and pulled out a wad of cash. It was more than she'd ever seen in her life.

'And don't ask, Carrie.'

'I don't think I wanna know, but listen, I can't take ya money.' She chuckled again. 'That's your hard-earned cash. I am sure you would have done the same for me.'

Sunny pushed the money into her hand. 'Take it, Carrie. You've done me a right favour.'

He took another deep breath. 'Shit, I really thought they had me. I can't believe you answered the door. Well, I didn't know it was you, at first. I expected Henry or Andy, one of the old girl's sons, to answer it. They were clearing out some personal stuff, 'cos she died, bless her. So what are you doing here?'

'This, Sunny Murphy, is my new pad. I got the keys just a few minutes ago.'

'Well, that makes us neighbours, then. I'm in the maisonette above. I keep meself to meself, like. I don't have people over. I don't like people knowing where I live.'

Carrie looked down. 'You know I'm married to Jimmy Carson, don't ya? He can be a right blabbermouth.'

Sunny scratched his sweat-covered head. 'Shame, Carrie, a right royal shame, that is. To think me and you would have been in-laws if me brother hadn't been killed.'

Carrie blushed. 'Er, is your James seeing Dilly?'

Sunny sat down on the sofa. 'Haven't you heard about Dilly giving evidence against Arthur?'

'No, my family aren't talking to me because I'm with Jimmy.'

'James heard about that. Arthur tried to . . .' He blushed. 'Well, you know, he tried to help himself to her.'

Hearing all of this again was making Carrie feel sick. She sat down in the armchair opposite Sunny and bit her bottom lip.

'James went mental. He saw your father and said that Dilly needs to have Arthur locked up for good, or he would kill the man when he gets off remand. It turns out that since the police – the bastards – won't give your Dilly protection, my brother has taken it upon himself to look out for Dilly, Mary, and Rosie.'

Carrie frowned. 'I live in that house, and none of the Carsons have said a word, although there has been a lot of whispering going on. But I'll be out of there tomorrow.'

He looked around. 'It's a right nice gaff. The old girl was lovely, always making me cakes. As I said, she has two sons. Oddly enough, one is from her husband's first marriage, but she ended up raising them both as her own. They did this place up for her. Loved their ol' mum, they did. Shame she died, but now you get to make memories here with your baby.'

'Oh, you know I'm pregnant, then?'

'Yeah, James told me.' He bit his bottom lip. 'I'd have whisked you away if you weren't, but you're a married woman now with a baby on the way. Right, I'm gonna head off.' Tugging the curtains aside, he checked to see if the coast was clear. It was.

'The filth don't know it's you, do they?'

'No, of course, they don't. They were chasing a man all in black. Please don't tell anyone. I mean Jimmy, especially Jimmy, the twat.'

'He is the fucking last person I'd tell.'

Sunny kissed her again and laughed. 'I would kiss you on the lips, but you'd either slap me or we'd end up in bed. Both ways, you'd feel bad afterwards.'

Carrie smiled coyly as she shut the door behind him. He was probably right about that. All the Murphys were exceptionally good looking, and she would have settled for any one of them over a Carson, that was for sure. *Still*, she thought, *you made your bed, you lie in it.*

Her thoughts then went to all the money he had given her. Eyeing up the bundle of notes in her hand – which was easily a couple of grand – all she needed to do now was to hide it somewhere. And somewhere where Jimmy wouldn't find it.

CHAPTER TWENTY-THREE

The room was warm forcing Dottie to remove her sweatshirt and sit in her T-shirt and jogging bottoms, which showed off her baby bump. She fingered the cross on her chain, while waiting for her visitor.

Ms Knight, the officer present in the room, was sweet, a quiet woman, who smiled easily and nodded a lot when she was listening, which at least showed that she was interested. She was one of the kinder officers; in fact, in the new part of Holloway, all the staff seemed friendlier.

'Is my brief late, or am I early, Miss?'

'Now, don't fret over it, Ellis. He has arrived, but you can imagine he must go through all the searches and form filling. Has the baby been kicking? Over the morning sickness now, I shouldn't wonder.' She smiled again.

'Yes, Miss, it feels like I've swallowed an alien.'

'It can feel like that. I know, having two of my own.'

Ten minutes later, the door opened, and Clive Clemence, Dottie's solicitor, entered. He, too, seemed to smile a lot. He had his tatty briefcase with him and was wearing a long overcoat over his dark-grey suit. Once he had sat down, he asked the officer politely to leave them alone.

'I'll be just outside, and I'll organise some refreshments for you.' She winked at Dorothy. 'A creamy hot chocolate, perhaps?'

'Thank you,' Clemence said, before he turned to face his client. 'And how are you doing, Dottie?'

'I'm okay. I'm good, actually. They treat me well. I've got a supportive friend. In fact, she's a birthing buddy called Billy, and so I really can't complain.' She raised her eyebrows. 'Do you have a court date yet?'

Clemence bit his lip, concerned that this young lady appeared to be quite comfortable in the prison setting. The young women he'd represented in the past wouldn't be acting like that; they would be hanging on to his every word and begging him to get them out. 'So we requested a psychological report.'

Dottie nodded and cheerfully replied, 'Yes, I've had several done on me.'

'Hmm, well, you would have because we requested one on behalf of our expert witness, and the prosecution have also requested one, and now their feedback is conflicted.' Suddenly, he stood up, removed his coat, and flung it over the back of his chair. 'It's hot in here,' he said, as he loosened his tie. 'So the trial date isn't set yet because of the need to carry out further psychological assessments.' He steepled his hands and leaned forward, maintaining his smile. 'We, I mean your appointed barrister and myself and also Mr Clarkson – who, by the way, sends his regards and has told me he has put some money in your prison account – need to examine the results of these assessments very carefully before the case can proceed.'

'I understand,' Dottie said, and then she beamed. 'So Mr Clarkson has put money in my account for me, has he? Really? For me? That's so kind of him.'

'Yes, and it's probably not allowed. But, still, it's done, so you can treat yourself. Now, back to the court case. They have deferred it until at least November. As I said, there is still the thorny matter of the psychological assessments to be concluded. So, in due course, depending upon the conclusions of these reports, you could in theory be released fairly soon after the trial, or, if the case goes against you, it will mean you being put in a secure prison for treatment, but at the moment, our plea of temporary insanity is the defence we are aiming for. In fact, it's the *only* defence.'

This didn't come as too much of a surprise to Dottie. She smiled and accepted her fate until a worrying thought popped into her mind. Her eyes bulged. 'Oh, and my baby. If they say I'm insane, then what happens?'

Clemence could see the panic written all over her face, and instantly, he felt sorry for her. 'I'm sorry, Dottie, but the social services may take the baby from you for its own protection, if they find you guilty of insanity. They may . . .' He held up his hand to reinforce his next point. 'I'm not saying they will, but they may take the baby away sooner than the eighteen-month period when they let some mothers – not all, but some – keep their baby.'

'Where will they take him . . . or her?'

He shrugged. 'Presumably to foster care, unless you can think of a family member who will take the baby. Or, of course, the child's father will have rights.'

Dottie nodded. 'Thank you, Clemmy, I do appreciate it.'

Surprised by her chilled-out attitude, he said, 'How do you feel about the trial being so far off and you having to remain here in custody?'

Dottie shrugged. 'I'm warm and fed. I can go swimming and I have friends.'

'But you're in prison, Dottie, locked up,' he said, somewhat baffled by her response.

'I can see what you are saying. But look at it this way, Clemmy. I'm freer now than I've ever been. I have had time to look back at my life. It's amazing how when you are locked up and away from what was your previous life, you suddenly realise how controlling those people around you made you feel. I felt just like a prisoner *then*. I was trapped by overcontrolling parents who brainwashed me. But now, I am free to think for myself.'

Clemence stared into Dorothy's eyes. Listening to this young woman – this articulate and intelligent woman – he could see that she had changed from the frightened teenager he had first encountered. She had grown up remarkably quickly in the space of a few months. She was no longer a child. She sat there with confidence, thoroughly composed, and not looking down into her hands, which was the case the first time he had met her.

***

As Clemence walked away from the prison, he sighed and shook his head. That meeting with his client was going around and around in his head. He still couldn't shake off what Dorothy had told him when she had compared her life before she had been arrested to the one she was living now. Her cold yet sobering words hammered away at his brain and made him wonder to what lengths Dorothy had suffered at the hands of her parents. She had also appeared, surprisingly, so normal. There was not a smidgeon of insanity about her; she spoke as if it was all par for the course.

As Clemence trudged across to his four-year-old Saab 900 Turbo, his feelings switched between sadness and apprehension. The reports were conflicting because the prosecution wanted to charge her with double murder, and yet the defence psychologist had said she was temporarily insane at the time. The circumstances leading up to the murders were so out of the ordinary that, from her account, they could easily have driven her to act in the way she did. But in the cold light of day, and under normal conditions, she would never have acted so sadistically. Her reports from school, the church, and the neighbours all painted her as a very kind, sweet, and polite child who worked hard with no history of violence. He only hoped the social services didn't snatch the baby the moment it was born and that they had some compassion for her, but, then again, that wasn't in his remit of professional concern. But it didn't stop him from thinking about how Dorothy would feel when her baby was taken away from her. He shuddered. The consequences just didn't bear thinking about.

***

When Dottie reached her cell, she noticed Billy was lying on her bed and staring at the ceiling with her arms on her chest. She appeared as white as a sheet, which was unusual since Billy's skin was olive. She didn't move either when Dottie walked in.

Holding up a paper cup, which Officer Knight had given her, Dottie said, 'I saved you a hot chocolate, Billy.'

When Billy didn't answer, Dottie knew something was wrong. She sat on the bed next to her and stared at the tears falling down the sides of Billy's face.

'Hey, Billy, what's up? You never cry. Tell me, please, what's wrong?' Leaning forward, Dottie wiped the tears from Billy's face and could feel herself welling up. She had never seen so much pain on her friend's face before. 'Do you want to talk about it? Was the visit a tough one?'

Slowly, Billy sat up, swung her legs around, and wiped her eyes with the back of her tattooed hand. 'The visit went exactly how I knew it would go.' She wiped another tear away from her face and then took a deep breath. 'Okay.' She sighed. 'You've been a good mate to me, Dottie. I mean you've been like a sister. You've even taught me how to swim.'

'Yes, so? We're friends, Billy.'

'When I was a kid, I read a book called *The Little Mermaid* by Hans Christian Andersen.' She laughed and blushed. 'I found the book in the bin down by the chippy where I used to live. I loved the book and always wanted to swim – to be like the little mermaid. I used to fantasise about it. It was the only nice thought I ever had, and you helped me to fulfil that dream. I can now swim.'

'Yeah, and it's a laugh, eh, so what's that got to do with the visit?' She shoved the hot chocolate under Billy's nose. 'Here, it's a nice creamy one.'

Billy sipped the drink and smiled. 'Thanks, Dottie. You are always thinking of me.' Her face suddenly hardened as she continued. 'But listen and listen well, right? There's something that no one in here yet knows about me.'

Dottie sat up straight, all ears, knowing this was serious.

'You know I'm in 'ere for killing me father, don't you?'

Dottie nodded. She was aware of it, but she had never felt it her place to delve into all the whys and wherefores.

'Well, my father and two of his mates – they called themselves my uncles – but they weren't – they were dirty ol' perverts – well, anyway, long story short, my father was a bit of a face, and so were his two mates, but, and this is the thing, neither of them would protect me against him. They'd turn a blind eye, and one even tried to get in me knickers when I was about ten.' Pausing, she sipped the hot chocolate and stared off into nowhere for a while.

But Dottie didn't interrupt her thoughts. She wanted Billy to control the conversation at her own pace.

'I hated them, I really hated them. I thought I could escape me father's clutches by running away with a boyfriend. I latched on to the first geezer that showed an interest. I got pregnant by him, but me ol' man beat the shit out of him and took him for a long drive in the boot of his motor. I think he left him in Wales somewhere.'

'Jesus, that's horrific.'

Billy nodded. 'But when me so-called boyfriend came back, he stayed away. In fact, he fucked off with some other girl, and that affected me badly. I was in a right state. All I wanted to do was run away. Then . . .' She paused and looked around to make sure the door was firmly shut. 'Me father and his mates did this job, on a post office. They were blaggers, you see. And one night, they were gathered in me father's living room. I watched from the landing as they emptied the money out of their holdalls and stuffed it inside the sofa. I saw them staple it up, and when they'd finished, you'd never have known the sofa had been tampered with. Except I did. I knew. Anyway, that night, after they'd gone, me father got drunk, and he didn't try to touch me like he had in the past. Instead, he fucking beat me for getting pregnant. When he kicked me in the stomach, I fell down the stairs, and for a moment, I thought he had killed me baby. I went into a rage. I understand the saying "blind rage" because that was how I felt. That was me. I got a carving knife from the kitchen, I ran back up the stairs, and I killed him. I fucking stabbed him to death. Admittedly I went a bit OTT, but I was fucking angry. The judge gave me a recommended sentence because the photos had disturbed him. I suppose stabbing someone through the eyes would make a mess.'

Dottie had her hands to her mouth. 'Oh my God.'

Billy laughed. 'Why are you so shocked, eh? You did much the same.'

Dottie shrugged. 'Yeah, I suppose I did.'

'Well, that's not the end of the story. While he was bleeding to death upstairs, I opened up the sofa, collected all the money, stuffed it into a few shopping bags, and then shoved them into me father's waterproof fishing bag. I got cleaned up. I took me father's shovel and his torch, and I ran all the way to the graveyard. I buried the money, *all* the money, the fucking lot of it.'

'Wow, you are a brave woman. At least, when you get out of here, you'll have money to start your life again. You could get a flat by the seaside and swim in the sea every day.'

Billy smiled, but it was a smile that was filled with sadness. She shook her head. 'No, Dottie, that visit I had today was from me father's two mates, me so-called uncles. They said I've got until the end of the week to tell them where the money is, or they will make sure I will leave this prison in a body bag.'

'What does that mean, Billy?'

‘That means they have someone in here who will stab me on the sly.’

‘No one in here will touch you, Billy. No one has the guts.’

Slowly, Billy shook her head. ‘Dottie, these men have money, or they did have. I saw how they were dressed – I saw their gold watches, their new teeth. They reeked of money, and I know how they get it. A couple of robberies, and they’re made.’

‘So if they have money, what’s a couple of carrier bags of cash to them now?’

She shrugged. ‘I don’t know. They’re getting on a bit. They’re not as young as they were and clearly not as tough. They look flashy, though. But they may have got too big for their boots. They’ve probably stepped on the wrong toes and need to pay someone off, and they don’t have the readies. But they have enough money to see someone all right to do away with me. I don’t know how much is in those bags, but it must be a lot.’

Dottie’s hands began to shake. ‘Billy, tell them where the money is. Just *give* it to them.’

‘Do you know what I love about you, Dottie? You never think of yourself, do ya? You are always thinking of me. You never asked me where I buried the money so that you could get your hands on it, did ya?’

‘Me? No, of course not. It’s not my money. Anyway, just tell them. Then at least you won’t be forever looking over your shoulder.’

‘No, Dottie, they ain’t ever having that money. They fucked me up as a kid, the three of them, so no, never. I would rather die than let them have the money.’

‘But you could end up dead.’

‘I don’t care, Dottie. I’m never getting out of here. Don’t you get it?’

Dottie’s shoulders slumped. ‘But we have a dream, a little house by the sea, me and you, drinking hot chocolate and feeding the seagulls.’

Billy wiped away another tear. 'Dottie, it was *your* dream. Mine was to swim like a mermaid, and I've done that. But I listened to you detail your dreams because it was like falling into this perfect world, even though it's not real. Dottie, you will get released one day. You will, but I won't.'

Dottie lifted her legs onto the bed and tucked her knees under her chin. 'I thought it was *our* dream, Billy.'

'Well, it wasn't. It was stupid, Dottie, just silly.'

Dottie turned on her side away from Billy and stared at the cold painted brick wall. She was angry with her – there's no two ways about it – but, at the same time, she had a feeling of dread tugging at her chest, making it harder to breathe. The fear of losing her best friend was like nothing she'd ever experienced – apart from the day her grandmother died.

'Sometimes, Dottie, you need to face reality. We are in a shithole and degraded to be made to feel grateful for a creamy hot fucking chocolate and on Thursday afternoons a doughnut for pudding. That's no fucking life. And to be honest, I don't care if they kill me. I'm not living, anyway. I'm just surviving, and there's a bloody big difference between the two.'

Rolling back over, Dottie faced Billy. 'I've only got you, Billy. That lot out there won't be so nice to me without you. Not that I'm being selfish about it, but, in a way, I suppose I am. I need you, Billy.'

'Well, Dottie, you'll have to survive alone one day, and' – she flicked her thumb over her shoulder – 'that lot all think you're a psycho, and most of them are more scared of you than me.' She screwed up her face and smiled. 'And you, Dottie Ellis, already know that, don't ya? I've seen you give them the evil eye for kicks.'

Dottie laughed because she had clocked how the women gave her a wide berth and were particularly nice; maybe they feared the unknown, frightened of the idea that she had a switch that could click at any moment and turn her into a cold-blooded killer.

‘Now listen, and memorise this.’ Once again, Billy looked about to make sure the door was firmly shut. ‘Annie Selby 1935 to 1967, Camberwell New Cemetery.’

Dottie frowned. ‘Who? What?’

‘She was me mum, thirty-two years old. I was thirteen when she died.’

‘Ahh, that’s a shame.’

‘Well, she left me father before that and left me with *him*, knowing he was a wrong ’un. So I had my reasons for not liking her either. But her name was Annie Selby. You remember that, yeah?’

With a firm nod, Dottie followed it with a compassionate smile. Maybe it *was* time she faced the reality of what may happen because Billy was no drama queen: she said it as it was.

CHAPTER TWENTY-FOUR

Staring at her husband snoring his head off, Carrie thought about the life she would have if she simply upped and left. That beautiful maisonette and the bonus of having Sunny upstairs was so appealing. But then feeling her stomach turning from the relentless morning sickness and living with the threat of the Carson brothers attacking her family, if she broke the agreement she had made with Albert, could she have the life she really wanted? Her shoulders slumped knowing her very existence was pretty much mapped out for her now.

Hearing Ginty's loud, husky, and brash voice call out into the back garden, Carrie suspected the whole street had probably heard her.

'Lenny, leave those fucking puppies be, will ya, and come back inside. You left the back door open, and you've let all the bloody heat out, you skinny arsed rat!'

His mother's screeching voice made Jimmy sit bolt upright. In a panic, he looked about him until he realised he was in bed, and then his shoulders relaxed. 'Fucking 'ell, what's she shouting about?'

Carrie tried to get out of bed, but Jimmy pulled her back. 'Hey, where are you going?'

'Get off, Jimmy. I'm getting up.'

'Carrie girl, last night muvver said something about the council giving us a place. Is that right?'

Carrie winced at his sour breath. 'Clean ya teeth. You stink rotten.'

'Don't be nasty.'

'Nasty? Fucking nasty? You came into bed in the early hours pissed out of your tiny mind demanding *sex*, you fucking animal.'

'Oh, come on, Carrie, I had a little bit to drink, and you are my wife. What is it with you, eh? Are you getting it from someone else?'

He ran his hands through his hair and coughed up a load of phlegm before running to the toilet to spit it out.

Carrie climbed into a pair of ski pants and quickly pulled a tight white jumper over her head before he could return and paw her again.

As he staggered into the room with as much finesse as a warthog, Carrie looked him up and down and wondered what she had ever seen in him in the first place. His hair was an uneven cropped style, which didn't suit him. He looked better with a skinhead, but his mates had grown theirs out, so he'd decided to do the same. And the winter months had taken away his healthy tanned glow, which used to make his eyes stand out. But now his skin was so white, he had this sickly pallor about him. All the drinking and snorting had given him brown rings under his eyes, and now he had cracks at the corners of his mouth, which made her pull away when he tried to kiss her.

Pulling on his jeans, Jimmy slipped his gold chain over his head and then looked under the bed for a top he'd worn yesterday. 'So your farver's moving out today, so me muvver said. His neighbour told her, but it's all hush-hush. In fact, Muvver asked if you knew where they were going. But I said they still weren't talking to you.'

Carrie stood motionless, her mouth wide open.

Finding his T-shirt and putting it on, he then noticed the shock on her face. 'Why do you care? They don't want nuffin to do with you.'

She wanted to cry. 'Are they all moving out?'

He sat on the bed and slipped his socks on. 'Yeah, they've got an exchange.'

'Where to?'

'Like I said, no one fucking knows. They are sly bastards, your family.'

Carrie would have thumped Jimmy for bad-mouthing them, but she was too shocked to think straight. Even though her family had disowned her, she had still felt a little comfort from knowing they were only living up the road. But now finding out that they were moving away – and not even nosy Ginty knowing where – it was definitely a worry.

Then she recalled what Sunny had told her about Dilly grassing Arthur for assaulting her, so maybe the council had offered them an exchange away from here for Dilly's protection. She trembled, and her heart ached. If they moved counties, it was conceivable that she might never see them again. Her baby would never know its grandparents or its aunties.

She slowly walked from the bedroom into the bathroom, where she closed the door behind her. Sitting on the edge of the bath, she placed her hands over her face and sobbed. Deep heart-wrenching sobs.

It had been a martyrish thing to go back to Jimmy to save her sisters, but she had never really given it all that much thought as to how hard it would be. Now, imagining she may never see them again was ripping her in half. She ran her hands over her belly, and for the first time since she discovered she was pregnant, she began to long for this unborn baby. This would be the one thing that she could have as a family: her own blood.

Like so many times when she was thinking about her own baby, her thoughts diverted to Dottie's baby, but she couldn't comprehend why she was drawn to the idea of taking on hers too. Maybe the gift of the beautiful maisonette, the plaque, and the history of the woman who had previously lived there had stirred a spiritual feeling. She'd never believed in omens, but perhaps this was a good one. It just seemed right, somehow.

After drying her eyes, she sauntered back into the bedroom. 'You were so drunk last night that I couldn't tell you that Lenny backhanded me and knocked me down the stairs.'

'I know. Muvver told me.'

'When?'

'I came home just after you went out. She said you got lippy with Lenny. There was a scuffle, and you fell down the stairs. So, I went looking for Lenny. I found him in the pub. He apologised to me, we had a few drinks, and that's why I came home late.'

Carrie shook her head in disgust. 'He apologised to you? But what about me?'

Jimmy threaded the last hole of his Dr Martens. 'He apologised for disrespecting me. You're my wife, not his.'

'Fucking charming!'

'Oh, for fuck's sake, Carrie, what does it matter? You're okay, ain't ya? And anyway, we've got a maisonette to view.'

Ginty leaned into the bedroom, her face beaming. 'Albert's gonna drive us to see this maisonette.'

Carrie rolled her eyes and wished she'd never told Ginty about it. But her mother-in-law, being the interrogator she was, had kept on and on until she had to let her know where she'd been all day. Ginty was good at making her feel like she'd been up to no good – even insinuating that any absence could only be explained by her seeking out other men.

'And if you don't like it, you don't have to accept it.' She went on. 'I know how these council people work. They'll pretend it's your only choice, take it or leave it, but that ain't the case. I know, see.' She gave an attempt at a sympathetic smile. 'It's probably not the right place for you two. You need your family close by. And the other side of the main road is a little too far away. Next door to my brother on the Ramsden estate, there is an empty flat. You can put in a word for that one. There ya go, Jimmy. You could have your Uncle Ernie right on your doorstep.'

Fuming, Carrie couldn't imagine anything worse, but she smiled politely and held up the keys. 'I've already accepted the place, Ginty, and it's not a flat. It's got a garden for the baby. It's better than a flat in a tower block, with pissy lifts and crack addicts for neighbours.'

Ginty stepped inside their bedroom and glared. 'You accepted the place without my Jimmy seeing it?'

'Yep, because it's beautiful. It's got two bedrooms and everything is all done up perfectly. I don't even have to buy a thing for it. The old girl left everything, all pukka stuff, proper nice, and it's done up like new. I've got the keys, and that's that, so you don't need to come with me and Jimmy to help us make a decision because it's already been decided,' Carrie said calmly, anxious not to wind Jimmy up.

Glaring at her son, she replied, 'Well, my boy will want me to see it, won't ya, Jimmy?'

But Carrie got in first. 'No, Ginty, it's mine and Jimmy's flat, and I want it to be just him and me for a while before we invite you over.'

She grinned, knowing it was boiling Ginty's piss. 'And we *will* invite you over. I'll cook a nice dinner, which will be lovely. But I want Jimmy and me to . . . well, you know, make it our own, test out the bed,' she said, knowing that talk of sex would always work on her husband, who was as thick as pig shit.

'Jimmy!' Ginty squawked.

'Nah, Muvver, Carrie's right. Me and her wanna stand on our own two feet, and I wanna see this place. Just me and her.' He winked at Carrie.

'You just think of your dick, Jimmy. You should be thinking of your muvver.'

But Carrie couldn't keep her mouth shut. Laughing, she said, 'Er, his dick and his muvver. A bit weird that, Ginty, if you don't mind me telling ya.'

Ginty flashed a death glare at Carrie. 'Oh, go on then, fuck off, you cheeky mare!' She stormed off and stomped down the stairs.

Carrie listened to her talking quietly to Albert.

'We ain't going now, Albert, so I'll have that three quid back for the petrol.'

***

As Jimmy and Carrie walked across the main road, he couldn't shut up. He was hyper about a job he and his brothers had been planning.

But Carrie wasn't giving him a second's thought; her mind was on her new home until she noticed that Jimmy had stopped talking and looked at her.

'What?' she said, having realised that she'd barely heard a word he said.

'Oh, nuffin,' he replied.

'What were you saying, Jimmy?'

He shook his head. 'Nuffin, it's not important, all right? Shut up about it.'

Carrie knew right then that whatever this grand plan was for him to get his hands on big money, it would involve something she would disapprove of because Jimmy wasn't shy to brag about all his scams and robberies, even if they could be classed as small-time ones. She could have kicked herself for not listening in the first place.

When they reached the maisonette, Jimmy stood with his mouth open. 'And this is ours?'

'Yeah, all ours,' she lied, because it was in her name only, but, then again, he wouldn't know. He could barely read.

As she was about to put the key in the lock, Sunny Murphy came bounding down the steps. His leather jacket was so new, she could smell it, as well as his fresh lemony aftershave. To her, he was the epitome of a young man who was going places. He looked so clean and fresh, his dark hair, with its natural wave, was flicked behind his ears, and his skin glowed an even sun-kissed colour. She wondered if he'd been abroad recently.

'Oi, oi, Sunny, so ya live upstairs, do ya?' asked Jimmy, holding out his hand in a gesture of friendliness.

Sunny paused and looked Jimmy up and down. 'You know fucking better than to ask me about my business.' He looked at Carrie and winked. 'Hello, darling, and how are you?'

Feeling embarrassed, but somewhat flattered, she smiled at him. 'I'm okay, Sunny. We got the keys to this place. Just having a look now.'

'Nice one, Carrie. It's respectable around here.' He looked at Jimmy. 'So don't fucking lower the tone, Jimmy. I don't want all your lot fucking burning out old motors in the street or piling your scrap metal in the drive.'

Jimmy laughed as if Sunny was joking, but he wasn't going to argue because Sunny and his brothers had a serious reputation, and there was no way he could afford to get on the wrong side of them.

As soon as they were inside the maisonette, Carrie expected a backlash from Jimmy, but the surprise of the new place rendered him momentarily speechless.

He was about to walk towards the living room when Carrie said, 'Oi, shoes off. This is our home, a clean home. I don't want no germs and no fucking dirt.'

'It's mine an' all, Carrie, and I'm the man of the house, so—'

'So do the right fucking thing, Jimmy, and keep it clean. Take ya boots off.'

Not wanting to spoil the occasion, Jimmy didn't argue.

Walking from room to room, Jimmy was quiet, taking it all in. Then he sat down, as his wife had done, on the sofa, stroking the velvet. 'Cor, this is nice, Carrie. Like proper nice.'

'I know.'

'But it ain't really us, is it? I mean, who do we know around here?'

Carrie was floored. 'What? You are joking, Jimmy? *Look* at this place. Fucking look at it. It's *ours*. Look at that lovely room for the babies, eh?'

Jimmy slowly turned his head. 'Babies? What? As in two?'

Realising that the word had literally popped out of her mouth, Carrie sat there rigidly, but she nodded. 'Yeah, Jimmy, two.'

'What? Are you having twins?'

'No, I'm not, but, Jimmy, you will have two babies.'

'Oh, not that shit again. I told ya that Dottie's kid ain't mine.'

'Stop it, Jimmy, just stop it. Her baby is yours, so stop lying.' Lowering her voice, she attempted a softer approach. 'I know you lied because you didn't want to rock things between me and you, but look, babe, we're married now. We've got our own home with a garden, so come on, Jimmy, be a man – a real man – and live up to your responsibilities. If Dottie gets a long bird, your baby will end up in the system, and fuck knows who he or she will end up with. That poor baby never asked to be conceived, Jimmy, and my baby will grow up with a brother or sister out there that our one won't even get to know. How fucking sad is that, eh?'

Carrie could see Jimmy's face change as if the penny was finally dropping.

'Jimmy, this baby is *your* baby, like mine is, who just happens to be carried by another woman.'

Jimmy's eyes widened as he pulled out a packet of cigarettes and lit one up.

Carrie wanted to tell him he couldn't smoke indoors, but, instead, she ran to the kitchen and returned with a saucer. 'It's your baby, Jimmy. Do you really want the poor little chavi in the system, no doubt being abused?'

He took a deep drag. 'So you reckon you could cope with two babies, do ya? But what makes you think she would let me have the baby anyway?'

''Cos she's got no one else, and you've got the right. You're the dad.'

Typically, once the burden was taken off his shoulders and passed on to someone else, like Carrie, Jimmy showed his more magnanimous side. He shrugged and said, 'Whatever. If you want another baby to bring up . . .'

'No, not *another* baby! *Your* baby, Jimmy, *our* baby's sibling.'

'Sibling? What the fuck is that?'

Carrie tutted. 'It means brother or sister.'

He shrugged. 'I suppose it's all right.'

'Of course, it's all right, Jimmy.'

'Carrie, she might not want you to raise her child.'

Glaring at him, she hissed, 'And what the fuck is wrong with me?'

He shrugged again. 'I dunno. Well, if you wanna put us forward, like however it works, then it's up to you, 'cos you know us men don't do the feeding and changing shitty nappies.'

Sensing Jimmy was nearly there with her plan, she decided to go for broke and play her ace. 'And, Jimmy, we get extra money for two babies.'

Watching her husband's eyes widen, Carrie sensed victory at last.

'Yeah, we do, don't we. All right, then, it's a deal. Tell her we'll have it.'

'And Jimmy, we'll bring our babies up in this home because you can't deny it is lovely, can ya. And how long did it take us to walk here? Less than half an hour, Jimmy. So, we ain't too far from your muvver.'

He smiled and stubbed his cigarette out. Now, bored with this conversation, he gave her a little wink. 'So shall we try out the bed?'

Feeling her insides turning cold at the thought of sex, she, nevertheless, gave herself credit for getting Jimmy onside. 'So we are gonna keep the maisonette and have Dottie's, I mean your other baby, as well, yeah?'

'Yeah, yeah, come on, let's try out the new bed.'

'Take oath, Jimmy.'

'Yeah, yeah, I take oath, on me muvver's life. Now get your clothes off.'

She wandered into the main bedroom, stripped off, and lay on the bed while he watched her. And the moment he climbed on top, she closed her eyes and imagined Sunny Murphy was there. When she climaxed, she had to bite her bottom lip to stop herself from calling out his name.

CHAPTER TWENTY-FIVE

Two weeks later

Thursday teatime, Dottie was in the middle of reading a book on breastfeeding, when she got a whiff of a warm bread aroma. 'Billy, it's doughnut day.'

Billy slapped the old *Jackie* magazine down and climbed off her bed, but the magazine fell on the floor. 'You love anything sweet. I bet you any money that baby is a boy. See, my baby was a girl and she had me craving for crisps and cheese. I thought I was having a boy, but it turned out the opposite.'

Dottie smoothed out her T-shirt. 'He is getting big now. It feels strange when he moves. It's like I've got a python inside me.'

'Come on, then, let's get those doughnuts. I think Janice and Sonia are saving theirs for you. Sonia's due to see the dentist and Janice is diabetic.'

'That's kind of them, Billy.'

'Kind? Nah, they wanna stay on your good side. Like I said, they are wary of you.'

As they approached the food hall, there was more noise than usual. Billy put it down to being doughnut day, but as soon as they joined the queue, she noticed a few new faces. One she knew well from way back starting from when they both lived in the same neighbourhood.

Candice Shipley was older, louder, and a good four sizes bigger. The top half of her body was huge, but her legs were thin, and to add to her strange appearance, she had a mass of wiry black and grey hair that stuck out in all directions. Deep crow's feet radiated from her eyes, making the creases in her leathery skin more prominent.

As much as she looked to Billy as though she was a complete fuck-up of a woman, Candice was a wily soul. She had practically run the old Holloway in the past. Which is why they had clashed and had a few run-ins.

Candice was not only devious and underhanded but she didn't care if she got sent down the block, and it never bothered her when they added time on to her sentence for her violent antics, including the day she ran a makeshift blade down Billy's spine. She got another five years for that and vowed she'd never forgive Billy because she assumed Billy had grassed. It would have made no difference, however, because she wasn't ever getting parole. Candice only cared about her feral kids. She was as happy as a pig in shit so long as they came on regular visits and were financially sound.

'I can smell the doughnuts, Billy. Doesn't it make your mouth water?'

'Not really,' Billy replied, her mind on Candice, who had not only run the old Holloway before she was shipped up to a prison in the north, but she was the only woman who could put the wind up her.

Deciding not to attract attention, Billy didn't look over at Candice. The last thing she needed was trouble. Everything so far was in place and all geared up to help Dottie when it came to the baby's birth. She couldn't let her down by being locked up in solitary confinement.

As Billy slid her tray along the counter and took the cheese roll handed to her, she heard the heavy breathing sound of a woman behind her.

'Oi, there's a queue,' said Dottie.

Billy froze when she heard Candice's distinctive growly South London accent. 'Don't you *oi* me, you pasty-faced cockroach. Who the fucking hell do you think you're talking to, eh? I'll put you on your arse!'

'You, I'm talking to you. You can't just push in.'

Turning around to shut Dottie up, Billy almost came nose to nose with Candice. Their eyes locked in a shared understanding. But the smile that stretched across Candice's crinkled face signified deep satisfaction, and it prompted Billy to swallow nervously.

Confronted with impending doom, cold perspiration broke out across Billy's forehead, and her skin tightened across her face. Before she could even look down at the woman's hands, she felt the thud, a resounding hard thud between her ribs. Petrified, she stood there in disbelief as Candice sadistically studied her reaction with a predatory unwavering stare. How could she have done it so brazenly in front of everyone? Another thud, this time to her stomach. She looked down and saw the bright-red blood and the weapon that would shortly end her life. It wasn't a two-inch blade. It was like a butcher's knife. Dripping in blood, the knife was too long to be anything but a lethal weapon.

Candice leaned forward. 'You fucked me over in Holloway. I said I'd get you back, and your uncles paid for this, so now, my kiddies will have money. So much fucking money. And now, you can rot in hell, bitch. Two birds, one stone. See you on the other side, you cunt.'

When the knife clanged as it hit the floor, Dottie's eyes were drawn to the noise and right away, she spotted the blade. And as Candice stepped away, Dottie could see the devastation. It took just a second to comprehend what had taken place. She realised that Billy was clutching her stomach, and her light-grey tracksuit was deep red, from the claret, which spread like ripples on a pond.

'Jesus!' The blood was everywhere. 'Noooo, please help!' Dottie looked around and screamed. 'Would someone fucking help!'

But all the women just gathered in a circle, and they watched as Billy staggered gasping and panting involuntarily. Her lips turned grey before she slumped to the floor.

Dottie dropped to her knees and hugged her, rocking back and forth. 'No, Billy! No! Please, Billy, don't leave me. Billy, don't die. You *can't* die, Billy.'

Moving her hands to cradle Billy's head, Dottie screamed at the top of her lungs. 'Someone help me!'

The buzzers sounded, and Officer Knight came flying over. She kneeled beside Dorothy and tried to assess the severity of the situation, but blood was pooling around them on the cold concrete floor.

Another officer came, took one look, and ran to the phone on the wall.

Dottie stared at Officer Knight, her eyes beseeching her. 'Please, please save her.'

Knight lifted Billy's top, but the sight was horrific. The two gruesome wounds were broad and deep, and the blood was gushing out. She couldn't do anything. No amount of pressure was ever going to stop the bleeding.

'Billy, stay with me. Please, you can't die.'

With the blood draining from Billy's face, she opened her eyes and stared at Dottie before whispering, 'Remember what I said.'

Dottie stroked her friend's cheek as Billy's eyes closed for the last time.

Like a wild animal, Dottie threw her head back and let out a blood-curdling scream.

Other officers appeared and ushered the women away from the scene and out of the food hall. They tried to pull Dorothy away as well, but she was so distraught, and her rage had reached a pitch.

She looked at the inmates, who were all being escorted away, except for one. It was the big ugly woman who had killed Billy.

Glaring at Candice, as they locked eyes, Candice suddenly looked away.

'You fucking murdered her, you evil bitch. I'll fucking kill you!'

Officer Knight slapped her hand over Dorothy's mouth. 'Shut up, Ellis, please shut up.' Because she knew that threats like that were recorded and would go on an inmate's record, making parole so much more complex, and she liked Dorothy Ellis.

'She's gone, Ellis. Come on, you have to return to your room. You can't do anything now,' said Knight, as she helped the girl to her feet.

But Dottie was limp with grief as she left the scene. 'She didn't deserve this. She wasn't a bad person. I can't leave her like that. I can't. It's wrong.' She looked back at the prone figure, all alone. 'She was my friend. She was like a sister. She didn't deserve this life.'

Knight slowly walked Dorothy out of the food hall. 'There are many women in here, my love, who don't deserve to be here. It's a cruel world. Let's get you back to your room, get you cleaned up, and I'll bring you a hot chocolate. It's been a shock, and you're having a baby. I think I'll get the nurse to check you over and see if you can have some kind of sedative.'

The room remained as Dottie had left it. The *Jackie* magazine lay on the floor, Billy's nightshirt was folded at the end of her bed, and the dent in her pillow remained.

Knight closed the door. 'Please, Dottie.'

Dottie looked up in shock. The officer had called her by her first name.

'Listen to me, love. You can't grass. Do you understand?'

But Dottie wasn't as naïve as she looked. Billy had taught her about life on the street, how to blag, how to fight, and what grassing could mean to a person. 'I don't care, Miss. That woman killed her in cold blood. Billy didn't stand a chance.'

Knight put her finger over her lips. 'Shush, you can't say anything. Look, you're having a baby. The likes of that Candice will stab you just like she did Billy, baby as well.'

With flared nostrils and harsh breathing, Dottie glared. 'Or I might just kill her first.'

Knight stood up straight, her head slightly turned to the side. 'You're not a killer, Dottie. Please, love, don't act like a psycho. You'll never get out of prison, ever.'

Staring into nothing, her face shaped into the epitome of sadness, Dottie took a few deep breaths. 'What happens now?'

'The police will be called. They'll take statements, but I think considering your condition, it's probably best that you go to medical because you look very pale.'

'Of course I'm pale. It's all been a total shock. I can't get it out of my head.' She suddenly burst into tears.

'I'll fetch a cup of sweet tea.'

Dottie nodded.

'You get into that shower and get cleaned up. It's not good to sit around in clothes with all that blood on them.'

Sitting on her bed, Dottie nodded again and Knight left the room.

The shower in the corner of the room was spotless. Billy liked to ensure their room was germ-free. And Dottie knew that from now on, she would think about Billy in everything she did.

The magazine caught her attention, so she got off her bed and reached down to pick it up. She wanted to see the last thing Billy was reading, but, to her surprise, her friend had left notes on one of the pages. Turning the page to the side, she read the message: **When you get released, go and get that money. It's for you. And don't do anything to get revenge. Go live your life and**

feed the seagulls, and then remember me, but get out of this hellhole first.

Tears fell like waterfalls cascading down Dottie's face. She stripped her clothes off in frustration and stormed over to the shower, and once she had turned it on, she let the fierce spray pummel her head. 'Damn you, Billy. You should never have left me. You should have paid them.' The tears fell like the spray until she felt calm. *But was it the calm before the storm?* she wondered.

Finishing her shower, she hadn't realised that Knight had returned and collected her ruined clothes. And there on the end of her bed was a new set of sweatshirts and joggers, and a mug of sweet tea had been placed on the side table along with her mail. Not bothering to dry herself, she slipped the jogging suit on and lay on her bed.

After a few minutes, Knight returned with a nurse who hardly spoke. She merely took Dorothy's blood pressure, checked her oxygen levels, listened to check the baby was okay, and left.

'Well, she was rude.'

'Dottie, you have to understand that what you have been charged with can put the fear of God in people. Besides, I shouldn't think that new nurse will last five minutes. She's not an ideal candidate for a position in a women's prison.'

'Suppose you're right.'

'Would you like another tea, Dottie?'

'No, I'm fine. Thank you for helping me.'

'Let me give you some advice. I can understand that losing your best friend is hard, especially here, in prison.'

Dottie nodded. 'It's going to be tough, I know that.'

'But you have a baby to think of, so you need to stay healthy and well and protect your child. If I were you, I would stay away from Candice. She's nasty, very violent, and she won't think twice about hurting you or the baby.'

'I get it, Miss, I do. I know Billy wouldn't want me to do anything stupid. Besides, I've got a few seagulls to feed.'

'Pardon?'

'Nothing. I have made a decision about my baby. I want to hand it out as soon as it's born. I don't want to raise it in this place, even though I can only keep it for eighteen months, if they let me, that is.'

Dottie looked down and began picking at the skin around her fingernails. 'The pain of losing someone you love is terrible. I can't get attached to my baby and suffer this pain again.'

Knight smiled gently. 'I hate to tell you this, but it hurts anyway.'

The way Knight spoke to her made Dottie wonder if the officer had given away a child herself.

'I'll get you some more tea – it'll do you a bit of good – as well as a couple of rolls and doughnuts. You must keep up your strength for the baby.'

'Thank you. I do appreciate this, Miss Knight.'

As soon as Knight left the room, Dottie glanced at the mail. She assumed it would be from the solicitor about the trial, but when she saw the handwriting and realised right away it was from Carrie, she quickly ripped the envelope open.

What she read had her heart thumping even faster than it had thirty minutes ago. Carrie and Jimmy were going to ask for custody. At first, she felt elated, but then she felt despondent. For a moment, she wanted to hold on to her baby and never let it go – this child she hadn't even seen, held, or known if it was a boy or a girl. The letter conveyed compassion and understanding. She got a sense of it by reading it multiple times. She opened the drawer, retrieved the writing pad and pen, and wrote back before she changed her mind. She gave Carrie the solicitor's details, and when she placed the letter in the envelope, with Carrie's new address, she hoped that her new-found friend would love her baby just like she would love her own and not favour one over the other.

CHAPTER TWENTY-SIX

Three months later

Jimmy pushed the double buggy back into what would be the baby's bedroom. 'The amount of shit in this place is getting outta hand, Carrie, and I'm done with fucking social services pestering us.'

'Well, they won't anymore. All the checks have been made, so you won't see them again.'

Carrie sat on the sofa fanning her face with an old magazine, while Jimmy stood at the front door dressed in a vest, his shirt tied around his waist, and his best jeans.

As he puffed away on a cigarette, Carrie struggled to bend over and do her shoes up.

He turned his head to see what she was doing and then yelled, 'Hurry up, for fuck's sake! Muvver will be fuming. You know what today is about. She'll be itching to get front-row seats.'

Carrie straightened up and took a few deep breaths because even a small task was hard to complete with a huge bump in the way. She certainly *did* know what today was, and even though the Carsons would be hoping for the best outcome for Arthur, she was hoping for another.

'I can't do everything, like I'm on speed. I'm carrying around this baby, remember.'

Jimmy knew that that was a dig at him for buzzing around at a million miles an hour because he did like his amphetamines, and he was also partial to the odd line of cocaine if it was on offer. And, lately, he had been snorting a lot. 'Just hurry up.'

Finally, Carrie was ready, and she waddled out of the front door and felt the warm breeze on her face. 'I hope it's not going to get any hotter. I can barely cope as it is.'

'Carrie, anyone would think you were the first woman to have a baby. My muvver said I slid out. She didn't even know she was pregnant with me.'

'Yeah, well, that's because she's so fat.'

'What did you say?'

'Nuffin, Jimmy.' She waved her hands. 'Don't blow smoke near me. It makes me feel sick.'

A souped-up Ford Escort XR3 pulled into the drive, forcing Jimmy to jump out of the way. He was about to give the driver a mouthful when Sunny jumped out of the car. 'Morning, Carrie, how you doing, love?'

Carrie hadn't seen Sunny in ages, and he looked more handsome than ever. His face was tanned, and his eyes sparkled. She felt dowdy in her maternity dress, which made her look larger than she actually was.

'Getting big, now, Sunny.'

'Nice set of wheels you have there, Sunny. Nick 'em, did ya?' said Jimmy, laughing it off as a joke.

'Now, tell me, Jimmy, why would I need to steal a car? When *I* can fucking afford one.' He stepped back and grinned. 'Off to court, Jimmy, to see your brother go down?' He shook his head with a smile on his face. 'They'll throw away the key, with a bit of luck.'

Jimmy clicked his jaw from side to side because he felt so uncomfortable. He couldn't argue with Sunny because he would get his head caved in; yet he was struggling to keep his mouth shut. 'Let's see how the judge views it.'

Sunny's smile evaporated, and his eyes darkened as he stepped closer and pointed a finger. 'Your cunting brother nearly killed Dilly. He tried to *rape* the girl. And as you fucking know, my brother Toby was engaged to her, and he would be turning in his grave if he thought for one minute his brothers weren't looking out for her, so, numbnuts, be careful what you say. And if I hear you ever say your brother doesn't deserve bird, then I'll rip your fucking tongue out.' He looked at Carrie. 'I know how you must be feeling, Carrie, but I bet your husband hasn't got a clue how this affects you.' He turned back to Jimmy. 'Or you know and you couldn't give a flying shit.'

Jimmy stared at Sunny, unable to respond, for fear of his backlash.

'You should think yourself lucky you have a girl like Carrie. You should be on her family's side, not those fuckwit brothers of yours. But, then again, all you Carsons are nothing but scroungers – sly fucking devious little mouthy shits.'

Carrie couldn't believe that Jimmy was standing there looking so gormless. She was more embarrassed because she was married to him. *If only it had been Sunny or any one of the Murphys that she had walked up the aisle with.* In fact, she couldn't think of one she would kick out of bed. As beads of sweat tickled the sides of her face, she quickly wiped them away.

Sunny offered her his most sympathetic smile. 'Bye, Carrie. I hope it all goes well in court. My brothers will be there.' He flashed a warning smile at Jimmy. 'I just might join them.'

'Your brothers? Why?'

'Ha, didn't you know? My brother Dylon is with Mary now, and, of course, Mary and Rosie will be there supporting Dilly. And my brother James is looking after Dilly these days.'

Even Carrie didn't know that Mary was with Dylon. She was pleased for her, though. And she now knew why Albert, Lenny, and Zachariah were spending so much time together moaning, groaning, and gossiping, and doing it behind her back.

'Gotta go, Carrie, I've got a meeting with Spud.'

Jimmy's eyes widened, and his throat felt like it was closing up. 'Spud?' he asked, nervously. 'How's he doing?'

Sunny's jaw shot forward, but he reined in his anger and substituted it with a smile. 'Spud is doing okay.' He winked. 'But we know what you and your brothers did, Jimmy.'

'What? I never—'

Sunny stepped closer, and then Jimmy clocked the golf club in his hand. 'What? Did you think Spud had lost his fucking memory?'

Jimmy's eyes were glued to the golf club. 'No, but it wasn't me.'

'D'ya know what, Jimmy, you talk the talk, but you can't walk the walk, can ya. Well, your card is marked, and one day, boy, your nasty ways will come back to bite your scrawny arse. The only reason you haven't been scraped up off the pavement with a shovel is because you're with Carrie.' He looked once more at Carrie before he stormed past and ran up the concrete steps to his maisonette.

Stubbing his cigarette out, Jimmy stomped on towards his mother's house in silence, until Carrie said, 'So Mary is with Dylon Murphy. That's news.'

Jimmy stopped dead and spun around, grabbing her arms. 'You think this is a fucking game, don't ya. Look at you, fucking flirting with that wanker.' His mouth twisted into a nasty sneer. 'Everything that's happened is all your fucking fault in the first place.'

'*Me?*' she said, trying to shake him off.

'Yeah, fucking you! Dilly was getting it on with Arthur, and you, who thinks she's Superwoman, attacked him with that shovel.'

'He was gonna rape me sister!' she snapped back.

But having been so totally humiliated by Sunny, Jimmy was in a vile temper. 'And you told your farver, and he had to get involved, didn't he! He ruined our fucking wedding and caused a riot. My bruvver was only defending himself against your farver when Silly Billy Dilly got in the way. But it started, Carrie, with you.' He poked her in the chest. 'You shouldn't go around acting like you're hard, like a man, 'cos you ain't hard. You're to blame for what happened to the silly tart. You're married now, so act like a wife and not some hard geezer.'

Those words had Carrie boiling. 'Hard? Fucking hard? Look at ya, you pissed your pants when Sunny had a go at ya. It was fucking embarrassing.'

Not having thought through the consequences of her words, she never expected her own husband to take his anger out on her. He pulled his head back, and without any hesitation whatsoever, he butted her hard across the bridge of her nose.

Carrie was completely stunned. Her eyes watered, her nose began to bleed, and she stumbled about dazed.

But Jimmy just stared at her as if he was about to hit her again. 'The Murphys ain't so hard, the wankers.' Then he gave a little chuckle and mumbled under his breath, 'They ain't that hard. Toby didn't fight back.'

No matter how quiet he thought his voice was, behind his clenched teeth, Carrie still heard those words. It wasn't a delusional thought. Oh no, she heard them all right.

Still reeling from the assault, Carrie gripped the nearest thing she could see. It was a hedge, and she almost fell through it, but she managed to steady herself just in time. Feeling the lump on her nose, she wiped the blood away with the back of her hand. 'You fucking bully, I won't fight you back, Jimmy, because I'm pregnant, but you shouldn't have done that to me.'

He pulled a handkerchief from his trouser pocket and handed it to her. 'Just get a move on. I ain't gonna be late because I'm rowing with you. You need to stop pushing my fucking buttons.'

Accepting the handkerchief, Carrie stared at him in disgust. It was not because he'd hit her – because she would get her own back – but because the mystery surrounding Toby's death may now have been confessed by her daft husband. She now had knowledge that would cause a war between the Carsons and the Murphys. She decided not to challenge him on it. For now. She couldn't give him any reason to wonder if she had heard him.

The intensity of the sun beating down made her head pound, and it was made worse by the crack on the nose. She knew Jimmy wouldn't feel even an ounce of guilt. She now wondered if he was more worried about how he came across to others; he certainly didn't show any concern for her wellbeing.

Her mind was on seeing her family again, not the case itself. It had been months, and she missed them dreadfully, especially her dad. And as she stared at her husband, who was now charging towards the main road, she wondered why, as Sunny had said, he hadn't considered how she felt about the court case. But, then again, Jimmy had clearly blamed her for the whole incident. Maybe it *was* her fault in some respects. If only she hadn't gone back to Jimmy. But it was all because she had been jealous, and she had wanted to test the water to see if he would come flying back to her. The jealous feeling was a moment of madness, and, worse, short-lived. However, the consequences of her actions were life changing for everyone.

Her thoughts turned to Dottie. Poor Dottie. She may not have done what she did to her parents if Jimmy hadn't dumped her.

Carrie wanted to cry but she knew she wouldn't stop if she started.

'Hurry up, for fuck's sake. Muvver will be spitting feathers if we miss the case. We have to show that we're supporting our Arthur. Now, fucking move it.' He stopped and stared at her disapprovingly. 'And wipe that blood off your chin.'

Carrie spat on the handkerchief and rubbed her chin. Her nose had stopped bleeding, although it was still pounding, and the pain was now behind her eyes as well.

***

Three old bangers were parked outside Ginty's house. There she was, hollering and hooting at people. 'Albert, you drive Lenny and Zachariah.' She suddenly stopped when she saw Carrie and Jimmy. 'About time. On me muvver's grave, Jimmy boy, if we miss the trial, I'll string you up.' She glared at Carrie. 'I bet it was your fault, fussing over how you look. It ain't a fashion show, ya know. This is my boy's life we're worrying about.'

Carrie could have said so much in retaliation, but she bit her lip.

'Uncle Rooster, you take Jimmy and his wife,' Ginty said, clearly enunciating the word wife.

***

By the time they reached the court, Carrie was ready to vomit. Rooster was hardly the best driver. He drove on his brakes and sped around the bends.

Jimmy didn't even bother to open the door for her. But Rooster did. At least he had some decency.

Getting out of the car, Carrie took a few deep breaths. Her heart was in her mouth when she saw her father outside the courts. He was with his brother Jack and also James Murphy. Gripped by an incredible urge to run to her father and fling her arms around him, she held herself back and hoped he would come to her.

Her father looked over as car doors from the Carson entourage opened and shut.

Her eyes instantly filled up when he glanced at her.

'Dad,' she whispered, as waves of emotion crashed over her. But at that moment, she knew he was hurt. There was no beaming smile that made his cheeks flush red and his eyes sparkle. His face fell into sadness, his eyes were cast down, and it was as if he had aged so much. 'Oh, Dad,' she whispered again, but as he looked away, she felt the sobs building up in her chest, and she fruitlessly battled with them until the tears fell like waterfalls, and her heart ached like never before, knowing that a few feet away were her family, and yet she couldn't join them. It seemed that she had lost them for good. If only they knew that she had done this because she thought she was saving them.

Suddenly, Ginty, who was marching on ahead, stopped when she obviously realised that James Murphy was there. She turned and faced Albert, Zachariah, Lenny, and Jimmy. 'Listen, we'll wait until they go in. I don't want no fight outside the court. I can't have another son in prison. Do you hear me?'

Carrie looked at the men, who were all nodding like schoolkids.

But when Ginty glanced her way with a clear mood shift, Carrie felt uneasy. She didn't like the way Ginty wore that satisfied grin.

'You, Carrie, will walk with me. You're a Carson now, and I want them to see you are on our side. You need to be supporting your husband. That's how it is now, so no fucking talking to them. Not that they will anyway, but don't you go and show us up by trying to worm your way back into their lives.'

The very thought twisted Carrie's gut and made her want to gouge out Ginty's eyes. 'I think I should wait outside.'

Ginty snatched her arm. 'You fucking won't. You will show them that we are a united family. We stick together.' She tutted loudly. 'And wipe your face. You look a mess.'

Lenny and Albert lit cigarettes and called Zachariah over. They huddled together, whispering. But that wasn't new. They were always whispering, planning, and scheming.

Jimmy looked over a few times before joining them, leaving Carrie with Rooster, Ginty, and two of Ginty's brothers she had never met.

The loud noise from a car exhaust and the high-pitched scream from the powerful engine had all the Carsons rubbernecking.

Carrie recognised the first driver who pulled up. It was Sunny, but the second driver, in a brand-new BMW 323i in

Henna Red – no less – was someone she couldn't quickly put a name to. That was until the man got out. It was Dylon Murphy, James and Sunny's brother. He was another tall, dark, handsome man.

When Dylon opened the passenger door, Carrie, just for a second, didn't recognise her own sister. She looked so well. Her face was tanned, her clothes were tailored, and her hair appeared thick and shiny. But what struck her the most was how alive Mary looked; her eyes were wide, and she walked with her head up, unlike when she'd been married to Lenny.

Sunny was with another man. Again, at first, Carrie couldn't place who it was at first, until he got closer, and then, she gasped. It was Spud.

Gutted that her family had to all intents and purposes blanked her, she felt so alone.

But when Carrie looked over at her mother-in-law, she took a crumb of comfort from the fact that they had probably done so more out of spite of Ginty.

She had her arms crossed, glaring defiantly with a sense of self-satisfaction on her spiteful fat face.

With her whole body trembling, Carrie felt rooted to the spot until Ginty snatched her arm. 'Come on, we're going in.' She waved her hand to her family, and they all marched towards the courts.

Inside, it was a hive of activity, with people walking to various hubs of the courthouse. Arthur's case was in courtroom two, and so they were advised to go to the waiting area just outside, which was a long wide corridor with about twenty seats bolted to the floor.

Carrie couldn't look up. She couldn't bear to see her family snub her. It was hard enough feeling her father's dismissal – just in his expression – but having to witness the rejection from all of them was cutting her in half. Expecting a backlash, or at least some mudslinging, there was nothing like that at all. It was the deafening silence, the perception of being not only snubbed but banished from a warm loving family – who had always stuck together through thick and thin – until now – that crippled her.

Slowly, she looked up to find all her family facing the other way; not one of them was facing the Carsons. She saw her mum being comforted by Rosie, and Dylon had his arm around Mary. Her father and his brother were staring out of the window. Meanwhile, Spud was seated at the end of the row with James.

Dilly wasn't present, but, then again, thought Carrie, *she wouldn't be there because she would be the main witness.*

Carrie wanted so badly to go to them. And she wanted to say to Spud how sorry she was. When he turned his head slightly, she could see the deep thick red scar that ran from his temple to the corner of his eye.

Now feeling even sicker, Carrie's head was pounding, her neck was burning, and she realised that if she didn't get to a toilet this very minute, she would spew her guts out everywhere.

Rising quickly from her seat, she turned to head to the ladies' room, but Ginty snatched her wrist and savagely pulled her back. 'Sit ya arse down,' she growled, under her breath.

'I feel so ill, I'm gonna puke.'

Ginty let go of her wrist. 'You come straight back.'

Carrie genuinely knew she *was* going to be sick. She tried her best to get to the door, but her legs unexpectedly felt like lead, her head spun, her skin felt as though it was on fire, and the room began to cave in before she dropped to the floor.

Jimmy, though, was too engrossed to notice that his wife had fainted. He was far too busy whispering secrets to his brothers.

It was left to Sunny, who was coming through the main doors, who spotted Carrie and instantly rushed to her side, saying, 'Hey, get an ambulance! Carrie has collapsed!'

Jimmy spun around, jumped up from his chair, and hurried over. But it wasn't out of compassion from a chivalrous husband.

It was more a case of being angry that Sunny had beaten him to it, and he had his wife – his prized possession – in his arms.

Jed, who had been gazing over into oblivion up to this point, heard Sunny, and, at that moment, putting all his pride behind him, he hurried over to his daughter.

But Jimmy stood in his way. 'Fuck off, Jed. She's my wife. Leave her to me.'

Hearing all of the commotion, Ginty was out of her chair and standing aggressively by her son's side. 'None of you wanted to know her. Now, go on, leave her alone. She doesn't want to be part of your family. I thought that was obvious.'

Jed glared at every Carson before Luanne pulled him away.

'Don't start. Not here, Jed,' she said, having seen Carrie come round. Assuming that her daughter was feeling faint because she was pregnant, Luanne felt reassured that Sunny was helping Carrie to her feet and guiding her to a chair.

But before Sunny had taken two steps, he stopped and glared at Jimmy. 'How did she get that bump on her nose? 'Cos it fucking wasn't there this morning.'

Ginty moved forward in front of Jimmy. 'That's the man's wife you're talking about. It was an accident, so best you back off and mind ya own business.'

Ignoring Ginty's threatening undertones, Mary had her arm around Carrie's shoulders. 'Are you all right, Carrie girl?'

'And you can piss off, an' all,' said Lenny, with his fists balled by his sides and his face tight with rage.

But Dylon, who was a good two feet taller, said, 'Talk to my fiancée like that again, and you will have a quick fucking course in sky diving.'

'She's my wife.'

'You thick cunt, a court official served you with the divorce papers. Which means you are *not* married.'

Carrie stopped the row from breaking into a fight. 'I'm fine, Mary, thank you,' she said, looking up through her long black eyelashes.

Mary nodded and headed over to her family just before the usher announced the court would be in session.

As the rest of them surged into the gallery, Carrie managed to slip away to the toilets. Once inside, she took a few deep breaths and sobbed her heart out. Unaware that her father had tried to come to her aid – that he did care – she was pleased that Mary had. She suspected that that was because she had suffered the most at the Carson family's hands – apart from Dilly – so she would understand what it was like.

Splashing her face with cold water, Carrie looked in the mirror and noticed that her eyes were now showing signs of bruising and the lump on her nose was beginning to be more prominent. More tears fell as she felt sorry for herself.

However, the sudden arrival of footsteps approaching the ladies' toilets had Carrie quickly drying her eyes.

To her utter shock, she saw Spud enter the room. His shoulders dropped as he tilted his head to the side in a sympathetic stance. 'Carrie, oh Carrie, look at you. Come here,' he said, as he held open his arms. 'Come here, girl.'

She literally fell towards him, allowing his massive, beefy arms to hold her tight. His embrace was more loving than she'd ever had from Jimmy, which reduced her to a quivering wreck. 'Oh, Spud, what have I done? What have I done? I thought you didn't want to ever have anything to do with me. And I've lost me family and . . . and . . .'

'Hey, listen, Carrie, you *haven't* lost them. I saw your mum's and dad's faces when you collapsed. They were frightened to death. Look, Carrie, they are hurt, but they still love you.'

'If I wasn't pregnant, I'd have fucked off miles away from those poxy Carsons.'

She stared at the scars on his face, and her guilt hung heavy like a lead brick sitting on her chest.

'Carrie, leave him. You can live at mine. I've got a nice place. Just leave him.'

'Me and you . . .'

'No, no, Carrie, I don't mean *us*. I mean as friends. Christ, it's not always about sex. Just leave.'

She searched his eyes to see the depth of his friendship. 'Spud, I can't leave him, not just yet, not till the babies are born.'

He looked down. 'You're having twins?'

'No, we are having this one and Dottie Ellis's baby, which also happens to be Jimmy's.'

'What? And he's making you raise another woman's baby an' all?'

She shook her head before he dabbed her damp cheeks. 'No, it's my idea. I want my baby to have a sibling, not for my friend's baby – Dottie Ellis's – to be sent from pillar to post around the countryside with no family, so, as I said, it was all my idea, and I need it to happen before I can fuck that cunt off.'

Spud smiled as he stared almost lovingly into her eyes. 'You amaze me, Carrie-Ann. You really do amaze me. What a woman, eh. Don't worry, I understand.'

She put her finger to her lips.

'I know, Carrie, I get it. I swear to you, I am the one person you can trust. I guess it takes someone as mad as me to get it.'

As they left the ladies' toilets, Spud let go of her. 'I am always here for you, Carrie, and believe it or not, so is your family. You let me know when, and I'll be there.' He winked before he left the courthouse.

Despite the case being in session, Carrie made the decision to wait outside. Her mind was still all over the place.

CHAPTER TWENTY-SEVEN

It took only two hours before the jury returned with a verdict, but Carrie wasn't there to witness it, which she regretted. She had prayed, though, that Arthur would get 'lifed off' because the terror in her sister's eyes that night still haunted her. She had waited outside the courts on the stone steps to breathe in the fresh air and to be away from the Carsons. But not just them. She wanted to be away from her own family as well; it was simply too hard to deal with the pain of rejection, otherwise.

Her two hours of peace were up when she heard the Carsons swearing and shouting and Albert being escorted from the courts by two security guards.

Then she caught sight of her father. He didn't look at all elated despite receiving some justice for the injuries sustained to Dilly. His eyes were drawn down at the sides. Perhaps all this emotional turbulence had taken its toll on him.

Attempting to rise to her feet, she winced and leaned against the wall, still feeling a little unsteady. Then she saw James guiding Dilly, and it was evident that he was more than looking out for her. The way he had his arm around her, it said it all, really.

When Dilly suddenly clapped eyes on her sister, she paused momentarily, giving Carrie a second of hope, but then she dismissively looked away. It was James who winked and mouthed the words *it will be okay*.

Carrie didn't move. She waited as her family walked down the steps past her. Her father came so close, and her eyes naturally followed him. Then, he put his hand on her shoulder. She so desperately wanted him to hug her, but even when he didn't, the mere fact that he had touched her made her believe he still loved her.

'Take care, my baby girl,' he whispered, as he continued walking.

'Dad?' she said, but he glanced back and said, 'No, love.'

Ginty came clambering down the steps like a hippo in stilettos. 'Get in the motor, Carrie. You could have supported me.'

Jimmy gripped Carrie's arm as though she was being arrested, and he marched her to Rooster's car. Ginty climbed into the front, and Rooster was off before she had even slammed the door shut.

Absolutely seething, Ginty craned her body around to face Carrie. 'You fucking let me down, hiding outside the courts like a coward, instead of showing me your support and standing by my side. My only daughter-in-law, and where was she? Hey? Fucking hiding! You should be ashamed of yourself. I won't forget this, Carrie-Ann.'

Carrie knew then that the outcome for Arthur had been bad. Yet, it seemed, the Carsons could only take their anger out on her – only her.

At that moment, suffering Ginty's rant, all Carrie could see was an oversized black caterpillar with rotten teeth and a fucked-up perm. But she paid no attention to her mother-in-law. Her mind was on her family and how well they looked, except for her mum and dad. They seemed drawn and tired. *Had she sucked the happiness right out of them?*

'Rooster, do you mind taking me home?' asked Carrie, feeling brave.

'No, he won't be driving you home,' said Ginty, turning her head again to face Carrie. 'We have a family meeting to discuss an appeal. That's what his brief said, and that's what we're gonna do. And you, Carrie, will be the miracle he fucking needs. I mean, what kind of judge gives a sentence like that? Eighteen fucking years? That's more than life.' She spun back to face the windscreen and lit a cigarette, forcing Carrie to practically hang her head out of the window, like the family pet.

It couldn't have been a better outcome, she thought. With glee in her heart, she was thrilled that the full-sized garden gnome had gotten his comeuppance.

'You are gonna tell the court that Arthur and Dilly were dating. They just had a tiff.'

Carrie's eyes nearly bulged out of her head. '*A tiff?* He fucking put a shovel in her shoulder. She nearly lost her arm and her life.'

Ginty spun her head around once again to face Carrie, this time as though she was possessed by a demon. Her eyes were red and her face looked just like a beetroot. Carrie expected to see smoke coming out of her ears at any moment.

'Are you fucking telling me you would let my son rot in prison for eighteen years?'

Carrie felt Jimmy dig his nails into her arm, letting her know he wasn't messing about. She could feel her skin tearing as though she was being bitten by a Jack Russell. But she didn't know what to say. How could she agree?

'Jimmy, you're hurting me. Get off.'

Ginty looked at Carrie's arm and grinned.

Carrie followed her gaze and looked down. To her horror, she could see the deep marks and the blood running out. In an attempt to pull her arm away, she was stymied by her husband, who gripped it even tighter.

'What do you say?' he said, with a hateful, cold tone in his voice.

'Let's see what the solicitor has to say, shall we.'

Unsure what that meant, Jimmy let go, and that's when Carrie saw the extent of the savage claw marks. As she trembled with the pain, she looked up.

Ginty's smug, satisfied expression said it all.

'I'm sorry, Ginty, it must be hard. I wish I could have been there for you, but I felt really sick. Anyway, let's see what we can do because eighteen years is a long time.'

Ginty frowned and wondered if Carrie was being serious or winding her up.

'So you've had a change of heart, then, 'ave ya?'

Carrie shrugged. 'My family don't want me, so yeah, I guess I am a Carson through and through.'

***

Ginty had laid the dining room table with rolls and synthetic cream cakes that Carrie never liked, but she nibbled at a ham roll. Meanwhile, the boys were outside in the garden, having greedily stuffed their ugly faces, and they were now supping cans of beer and smoking joints.

'So I guess if it's a boy, you're gonna call him Jimmy?'

Carrie smiled. There was no way the baby would be named Jimmy.

'Not sure yet. Maybe. It would be nice if the baby's name matched Dottie's baby's name.'

'Fuck me, she could call it Tarquin.'

Carrie nodded and laughed. 'As long as it's healthy, she can call it 'fuckwit' for all I care. At least the babies will have each other.'

Ginty's eye twitched. 'You're mad.'

'No, not really, Ginty. I'm just doing right by Jimmy's babies.'

'You must love him.'

Ginty's calm voice, devoid of the usual venom, shocked Carrie.

'Oh, I do, Ginty. I do love Jimmy.'

Carrie smiled sweetly, and then as she gazed out of the window at her husband, she imagined where she would place the knife in his back.

Once the ham rolls were eaten, Carrie got up and took the dishes to the kitchen. She washed them up and called out, offering to make Ginty a tea or a stiff drink.

'I think I need a brandy. Seeing my dear Arthur's face like that has knocked me sideways.'

'Yeah, you sit there. I'll do you one.'

When she opened the drinks cupboard, she spotted three bottles of brandy, two bottles of vodka, and a half-empty bottle of sherry. At the very back was a bottle of whisky. Yet when she pulled out the dusty bottle, she spotted something gold at the back of the cupboard. Checking no one was watching her, she slid her hand inside and retrieved the object. It was a very expensive gold watch. Her first thought was that it belonged to Jimmy's father, but, oddly, it felt familiar. However, when she turned it over and read the engraving, she almost dropped it on the floor. She blinked to clear her vision and had to reread the words. With her hands shaking, she slid the watch back into the cupboard, but, in the process, she knocked a bottle of vodka on the floor, where it made a hell of a racket.

Albert and Lenny came barging in through the back door, looking at her startled.

'What the hell are you doing in there?' shouted Albert, as he pushed Carrie aside before gawping into the cupboard.

Fortunately, Carrie had had the presence of mind to push the watch back behind the old whisky bottle, so when Albert looked, the watch wasn't visible.

He glanced back at Lenny, who seemed more than uneasy. He looked ready to throw up.

'Why have you got the bottles out? What are you doing nosing around, eh?' he hissed.

‘Carrie, where’s me drink! I hope you ain’t dropped the bottle of brandy,’ Ginty hooted.

Carrie glared back at Albert with an exaggerated frown. ‘I was getting your muvver a drink.’

‘Carrie?’ Ginty yelled.

‘I’m coming. Sorry, I dropped the vodka bottle, but it ain’t smashed,’ she said, as she quickly grabbed a glass from the draining board and poured a generous shot. She glared at Albert. ‘Why would I be nosing around in a kitchen cabinet? Fucking hell, Albert, does it look like I can even fucking drink?’ She stroked her bump. ‘I’m hardly gonna chore the booze, am I?’

‘Suppose not. Anyway, Muvver’s calling.’ He nodded for her to leave.

‘Bloody hell, what are you trying to do? Get me drunk?’ said Ginty, as she eyed the generous amount in the glass in Carrie’s hand.

Carrie leaned forward to remove the glass. ‘I’ll pour some back.’

‘No, you won’t. Leave it alone. I’ll tell you what: why don’t you put some music on, call the lads in, and see if they want a good drink, will ya? I know my boys like a brandy.’

Carrie knew they did too, but the more drunk they got, the more aggressive and argumentative they were likely to be, and since the slating of her parents and sisters was on their tongues now, she knew it would only get worse, and they would aim their anger at her. And she knew damn well that if Jimmy was drinking, which was often on Sundays after dinner at Ginty’s, then they would have to stay the night, and she hated every bit of it. She loved her maisonette and felt dirty when she stayed at Ginty’s. The bedding was never changed and it smelled of wet dogs. She liked to be the queen of her own castle, not the lady-in-waiting at Ginty’s. Still, she didn’t want to upset anyone, not now, not after what she had seen. The thought terrified her.

But she had a plan. She smiled and winked before she returned to the kitchen, grabbed the bottle of brandy, and placed it on the coffee table. 'The boys are outside drinking beers. How about it be just me and you, 'cos me muvver's not around to tell me what it's like giving birth, so I thought you might like to give me some advice.'

Instantly, Ginty's eyes lit up. Pouring another shot of brandy, she shuffled in her seat until she was comfortable and took a big gulp before going into a long and tedious story of how she went through each pregnancy. And how she was the best mother there ever was, describing how white her nappies were hanging on the line and how the women in the street admired the way she raised her babies.

Ultimately, Carrie realised she was talking about herself and what a wonderful mother and mother-in-law she was. However, she decided to nod, smile, and praise her because the only way she could protect herself from the Carson men was through this mouthy violent bitch of a mother-in-law.

It was plain that Jimmy didn't care about her. He hated the fact that she wasn't so sexy anymore with the big bump in the way. Which suited her. But even living with him was unbearable. He had now turned violent. Which was evident from the bump on her nose, which had led to her having two black eyes now, and the vicious claw mark on her arm.

Albert's expression of suspicion kept playing out in her mind. *Did he know that she'd seen that watch?* If he did, he could do something stupid. He was the one man she trusted the least.

With her legs curled under her on the sofa, in the most relaxed pose she could muster, she continued to listen to Ginty, whose words were now a little slurred and whose descriptions were exaggerated to the point where she had a completely fictional storyline going on in her head.

Albert came into the living room and looked at Carrie. Nothing was said until he turned to Ginty. 'All right, Muvver?'

Ginty nodded. 'I am having a good talk with my daughter-in-law about women's stuff, so fuck off, Albert. In fact, bring in another bottle of that brandy and leave us to it.'

Albert looked back at Carrie, who smiled, but it was not her usual sarcastic smile.

'Do you want a drink, Carrie?'

'No, I can't, 'cos of the baby, or I would. You know me, Albert.'

He shifted from one foot to the other. 'Actually, Carrie, I don't fucking know you at all. You're just Jimmy's wife who strangely wants to raise his two kids and one might not even be his. It's all fucked up to me.'

'Oi, shut that bloody great mooi of yours, Albert. If me daughter-in-law wants to do the kind thing and take on Jimmy's other baby, then I take me hat off to her. It makes her a real woman, in my eyes.'

'I'll get that brandy.' About to walk away, he glared at Carrie. 'I'm watching you.'

'Oi, leave the girl alone. Go on wiv ya, and get me that bottle.'

But Albert nodded slowly, letting Carrie know he had his eyes on her.

Ginty began fanning herself. 'Cor, Carrie, open the window, will ya. I feel as hot as Satan's bollocks.'

Once Albert returned with the bottle of brandy, and he had left the house to rejoin his brothers, Carrie edged her way off the sunken sofa and waddled to the window overlooking the back garden. All the brothers had congregated by the shed at the end of the overgrown scruffy plot, which was dotted with old tyres, dog cages, an old sofa, and one half of a scrap metal container.

Albert was talking while the others gathered around. He was aminated, and yet the others weren't joining in as though they were having a laugh, even though they all had beers in their hands. She stared for a moment at Jimmy, who was so attentive.

He was nodding, acknowledging everything Albert was saying. Then, Albert took the keys out of his pocket and began unlocking all the padlocks that locked the shed.

When he suddenly looked back at the house, Carrie almost jumped. She knew the instant their eyes connected, he was angry. He turned his attention back to his brothers. He obviously gave Jimmy an order because her husband was now stomping towards the house.

Carrie pushed the window wide open and hurried back to her seat.

While Ginty was pouring another drink, Jimmy burst into the room and hollered, 'Carrie, what the fuck are you doing watching us through the window, eh? We're having a men's meeting, you nosy bitch. Albert just said—'

'Now, hold on a minute. Carrie's been talking with me. I asked her to open the window, so, ya lairy prick, she ain't been watching you. And what makes you so special, anyway?'

Jimmy looked from Carrie back to his mother. 'She was staring out the window, Muvver, and we're having a men's meeting, not for her ears.'

Ginty roared with laughter. 'A men's meeting? Oh dear! So what are you doing there, then, eh? For Gawd's sake, Jimmy, grow a pair, will ya, and start defending your missus. She was opening the window for me, so reel in your scrawny neck and apologise.'

Jimmy's eyes moved like a ferret's, and his lips tightened in annoyance. 'I'm not apologising to me own fucking wife. You were staring out the window, Carrie. I saw you.'

Carrie rolled her eyes. 'Jimmy, I was struggling with the lock. I don't care what you men talk about. I am going to be a muvver soon enough, right? Do you think I care what dodgy shit you get up to, eh?'

Jimmy looked nervously at his mother, expecting another backlash.

'Go on, Jimmy, run along. I'm talking to Carrie, and you are ruining it.'

As soon as he left the room, Ginty waved her hand. 'He has always been the same. He wants to be like his big bruvvers, and no doubt he will be, but he needs to grow up before they let him loose with any ideas that will make them serious money.' She winked and tapped the side of her nose. 'But, listen to this. Albert has been bringing him into the fold for a special job they've got coming up. That takes brains. And my boys have business heads on their shoulders. This will make 'em a mint.'

Carrie could tell that Ginty's tongue was loosening because she was speaking so freely and evidently feeling thoroughly safe in her daughter-in-law's company to do so.

Wanting to know more, Carrie said, 'I know. Jimmy was telling me the other night. I'm excited for them, and I hope it makes them a lot of money for all of us.'

Ginty rubbed her hands together. 'Yep, and I'll get my cut.' She laughed. 'I mean, I'm risking me own liberty. If they get caught, the filth could do me for . . . harbouring . . . No, I don't mean that. I mean . . . What's the word?'

Carrie was on the edge of the sofa, leaning forward, hoping that Ginty would spill the beans. 'Harbouring stolen goods?'

'No, not goods. What's it . . . when it's a . . . person, er?'

It was obvious that Ginty was slurring her words. It took all of Carrie's strength not to gasp. She had to extract the information without sounding like she was fishing. The way the boys were huddled around the shed and the number of padlocks used to secure it made her wonder if what she had seen and what Ginty was saying were connected.

'Yeah, and it's your shed.'

She put the bait out there, hoping to reel Ginty in, but she knew it was a risk. If she got it all wrong, Ginty would know she was digging for information.

The fresh air coming in through the open window had an effect and Ginty's head fell back against the armchair. With her eyes closed, she nodded. 'Ahh, Carrie girl . . . you're a good daughter-in-law . . . Ya know that . . . I knew you'd be a good 'un.'

Carrie stared and realised that Ginty had fallen into a drunken stupor, but not before her mother-in-law said, 'And we'll be rich . . . proper rich . . . Those greedy pricks will have to share some of their money soon enough . . .'

Trying to put everything she heard together, Carrie felt sick with unease. Today had been a day that she had learned so much, and now she needed to be alone to process it all. And to try to marshal her thoughts as to what to do next. Surely, the Carsons weren't now crossing into a crime that they weren't bred for, were they? The Carsons had always been chancers. They had never carried out a crime that took a clever execution.

Looking at her watch, she left Ginty to sleep in the armchair and called from the back door. 'Jimmy, I'm heading home.'

But Jimmy was so engrossed in the conversation, so desperate to be part of the Carson gang, that he waved his hand dismissively.

'I'll leave the keys under the stone, Jimmy.'

'Yeah, yeah!' he yelled back, again dismissively.

It pleased her. She hated him being around, anyway.

Slowly, creeping out of the house, Carrie was desperate not to wake Ginty. Quietly, she closed the front door behind her. As she walked along the path, she noticed something that immediately caught her eye. It was her old dressing gown that she had left at her parents' home. She pulled it out of the bin and saw the wrapping paper underneath. She knew it had been sent by Dilly because she always used that particular floral paper.

Pulling the dressing gown over her injured arm, Carrie rubbed it gently before glancing back at the house and whispering, 'You cruel, evil bastards.'

As she walked away, she felt slightly light-headed – the oppressive sense of dread and doom leaving her – until her thoughts went back to what she had seen in that cupboard and what Ginty was trying to tell her. It made her stomach tighten and her temples pound.

CHAPTER TWENTY-EIGHT

Carrie took her time strolling home. It was getting late, but she was still hot and uncomfortable. There was some relief, though, from the cool night air that was helping to soothe her sweaty skin and clear her mind. She liked the summer, but being pregnant in the heat was harsh. Still, she didn't have long to go and wondered if Dottie had given birth yet. She was overdue, that was for sure.

She carried her dressing gown rolled in a ball as though she was carrying a baby, and that was when she caught a glimpse of her arm. She stopped dead in her tracks and noticed how swollen it was. 'Spiteful bastard,' she mumbled, under her breath. 'You will pay one day, Jimmy Carson.'

When she reached her home, she noticed that Sunny's car was in the driveway. For a moment, she wanted to run to his place to tell him what she knew, but hearing the gentle beat of a song he was playing, she thought better of it. He was probably entertaining someone. A pretty girl probably – because he could have anyone.

However, Sunny must have seen her from his window because she heard him call her name before he came pelting down the steps dressed only in a pair of boxers.

At first, she looked at his big eyes smouldering in the moonlight. Then, she couldn't help herself but look at his chest, which was so defined by his popping muscles, and clearly twice the size of Jimmy's. She admired his tan and he smelled good enough to eat. Jimmy always stank of sour beer and fags.

Sunny chuckled. 'Sorry, I should have got dressed. So you're home.' He looked over her shoulder. 'Where's Jimmy?'

'He is drinking with his brothers. I snuck away.'

'Commiserating now, no doubt.' He punched the air. 'Eighteen years, fucking get in there!'

Feeling awkward holding her dressing gown like a baby, she flapped it over her injury-free arm. 'Good job an' all,' she replied.

Sunny instantly seized her other arm, and he pulled it closer. 'What the hell is this, Carrie?' He pointed to the deep claw mark.

'Aw, it's nuffin.'

'Carrie, I saw you this morning. You didn't have a red nose, two fucking black eyes, and what looks like a dog bite on your arm, did you? Did that cunt do that to you? 'Cos, one word, Carrie, and I'll bury the bastard.'

'You hate him, don't ya, Sunny?'

He ran his hands through his hair and sighed. 'Do you even *know* him, Carrie? Because I still can't get my head around why you married him. I always thought you were sensible, going places. You could have been a model, Carrie.'

She blushed. 'Sunny, I'll be honest with you.' She stroked her bump. 'I never would have married him if he hadn't deliberately got me up the duff.'

'The fucking arsehole. And, yeah, I do hate him, Carrie. Us Murphys hate all the Carsons. It spans way back. Arthur, Albert, Zachariah, and that mental piece of shit Lenny have spent their lives trying to fuck us over.'

'How?' asked Carrie, genuinely interested.

'Didn't you know about James's car accident? You were probably about thirteen. Anyway, James was in a bad pile-up. His brakes failed. The old girl, next door to my mum, described Albert and Arthur as the lads she saw ducking down behind his car the night before it happened.'

'And she was sure it was them?'

Sunny looked at her in amazement and shook his head. 'And I thought you knew how bad they were, and there you go defending them.'

Carrie was gutted. Why did she even ask that question? 'No, Sunny, I don't doubt it. I was just asking.'

He smiled. 'Sorry, love, it's a raw subject. Anyway, our neighbour was walking her dog and saw them. She knew who they were. She said they were Ol' Man Carson's boys, and, at the time, Jimmy was too young, Lenny and Zachariah were in prison, so it was a wild guess who the two culprits were. We couldn't prove it, though. Still, my brother Toby gave Albert and Arthur a good hiding as a warning to stay away.'

'But why did the Carsons want to, as you put it, fuck you over?'

'Blimey, Carrie, what have you been doing? Living under a rock?'

'Maybe I have. So tell me.'

'Why do you want to know now?'

'I think I have a right to know what I've married into.'

Sunny looked at her arm again. 'Come upstairs with me. We need to clean that up, for starters.'

Carrie looked about her. 'Jimmy, I mean if he . . .'

'If he is on the lash with his brothers, I can't see him coming home, can you?'

She shook her head and nervously followed him up the steps, while checking that none of the neighbours could see her. Although it was hardly likely since directly in front of her maisonette, there was a long thick bush hiding the house behind it.

Once inside, her eyes nearly popped out of her head. His living room was so modern, with a leather Chesterfield and a large TV cabinet in teak. And on the floor, there was a Chinese rug. Under the window was a single armchair, and in the middle of the room, there was a coffee table with brass legs and a glass top. She immediately saw that it was classy. She had always wanted a leather Chesterfield and a Chinese rug for her home. She had seen them in magazines and imagined that only the rich people in big houses could afford them.

‘Sit yourself down, Carrie. I’ll get my first-aid kit.’

She sat on the leather sofa while her eyes roamed the room. He was into his cars because there was a framed picture of a Ferrari on the wall and a pile of car magazines on the table. Then she clocked the huge Bang & Olufsen music centre and the records, all neatly secured in a glass-fronted teak cabinet.

He hurried back with a bowl of water, and it was clearly laced with Dettol from the smell. Tucked under his arm were rolls of bandages and a first-aid kit, which amused her. The irony wasn’t lost on her.

Kneeling beside her, he stretched out her arm and carefully dabbed the warm water.

Watching what he was doing to her arm, she stared at his face and noticed how the intense concentration made him appear quite studious and even more attractive.

‘This is really nasty. Do you want to tell me what happened?’

‘It was nothing I couldn’t handle, Sunny.’

He stopped dabbing and looked her in the eyes. ‘He will do something you won’t be able to handle if he is anything like his brothers. They are bullies, Carrie, cowardly bullies.’

She thought about what she’d learned today. There was so much she could tell him. But instead, she bit her lip and pushed the thoughts to the back of her mind before she blurted them all out.

He turned his attention back to bandaging her arm. ‘Yep, proper bullies.’

Carrie was curious about the Carson family’s past history with the Murphys. ‘Please, Sunny, tell me why the Carsons wanted to mess with your family?’

Sunny finished bandaging her arm and leaned back on his haunches. 'So, has no one ever told you about the feud that started with my grandfather Joseph Murphy and Jimmy's grandfather Benny Carson?'

Carrie shook her head. 'No.'

'Well, I don't suppose the Carsons brag about it. So, in brief, they were mates as kids, both from large families. When they were older, they planned a big job together. Joseph drew up the plans, the timings, the getaway, and everything to rob a Royal Mail train. Anyway, Benny Carson didn't follow instructions to the letter because he thought he could outdo Joseph. Benny was jealous and greedy, you see. When they jumped from the train, Benny had his own men waiting, and they fucked off with the bulk of the money, leaving my grandfather alone on the run. But Joseph was no fool. He got away because he stuck to the plan. But thick shit Benny and his mates, in a panic, drove their two bob getaway van into a walled garden, and eventually, the police caught them. Instead of taking the nicking on the chin, though, Benny wanted a lesser sentence and grassed on the brains of the outfit – my grandfather Joseph.'

'Oh, so Joseph went to prison, and that's why the two families are feuding, is it?'

Slowly, he shook his head. 'No, the Murphys could have stomached that, but while Joseph was inside, Benny, having served only two years, came out and went after my grandmother.' He shook his head. 'Benny did stuff to her believing that no one would come for him because Joseph was inside. But he seriously underestimated the bond between Joseph and his brothers. So when they found out what happened, there was a war.'

Carrie nodded, anxious to hear what happened next.

'So, Carrie, it's been bred into us, and it certainly has been bred into the Carsons. My father, God rest his soul, and Ginty's husband had many a brawl, and before Jimmy's father got with Ginty, he wanted me mum. She was a looker in her day, but my father married her, so the feud continued. You would have thought it would have died out when Ginty's boys were born. But no. Ginty was always jealous of my mum and spurred her sons on to hate us all. Especially when her husband died. Although everyone believed he took his own life to get away from Ginty. Anyway, it began with Arthur, Albert, and Lenny letting down our bike tyres and flinging dog shit at my mum's windows, and then it slowly escalated. The hate was bred into them. They hate that we've done all right for ourselves. Jealousy turned them inside out.'

Carrie smiled. 'They are fuming now because Mary is marrying Dylon, and James is seeing Dilly.' Her eyes suddenly cast down. 'They have me, though.'

Sunny jumped up. 'Yeah, a fucking shame that, but listen, I'm here if you need me, okay, and don't let that prick hurt you. Carrie, fuck him off. I mean, I'd love to kick him out of the house.' He laughed, and then he stopped to help Carrie to her feet. She was practically nose to nose with him. They remained like that for a moment before he breathed. 'I could, Carrie, I really could kiss ya.'

'I wish it was you,' she mumbled, under her breath, as she grabbed her dressing gown and left the living room. She didn't think he'd heard her until he called after her. 'Me too, Carrie, me too.'

She paused at his front door, and a sudden thought flickered across her brain. 'Sunny, are your brothers wiv me sisters to get their—'

'Were you going to say to get their own back? Noooo way. Oh, come on, Carrie, look in the mirror. You and your sisters are all stunning. You must know that. Mind you, you were always hanging around the high street with the scallywags because I suppose you were the little rebel in the family. A tough little cookie on the streets, with all the Orpington lot looking up to you because you could have a ruck and you were pretty. Miss Popular, eh?'

Carrie blushed again. 'Well, me life is very different now.' She stroked her bump again.

She hurried away before she burst into tears – tears of regret.

***

Once she opened her front door, a slight sense of contentment rippled through her. It was her home, which made her feel grown up. A couple of letters lay on the mat. One was a handwritten note. It was from social services. The other letter was a bill.

With anticipation, she read the one from the social services. Dottie had given birth, and since everything was in place to bring the baby home, the social worker would be arriving at their house a week from today at nine o'clock in the morning to escort them personally to pick the child up.

Carrie reread it and frowned. Even though it had been handwritten, it didn't say if the baby was a boy or a girl. She had been in constant contact with Dottie via letters and a couple of visits and had done her best to reassure Dottie that she would love this baby. She sighed. The very least the social worker could have done was to tell her the sex of the child. Let alone say if the baby was healthy. Her mind was now spinning. There was so much gloom over the day, with mysteries and secrets, and now she had one more to contend with: what was she collecting from the prison?

***

A week later

Carrie was flapping. She had cleaned the maisonette so thoroughly, her nostrils were burning from the bleach. Jimmy had spent most of the week at his mother's, but even when he was around, he seemed very distant, as if he had a lot on his mind, which often made her wonder what this big job was all about. They had barely spoken, apart from her informing him of the arrangements for collecting his new baby.

The social worker was escorting them to the prison herself. Even though her previous visits had been intrusive, she was actually a lovely woman, starchy in appearance but soft in her words.

When the taxi arrived outside, Jimmy sighed. He looked at Carrie. 'So we're off to see the baby, then, are we?'

'No, Jimmy, we're going to bring *your* baby home.'

He mustered a fake smile. 'We don't know what she's had yet.'

'No, but it's your baby, Jimmy, so please act like you care and show some excitement.'

He glared at her. 'I think you have enough for the two of us. Why the fuck you dragged me into this idea, I don't know. Still, I've signed the papers now. I can't go back on my word.' His face fell into one of regret.

The knock at the door had Jimmy on his feet. 'So, this is it.' He nodded for Carrie to open the door, and there, with a beaming smile on her face, was Ms Palin, a woman in her thirties, who moved quickly and spoke fast.

'Are we ready?' she said, positively glowing.

Carrie nodded. 'Shall I bring anything?'

'Oh yes, the car seat.'

Carrie hurried to the nursery and snatched the car seat, but Ms Palin frowned. 'Oh, Jimmy, maybe if you carried it. I find them rather heavy, and with Carrie in her condition . . .'

Jimmy nodded, feeling awkward. As soon as Ms Palin's back was turned, he snatched the car seat and grumbled under his breath, before marching towards the taxi.

Carrie felt on edge because she did not want Jimmy to mess it all up with his moody attitude. But, at least, he was better dressed for the occasion today. He was wearing his smart black trousers and a white shirt.

CHAPTER TWENTY-NINE

Carrie nudged Jimmy as they stood outside the medical room with two prison officers hovering awkwardly about.

'Try to look happy, for fuck's sake,' she whispered, through gritted teeth.

He nudged her back. 'Why didn't you ask if it was a boy or a girl? We've sat in that office filling out form after fucking form as if I have to adopt my own kid. It's bollocks. And no one even mentioned if it's a boy or a girl.'

Carrie looked at the two female officers, who were talking to each other and not paying any attention to her or her husband. 'I didn't like to ask, in case they think we prefer one over the other. That would make us look pretty shit.'

'I do have a preference. I want boys. I told ya. I'm not into daughters. I want a son I can teach everything I've learned.'

Carrie laughed. 'That will take two minutes, then.' She meant it as a joke, but he wasn't in the mood to take it that way.

'You can be fucking nasty, Carrie.'

'I was joking.'

'Yeah, sure you were.' He tutted. 'How much fucking longer are they gonna be?'

'Shush.'

'And I don't wanna see that Dottie. She gives me the creeps.'

'She didn't give you the creeps when you put that baby inside her.'

'She hadn't murdered her muvver and farver then.'

'You don't know that she has.'

The door opened before he could say another word, and Ms Palin ushered them in.

Dottie, with her hair tied up in a loose ponytail, her face white and sad, was dressed in a tracksuit and was sitting on the bed. Her hands were helplessly resting in her lap as she stared at the cot beside her bed.

Carrie guessed from the gentle, sweet gurgling sounds that the baby was inside. To her surprise, Jimmy barged past her. And instead of being respectful and kind, he walked over to the cot, ignoring Dottie completely, and peered in.

Carrie wanted to punch him in the face for being so tactless. She hurried over before he made any other move, but then, she herself was drawn to the cot and had to gaze inside.

'Jimmy's been excited to see the baby.' Carrie smiled at the social worker to excuse her husband's bolshie behaviour.

It was clear the beautiful baby was a boy. His blankets were blue, and his hat was coloured in blue-and-white stripes.

Carrie shuffled around the cot to sit on the bed with Dottie. Looking up at Jimmy, she flicked her head for him to leave.

Ignoring his wife, he said, 'So, it's a boy.' Then he glared for a moment at Dottie.

Dottie, though, kept her head down. She refused even to look at him.

''Course it's a boy, Jimmy. And he's a beautiful boy, too. Now, I want to talk to Dottie on me own.'

Jimmy didn't need to be asked twice this time. He wanted to leave anyway.

Ms Palin was standing with a nurse in the corner of the room watching, and Carrie spun herself around to face them. 'Can we be alone, please?'

Ms Palin looked at Dottie, who nodded, and they both left, leaving Carrie with Dottie and the new baby.

'He's beautiful, Dottie.' She stroked the baby's cheek. 'This must be so hard.' An unexpected tear fell down her cheek, and she choked on a sob.

Dottie put her arm around Carrie. 'Please, Carrie . . . he is all I have.'

Carrie stood up, reached into the cot, and scooped the baby out, pulling him to her chest.

'Dottie, I swear to you, I will love this child like me own.'

Dottie smiled. 'You probably won't, but just try not to treat them differently, eh?'

'I've been thinking about it a lot, and when I give birth, they are gonna hand me a stranger. It might be my baby, but it's still a stranger, just like, er . . .'

'He's called Billy. Will you call him Billy as well? It will mean such a lot to me.'

'Ahh.' Carrie looked down at the baby's face. 'I love the name. Billy. Yeah, it's perfect. Baby Billy it is, then.' She smiled and kissed the baby's forehead.

'I named him after my best friend.' Her face melted in sadness.

'Yeah, I remember you mentioning what happened to Billy, on my last visit.'

Dottie nodded, smiled at Carrie, and hugged her tightly.

'Listen.' Carrie lowered her voice. 'I heard the social worker talking on the phone to someone a few minutes ago. I dunno who it was, but they said that you might get out. Is that right?'

'Temporary insanity, they say, but who knows. Look, Carrie, don't worry, I'm giving my baby to you because I want him to have a life. A complete life with you as his mum. So now I've got nothing and no one.'

'Dottie, listen, when you get out, come and see Billy, and of course I'm gonna love him, but in my mind, I'll always think he's on loan to me.'

Dottie's eyes widened. 'But they said I can never see him again.'

'Who do they think they are, eh? That's all bollocks. Fucking bollocks. If you wanna see him, you come and see him. I can bring him up to visit you, if you want.'

'No, Carrie, not while I'm in here. It would do my nut in.'

For a split second, Carrie wanted to laugh because Dottie was talking differently. Still, then again, she was in prison, so perhaps the lingo was rubbing off on her, or maybe the lack of parental influence was allowing Dottie to talk how she wanted to and be who she wanted to be.

Suddenly, Dottie burst into tears and hugged both Carrie and Billy. 'Will Jimmy l-l-l love the baby?' she stuttered.

'Dottie, I've got enough love for the both of us, so don't you worry about that. Anyway, what man changes nappies and does the night feed?'

'I can do my time in peace now, Carrie. Thank you very much.'

The tears flowed and set them both off. Even Billy began to cry, and Carrie immediately began to rock him. 'There, there, Billy boy. I've got ya.'

Dottie smiled and her whole persona relaxed because she knew now that her baby was in safe hands.

When it was time to leave, Dottie held the baby one last time, smelled his black hair mop, and kissed the heart-shaped birthmark on the back of his neck.

'Carrie, if I never see you again, please tell Billy that the birthmark is where I left him with a kiss.'

'I will, Dottie, I will,' Carrie said, her voice trembling with emotion. It was the saddest thing she'd ever heard.

***

Carrie spent the journey home gazing at the baby, while Jimmy spent it staring out of the window. The social worker had escorted them only to the taxi before she went off to her office to complete the paperwork. As the two of them headed home, you could cut the tension in the car with a knife.

'Jimmy, don't you want to look at him? He is such a dear little thing.'

Turning to his wife, he said, 'And she called him Billy. He should have been Jimmy or named after one of me brothers, or me ol' man, but not fucking Billy.'

'Never mind about that. Look at him. He is perfect.'

Jimmy turned his gaze back to staring out of the window, evidently in a bad mood. Then he called out to the taxi driver. 'Hey, mate, how long's it gonna be before we're back in Orpington?'

The driver shrugged. 'I can't predict the traffic, mate.'

'Jimmy, what's the rush? You should be grateful that the poor baby's not screaming his head off.'

'I've got a meeting.'

'Oh yeah, what, with the Carson clan?'

Jimmy shot her a questioning glare. 'What do you mean, the Carson clan? You're a Carson an' all, and don't you forget it.'

'How the fuck can I, Jimmy, eh?'

Ignoring him, Carrie stared at the baby, who was sound asleep in the car seat. As much as she knew the baby wasn't hers, she was falling in love with him. She wondered what colour his eyes would be and whether or not he would keep his mop of hair.

'Did you have black hair, Jimmy, when you were born?'

'How the hell do I know.' He glared at the baby. 'It looks nuffin like me.'

'Babies don't look like anyone until they are properly unfolded. I'm sure he will be a handsome lad, just like his father.'

Jimmy would have sucked in the compliment and grinned like the narcissist he was, but instead, he shot Carrie another glare. 'Are you being fucking funny?'

'No, I wasn't. Actually, I was trying to be nice.'

'Well, don't bother 'cos it don't suit you. In fact, fuck all suits you.'

Carrie frowned. She couldn't believe how spiteful he was acting.

Once again, Jimmy looked over at the driver in frustration. 'For fuck's sake, mate, I need to get home. Can't you put your foot down?'

'It's the rush hour, mate,' said the driver. 'I can't move because there are cars are in front.'

'All right, can you go via Chislehurst?'

'I was, anyway, mate.'

'Good.'

Carrie frowned and eyed her husband suspiciously. 'Why Chislehurst?'

But when he turned to face her, she wished she hadn't asked because his underjaw shot forward, and he said spitefully, 'Mind your own business, woman. You're too fucking nosy.'

Carrie nodded. 'Fair enough,' she replied. She turned her attention back to the baby. But every so often, she studied her husband's face. Something was bothering him, and she assumed it was due to this big so-called job he and his brothers had planned. Or was he seeing another woman? It wouldn't surprise her. He had always thought of his dick before anything else. He'd even told her straight-out that he found her disgusting because she had gained so much weight – baby weight. She didn't care because she felt the same way about him. Even sitting in the same room as Jimmy made her hate him. Her eyes drifted to the pink scar on her arm – a reminder from when he'd clawed her. She would never forget that. It was strangely sickening because he hadn't thumped her out of temper. He had slowly dug his nails into her until her arm bled. It was as if he was getting some sort of sadistic pleasure from hurting her.

As the taxi took them through Chislehurst and continued along St Paul's Cray Road, Carrie wondered if Jimmy would ask the driver to turn left into Leesons Hill and drive straight over Sevenoaks Way towards his mother's house. But he didn't, so she naturally assumed he was going home. Because as they passed the woods and continued on, the second left would take them towards their home.

Just as they reached the big gated houses on the left, Jimmy craned his neck.

Carrie followed his eyeline and clocked the big house with the double gates. In the front garden there was a child's tricycle and a doll's pram. Her heart was in her mouth. Why would Jimmy be interested in that house? Even the block paved drive looked brand new, so it wasn't as if they could con the owners into having a tarmac driveway.

She was about to ask him why the interest in that particular property when the baby let out a cry, which was more like a whimper, but it was high-pitched enough for Jimmy to tell her to keep Billy quiet.

The driver had been given their address, so they drove straight to their maisonette. Carrie thanked him, and she assumed that Jimmy would help carry the baby, who was still in the car seat, into their home, but he remained in the car, sulking like a spoiled child.

'Jimmy, are you coming in?' she asked.

But he waved his hand contemptuously again. 'Nah, I told you. I've got a meeting. And I'll be back in a couple of days.'

'But, Jimmy, what about the new baby? And I'm due myself soon, so what if—'

'Your choice, Carrie, not fucking mine.'

'But what if I come into labour?'

He growled. 'You got that bloody phone installed.' His eyes narrowed. 'But what I wanna know is where did you get the money from to have that put in, eh?'

Annoyed, she said, 'I sold some of my jewellery. We needed a phone.'

'Well, you've got what you wanted. Now, get on wiv it. I've got business to attend to.'

The driver got out of the car, stretched his back, unclipped the car seat, and then offered to carry it, making sure Jimmy heard him. As they reached the front door, the driver whispered, 'Watch that baby. He might be your husband, but I've known men like him. My father was one of them. A nasty piece of work. You take care, love. God be with you.'

Carrie suddenly felt as if she was carrying a lead brick – dread was taking its toll on her.

***

As soon as the front door closed behind her, she hurriedly took the baby out of the car seat and placed him flat in the cot. She warmed some milk and took a note of the time before she changed his clothes and nappy, and then she gently poked the bottle into his mouth to suck on. And like a dream, he drank the milk and brought up the air right away before she put him in the cot again. *Surely, it's not this easy, is it?* she questioned.

Leaning over, she kissed his peachy cheeks. He opened his huge blue eyes, and she fell more in love with him. But every time she smiled at the baby, she felt Dottie's heart breaking, all alone in the prison cell with no baby to cuddle. She looked at the plaque she had screwed to the wall and reread it, determined now that she would do right by the children.

As soon as Billy drifted off to sleep, Carrie heard someone trying to get into the house, but then, whoever it was, who banged on the door, called out, 'Open the fucking door, Carrie.'

It was Jimmy's penetrating voice. Hurrying to the door, she had barely unlocked it to let him in when he pushed the door open, smacking her hard against the wall.

'The fucking taxi driver took me two minutes down the road and told me to get out. I swear to God, he is lucky I didn't chin the old bastard.'

Carrie was stunned that he had blatantly forced her out of the way and was now moaning about the taxi driver, regardless of the fact that she was pregnant.

'He reckons he was only paid to take me that far.'

'Oh yeah, I suppose the social worker paid him the exact amount she was charged to take us to the prison.'

'Oh, I see, and you reckon that's all right, do ya?'

Seeing the rage in his eyes, Carrie knew that no matter what she said or did, he was itching for a fight. Ignoring him, she checked on the baby. Luckily, he was still sound asleep. But the racket Jimmy was making, in opening and shutting the kitchen drawers and swearing, compelled her to leave the nursery.

'What are you looking for?'

'The number of a cab firm. It's too late to walk to me muvver's. I'm fucking late as it is.'

Ripping the last drawer from the cabinet, he threw it on the floor. The utensils clanged and banged like a beginner's practice band.

Carrie could see that Jimmy was literally foaming at the mouth, but she wasn't going to put up with that. 'What is going on, Jimmy? Look at ya, wrecking me kitchen. And you're gonna wake the baby.'

'The baby? That fucking scraggy runt! We should never ever have got involved. We should have left the kid with its psycho muvver. But, oh no! You, Carrie!' He pointed in her face. 'You had to have your own way. Well, I'm telling you now, you're gonna change, woman. You're my wife, and that means you're gonna do as I say from now on. Now, find me a cab firm number.'

The shock from hearing Jimmy's rant rendered Carrie speechless. Who the hell did he think he was!

'Don't you dare talk to me like that, Jimmy. Have respect for me, will ya. Look, I'm carrying *your* baby.'

Once again, the rage showed in his eyes, and she watched as his fists balled, and his biceps tightened. She stepped back and stumbled over the utensils he had thrown all over the floor.

'My baby, Carrie, is it?'

Jimmy stepped over the drawer on the floor and snatched Carrie's wrists, pulling her close to him, before he gripped her hair and tried to bend her back. 'My baby? I bet it ain't, you dirty whore!' he yelled.

'Get off me, Jimmy. You're hurting me. Get off, please.'

'Hurting you? I thought you were hard, Carrie.' He bent her back even more until she fell and her shoulder hit the kitchen side.

Instantly, pain shot down her arm, taking her breath away and blurring her vision. She couldn't move, but the intensity of the pain made her scream. 'Ahh, Jimmy, me arm. I've broken me arm. Help me!'

But the pure loathing in Jimmy's eyes told her he didn't care. He curled his lip in disgust before he stormed off, shouting, 'Clean this mess up! I'll be back when I'm fucking ready. It's *your* fault I'm late.'

As Carrie took a few deep breaths, hoping the pain would ease off, she called out, her voice strangled by tears and agony, 'Jimmy, please, can you help me? I'm hurt, Jimmy.'

But by this time, he had stormed off, heading to the front door, but only to march back and straight into their bedroom. And to her surprise, she heard what sounded like him lifting the mattress. She wondered if he'd hidden some money there. Fortunately, her secret stash was under a loose floorboard in the kitchen, covered with lino and a small rug.

'You won't be needing this fucking thing either, calling all ya fellas when I'm out, you old whore!'

She then heard him rip the phone from the wall and smash it against something. What the hell was the matter with him? Her husband was turning into a lunatic by something sent from hell.

Hearing a ringing in her ears – which clearly wasn't from the newly installed phone put in at great expense – she then heard him slam the door shut.

Easing her throbbing arm onto her lap, she waited until she felt she could push through the pain and get to her feet. The time ticked away, and she listened for Billy, but he was quiet; the only sound came from the kitchen clock ticking.

Looking up at it, she now wished she could turn back the hands of time. Marrying Jimmy had not only been a monumental mistake but his anger could actually cause serious harm to her and her baby. What was she really doing, a baby in one room that wasn't hers and one nearly due?

There was no point, though, in feeling sorry for herself. She had to get up, make up some bottles for the night feed, and find a way to do it with one hand, for now. However, as soon as she got up, she felt a pain not only in her shoulder, which spread down to her arm, but in her stomach as well. A tight, quick pain took her breath away. 'Oh no, not now. This *can't* be happening.' It was too soon, but there was no going back now. Her waters had broken.

Fear forced the pain to the back of her mind as she hurried to the bedroom, but the moment she had confirmation that Jimmy had indeed smashed the phone to smithereens, she threw her hands to her face in alarm. She had to find a way to get to the hospital with a possible broken collarbone, a newborn baby, and her own baby coming anytime soon.

'One day, Jimmy, you will wish you had never crossed me.'

After calming herself down, she moved her arm to see how bad it was and concluded that it was probably no more than a sprain. So she quickly made up a baby bottle, wrapped Billy in a blanket, and put him in the car seat. Billy wriggled but then he fell straight back to sleep.

She waddled to the bedroom where she stripped off and put on clean underwear and a fresh dress. She'd already had a bag packed for the hospital for at least a week.

Just as she was about to drag the bag from her side of the bed, she saw something on the floor. It was a photograph. When she peered closer, she saw it was a picture of the back of a very grand-looking house, and in the rear garden, there was a paddling pool. It was so odd, but she didn't have time to give it too much thought because she had experienced what she assumed was another contraction. Sliding the photo into her bag, she continued towards the front door.

With the car seat swinging in one hand and her heavy hospital bag in the other, she groaned with the pain that shot down her arm. It was making her feel sick. The cool air made the baby gasp for breath, and yet she was sweating. Another contraction came, and this one brought her to her knees. She had to find a neighbour to use their phone, but no one had their lights on, and Sunny was clearly out. Another pain gripped her so hard, it stopped her from moving.

'Damn you, Jimmy. Damn you!'

CHAPTER THIRTY

Ray Clarkson tutted when his restless dog Jack pawed his leg, having sat patiently waiting for his evening walk.

'All right, we'll post the letter on the way,' said Clarkson, shaking his head because all he had to talk to now was his dog. Their usual walk would have taken them past Dottie's house and left at the end of the road where the nearest postbox was. However, as much as he was a senior detective and was used to everything the Devil himself could throw at a person, there were some things he couldn't bring himself to do, and walking past Dottie's previous home was one of them. He decided to turn right and then left and walk down to the nearest shops, where there was also a postbox. The evening was pleasant with a breeze, so wearing his jeans and T-shirt, he slid his door keys into his pocket and tucked the letter under his arm.

As if Jack could read his master's mind, he pulled on the lead in the direction Clarkson wanted to go. However, as soon as they turned the corner, he could see a young woman on the footpath and beside her was a baby in a car seat. Being a detective, he was always curious, and the position the woman was in didn't look natural. Hurrying over to her, his first thought the moment she looked up was that she was distressed.

'Please, could you help me? Arrgghh.' She doubled over.

'Yes, certainly, I'll help you to the wall.' He reached down to offer a hand, and as she grabbed it to pull herself up, he realised she was pregnant. Yet, right away, he noticed the newborn in the car seat. 'Are you in labour, Mrs . . .?'

In pain, Carrie didn't think to offer her last name. She blurted out, 'Please, mister, can you call an ambulance? Yep, I'm in labour.' She smiled when she looked at his sympathetic face. 'I think I need to get to the hospital, like now. Me waters have broken. I flooded the kitchen.'

'Yes, yes, I live literally around the corner. Will you be okay for a minute?' Clarkson said, as he helped her to the small garden wall. He then lifted the car seat and brought it closer to the young woman.

She nodded and thanked him before he returned to his house and called for an ambulance.

'Sorry, Jack, your walk will have to wait.'

Before he hurried back to where the young woman was, he reached under his arm for the letter and realised he must have dropped it. But as he approached her, he saw she had it in her hand and was staring at it.

She held it out as he approached. 'You, er, dropped this.' She handed it to him. 'Did you call an ambulance?'

'I did, yes.' He took the letter. 'Thank you.'

'So you know Dottie, then?'

Startled, he replied, 'Well, yes, I do.'

'Are you a friend?'

'Yes. I've known Dottie from when she was very young. She was my daughter's friend, in fact.'

Carrie panted momentarily as another contraction passed. 'She's my friend too, ya know.'

Clarkson raised his brow. 'Really?'

'I don't tend to talk to strangers, but if you're writing to her, then I guess you must be a mate or something.'

'I'm Ray Clarkson.'

'Gawd blimey, Dottie mentioned you. She wears your necklace, ya know.'

He smiled. 'How do you know that?'

'I've been to visit her a few times. We talk, and I write. Not too much 'cos I'm not that good at it.'

'She's just had a baby herself, a little lad,' Clarkson said.

Carrie studied the man's face. 'If she told you that, then I might as well tell you something else as well.' She pointed to the car seat. 'Meet Billy, Dottie's baby.'

Clarkson felt his whole body come alive with goose bumps. He crouched down and stared at the baby before gently touching the little one's cheeks. Then he looked over at the young woman. 'So you must be Carrie Carson, Jimmy's wife, then?'

'She told you about me?'

'Yeah, she did, and I will be frank with you, Carrie, I know your husband and his brothers because I'm a local detective.'

Carrie's eyes widened. 'Oh really? Actually, Dottie never said you were a detective. She said you send stuff in from time to time and you have given her money.'

'It's okay.' He laughed. 'I'm not judging you, not my place, but, Carrie, if you ever need me or need help with Billy, you come and see me, okay? But I would rather you didn't mention me to Jimmy Carson or any of the Carsons because I like to live a peaceful life.'

'Believe me, Mr Clarkson, I understand that.' She sighed. 'But you ain't gonna be watching me, 'cos I promise I know it ain't easy having two babies, but I will do me best. I'm gonna have the social services breathing down my neck, anyway.'

Clarkson waved his hand. 'Not at all, Carrie. All I meant was if you ever get into difficulty – and only you can be the judge of that – then you come and see me.'

'You really cared about Dottie, didn't you?'

'I still do, Carrie, I still do. Now, shall I escort you to the hospital because you can't be worrying about giving birth and seeing to this little one.' Clarkson heard the ambulance in the distance. 'When we get to the hospital, I can call your husband.'

Carrie summed up Clarkson right away. He was kind and seemed so genuine, and, in any case, she recalled her mother telling her *never look a gift horse in the mouth.* 'No, don't call him. He's not the type to fare well in a labour ward. But maybe I could beg a favour.'

'Go on,' said Clarkson, as he gripped the handle of the car seat.

'A man called Sunny lives upstairs.' Carrie pointed to the maisonette. 'If you see his car in the drive later, maybe you could ask him to come to the hospital. Only, he knows where my mum has moved to, so he could help me.'

'What about Jimmy? Sorry, it's not my business. Of course, I will.'

She smarted again and breathed deeply. 'Cor, it hurts.'

He smiled. 'I know, but you see, it will all be worth it.'

Carrie looked at Billy and nodded. 'Oh yeah, it definitely will be. Just look at this one. You couldn't get more perfect, could ya. I just wish Dottie . . . Oh, never mind. I promised her I'd love him, and I already do.'

'I can see that.'

Just as the ambulance pulled over and two paramedics opened the rear doors, a car came tearing down the road.

Clarkson stared in horror as the car didn't look as though it was going to skirt around the ambulance until he realised it was coming to a stop.

'That's Sunny, who lives upstairs.' She winked at Clarkson.

'A Formula One driver now, is he?'

Sunny leaped from the car and hurried over to Carrie. 'What's he fucking done now? I swear, Carrie, I will fucking kill him if he touches you again.'

'Shut up, Sunny, I'm in labour, you crank.' She glanced at Clarkson.

Sunny followed her eyeline. 'Oh, er . . . all right, mate?'

'High, Mr Murphy.'

Sunny's eyes narrowed. 'Oh shit.' He suddenly stood up with his back straight. 'It's Chief Inspector Clarkson, right? I didn't recognise you.'

Clarkson had that effect on people. It would compel any grown man to stand to attention. Maybe his cool, calm voice had a subconscious effect on people in the same way an off-duty sergeant major might.

Clarkson nodded. 'Yes, er, I was helping Carrie and the baby.'

As the paramedics took over and helped Carrie onto the stretcher, Sunny looked at the baby. 'Is this, er . . .?'

'Dottie Ellis's baby, you mean? Yes,' said Clarkson. 'I was going to go to the hospital with Carrie to watch over him. She did ask for you.'

Sunny's eyes sprang open. 'Really?'

'Yes, so I don't know if you want to take over?'

'Yeah, sure, of course I will.'

Clarkson flicked his head for Sunny to move out of Carrie's sight. 'Sunny, look, I know I let your family down. I know we didn't solve your brother's murder, but I'm back at work now, and I want the case reopened.'

Sunny's eyes welled up. 'Thank you. Yeah, I did hear you were off work and I'm sorry for your loss.' He coughed to hide the awkward tension. 'Thanks for helping Carrie.'

'Look, I know I didn't end up being much help to your family, but, Sunny, may I ask a favour?'

'Sure,' he said, anxiously, looking over his shoulder to check that Carrie was okay.

'I know what the Carsons are like, and I heard what you said about Jimmy when you got out of your car. Would you keep an eye on Carrie and the babies?'

'You didn't need to ask. She's like family. You may know that her sister Dilly was engaged to Toby. They were getting married the day after he was killed.'

Clarkson nodded. 'Yes, I did know.' He smiled sympathetically. 'You're a good lad, Sunny. Can you handle this?' He handed him the car seat.

'It looks like I'm gonna bloody well have to. Cheers, Mr Clarkson.'

Clarkson felt Carrie was in safe hands as soon as Sunny clambered into the back of the ambulance with the baby.

Once the ambulance was on its way, Clarkson decided to go home, get changed, and then head to the station. He was determined now to make a conscious effort to reopen the Toby Murphy file. He couldn't get the sadness in Sunny's eyes out of his head and the flashbacks of the day he was present when they told the family that Toby had been killed. That scream from the mother was still ringing in his ears. Now he was back at work and in charge of his team, a few things would change.

***

The office was quiet because it was now ten o'clock at night. Kenneth Granger was at his desk and going through some paperwork. He looked up and politely gave a nod of acknowledgement.

However, their relationship was now strained. Previously, Granger had assumed that Clarkson would never return to work. He had been in his element swanning around in his place. However, now that his boss was back and he himself was down the pecking order, he was finding the role adjustment hard to swallow.

Sitting at another desk with a lamp on was Detective Constable Susan Ring, a favourite of Clarkson's.

'Susan, I see you're burning the candle at both ends and all that.'

'Gov, haven't you heard?'

'Heard what?' A deep furrowed frown turned his otherwise deadpan face into one of annoyance. He looked at Granger, who was seemingly uneasy.

'Sorry, Ray, I was going to call you, but we've only just got the call ourselves, haven't we, Susan.'

'Oh, er . . . yes, Ken.'

'So what's the news?' Clarkson asked, as the door opened, and in walked Colt, the detective with whom Clarkson struggled to get along.

'Chief, I didn't know you were coming tonight. You can't seem to stay away these days.'

'Is that a problem, Colt?'

Colt looked down. 'No, sorry, Chief.'

Clarkson pivoted to face Granger. 'So what's the new case about?'

'We've had a call. A child has been kidnapped or most likely gone for a wander. The family lives in the Petts Wood area.'

'Your neck of the woods, Gov, isn't it?' asked Susan.

'Well, yes, within walking distance, I suppose. Who's there now with the family?'

Granger coughed. 'I sent a couple of uniformed officers.'

'How old is the child?'

'Three, apparently.'

'Uniforms!'

'Well, yes, just to get the facts. Look, Gov, it's only just happened. They might find her playing in a cupboard, or she may have fallen asleep under the bed. You know what frantic parents can be like, especially the ones with money. The child's called Annabelle.' Granger stopped talking and began chewing his bottom lip.

Clarkson glared in horror at the flippancy of Granger. 'Or, Ray, the kiddie could have been kidnapped, and the family will have no damn idea what to do if the kidnappers receive a call demanding a sodding ransom. What in God's name were you thinking sending two uniforms over there?'

Ray looked up sheepishly at his boss and blushed.

'What's the address? I'll go over there my bloody self.' He looked across at Susan. 'Would you like to drive?'

Granger flared his nostrils because it was becoming evident that their once close relationship had taken a nosedive. 'I'll go, Gov. Susan, you get off home.'

Clarkson stopped and spun around. 'No, Ken, you're not the lead anymore. I want Susan to come with me. The mother might warm to her. Oh, and what's the name?'

'Annabelle.'

'No, you fool, the surname.'

But Susan answered for Granger. 'The father's name is Charlie Murphy.'

Clarkson froze for a moment. 'And why wasn't that the first thing you told me? Christ, Ken, it wasn't so long ago we buried his nephew Toby. We never found the killer, did we, so you can imagine how his other nephews, James, Dylon, and Sunny will react if we don't pull out all the stops.' He walked over to Granger, placed his hands flat on the desk, and said, 'Is this your way of getting your own back on Charlie Murphy because you couldn't find the evidence – if there actually was any – to have that man convicted of the post office job in Leeds?'

Granger leaned back, shaking his head.

'How you got to be the governor puzzles me, Ray. You seem to be on the side of the criminals.'

'Well, Ken, it seems to me that you are letting your personal vendetta with Murphy affect *your* job because our duty right now is to find a three-year-old child.'

Having been slapped in the face with the morality card, Granger looked away, embarrassed.

Susan printed off the details, including the address, and followed Clarkson out of the building.

***

As Clarkson and Detective Constable Ring stood at the main gates, Clarkson did a quick survey of the front garden. He then glanced over at the security pad, which was used to gain entry to the house; it was an intercom system with a number keypad, but he didn't need to buzz through because the gates were open. As they walked towards the front door, he clocked the fences, the bushes, and the potential few gaps where someone could have climbed in, which would make the secure main gates a joke. Because although it would appear to be a secure property from the front, someone who knew this place well would know it wasn't.

Susan Ring knocked at the door while Clarkson was still absorbing the surroundings.

Hearing footsteps hurriedly approaching impressive heavy double oak doors, Clarkson turned to face the occupier.

When the doors were opened, Clarkson came face to face with Bella Murphy.

She was a woman in her forties, who was blessed with a beach tan and highlighted blonde hair that was tied up in a high ponytail. Recent events, though, it appeared, had aged her considerably. Her mascara-smudged eyes and her body language spoke volumes – head down and shoulders slumped.

Clarkson gave Mrs Murphy a sympathetic smile. 'Hi, I'm Chief Inspector Ray Clarkson.' He felt it best to remain formal because he wasn't sure if she remembered him. 'And this,' he gestured to Susan, 'is Detective Constable Susan Ring.'

'Have they found her yet?' was all Bella said.

'May we come in?'

Bella stepped aside and looked towards the road. 'God, what if someone's taken her?'

'May we talk somewhere more comfortable?' asked Clarkson.

Bella ushered the officers into the grand hallway. It was so large that there was room for a round table to display a tall vase and a mass of expensive fresh flowers.

She pointed to the room on the right. 'You can join the two PCs. They are in there.'

As Clarkson entered the lounge, he noticed that two uniformed officers were sitting on a sofa looking more than relaxed and drinking tea and nibbling on biscuits.

When the officers saw Clarkson, they jumped to their feet. His stern expression alone had them out of their seats.

'Have you radioed through the child's description? Do you have photos to take back to the station?' he said, expecting that they probably hadn't.

The younger of the two officers shook his head. 'We were just going over the details. Well, I mean, we haven't been here long. Mrs Murphy made us tea and . . . she gave us one photo, er . . .'

'Do you have anything in your notebook?'

The officer shook his head. 'No, not yet, Gov.'

'Right, the pair of you, take the photo back to the station. Make everyone aware we have a missing child. I want the whole of the bloody Met and every station in Kent on board.'

Without further ado, the two officers hurried out of the house.

Clarkson then turned his attention to Bella. 'Can you take a seat please, Mrs Murphy? I want every detail of today's events. I will want you to walk me through them. Now, before that, I need to know where Mr Murphy is.'

Bella grabbed a tissue from a box on the long marble coffee table and blew her nose. 'He's in France fishing. He goes there the same time every year, the anniversary of his father's death. The family go fishing at some lake or other.'

Clarkson looked at the three cups on the table. Clearly, tea had been made and yet Bella smelled of alcohol. Looking at her glazed eyes, he figured it was probably down to the amount of liquor consumed.

But the tears came now. And her hands were shaking as she gripped her tissue. She went across to an armchair, sat down, and invited the officers to sit down on the sofa.

'Sorry, Mrs Murphy, but I want to ask you a question. Please don't think for a second I am laying any blame on you, but have you been drinking today?'

'Yes, I have. Oh my God, if only I hadn't, I would have noticed much sooner that Annabelle was missing.'

'It's not your fault, Mrs Murphy.'

'Bella, please call me Bella. Annabelle was playing in the garden. I like to let her play for as long as she wants because she doesn't go to bed until late, and when I called her in for her bath, she didn't answer. She'd just vanished.' Bella covered her eyes and sobbed.

Susan took over. Going across to Bella, she kneeled by her side and rubbed her back. 'It's okay. But we need you to recall everything you can about today.'

Bella blew her nose again and wiped her eyes before she composed herself. 'I took Annabelle to her nursery in Petts Wood, and my neighbour, Jilly, picked her up for me. She does this on a Thursday. She keeps her at her house until I get home. Thursdays is the day I go and have lunch and a few drinks with my friends at Minstrels in Orpington High Street, you see.'

'Is that every Thursday?' asked Susan.

'Yes, and I always get a cab home. I ring Jilly and she brings Annabelle back to me. But I'll be honest.' She looked up to the ceiling and had to compose herself again. 'I don't know why, but I was seemingly quite drunk. I normally have three drinks, but it was as if I had drunk six or seven or someone had spiked my drink because I never doze off. Not when I'm alone with Annabelle. But I did today. Oh God, forgive me, I did, and now she could be lost in the woods or taken. Oh my God, what if someone took her?'

‘And the relationship with your husband. Is that good?’ asked Clarkson. He knew that question would have Bella sobering up.

Bella looked at Clarkson as if he was completely mad. ‘Yes, very good. He’s a good man.’

‘I need you to think very carefully about the next question.’

Even Susan was now paying attention because as far as she was concerned, Clarkson was the man to learn from.

‘Is there anyone who would want to cause you, your husband, or your family harm?’

Bella shook her head. ‘No, we don’t have enemies. There’s no one who’d want to take our sweet Annabelle.’

‘Bella, cast your mind back to when your husband’s nephew, Toby, was murdered. Now, again, I need you to think carefully. We are aware of your husband’s past, but I am not concerned about that.’ He held up his hands. ‘I’m not interested at all. All I want to focus on today is getting Annabelle home. So do you know anyone who has any connections with Charlie or even Toby, who, shall we say, is less than honest? A disgruntled business partner perhaps or a dissatisfied colleague, friend, or associate? Because Toby and Charlie did work together, didn’t they?’

Bella sighed. ‘Detective, I know what you’re getting at. My Charlie had a bit of a past. Everyone knows that. But he served his time and worked hard to build his business, and he doesn’t want that life anymore. He has no need for it. This house, we built it, and the business from scratch.’

With a smile and a nod, Clarkson said, ‘As long as there is no one on your mind who would have a reason to take your little girl.’

She shook her head, her voice trembling with emotion. ‘No, honestly, I really can’t think of anyone because if I could, I would say so. My Annabelle means more to me than anything.’

Clarkson could see she was being honest.

‘Does your husband know yet?’

'Yes, I called the hotel he is staying in. He's on his way back.' Fresh tears tumbled down her cheeks. 'I hope you find her before he arrives. She is his world too.'

'I will promise you this, I will do everything in my power to find her.'

Bella stared at Clarkson for a moment, and then, with a cold, emotionless tone, she replied, 'Didn't you say something like that when Toby was murdered? Only, you never did find his killer, did you?'

Clarkson stood up and rolled on his feet. 'So you remember me, Bella? I was beginning to think you didn't.'

'Vaguely, but it was your promising words I recall the most.'

Clarkson felt his stomach clench because he had let this family down. It was just before the car accident. He was then in hospital, and he had to take time off to grieve for his daughter and get well himself. Granger took over, and instead of finding Toby's killer, he went off on a tangent trying to pin the Leeds post office robbery on Charlie, all because, at the time, Charlie was in Leeds looking at a pub to buy, and the description of the robber matched Charlie, and they found a crowbar in the boot of his car.

CHAPTER THIRTY-ONE

Feeling exhausted yet exhilarated, Sunny embraced the soft cushioned hospital chair with Billy sleeping in his arm. 'Ya know, I never imagined having kids.'

'Sunny, you would make a wonderful dad,' said Carrie, sitting upright in the hospital bed.

He looked over at her and stared for a moment. The sun shone through a gap in the blinds and it lit up Carrie's face. Her hair was still wet from where he had overzealously sponged her forehead. Her eyes sparkled, and her cheeks glowed as she held her newborn son in her arms.

'It's mad how they look the same.'

'Well, all I can say is the only sound thing Jimmy has is his genes.'

'Carrie, you know I hate Jimmy, all of them, but what's he gonna do when he knows I was holding your hand when you were pushing out his son?'

She kissed her baby's head, and another tear trickled down her face. 'This little fella is a month early. Luckily, he's big enough to have escaped a month in an incubator. But imagine if he *wasn't* okay. I could have lost him, Sunny. And I would have blamed Jimmy because he really hurt me. He bent me back right back, and I thought he'd broken my arm, and I begged him to help me, but he just left.' She kissed her baby's head again. 'So I couldn't really give a toss what Jimmy thinks.' She sighed and wiped away her tears. 'The truth is, Sunny, I look at these two babies, and I don't think of them as being part of Jimmy. I only stayed with him because of what Albert threatened. I couldn't bear to think of my sisters being tortured by the Carson brothers. So I stayed, and I tried, but I hate him, I hate *all* of them, and if their house burned down with them all in it, I wouldn't shed a single tear.'

'You should have said something because Albert and Lenny are seriously nasty bullies who don't hold that much power. And especially not now. James and Dylon are dating Dilly and Mary, and Rosie is always with one or the other. Why don't you tell your father the real reason you went back to Jimmy?'

Her eyes cast down and the tears came again. 'If I told them now, they'd never believe me. And if they did, imagine how guilty they would feel, and as much as I can be a mouthy cow, I would never hurt me family. Anyway, I've two boys to bring up now and to protect from the Carsons.' She tutted. 'And they are little Carsons themselves. So, I only pray to God they don't turn out like their farver. Fingers crossed, Jimmy fucks off with his new tart.'

'*What?* He's seeing someone else as well, is he?'

'I reckon so. He had a lovebite on him last week. He came home stinking of cheap perfume and had lipstick on his white pants. He's always out, never in now, which suits me. And when I washed his jeans, in the pocket, I found a condom.'

'It's a shame it weren't you and me, Carrie.'

She cried. 'Oh, Sunny, don't . . .'

Suddenly, he got up from the armchair and carried Billy over to her, placing the baby in the crook of her free arm, before he put his arm around her and sat on the edge of the bed. 'Do you know what, Carrie-Ann, when you were gripping my hand and pushing the little bugger out, I thought the whole ordeal would turn me off, and I wouldn't see you as this sexy woman that I'd want to get my hands on.'

She chuckled. 'Sexy, eh?'

'Yeah, sexy, but, Carrie, we went through something special together, didn't we.'

'We did, Sunny, and it fills my heart with pleasure, but at the same time, it kills me because it bloody hurt, and yet you were there with me, being so kind and sort of loving. It won't be long before I'm back home with that horrible bastard Jimmy hollering and hooting, while I'll be dreaming of you upstairs and listening to your records on your big music centre while you entertain some hot chic.'

Sunny wiped the tears away from her cheeks before leaning in and kissing her on the lips. 'No chick will ever be as hot as you, Carrie-Ann.'

A gentle tap at the door made Sunny jump off the bed.

'Sorry, the doctor is on his way to check the baby . . . Do we have a name yet?'

Carrie looked at Sunny. 'What's your middle name?'

'Jesse.'

'Aw, perfect, he's called Jesse.'

Sunny kissed her cheek. 'Our secret.'

The nurse looked at Sunny. 'You're not the father, are you?'

Sunny laughed. 'No, but I wish I was.'

'I thought you were.'

Carrie sighed and tutted, annoyed that she had to explain herself. 'Does it matter? He was with me throughout. So the doctor wants to check Jesse over. Is everything okay?'

'Er, yes, sorry, he will be along soon. I would like to check you over, if that's all right.'

'Carrie, I'm going to call James, yeah? He can let your sister know you have the baby now. He's always with her these days. I'll be back in a minute. Do you want anything?'

In her mind, she was thinking *You, Sunny, I want you.*

'I'm fine,' she replied. Then, she thought of Dilly. And that watch. It was sending her around the bend with curiosity. 'Oh, would you ask if Dilly would come and see me? I really need to talk to her. She probably won't but all I can do is try.'

Sunny winked. 'I will do, darling.'

Feeling awkward about questioning Carrie about the father, the nurse gently removed Billy and placed him in a cot that the previous nurse had kindly allowed Billy to sleep in. The nurse then placed Jesse in the cot beside the bed.

'I, er, I thought that man was the father only because he acted like it. In fact, he was so supportive, I would never have thought otherwise. You are lucky to have a friend like that. But, then again, Carrie, to take on another woman's baby when yours is the same age is admirable.'

'Thank you, nurse, that's nice of you to say, but I want the boys to be close. I grew up in a big family, and we always had each other. It was noisy at times but fun. I couldn't imagine being an only child. These two babies will have each other and hopefully be best friends.'

'Will your family be coming up at visiting time, if, of course, you don't get discharged?'

Carrie stared, her voice paralysed with emotion. Biting her lip, she shook her head.

The nurse nodded in understanding before she wheeled Billy next to Jesse.

'Apart from Jesse being smaller, they are identical.'

'Yeah, except my little Billy has a kiss birthmark on his neck from his mum. His real mum.'

***

After the thorough check-up, the doctor gave both Carrie and Jesse the all-clear to go home, which suddenly sent a shiver of terror up her spine. She stared at the babies and her heart filled with so much love, and yet the whole experience was scaring the living shit out of her. She would never want anything or anyone to hurt them.

She imagined Jimmy would be a nightmare because the babies would cry and wake up through the night. Jimmy's patience wore thin at the best of times, and his tolerance for anything that slowed him down or irritated him was practically zero. The more she thought about Jimmy and how so very cruel he had been, the more she wished him dead.

The nurse helped her to get dressed. 'When I had my babies, we had to stay in hospital – bed rest and all that – but now they chuck you out as soon as they can. But, Carrie, you'll be carrying two babies. Please don't overdo anything. We don't want you back in here with a haemorrhage. I'm sure you'll be fine, but rest as much as possible.' She looked at the babies. 'They are lovely and all that, but they're hard work. Now, you cannot leave the hospital unless someone drives you home or accompanies you in a taxi. Will Sunny do that?'

'Yes, yes, he will.'

'Great, I'll leave you to it.'

The moment the nurse left the room, Sunny came flying in. His face was white, his eyes frantic. 'Carrie, I've gotta go. I can't stay.'

'Please wait. What's happened?' She could see something serious had occurred.

'My Uncle Charlie's baby girl Annabelle has been kidnapped.'

Carrie's whole body felt as though it was turning to ice. 'Jesus!'

'So I have to go.'

'Sunny, I would never ask this – ever – not in this situation, but please could you drop me and the babies off at home. I can't leave unless I have someone to take me.'

He ran his fingers through his hair. 'Are you ready to go now?'

She nodded. 'Yeah, they discharged us.'

'Of course I will, but I can't stay with you. I need to find out what's happened.'

'I'm sorry to ask.'

He waved his hands. 'No, Carrie. Honestly, it's no problem. There's not much I can do for Charlie until we get an idea who would have taken her.' He shook his head and swallowed to stop himself from crying.

***

Driving away from the hospital, Carrie hardly said a word for two reasons. Firstly, she didn't want to distract Sunny from driving when clearly he was beside himself with worry. Secondly, she experienced an unsettling in the pit of her stomach and wondered if she was putting two and two together and coming up with ten. Biting her nails, she went over in her mind what she sensed back at Ginty's house, and she tried to work out if there was any possibility that what she had seen could be connected.

As soon as the babies were in the nursery, safely tucked in their cots, Sunny kissed Carrie's forehead and hurried to the front door.

'Sunny, please wait a minute.'

'Carrie, I must go, love. Jimmy will be back soon, and I'm not in the mood to row with him.'

'Please, just wait a moment.'

He spun around. 'Carrie?'

'Sunny, you don't think the Carsons kidnapped Annabelle, do you?'

He frowned. 'The Carsons?' He looked at her as if she was mad. 'No way. Listen, I know you hate Jimmy, but let's be honest. Even if his brain was made of dynamite, there still wouldn't be enough to blow his bloody head off, and, Carrie, he's not even house-trained. So, no, I don't think he'd have the balls. Or his brothers. Look, I've gotta go.'

'Sunny, what if they planned it over months? I mean scheming?'

Sunny was irritated now. 'Carrie, please don't give them that much credit. It's not a good look. Now, I'm *going*. Sorry, I didn't mean to raise my voice.' He shook his head. 'She's only fucking three years old. You've gotta be sick to do that *and* fucking brave.'

Carrie grabbed his arm. 'There are padlocks on Ginty's shed. A load of them.'

'So?'

'They've been planning something big, Sunny. Very big. Ginty said something about greedy pricks sharing their money.'

'*What?* What are you talking about?'

'Sunny, I don't know. Ginty was drunk, and she was talking about the boys' plan. She said they were planning a special job that would take brains. I'm sorry, Sunny, it may be nothing, but what if they've taken Annabelle?'

Sunny's eyes darkened. 'Believe me, if they *have* kidnapped her, they won't be carried out in body bags. They'll need a shovel and a bin.'

'I might have it all wrong. But the padlocks are on the shed.'

Sunny shrugged. 'They breed dogs, don't they?'

She nodded. 'Yeah, of course, they do. Sorry, I just see the worst in them, and their big clever job is probably robbing the sweet shop.'

'I'll see you, Carrie.'

She closed the door behind him and dragged her baby bag into the kitchen. She wanted to get all the bottles washed up and her nightwear in the washing machine before the babies woke up. Yet, she couldn't get the idea out of her head that the Carsons were somehow involved in this girl going missing. *Were her hormones playing havoc with her mind, or were the Carsons really capable of pulling off a kidnapping?*

Billy started to cry, and then Jesse joined in.

Now shattered from not having had a wink of sleep, let alone from giving birth, she just wished she had a little more strength in her. But with no husband around and none of her family, she knew she would just have to suck it up and get on with her life.

She made up a few bottles and then hurried to feed her babies before their cries reached a hysterical pitch. At first, she panicked because everything was new to her, and, again, there was no one to help. As she picked up Billy, she realised he'd messed his nappy and it was leaking out of the side. 'Stay cool, Carrie, you can do this,' she told herself, as she tried to ignore Jesse's cries and get on with the rotten task.

But when there was a knock at the door, she began to flap. *Please don't let it be the social services.* 'Hold up!' she yelled out. Hurriedly putting a fresh nappy on Billy, she held him in her arms, and rushed to the front door.

As she pulled the door open, she was struck dumb. There standing with their hands full of Mothercare bags and beaming smiles were her mother and Dilly. She was so overwhelmed, she wanted to burst into tears.

'Well, are you gonna stand there gawping, or are you gonna let us in?' said Dilly, with a cheeky grin on her face.

Luanne dropped her bags in the hallway, immediately took the wriggling baby from Carrie, and said, 'You'd better see to the other one.'

'Oh, er, yes, they need feeding. It's all new. I don't know if I'm doing it right and . . .'

Dilly had already made her way to where the wailing was coming from. 'Ahh, look, he's so tiny,' she said, scooping him out of the cot. 'So which one is which?' she asked, rocking Jesse and admiring him.

'That's Jesse, and that one you're holding, Mum, is Billy.'

She realised she hadn't said which was her own child and she wasn't going to. Not now.

'They are going to be a handful. It's going to be hard work, Carrie-Ann,' Luanne said. Then she glanced at Dilly. 'But we're here, now.'

Carrie was suddenly so overcome. Leaning against the wall, she covered her eyes and sobbed.

'Hey, Carrie, it's going to be all right. I wish you had told us why you went back to Jimmy.'

'Yes, so do I,' said Dilly. 'I can fight me own battles. You didn't need to do that.'

Carrie moved her hands away from her face. 'I did, though, Dilly. If you had heard what Albert was saying he'd do to our family, I couldn't risk calling his bluff.'

Dilly looked down at the baby, who was still yelling. 'Carrie, where are the bottles?'

'Oh, on the side in the kitchen, already made up.'

Luanne rocked Billy as she walked into the living room. 'Oh, wow, Carrie, you've got ya place proper nice, eh. You've done well, my girl. I'm proud of you, I am. And . . .' She paused to stop herself from choking up. 'I'm sorry, we shouldn't have disowned you like that. Your farver's at home. He's ashamed to show his face now. Sunny Murphy has only just told us what's been happening.'

Dilly returned with two bottles and handed one to her mother. They both sat on the sofa while Carrie sat on the chair under the window. 'Have the police found the little girl yet?'

Dilly shook her head. 'They're at Bella Murphy's house, going through every person they can think of who may know something.'

Carrie cuffed her renewed tears away. 'I can't believe you're here.'

'Don't cry, Carrie, you'll set me off.'

'You didn't ask me which one is my own birthed baby.'

Luanne looked up and smiled. 'I don't need to know because you've taken one on as your own, and that's enough for me. They are both my grandbabies. And I love them already. Now, get that sixpence out ya pocket, Dilly. One each, cross their palms with silver.'

Carrie bit her bottom lip to stop her tears. Seeing her mum and sister loving the babies as they did was a dream she would never have thought possible.

'Ya know what is strange, Carrie? Both babies are so much alike, I couldn't tell them apart, except one's smaller, but they both look like you. I swear, they are the spit outta your mouth.'

'Thank Gawd,' said Dilly.

Carrie laughed. 'I don't know how that's even possible.'

'God works in mysterious ways.'

'Where is that husband of yours?' Luanne asked, in a bitter tone.

Carrie shrugged. 'Out with his brothers or his fancy bit, I s'pose.'

Dilly raised her eyebrow. 'Well, more reason to divorce him, then. Who's he supposed to be seeing? Not your ol' mate Misty, is it? Because she's always had her eye on him, ya know.'

'I dunno. But he's gonna be shocked when he comes home and finds two babies.'

'And a mother-in-law and a sister-in-law ready to give him what for.'

Carrie chewed her bottom lip again. She now wondered if, in fact, it was Misty who Jimmy had been sleeping with because Misty always wore a specific perfume that she couldn't stand, and Jimmy had come home stinking of it. Perhaps, though, it was a coincidence. Yet there seemed to be a lot of coincidences happening lately.

***

After the babies were put back in their cots to sleep, Luanne made the tea, and the conversation became more serious.

'Dilly, can I ask ya something? Before Toby got shot, right?'

With her face drenched in pain, Dilly nodded.

'Did you give him that watch, you know, the one you got for his wedding present?'

'Why?'

'Well, where is it? Do you have it?'

Dilly shook her head. 'I gave it to James to give to Toby before the wedding, but . . .' She took a deep breath. 'The wedding never happened. I should think James still has the watch in his suit pocket.' She suddenly shuddered. 'It's hard because I loved Toby so much and yet . . .' She glanced at her mother. 'I love James as well. Do you think it's wrong?'

Carrie beamed. 'Wrong? No, not at all. Toby would love you to be with his brother. He'd know that James would look after you.'

'Carrie, why are you asking about the watch?'

'I dunno. I may have read into something that wasn't there.'

'Carrie, tell me?'

'I found a watch at Ginty's house. It was hidden at the back of a cupboard. It looked like the one you bought for Toby.'

'You would know it, Carrie. I had it engraved.'

Simultaneously, they said, 'Forever and a day.'

'How did you know that, Carrie?'

Carrie threw her hands to her mouth in utter shock. 'Christ, Dilly, it's Toby's watch. I mean, I read the engraving, and I knew whenever you ended a call or kissed Toby goodbye, you'd both say: love you forever and a day. I thought it was beautiful.' Suddenly, her eyes filled up again. 'Oh, Dilly, what does it mean? Why would they have his watch?'

'Mother of Mary, what have those fucking Carsons done? Surely, it wasn't them who shot him, was it?' said Luanne.

Dilly stared off into space. 'Well, there's been a long-standing feud, but *murder*? I dunno if they have it in them.'

'Dilly, Arthur nearly killed *you*, remember.'

'And . . .' said Luanne, 'any fucking mongrel can pull a trigger.'

CHAPTER THIRTY-TWO

As Carrie opened her eyes, she felt a pang of guilt. And then guilt changed to one of sheer panic. How could she have fallen into such a deep sleep? Had she slept through the babies crying for their milk? Gasping, she quickly got out of bed and swooned for a moment from a head rush. She then hurried into the nursery at full pelt, only to find the babies asleep. Taking deep breaths, she leaned on the side of Billy's cot, in relief.

'I let you sleep, Carrie, but I need to get home meself, love', whispered her mum, as she appeared with a mug of tea. 'Here, drink this. The made-up bottles are in the fridge, the dirty ones are washed up, and I've empty the bins. And' – she nudged her daughter – 'those two little angels won't want feeding again until twelve.'

'Mum, thank you *so much*. I'm not sure what I would have done if you hadn't helped me.'

'And I should have done a lot more before now.'

'You didn't know the truth then, though, did ya? Anyway, Mum, I am just thankful that I've got you and all my family back. D'ya think Dad will come and visit me?'

Although Luanne looked tired, having been up most of the night, her cheeks were rosy, and her eyes glistened. 'You try and keep the ol' bugger away.'

'Where's Dilly?'

'She went home. She wants to talk to James about the watch, and we noticed your phone was smashed to pieces. Was that your fit of temper or his?'

'His, Mum. He smashed it up when I needed it the most. I was lucky this detective bloke, er, Mr Clarkson, came past. He called an ambulance just before Sunny arrived.'

'Clarkson?'

'Yeah, do you know him?'

Luanne nodded. 'He's one of the good ones. I'm sure he was the one leading Toby's murder case.'

'Mum, I have this feeling. I can't shake it off, and I can't make sense of it, either.'

Luanne leaned into each cot and kissed each baby. 'Do you wanna talk about it now, Carrie?' She sighed because she was tired and wanted to get home to her bed.

'No, it's fine. You go home and rest. Er . . . Mum, where is home? . . . You moved and . . .'

Luanne swept Carrie's wayward curl out of her eye and around her ear. 'I'm sorry we didn't tell you. But we didn't want Ginty knowing. We moved just the other side of Poverest School, the third house next to the school, number seven.'

Carrie was shocked. 'So you live *this* side of the main road?'

'Yep. The neighbours turned their noses up at us at first, but after I baked them a rhubarb and apple pie each, they soon changed their tune.'

'So you're literally a five-minute walk away?'

'Yes, so we're here to help you, Carrie-Ann.'

Their conversation was interrupted by a gentle tapping at the front door. Carrie knew that knock was Ms Palin's, and the timing couldn't have been better, really. 'Stay for a moment, Mum. It's the social worker.'

Luanne hadn't put her shoes on yet, so she stayed because it looked good that Carrie had support.

When Carrie opened the door, she was greeted with Ms Palin's beaming smile.

'I received a call from the hospital. You have the baby and are home already. How are you, Carrie?' she asked, in her sweetest voice.

'I'm good, actually. Me muvver and me sister have been over. They're gonna—'

'Help out,' Luanne jumped in. 'We're all hands on deck in our family, so Carrie will not be alone, and I live just a few minutes' walk away. And I've raised five kids of my own, including my husband.' She chuckled.

Ms Palin was taken aback. It was as if Luanne was the great protector. 'Oh, what a huge relief, Mrs . . .'

'Call me Luanne.'

'Luanne, I came because I thought the first few days Carrie may need some help. But you seem to have everything under control,' she said, as she eased past Luanne and walked into the nursery and checked each baby. 'And they are both feeding okay, are they?'

'Guzzlers, the pair of them.' Luanne smiled. 'I stayed to do the night feed and give Carrie a break, so I'm off home to get some rest, but her sister will be back shortly.'

Ms Palin beamed again. 'Well, there is nothing for me to do, is there? I can see you have everything completely taken care of.' She winked at Carrie. 'You're doing very well, Carrie. I won't be popping in every five minutes. There's really no need.'

'Thank you, Ms Palin.'

As soon as the door was shut, Luanne slipped her feet into her flat sandals. 'You don't want those social services busying themselves.'

'She's okay, Mum, but I think she was a bit wary of you. Still, if it keeps her away from my door, all the better. I can't be done with being watched and judged.'

No sooner had Ms Palin left than James arrived with Dilly, so Luanne took off her shoes again and followed them into the living room. James looked as washed out as Luanne. He obviously hadn't slept either. But there was an urgency about him.

'Carrie, sorry to barge in, love. Oh, and congratulations, by the way. Two babies! Wow! Look, I'm gonna cut to the chase. Dilly informs me that you saw Toby's watch in Ginty Carson's house. Is that right?'

Carrie had never seen James so stern, and it made her feel as though she was in trouble.

'Yes.'

He spun around. 'Where's Jimmy?'

'I, er . . . I don't know, James. I really don't know. He said he was doing business with his brothers and would be away for a few days.'

The car roaring up to the property outside had James looking out of the living room window. 'Here's Sunny.'

By the time Carrie could catch her breath, Luanne had let Sunny in, and both brothers were almost towering over her, demanding answers. That's how it felt to her, at any rate, and so she nervously backed away.

Sunny, however, instantly realised that he and James were putting Carrie through the wringer, so he put his arm around her shoulders, much to Luanne's surprise.

'Carrie, darling, we're not having a go at you. We just want to know what you saw.'

'Christ, sorry, Carrie,' said James, running his hands through his hair. 'Sweetheart, I didn't mean to barge in like a copper. But it's been an anxious time. It still is, and now to hear that you saw my brother's watch, when I had given it to him the night before the wedding, it suggests it was on him when he was shot. You know what that means, love, don't ya?'

She nodded. 'Yeah, I do. James, you don't need to worry about me. I don't care if they're all locked up. They mean nuffin to me.'

James put his hands on his hips and nodded. 'And you, Sunny, you dismissed the idea of the Carsons being involved in Annabelle's kidnapping, didn't you.' He looked at his brother ruefully. 'Well, if they had the fucking balls to shoot Toby, then nothing would surprise me. Whereabouts was this watch?'

'In Ginty's kitchen, in the cupboard to the right of the sink, at the back, behind the bottles of spirits.'

'Come on, Sunny, bring your crowbar and your bat. This is fucking war.'

'Wouldn't it be better to call the police?' asked Carrie.

James looked at her as if she was mad. '*The police?* By the time the police get their act together and knock at Ginty's door, the Carsons will have had time to hide the watch.'

Luanne looked at Dilly, who was as white as a ghost. 'Dilly girl, you sit yourself down before you collapse, love.'

'I wished to God I'd never given him that watch. He might still be alive.'

James pulled Dilly close. 'I might as well tell ya, Dilly. Toby was robbed for a bag of money. Charlie, Tony – you know, Spud's uncle – and Toby had a business going with the burger vans. Anyway, they were selling more than burgers.' He winked. 'And on the night before the wedding, Toby collected a chunk of money from a dealer. It was for the honeymoon, but on his way back, he was shot, and whoever shot him robbed him of the money. We never told the police about the money, and I'll be honest, I didn't think too much about the watch. In fact, I just assumed the police had returned it to you, Dilly.'

Carrie leaned against the wall, her arms folded. 'So, then, could it have been the dealer?'

James shook his head. 'No, because when we paid him a visit, he offered to give Charlie the money that had been stolen. We knew it wasn't him.'

'Then it must be them, yeah? Why else would they have the watch?'

James turned to Sunny. 'Go upstairs and call Charlie, Dylon, and Spud. I want to turn Ginty's lair upside down and the Carsons inside out, even if I have to skin the fuckers alive,' he spat. 'And bring your cordless and some screws.'

Sunny winced. 'Nasty.'

'Nasty ain't the fucking word. I will be unforgivingly brutal.'

Sunny hurried to his maisonette while Carrie turned her attention to James. His expression spoke volumes. His wrath was palpable, and she certainly wouldn't want to make an enemy of him. Even his muscles appeared to have inflated, and his face stretched tight in rage. In fact, the man standing a good six feet seven inches in front of her looked like a monster, ready to kill.

He turned to Dilly. 'If they killed Toby, they'd have the balls to take Annabelle.' He chewed his bottom lip and breathed deeply. 'We will find Annabelle, and I'm gonna avenge my brother's killers.'

'James, please be careful. I can't lose you as well.'

He sucked air through his teeth. 'Those rats can't hurt me, they're weak.'

'Not if they have a shooter,' said Luanne.

Without even answering her, James kissed Dilly on the cheek and left.

The three women gawped out of the window as Sunny and James tore off in two separate cars.

'Please, God, let them find that little girl,' said Carrie.

CHAPTER THIRTY-THREE

James parked his car at the end of the street, and Sunny drew in behind him. They had already put a plan in place. Spud drove Charlie and Dylon but he parked at the other end of the street. The neighbours were quiet, but it was still fairly early for barbeques and gossiping. A lurcher stuck his nose out of a bush, but the dog quickly retreated when he saw James with a torque wrench in one hand and a crowbar in the other. Shoulder to shoulder beside him was Sunny, who carried a cordless screwdriver and a bat. The two men marched like soldiers, ready for action.

When Martin Shedder, a close friend of Ginty's, stepped out of his garden on to the pavement, his eyes bulged.

James gave him a warning nod.

Hopping back behind his gate, allowing them to pass, Shedder watched to see where they were heading. It reminded him of the day the Carsons and the Murphys fought in the middle of the street. Of course, the Murphys won, and today, he wasn't so sure the Carsons would survive at the hands of the younger Murphys either, especially given that James, a mountain of a man, with a fifty-four-inch chest and hands like shovels, looked as though he meant business.

As James rounded the bend, he saw Charlie, Dylon, and Spud. They were all tooled up, and so by the time they reached Ginty's house, they were together.

Charlie's skin was coated in raging sweat, and his face was an angry white. His incentive was to get even with Albert because he was the sly bastard in the family who had got away with way too much in the past. And the one who would be reckless enough to kidnap his little girl.

Spud, who had been working out at the gym daily, was a size now because he had been building himself up and waiting for this day. His hate towards the Carsons had grown inside him like a tumour. Jimmy, the turncoat, the two-faced bully, would get it from him. He'd already made his claim to being the one who would beat Jimmy to within an inch of his life.

And, of course, Dylon wanted to have Lenny for all the shit he'd done to Mary.

With a confirmatory nod to each other, they knew the arrangements. Charlie, Spud, and Dylon would take the back door while James and Sunny took the front. Sunny was about to kick the door in when James pulled him back. He put his finger to his lips. 'We don't want to draw attention, Sunny. Just knock, will ya.'

Sunny gave his brother a cheeky grin and gently tapped at the door.

James didn't expect anyone to answer. However, when the door opened only slightly, Ginty's fat round face appeared. James could see she was about to shit a brick and slam the door on them, but he shoved his foot in the gap and pushed the door open, knocking Ginty against the wall.

Sunny stormed through the hallway to the kitchen, unlocked the back door, and ushered Charlie, Spud, and Dylon inside.

Before Ginty could scream out a warning, James grabbed her by her mouth and walked her into the living room, where he pushed her down into the armchair and pressed the crowbar against her chest. 'Now, missus, you're gonna tell us where our little Annabelle is, or I'll start ripping your teeth out.'

Ginty glared, almost calling James's bluff, but he leaned closer, twisting his mouth to one side, in fury. 'I'm gonna turn your boys into mashed potatoes unless you tell me where that kid is, and I swear, Ginty Carson, if any of you have hurt a hair on that baby's head, I'll kill all of you.'

Her eyes darted to the doorway, where she could see the staircase.

He prodded the crowbar hard in her chest. 'Upstairs, is she?'

Ginty didn't answer. She listened to the men running upstairs before Dylon suddenly called out, 'She ain't up here, but this cunt is.' Suddenly, Lenny came tumbling down the staircase. Ginty attempted to get up to help him, but James pushed her back down.

The noise of heavy feet hurtling down the staircase heralded the arrival of Dylon and Spud. 'The others ain't here. Just that one.'

'Arrgghh, please don't hurt me!' screamed Lenny.

'Not so hard now, are ya, cunt,' hissed Dylon, as he pulled Lenny to his feet and shoved him against the wall.

Meanwhile, Charlie went outside. He hurried to the shed, and, like Carrie before him, he noticed the new padlocks. He had his own crowbar, his weapon of choice, because in a fight, he liked to leave a mark or two or use the weapon to pull teeth out.

Being the youngest uncle, and the same size as his nephew James, it wasn't really surprising that he was known for taking no prisoners. His heart raced as he used all his strength to snap off the padlocks, one after the other, until he could rip open the door.

The smell hit him first. The stench was awful. There in cages were three Staffordshire Bull Terrier bitches, which were emaciated with heavy teats. He knew they had been cruelly bred year after year, but he couldn't help them now. He would sort them out later. He searched for his daughter, and his heart sank. He had been certain he would find her here. However, in among the straw, shit, and an old mouldy blanket, he saw something bright red. He lifted the muddy and mildewy throw and retrieved a teddy. He recognised the fluffy toy as the one he had bought for his daughter. Pulling the teddy to his chest, he left the shed and raced up to the house.

The scream from the hallway was like that coming from a kid. But when Charlie ran in, he saw Dylon smashing Lenny all over the place. Moments later, a stream of blood shot out of Lenny's nose and covered Dylon's white T-shirt.

Charlie pulled Dylon away and shoved the teddy in Lenny's face. 'Where is she? Where the fuck is my child?'

Lenny writhed in pain. 'Arrgghh, please don't hit me,' he begged. 'I don't know. On me muvver's life, I don't know.'

James, who was in the living room, holding the crowbar to Ginty's chest, turned around for a moment to see what Charlie was doing. He saw the red teddy in Charlie's hand, and so he knew then that the Carsons must have been involved in her kidnapping.

Before James turned back to interrogate Ginty, she had managed to sidle out of her armchair, snatch the poker, and smash him in the forehead. She hadn't held back either; she went in again to smash him in the face, ready to kill him. But her second action was futile; she missed and lost her balance.

James staggered backwards for a moment. Then, a deranged look clouded his eyes, his lip curled like a dog's, and he grabbed the poker, ripping it out of her hand. Pushing her towards the armchair, she fell into it.

The shock on her face was not because of what James had done to her but because he was still standing after that blow to his head. She was now certain he was going to kill her.

'You're no woman, Ginty Carson, you disgusting cunt. Now, where is the baby?' He took the teddy from Charlie and smashed it in Ginty's face. 'This is hers. Now, where the fuck is she?'

The thin smile of satisfaction on Ginty's face almost sent James over the edge. He raised the poker to batter the woman, but

Spud stopped him. 'James, no, we need to find Annabelle. You can finish her off later.'

Charlie's voice, however, was overpowering everything. He was screaming at Lenny in between punching seven colours of shit out of him. 'Where's my baby? I'll kill ya. I will fucking kill the lot of ya.'

James knew then that the Carsons weren't going to talk. It didn't really surprise him, if he was being honest with himself. Still they had a plan.

'Sunny, get ya cordless screwdriver and screw that cunt to the door. Dylon, turn this house upside down. And while we're at it, Spud, check the kitchen cabinets for that watch.'

He saw Ginty's face suddenly change. Her eyes widened, and her mouth gaped open. 'What watch?'

'What watch?' James yelled. 'You know what watch I'm talking about, don't ya?'

Terrified, she shook her head. 'No, I don't. You've turned the place upside down. This kid ain't here, so, look, we've done nuffin wrong.'

'The fucking teddy, Ginty, the teddy. You had the child here. Why would you have her toy?'

Ginty snatched the teddy and shook it. 'It's a fucking teddy. I give the dogs toys to play with.' Her eyes nervously shifted to Charlie, whose hands and face were covered in blood and whose shoulders were slumped.

'I've knocked him out,' said Charlie. 'We're gonna have to wait till Lenny comes to.'

Ginty tried to get up. 'Have you mullered me boy?' she asked, her voice strangled with fear. She tried to look over Charlie's shoulder. Then she heard the cordless screwdriver buzzing. 'No, please don't hurt him. He ain't done nuffin wrong.'

'Am I screwing his hands to the bannister, James?' Sunny called out, as cool as a cucumber.

It made Ginty question which one of the Murphys was the most dangerous. Right now, her money was on Sunny. 'Please no, listen, we haven't got the kid. I saw it on the news . . .' She stopped dead in mid-sentence, terror playing out across her face.

James turned around only slightly and saw Spud holding up the watch. 'I've found it.'

Shaking her head in denial, Ginty knew she was going to be hurt.

'Who killed him, Ginty? Which one of your lot pulled the fucking trigger? Tell me.' He dug the poker into her cheek, pressing hard, hoping her eyes would pop.

Hearing the police sirens, Ginty's expression was one of relief and huge hope.

CHAPTER THIRTY-FOUR

Shedder and another neighbour had both called the police. The details they gave were alarming enough to send two police cars and four officers to the scene, and, on their arrival, they were geared up to storm the house.

However, as they were in position to gain entry, the front door opened. Sunny Murphy greeted them with his wild eyes and a smile on his face. He instantly recognised the infamous PC Gant, who had walked the beat for years and clipped the lads around their earholes if they were cheeky, although now, it wasn't allowed. But still, Gant knew everyone and everything about them.

'Officer Gant, come in. You'd better call Detective Clarkson. He'll wanna hear this.'

Gant, a tall man with a square jaw and ferret eyes, turned to face the officer behind him. 'No arrests just yet. Let me sort this out.'

It was a warning remark, and Sunny guessed that the younger officers, who had accompanied Gant, were probably a bit too keen.

As Gant stepped inside and was level with the doorway to the living room and the bottom tread of the stairs, he quickly clocked the dynamics of the situation. One of the Carson lads had been beaten up, but which Carson he was, was hard to tell since his face had been rearranged, and his eyeballs were barely intact in his sockets. He radioed through to call Clarkson to the scene.

When one of the younger officers saw Charlie Murphy's bloodied knuckles, the claret on his shirt, and the angry look on his face, he was minded to step forward with his handcuffs to the ready, but as Gant had given the instruction for there to be no arrests at this stage, he hung back.

Charlie raised his hands. 'I'm Charlie Murphy. My daughter's been kidnapped.' He grabbed the red teddy from James. 'This is hers. It was left here. These cunts have her.'

Gant realised that the man was indeed Charlie Murphy. 'Please continue, Mr Murphy.' He was aware of how high profile this case was. A large number of police officers were already searching the woods for Murphy's daughter.

'They've had her here.'

Ginty, who was still being held back by James, yelled out in a gravelly smoker's voice, 'Thank Gawd you've come. They've attacked me son. Look at him. He needs an ambulance.'

Gant glared at Ginty, knowing exactly who she was and what she was. He had no sympathy for any of the Carsons. He'd never met a good one, and for years, they had escaped a lot of prison time with their fake but watertight alibis.

He looked at Lenny, who he now recognised. Lenny was sitting up but leaning against the wall moaning. 'Fell down the stairs, did he, Mr Murphy?'

Sunny jumped in. 'Yeah, he's a clumsy cunt.'

'He ain't clumsy nor a cunt!' squealed Ginty, as she jumped up from her seat.

But this time, James didn't use the poker or his crowbar to force her back down. He backed off, now there were coppers in the room.

'Why ain't you arresting these men? They broke into my house and beat up me boy. Now, are you gonna cuff 'em or what?'

'Take a seat, Mrs Carson. A serious allegation has been made,' said Gant, cringing at the coarse manner in which Ginty spoke.

'Who by?' she said, with a shrill voice.

Gant rolled his eyes. 'Are you deaf? By Mr Murphy. He's just accused your family of kidnapping his daughter.'

Ginty was stunned. 'They can't do that. They've broken into my house. My fucking home. They've battered me son, and you're not even nicking 'em?'

Gant turned and looked at the front door. 'I can't see any evidence of breaking and entering.'

James smiled. 'She invited us in.'

Gant nodded. 'It does appear that way.'

Charlie thrust the teddy under Gant's nose. 'They definitely had her here. I bought my baby this teddy in Spain.'

Gant nodded and turned his head to the side when he heard the crackling on his radio, and Clarkson said, 'Gant, what's happened?'

'Gov, the Murphys are at Mrs Carson's house. They have got . . .' He took the teddy from Sunny and turned it over in his hands. 'The child's teddy, potential evidence that Annabelle Murphy was here.'

'I'm on my way. I want the Carsons secured.'

Sunny, who could just about hear the radio conversation, piped up, 'There's only Ginty and Lenny here.'

'Gov . . .'

'I heard. I'll be there shortly.'

Ginty's face was red with rage. 'Me boy needs an ambulance. Look at him. Are you fucking blind, you wanker?'

Gant stepped closer to Ginty, his shoulders square, and his eyes narrowed to slits. 'Where's the kiddie, Mrs Carson?'

Her eyes ping-ponged from James to Gant and then to her son, who was coughing up blood. 'Jesus, me boy's gonna die. Fucking *do* something . . . I'll report you.'

James sniggered. 'There are enough witnesses, Ginty, who saw your boy fall down the stairs. Now, tell Officer Gant here where the toddler is.'

Having only just recognised James as well, Gant looked him up and down. 'Bloody hell, James Murphy, well, your dear mother didn't stick you in a grow bag, did she?'

James smiled. 'All the carrots she made me eat.'

Ginty was panicking. 'Fuck me, are you not gonna help me boy? You'll have murder on your hands if anything happens to him. I'll see to that.'

Gant's smile instantly disappeared. 'Murder? Oh, Ginty Carson, I will make sure you are charged with a string of offences that will see your backside in prison for the rest of your life.'

She swallowed hard. 'You can't.'

He towered over her. 'You've been the alibi for your sons for years. They've got away with . . .' He showed his hand and counted using his forefinger. 'Rape, theft, violence, animal cruelty, GBH, ABH.' He stopped because the rage he was feeling was giving him palpitations. 'Well, you're going away for this, if it's the last thing I do.'

Ginty swallowed again, but, as always, flames of anger flickered through her. 'You can't. The kid ain't here, and like I told that mouthy bastard' – she pointed at James Murphy – 'I bought the teddy for my dogs.'

Gant flashed her a look of contempt. 'Oh, we will find the child, and when we do, you're going away for a very long time. I doubt you will see the light of day . . .' He paused and took a few deep breaths, before clocking the pain and helplessness on Charlie's face.

'You are a cruel woman, Ginty Carson.'

'Thank you,' she replied, with a mocking grin.

Gant whispered to the young officer. 'Cuff her tight so her wrists bleed.'

'Yes, Gov.'

***

Clarkson arrived at the Carson home with Susan Ring, much to the annoyance of Granger, who had to all intents and purposes been pushed off the case. The chief inspector took one look at Lenny and shook his head. 'Is he able to speak?'

Gant shook his head. 'No, Gov, I'll get him checked over at the hospital.'

Clarkson gave him a confirmatory nod. 'Keep him cuffed. We want him talking.'

James approached Clarkson. 'As well as Annabelle's teddy that Charlie found in the shed out at the back, we also found Toby's watch in the cupboard.'

Clarkson's eyes widened. 'Are you sure it was his? Although that doesn't mean much, James.'

'I presented Toby with the watch the night he was killed. 'Course, when we found out he'd been shot, it went out of my head, but that's the watch.' He nodded at Spud who was holding it up. 'It's engraved.'

Clarkson carefully removed an evidence bag from his pocket, and Spud dropped it inside.

'It's not enough to convict anyone, but enough to add credence to reopening the case with the Carsons as the suspects. Do you know where the other brothers are?'

James shook his head.

'Where did you find the teddy?'

Charlie flicked his head for Clarkson to follow him to the shed.

When the men arrived there, the sight of the three sickly dogs immediately captured Clarkson's attention. 'Oh, dear God, how could anyone do this.'

Charlie used the toe of his shoe to lift the stiff and muddy blanket. 'Her teddy was under there.'

Clarkson looked grim-faced. He studied the floor, now in deep thought.

Holding his nose, Charlie's eyes streamed. 'If they kept my baby in here, in this shithole, she would have been terrified. I swear, I will do time over this.'

'Let's see if we can avoid that, Mr Murphy.'

Clarkson pulled on a pair of plastic gloves and dragged the blanket out of the shed. He then looked down at the floorboards, gripped a loose one with his fingertips, and pulled it up.

Charlie was peering over his shoulder, and there, in clear view, was a gun. 'Now, that is what I call *real* evidence,' chortled Clarkson.

'Mr Murphy, er . . . Charlie, I will call in forensics and the dogs, so please don't be alarmed, okay. I am just taking precautions. I want the dogs to follow a trail using the teddy bear.'

'Not cadaver dogs, then?' Charlie asked, hoping that this wasn't going to be a murder investigation.

'No, I don't think so. As much as the Carsons are scumbags, I can't see them hurting a child. I don't believe they kept her in here, either. I reckon her toy spooked them and they threw it in here, out of the way.'

Charlie nodded. He now hoped that Clarkson would have more luck this time in dealing with his daughter's disappearance than he'd had with his nephew's murder.

Clarkson dropped to his haunches and used his pencil to hook the gun before putting it into an evidence bag. Then, he put his hand under the next floorboard and found a bag. When he pulled it out, he saw that it was an unusual leather sports bag.

'I wonder if this was Toby's?' said Clarkson. But as he looked at Charlie's face, he knew the answer.

'They killed Toby, didn't they?'

Clarkson rose to his feet. 'If this *is* Toby's bag and this gun is the weapon used to shoot him, then this points to their involvement, yes.'

Charlie sighed, took a slow breath, and looked at the sky. 'Well, it is definitely Toby's bag. I know it is because I had it made for him. He liked mine, you see.' A tear plummeted down his face, before he quickly wiped it away.

Clarkson gently rubbed Charlie's shoulder. 'We will find her.'

'Well, apparently, I've got Carrie Carson to thank for getting us this far.'

'Carrie?'

'Yeah, she was the one who told us about the watch.'

'Hmm, yes, and she might be able to help me some more,' mumbled Clarkson.

***

As soon as Ginty and Lenny were escorted out of the house and the forensics team arrived with the dogs, Clarkson left Susan to run the show while he headed over to Carrie's home.

If the Carsons were hiding that child somewhere, Carrie might have a clue. After all, she knew Jimmy better than anyone, he thought.

There was no point in interrogating Ginty and offering her less prison time if she cooperated because her loyalty to her sons was the one admirable quality she possessed. As for Lenny, he was just a waste of space.

***

Dilly and Luanne had only just left Carrie's home, when Mary arrived. She was dying to see the babies.

Mary was about to ease one of them out of his cot, when there was a knock at the door. She peered down the hallway as Carrie held the door wide open for Chief Inspector Clarkson to come in.

Carrie could tell instantly from the detective's grim expression that this was not a social visit. *A pity*, she thought. *It would have given her so much pleasure to show Dottie's friend her new home, one which she was so proud of.* But the manner in which Mr Clarkson hurried inside and spoke fast told her he was on a mission.

'We need to find Jimmy, Carrie. I believe he may have Annabelle Murphy, the missing child. Think carefully, please. Where would Jimmy take her? Where would he feel safe?'

Mary could see the detective's mouth was dry, and beads of sweat had gathered around his forehead. 'Would you like a cup of tea or something cold, detective?'

'Oh, I would welcome a cup of tea. Thank you, er . . .'

'It's Mary. Me sister Mary,' said Carrie. 'And, Mary, this is . . .'

'Detective Chief Inspector Clarkson. I remember,' Mary said, before she hurried to the kitchen to put the kettle on.

'Do you think Jimmy took the little girl?'

Clarkson shrugged. 'We have reason to believe the Carsons are involved, but you know Jimmy well, don't you. Where would he take a child, or where would his brothers hide one?'

Carrie walked Clarkson into the living room. A whiff of her new air freshener tickled her nose, and she sneezed. 'Oh my God, not that cheap perfume smell again. That's gotta be Misty's.'

Clarkson frowned. 'What?'

'Look, Mr Clarkson, I think Jimmy's having an affair. Now, I know it's a long shot, but me sister Dilly joked that maybe he is seeing an old friend of mine called Misty. It was a tease that Misty fancied Jimmy, but maybe it wasn't such a joke after all. Anyway, she wears this cheap perfume, and when I washed some of his shirts recently, I could smell the perfume on them. And another thing, Mr Clarkson. Wait here a sec.'

Carrie scooted into the bedroom to find her bag. She looked inside for the photo she found just after Jimmy trashed the phone, and then rushed back into the living room.

''Ere, Mr Clarkson, 'ave a look at this.'

Clarkson studied the photo and instantly visualised Charlie Murphy's back garden, before he popped the photo into an evidence bag.

'Carrie, you might be on to something here. Where does this Misty live? Does she live on her own?'

Grabbing an old envelope from the coffee table, Carrie scribbled down the address and gave it to Clarkson. 'She lives with her muvver, but her muvver's got that dementia, so she doesn't know what day of the week it is. Misty might be at work, though. She works in this wine bar in Orpington called Minstrels.' She shook her head. 'I dunno, Mr Clarkson, Jimmy kidnapping someone? He can barely do his shoelaces up, the tosser.' She clocked the stern look on the detective's face. 'You do think Jimmy took the little girl, don't ya?'

Clarkson held up the evidence bag and nodded before a deep frown creased his forehead. 'Sorry, Carrie, did you say Minstrels?'

She nodded, hoping she was being helpful.

Mary came into the living room with a tray on which she had placed a cup of tea, a bowl of sugar, and a jug of milk. 'There you go,' she said, as she put the tray on the coffee table.

But Clarkson didn't have time to sit and enjoy the tea. He gulped it down, scorching his throat.

'Thank you, Mary. Carrie, don't say anything to anyone. If Jimmy returns, please find a way to leave and let someone know he's here. I don't know how dangerous he is.'

Carrie nodded, her face drained of blood. 'Like I said, you really do think he's kidnapped her, don't you? But he's not that dangerous, surely?'

'He could be because I also have reason to think that the Carsons were involved in Toby Murphy's murder,' he replied.

'I knew it! In my heart, I bloody knew it. Ya see, Mr Clarkson, not long ago, Jimmy said something to me about the Murphys, which I don't think he meant to. He said, "They ain't that hard. Toby didn't fight back." That sort of says everything, really, don't it. So, if Jimmy does come back, I'll let you know, I promise.'

Once Clarkson was in the car, he called through to the station to have Misty Jacobs's address raided by armed police. The suspects of the kidnapped child could well be inside, armed and dangerous.

***

By the time Clarkson read the address on the street sign nearest to the tower block where Misty lived, he could see that the place was swarming with armed police. He knew he was staking his professional reputation on this hunch of Carrie's. But she probably knew Jimmy better than he did himself. It was worth a shot, but if it all came to nothing, Annabelle would still be missing. And time was ticking away.

Approaching the entrance, Clarkson was aware that word must have spread on the grapevine because already a very sizeable crowd was building up. Police officers had cordoned off the perimeter of the tower block, and they were trying to hold the onlookers back. Clarkson noticed that Susan was already there.

In fact, Detective Constable Susan Ring, having finished up at Ginty Carson's house, had arrived a while ago at the block of flats. Knowing the area well, she had given Charlie a lift to the scene for the purpose of taking charge of his daughter, if, of course, she was there. Prudently, she had instructed him to remain in the car while her colleagues did what they were good at.

Clarkson nodded at Charlie, in acknowledgement. He was at the point of opening the main door to the block of flats, when he was pulled back by McAree, the lead armed officer.

'They're coming out, Ray.'

'Have they got the kid?'

'Yes, she's alive. They are bringing her down now.'

'Who was in that flat?'

'I don't know who they are, but there's an elderly lady, a young woman, and two men.'

The main door opened, and two armed police officers escorted a young man who had his hands cuffed behind his back. When he glanced up, Clarkson saw Jimmy Carson looking absolutely terrified, with tears running down his face. Behind him and also escorted by armed police was Zachariah Carson, who had clearly wet his pants. His pale-blue tracksuit was dark around the crotch with an unsightly urine stain.

Charlie couldn't wait. He leaped out of the car, and in two fast and hard, brutal punches, he smacked Jimmy off his feet, and he did the same to Zachariah before anyone could stop him.

But the cry from his daughter had him running to her with his arms out. 'My baby!' he cried, as he pulled the child from the female officer's arms and squeezed her tight.

Despite cradling his child, Charlie still managed to deliver a swift backhander to Misty while she was also being escorted out. Before he stormed away, he acknowledged Clarkson. 'Thank you, mate, thank you.'

Clarkson nodded but he was worried. He looked about before he said to McAree. 'One's missing.'

'Gov?'

'Albert Carson. Where is that bastard?'

'Sorry, Gov, the flat's empty. There were only two men, one young woman, and, as I said, the old lady, but she's away with the fairies.'

'Damn it! Fucking damn it!'

CHAPTER THIRTY-FIVE

July 1983
Carrie was grateful that Sunny had levelled out an area of the back garden so that she could have a couple of sunloungers and a paddling pool for the boys, which they both loved. They would slip over the edge together and slide into the pool in the three inches of water. She was amazed by their motor development skills. They had learned to walk on the same day. And comparing them for size, they were practically the same. Even she had to look twice to tell them apart.

The family were up early, and the boys were in their high chairs enjoying breakfast when a handful of letters came through the letterbox.

Carrie hoped it wasn't another bill because up until now, she had been managing very well to pay for all the monthly household expenses as well as the day-to-day ones. She even had spare cash left over for the kids' treats.

Spud had been her saviour in that respect. His kind offer of a job collecting the takings had made all this possible.

And Sunny had taught her to drive, so she'd passed her test, and with the money that she had stashed away, she had bought an old Ford Fiesta.

As she approached the front door, she eyed the white envelopes and smiled. There were no brown ones. On closer inspection, the first letter she picked up was from Jimmy, which she didn't even bother to open. She would throw it in the bin later, along with all the others. And when she had time, she would write to Wandsworth Prison informing the governor that as she was now divorced and since Jimmy would be serving twelve years for his involvement in kidnapping that poor little girl, she didn't want to see any more letters from him on her doormat. She had no interest in waiting for him. And when he came out, assuming he did, she would put a restraining order on him, if he ever tried to knock at her door. His constant barrage of letters reminded her of what he'd done; his begging forgiveness and demanding persistence to see his sons was grinding her down. Hopefully, the governor would put a stop to it all.

The second letter was handwriting she didn't recognise, but the franked stamp was a dead giveaway. It was from Holloway Prison. Her hands hovered over the seal because her initial impulse was to throw the letter in the bin. However, curiosity got the better of her.

But as she read it, she was relieved to see that there was nothing for her to worry about.

Having been sentenced to twelve years for her involvement in the kidnapping of Annabelle Murphy, Ginty would possibly die in the nick.

The letter wasn't filled with threats because the officers read every inmate's letter first, and had she tried to pull a fast one, she would probably have received a longer sentence.

But, as Carrie read the letter for a second time, she could see that like all of Jimmy's correspondence, this was very much a pleading one. Saying she forgave Carrie for being a prosecution witness, even though it went against her beliefs, but she still considered her as a daughter-in-law, regardless of the divorce, and so could she see it in her heart for Carrie to visit her because all her sons were in prison. She had no one, and she longed to see the babies.

'Tough titty,' said Carrie, as she screwed up the letter and placed it on the console table along with all of Jimmy's unopened missives.

The last letter she could see was from Dottie. She smiled and decided to take it to the living room and read it while she drank her tea. The boys were sucking on the toast and jam, so she got stuck in to reading the letter.

'Mummy says she is painting the spare room ready for if we visit. She has also got a friendly seagull who sits on the window ledge. She's calling him Ray, after Detective Chief Inspector Clarkson.'

She wasn't in the least surprised that Dottie held Clarkson in high regard after all the work he had done in getting the young lad Lucas to tell the truth about what happened that day and to get a statement from Maggie Lawson, the woman in the church, who'd had the conversation with Dottie's mother regarding having her daughter committed to a mental hospital. It had all been relevant in the case.

Looking back to last November, when Dottie had gone back to court for her trial for the murder of her parents, she recalled how worried she had been about the outcome for her friend. Obviously, with Dottie being pregnant, and with the mitigating circumstances, which included her parents trying to drug her, and the fact that they were social deviants of the worst order, the court threw out the prosecution's case for double murder. Instead, at the time of murdering her parents, she was found to have a disorder of the mind, which impairs an individual's ability to know right from wrong. In short, she was declared to have temporary insanity.

So Dottie had been freed from prison, but restrictions were placed on her. She was under the strict supervision of a psychiatrist, whom she had to see every week. And a further order was placed on her: she wasn't allowed to return to

Orpington or have access to her son, but she was given a flat in Margate overlooking the sea.

'I'm sure they'll love that.' She sipped her tea. 'How about it, boys? A long weekend by the sea. She says she thinks you're clever for learning to walk.'

Suddenly, she stopped reading. A deep frown creased her forehead. 'How do you know they can walk?' Her body turned cold as she tried to recall if she had told Dottie the boys could walk. Then she smiled. 'Silly me, I bet Ray Clarkson told her.'

He often popped in when he passed, if he wasn't walking one of his three Staffordshire Bull Terriers with Jack, who, by all accounts, loved the company of three bitches. Although they certainly wouldn't be breeding again.

Thinking that maybe it was a good day to take the babies to the duck pond, she walked over to the window to see if the sun was out and to decide whether or not to pack the sunscreen and sun hats.

Just then, she thought she saw a movement behind the bushes that faced her house. She stared and realised a sudden gust of wind had moved the bush. Was she merely imagining things? Yet, it wasn't a new occurrence. Since the Carsons had been sentenced, all serving a significant time inside, she had felt continually on edge. The reason for that was Albert Carson. She knew how evil Albert could be, and the police hadn't caught him yet.

On the positive side, it had been almost a year now since she had last seen him. In fact, no one had. The police had had his mugshot on the TV for several weeks, on and off, stating he was dangerous because his prints were found on the gun that was used to kill Toby Murphy. His prints, and those belonging to Lenny and Zachariah, were also on the leather bag, so they had all played a part in Toby's death. Jimmy managed to escape any charges connected with Toby's murder, but he was considered the lead in the kidnapping case.

Knowing how dangerous Albert was, she now understood why, so far, he had got away with Toby's murder. This was something she hadn't envisaged when the Carsons were arrested. *He was a clever bugger*, she thought. With a loud tut, she pushed the thought to the back of her mind and got the boys ready for a day out.

Billy was particularly troublesome; he wouldn't stand still to have his sunscreen put on, and Jesse was also a nightmare. He just ran around in circles until he was dizzy, and then he would wobble about all over the place. Finally, she managed to strap her sons in the double buggy before collecting the things she needed for the day out.

Just as she was about to take the brake off the buggy, she remembered the juice bottles and hurried back inside. When she emerged from the maisonette, she noticed that Billy was about to fall out of the buggy. She ran to him and caught him before he fell. Then she ensured the harness that strapped them in was tighter. Billy was a genius when it came to getting out of things; he could already take his clothes off, and his nappy, which he found highly amusing, although this was proving another nightmare for her.

'Right, we're away,' she said, as she flicked off the brake and walked ahead, mentally recalling if she had packed everything she needed in the bag. Raising the two babies required careful planning; she could never go out at the last minute.

As she walked along the road, soaking up the cool breeze on her face, she unexpectedly felt a presence, like a ghost following her. Ice ran through her veins as she spun around, but no one was there. This feeling had been getting worse, she realised, but it was always exacerbated when she received letters from either of the prisons – Wandsworth or Holloway. As was the case this morning. And when she thought about Albert. She knew she needed to stop worrying. After all, she had two little boys to make happy.

Having spent two hours walking along the river down to St Pauls Cray and then pushing the boys on the swings, she looked up and saw the black clouds rolling in. 'Damn!' she said, wishing she had checked the weather forecast.

The boys kicked off when she strapped them back into the buggy because they were having so much fun, but the threatening rain compelled her to search the undercarriage of the buggy, only to discover she had left the rain cover at home.

When she heard a crack of thunder, she knew she had to run; the heavens opened, and the rain pelted down. 'Oh no!' she cried. The babies would get soaked, and she was far away from home. Still, she could run; she was fit. But she wasn't going to be able to run far in wet squelching sandals. So she stopped, took them off, and legged it.

The rain became heavier and heavier until the babies began to cry because they were soaked, and she cried because she felt like the worst mother on the planet. As the heavens really opened, her tears were flowing nearly as fast as the rain. But she kept on running while telling her sons they would be home soon and everything would be okay.

Finally, they were home, and as she pulled out her house keys to unlock the door, she was shocked to find that it was actually slightly open. She decided that she must have forgotten to close and lock it when she left the juice bottles behind.

Walking backwards into the maisonette, she dragged the buggy inside and then picked up her babies. 'Oh no, look at you two. I'm so sorry.' She hugged them both, pulling them close to her. Then she peeled their clothes off. Billy was trying to take off his own, but Jesse was still sobbing. The whole incident had frightened the life out of him. Once they were stripped off, she ran a warm bath. 'This should put smiles on your faces,' she said, squeezing Jesse's cheeks and gently prodding Billy's pot belly. Kneeling on the floor, she washed the boys until she could feel their skin warm enough to get them out of the bath and into some clothes before they had a nap. And she hoped that after all the drama they had witnessed, they would be dead-beat for quite some time.

Right on cue, as soon as they were lying in their cots with their warm bottles of milk, they closed their eyes and were out like a light.

She then stripped off her clothes and towel-dried her hair and put on a T-shirt dress before cleaning the kitchen and drying the buggy.

Moments later, she heard Sunny's car pull into the drive and she hoped he would pop in. He was good with the boys, and despite the sexual tension between them, he hadn't pushed it. Even though she really wished he would.

The knock at the door had her grinning, and she hurried to open it.

Sunny leaned against the doorframe. His hair had grown, and he flicked his long fringe out of his eyes. When he smiled, her stomach was a party of butterflies.

'Fancy a coffee?' she said, hoping he could come in.

'Go on, then,' he said, gazing at her with so much love.

He looked more handsome than ever since he had got bigger from working out at the gym, and his summer tan added definition to his striking blue eyes.

'The boys are asleep. We got caught in the rain.'

'Friday night, your sisters are having their joint hen do, and I thought it's not fair if you can't go, so I'll babysit. Besides, my brothers' joint stag do is on Saturday.'

'Ahh, Sunny, that's so kind of you. Thanks.'

'It's only fair, ain't it? Anyway, I enjoy it, really. They're right little characters. So I'll pop in at five to take over, if you're doing the van rounds.'

'Cheers, Sunny. I know it takes a few hours out of your day just so I can earn a few bob.'

He gently touched her cheek. 'In a couple of weeks, we'll be in-laws.'

Carrie wished she was getting married again, but to Sunny this time. Although she never expected it to happen, she was grateful for his friendship and help with the boys.

After they had sat down and talked for an hour while they drank their coffee, she wondered if she had taken in anything that Sunny had said because she enjoyed looking at him so much. In fact, she only wished he loved her as much as she adored him. The way he winked and smiled at her often made her wonder, but, then again, was he the same with other girls? She wouldn't know.

After glancing at the clock, Sunny jumped to his feet. 'Right, I must dash. I'll be back at five.'

She nodded and hoped for a kiss, but he was in a rush, so she saw him to the door and checked on the boys. They were still asleep.

***

As soon as Sunny arrived later that afternoon, Carrie left to do her work. When she drove into Brands Hatch, she clocked the old man closing up, and when he saw her, he held up a hot dog, with mustard, onions, and tomato ketchup, one of her favourite go-to meals.

'Oh, Frank, you darling, thank you.'

He also gave her some envelopes and then waved goodbye. That was the last collection before she met up with Spud. However, when she drove into The Fighting Cocks car park, she noticed his car wasn't there. Where was he? He was always on time.

Glancing at the six fat envelopes, she felt uneasy, so she locked the doors. She sighed. It wasn't like her to be so on edge.

Finally, Spud pulled into the car park and hopped out of his new car with a look of satisfaction.

She wound down the window and handed him the envelopes, and he handed her one in return. 'A bonus, Carrie. We've done well this month. Gotta run.' He winked. 'Seeing a man about a dog.'

She chuckled. 'You've been saying that for as long as I can remember.'

'No, seriously, I'm getting a dog. I've always wanted one, and I'm off to have the pick of the litter.'

'Spud, why don't you get two, so they have each other?'

'Because, Carrie girl, I'm getting a Great Dane.'

'Oh, I see, but it might be better to get a nice girlfriend as well, though.' She laughed before she drove off, heading for home.

***

Disappointed that Sunny wouldn't stay – he was going to meet Spud to pick out this Great Dane puppy – Carrie thanked him and waved as he headed over to his car. Once again, she really had hoped that he would have kissed her, but he hadn't. Closing the door, she leaned against the wall.

The boys looked exhausted because Sunny was always throwing them around. He loved to hear them laughing hysterically, and now they were walking, he chased them, making them fall over from laughing. So now they lay in their cots hugging their teddies and listening to a *Mother Goose* story on the tape recorder that her father had bought them.

Feeling fed up, Carrie dragged her feet to the bathroom and stared in the mirror. Her eyebrows needed plucking. She found the tweezer and a magnified mirror and took herself back to the living room. The light was better there. As she sat cross-legged on the floor and set about plucking her brows, she suddenly felt a cool draught and saw the flash of something dark.

Thinking it was a figment of her imagination, she calmly put the mirror further away from her face so that she could get it in focus. But then, her heart missed a beat and cold perspiration broke out across her forehead.

The unmistakable figure of a man – all in black and wearing a beanie – was lurking in the hallway.

Confronted with impending danger, Carrie had to think quickly, but she was frozen in terror. There was no doubt she knew who he was and what he was capable of. Her brain shot into gear, and she hoped he would edge his way to the living room away from the boys' nursery; she had to protect them at all costs. But he didn't come closer. He shot into the nursery, and fear ripped through her like a spear. She leaped to her feet and heard one of her sons scream. It was Jesse; he had the higher-pitched voice, followed by Billy, who always screamed, if Jesse cried.

Carrie didn't think to grab a knife. Her only mission was to get to her boys. Holding her breath, she ran to the nursery to find Albert pointing a gun at Billy, and then at Jesse.

Billy was screaming, with snot pouring down his face, as he held out his hands for Carrie to take him. Jesse was doing the same.

But Carrie was rooted to the spot, even though she could see the absolute terror in their eyes. She had never seen them so distraught.

'No, no, Albert, please don't hurt them. They're babies.' Her eyes flicked to and fro, from her sons to Albert, who, strangely, seemed very calm and collected.

'Which one is yours?'

'They're both mine. Albert, please.'

He waved the gun back and forth. 'Fucking choose which one lives and which one dies.'

'Oh no!' she gasped. 'Please, Albert, please. I'm begging you. Don't, look . . . look . . . they're your nephews. They're both Carsons. Look at them. They look like you.' She lied.

'Bollocks, they don't look like me, neither of the little bastards.' He pointed the gun, still swaying it from one baby to the other.

'Please shoot me. Kill me, but don't hurt them.'

Their screams became louder until Albert yelled, 'Shut the fuckers up!'

'All right! All right!' She held up her hands and moved between the two cots, grabbing both babies and holding them to her. 'Please, Albert, I know you hate me and wish I was dead. Kill me, then, not these two.' She could feel the children shaking with fear, and she hated Albert with every part of her being. Hugging them tightly, she knew they could feel her heartbeat racing. Then she backed out of the nursery.

Albert pointed the gun in her face. 'Where are you going? Get back here. I want you to feel the pain I've been feeling. You destroyed my family. You went prying around me muvver's kitchen and had to find that fucking watch, didn't ya? And then, you sly cunt, you pretended you didn't see anything. My Jimmy trusted you. You should have been on his side, like a proper wife would. You should have been his alibi, not grassing him up to the fucking filth. No one was gonna hurt that kid. We just wanted some of what that greedy bastard Charlie had.'

Carrie nodded, agreeing, hoping he wouldn't hurt the boys. They had calmed down now, but she could feel their little fingers gripping her for dear life as their chests heaved with dry sobs.

'I understand, Albert, I do, and I'm sorry, I didn't realise the facts, or I would have stuck by Jimmy.'

'You fucking liar, Carrie. You've always been that mouthy bitch who walked around like she owned the place, and it's all your fault that me family are locked up. My dear ol' mum is rotting away in prison in Holloway, and Lenny and Zachariah are in Wandsworth with Jimmy. And there you are in ya fancy house with your boys and a job. A fucking job earning money from that cunt Spud. You should have stayed a Carson, Carrie. But now you're divorced, I have no loyalty to you or those brats. So you're gonna know what it feels like. You're gonna have to choose which one lives!'

Carrie fell to her knees in the hallway, holding on to her babies so tightly, she wondered if she was squeezing the life out of them. How could she choose which one would die? It was impossible. 'Please just kill me, instead,' she said.

Albert was now standing in front of her with his back to the front door. He laughed in her face. With the gun by his side, he said, 'Seeing you begging is the best tonic ever. Go on, do it once more.' He laughed again.

Carrie didn't have the option to jump up and grab the gun. He would shoot her or one of the boys first. Seeing that there was no way out of this mess, she said, 'Albert, listen, I've got money stashed away. You can have it.'

'Money?' He mocked her. 'Fucking *money*! I don't want ya fucking money. I want you *hurt*, Carrie-Ann.'

With nowhere to run and nothing she could do except to try to talk her way out of him hurting the boys, she felt helpless. But as the front door opened a little more, which he had clearly left open, probably because he wanted to sneak back out again, she hoped it was a friend not a foe.

Her eyes flashed a look over Albert's shoulder, but he laughed. 'That old trick, Carrie? I ain't falling for it. Sunny's gone out. We both know you are home alone. And I know you're not expecting anyone, so if you want to play games, I'll ask you to choose which baby dies.'

Carrie had seen who was in the doorway, but she chose not to look again in case Albert decided to spin around.

'This is the last time, Carrie. Now, choose.'

He lifted the gun, but before he could engage the trigger, Dottie whacked him hard with a brick. She hit him so hard, his head bounced off the wall. He dropped the gun and slumped onto the floor like a sack of shit. Dottie kicked the gun out of his reach before she hit him again with the brick, making sure he was well and truly out cold.

Completely stunned, Carrie got to her feet.

'What the fuck! Well, bugger me, Wonder Woman. How . . .? I mean, when . . . I mean . . .' Carrie was stumped.

Dottie, who seemed to have filled out, dressed in jeans and a tight black sweatshirt, put her finger to her lips. 'I'm not supposed to be here.'

'Well, I know that, but by Christ, Dottie, I have never been more grateful to see you in my life. Jesus . . .' Her chin trembled as she tried to put the babies into their cots. 'He wanted me to choose, Dottie.' She cried. 'Oh my God.'

Dottie kicked Albert, to check he was still out cold. Then she joined Carrie in the nursery. She didn't touch the boys. She looked from one to the other before putting her arm around Carrie. 'It's all right, Carrie, he's more than likely dead, and if he isn't, I'm gonna finish him off. He doesn't need to be alive. Does he?'

Carrie kissed each baby's head and gently closed the nursery door behind her.

'What did you say, Dottie?'

She shrugged. 'I said, I might as well finish him off.'

'Dottie, that's murder.'

Dottie chuckled. 'Murder? Don't you think I know that? Besides, if they arrest him, he could get off. You know, they call it temporary insanity. Look at me. They let me out.'

'Dottie, that's completely different,' Carrie said, as she stared at Albert's lifeless body. 'You were judged as insane at the time of your, er . . . crime.'

Dottie rolled her eyes. 'No, I wasn't, Carrie. I *meant* to kill them. It wasn't some mad moment where I lost it. No, I hated them. I wanted them dead.'

Carrie stared at her friend fleetingly. 'So I guess what you're saying is you're a psychopath. Is that right?'

'No, I'm not a nutter, either. I just think life can be so unfair, and there are some people in this world who shouldn't be in it.'

'What the hell are we supposed to do, then?' asked Carrie, feeling very uneasy about this conversation.

'We'll make it look like a suicide. Get some rope, tie him to a chair, and I'll fill his belly with spirits. As much as he can take. Then, we are going to pour every drug we have down his neck.'

'What, and that looks like suicide, does it?'

'Maybe not exactly, but it will look like he overdid it with the drink and drugs, and, well, when they find him, he'll be so decomposed, they won't look too deep. I mean, he's been on the run for a year. Mind you, they didn't look too hard. I saw him come out of the Carson's house, which has been boarded up. I sometimes come over just to see the boys. I keep away, Carrie, because I don't want it to be awkward for you, and plus, I'm not really allowed in the area.'

'Oh, so you've seen the boys walking, 'ave ya?'

'Yeah, you've done a good job, Carrie. Now, let me get rid of this rubbish. Get some rope.'

Carrie was in awe of Dottie. She seemed to have everything under control, a fearless woman. She hopped to it, and within minutes, she and Dottie had lifted the stinking man onto the dining room chair and held him in place to tie the rope around him.

'I've got a bottle of whisky,' Carrie said, as she grabbed it from the cabinet. 'And Jimmy's got a stash of pills. I'll get them.' She scooted away but quickly returned with her hands full.

'God, he is ugly,' said Dottie, as she peered into his mouth. 'Look, his teeth are all rotten, and he already reeks of booze. I saw him hovering around the street. But I never thought you'd let him in.'

'I didn't let him in. He must have known I kept the spare key under the stone. Damn it! I'm so stupid.'

'You're not stupid, Carrie. Pass me that bottle and point that gun in his face.'

Carrie nodded, more than happy to let Dottie take the lead.

Dottie poured the whisky into his mouth, but he choked and momentarily opened his eyes. '*Drink!*' she hissed.

He choked again, and then his eyes were wide open in horror, as he tried to wriggle free. When he realised he couldn't move, he looked up at the two young women. 'You cunts!' he growled.

'Shut the fuck up and drink.'

'What? No, I ain't drinking that.'

'All right don't drink it, then. I'll cut your balls off with a rusty knife without a pain relief.'

He began to shake, almost convulsing. 'No!'

'No? Then drink.'

He glared at Dottie as he drank the whisky.

Taking some tablets from Carrie, who had raided Jimmy's drawers, Dottie said, 'Good man, now swallow these. It's all right, they're only uppers.'

He frowned, but the whisky was hitting his empty stomach and instantly sending him into a relaxed state. He opened his mouth, and Dottie popped more tablets inside and added even more of the liquor down his throat.

'That's it. You'll feel so much better in a minute.'

His face turned grey, and he tried to vomit, but Dottie held his head back.

Then the girls watched a man slowly dying in front of them. It began with Albert gagging on his own vomit because he couldn't move his head to expel the contents. Then he gasped. But the vomit went down the back of his throat. Albert tried to cough. But his windpipe was solid with puke.

Now, as his eyes bulged in terror, Carrie recognised that look she'd seen in her two boys, and at that moment, she felt as calm and murderous as Dottie.

'He's gone! Look, Carrie, he's choked on his own vomit.' She shrugged her shoulders. 'Well, that's one less thing to worry about. Now, I will reverse my car into the driveway and we'll load him into the boot.'

Carrie nodded, still in shock. Then, she began to focus on what Dottie had just said.

'A car?'

'Yeah, my friend Billy left me some money. It's a long story. I thought I'd put it to good use.'

Carrie peered out of the window and saw the silver Ford Escort. She frowned. 'I've seen that car around.'

Dottie nodded. 'When I say I've put it to good use, I learned to drive as soon as I was released back in November. I just wanted to make sure you and the boys were okay, knowing that Albert was on the run. Listen, Carrie, you can say no, but can I see Billy and give him a hug before I go?'

'Yeah, Dottie, 'course you can. He's your boy. He's just on loan to me.'

As Dottie held her baby, he didn't scream in fear; he nestled his head into her neck and curled his fingers around her red locks.

'He knows you're his mum, Dottie.'

'I know I wrote to you about coming to Margate and staying, and I appreciate you probably won't come, but, one day, if you want to, I would love it if you came to see me.'

Carrie smiled. 'You try to stop me. Fresh air, seagulls, fish, chips, and sandcastles. I always thought you were serious about the long weekend. I've been telling the boys we're coming to you. To feed the seagulls.'

Dottie's eyes welled up. 'It was a dream I once shared with Billy, but I would love to . . .'

'Dottie.' Carrie put her arm around her. 'We're in this together. Jesus, you're like the guardian angel.' She looked down the hallway at Albert's dead body. 'Dottie, promise me we won't get caught hiding Albert's body. We have our sons to watch growing up.'

CHAPTER THIRTY-SIX

Six weeks later

Carrie lay a large blanket on the sand. She then unwrapped the fish and chips and blew on them before giving Jesse a portion. She smiled at Dottie. 'Look at Billy. He's just a greedy bugger.'

Dottie held her son in her lap while he stuck his chubby hands in the newspaper and grabbed a handful of chips. 'His birthmark is fading.'

'Yeah, probably because you keep kissing it.'

'I saw the news. They found Albert, eventually. They reckon he drank himself to death and choked on his own vomit.'

'Yeah, the council who went in to renovate Ginty's place for the new tenants found his decomposing body there,' said Carrie, as she winked.

'Carrie, so show me the ring again.'

Carrie wiggled the third finger on her left hand. 'I never thought Sunny was that romantic, but it turned out he is. It was at me sisters' wedding. They had a joint one. Anyway, when they went to throw their bouquets, they stopped, turned around, and handed them to Sunny. Of course, everyone was baffled until Sunny gave them to me. And then' – she nudged Dottie – 'he got down on one knee in front of all the guests.'

'I'm so pleased, Carrie. You deserve a good bloke.' She looked up. 'Oh, speak of the devil.'

'Here, girls, I got us some jellied eels,' said Sunny, as he sat down beside his fiancée. 'Well, this is nice, ain't it. I could make this a regular thing.'

Dottie blushed, as Spud came over and sat beside her. 'I've got you cockles, Dottie. I hope you like them.'

Now lying down on the warm sand to soak up the sun, Sunny sighed. 'I was just saying, Spud. I could make this a regular thing, couldn't you?'

Spud looked at Dottie and smiled. 'Oh yeah, I definitely could. Tell me, Dottie, do you like Great Danes?'

Printed in Great Britain
by Amazon

40873220R00216